McCormac

Volume II of the
Cleanskin Short Stories

John Benacre

Reviews

"The author's depiction of the historical backdrop is profound."
– *Kirkus* Reviews

"A likeable, pragmatic protagonist comes of age in a
comprehensively detailed, chaotic period in history."
– *Kirkus* Reviews

"... a worthy counterpart to the first volume."
– *Kirkus* Reviews

* * *

Also by John Benacre

Easter, Smoke and Mirrors

Shape, Shine and Shadow

McCann

McCormac

Published in the United States of America by John Benacre Inc.
This paperback edition November 2016.

This book is dedicated to Peter, who would have just turned thirty, and to Dee, who boldly showed us the way to ninety-five.

Acknowledgements

Thanks to Pauline, Henrik, Michael, Paul C, Paul G and Steve; also to David McKittrick, Seamus Kelters, Brian Feeney and Chris Thornton for the wealth of detail in their 1999 book *Lost Lives;* and to Lewis Carroll, for four lines borrowed with respect and affection from *The Walrus and the Carpenter*. Thanks also to Inniskeen fishing guide, Paddy Keenan, for his help and great craic when researching the River Fane, and to Brian O'Coill for hosting us in Dublin and for his generous hospitality. Thanks as always to Wikipedia for its user friendliness and continued excellence.

Contents

Author's Note to the Reader

This collection of short stories expands the contextual backdrop to the novel *Easter, Smoke and Mirrors*, and its sequel, *Shape, Shine and Shadow*. It complements Volume I of the Cleanskin Short Stories, entitled *McCann* (which was named to *Kirkus Reviews* *"Best Books of 2015"*), and it will be followed in due course by Vol III, *The Elders*. Whilst I hope you appreciate the stories in this book as stand-alone tales in their own right, they are largely set down in chronological order and all are inter-related. In reality it reads like a novel. Some are mere seconds apart, others weeks or whole months, and a few leap several years at a time; so that you will doubtless appreciate them most if you read them sequentially.

I hope you enjoy them all. JB

God's People

"So what's it going to be, MFI or MI5?" a twenty-seven-year-old Bill Wallace asked with a grin.

"MFI? The furniture people?" a young and pretty Maggie Allinson smiled in return, "God you're kidding, it would have to be something a whole lot better than that to get me turning the wheels of industry. Now let's see, let me run British Steel for a few years. That I could get my teeth into."

"Oh, I don't know," Bill grinned again and sipped at his pint, "I'll bet the Managing Director of MFI earns a lot more than the Director General of MI5."

"Um, I'm sure he does..."

"And you'll notice that I'm presuming you'll be aiming for the top job as always?"

"Of course, in time," she chuckled, "but as you well know this isn't going to be about the money for either of us."

"Yeah, hardly," Bill laughed, "I think even I'm going to take a pay cut, and that says something on army pay."

"Besides," Maggie sipped from her glass of wine, "MFI's on borrowed time. That was a bad example even if you were just teasing. Some intelligence officer you're going to be if you don't do your homework properly."

"Why?"

"Because IKEA's coming, and Do-It-Yourself stores like B&Q and Homebase."

"IKEA? You reckon?"

"No, I'm certain."

"And so what? They've only got stores in Scandinavia and Germany, haven't they?"

"Not anymore they haven't, shows how much you know," Maggie said confidently, "they're setting up in France and Spain as we speak..."

"Really?"

"Really, and they're in Japan, Hong Kong and Singapore already; I read an article about their expansion yesterday. What's more they're in Australia and Canada as well, and so the USA will be next. And then of course, once they're in the US, there'll be here in the UK too. You watch. God, everything in America comes here eventually, even hot-dogs, bagels and AIDS."

"And you know this how," Bill chuckled, "because you've got shares I suppose?"

"In IKEA, yes of course, they're going places, but I've sold my shares in MFI. The retail furniture bubble's about to burst, so time to move on."

It was indeed time to move on, for both of them, and this was the latest of several discussions they'd had in recent days about launching a second career. But unlike any of their previous circuitous chats, this time they were both acutely aware that they'd reached a decision point. That can wasn't going to be kicked along any longer.

Both were the same age and ready to set the world on fire. Bill Wallace had just resigned his commission in the British Army after six busy and demanding years of counter-terrorism in the Intelligence Corps, and Maggie Allinson had just decided that after five years in the Stock Exchange that she was worthy of something better. Something more fulfilling and with a greater challenge. But not before she'd made a small fortune though. No, now she'd have to find other ways to prove herself outstanding in the workplace, and Bill reckoned he knew just the organisation. He'd been on at her for over a year, and indeed they'd both considered it at one time when they were still at university.

They'd been inseparable at uni' - until bedtime at least - and they'd always known they'd finish up in some sort of a joint venture one day. A meeting of like-minds was a good way to describe it. Maggie had always intended that would be in some sort of a financial enterprise that would make Bill a millionaire, but Bill hoped he was about to enlist her help instead in saving the Free World. For him it was no contest, and in his heart of hearts – once she'd got the Stock Market thing out of her system – he knew that Maggie was made of the same stuff. He knew from his own experience that she felt the same way about patriotism, duty and the security of the nation, and her drive and sheer intellect would be an asset to any organisation. Now it was simply a case of taking the plunge... hopefully together.

Bill was about to join MI5, the Security Service, with or without Maggie Allinson in tow. Maggie was pretty sure she was about to as well, largely because of the constant challenges it would present; but she would be giving up a whole lot more than he was. Millions in all probability. And she was a woman of course. That made a difference. Back in 1981, and in what was still very much a man's world, that always made a difference. She reckoned the Service would provide a level playing field though, and given that she reckoned she could give any man a run for his money.

For Bill the decision had been easy. In places like Bünde, Belize and Berlin, and for more than three years in Northern Ireland in particular, he'd had a taste of a world he knew was for him and at which he'd proved to be highly competent. But he also knew that in a peace-time British Army such opportunities might be few and far between in the future. He'd felt at home 'in the know' and in the shadows, and so he wanted more of the same. But first he had to convince Maggie.

"And look," he said with childlike enthusiasm, "you know they're an Equal Opportunities employer?"

"Yeah, right, I've met a good few of those before," she said. "I even had to fight one off recently, he thought we were so equal. It didn't stop him making a grab for all the bits that he didn't have though. Arsehole."

"Yeah, I can imagine," Bill scowled, "but look, the Service are really serious about it Maggie. And I believe them. There's a larger than normal percentage of women as it is, and the people I've been working with are predicting a female DG within the next twenty years." In fact, when Dame Stella Rimington later became the Director General in 1992, that significant milestone was achieved in just eleven.

"Twenty years? Well that can't be me," Maggie said.

"No, but it could be you in thirty."

"Jesus, that'd be a laugh," she grinned, "if we're in the same intake. Just imagine. You and I might be competing for the top job thirty years from now."

"Yeah," Bill chuckled, "I think we both know each other well enough to know that's not going to happen. If there's a fast lane, you'll be tearing-off along that quite nicely by then. And you know me, I'm going to be perfectly happy caught up in all the tactical weeds somewhere."

"Don't worry, I'll look out for you."

"Shit, I've no doubt about it," he laughed. "That's half the reason I want you there with me."

9

Bill wasn't entirely joking. They both chuckled at each other though and sipped their drinks for a moment in silence. Neither had ever felt the need to talk when in each other's company, and so they normally only spoke when there was something meaningful to say. For long moments there wasn't, so Bill left the ball rolling gently around on Maggie's side of the net. After a while she picked it up and tossed it back.

"So, if I say yes, how do we actually go about it?" she asked.

"I make a phone call."

"That easy? Surely not."

"Well not normally, no, but I've just been working with a bunch of them don't forget, and well, it's a phone call they're half expecting."

"Yeah, from you maybe."

"No, from both of us, if I manage to persuade you."

"So you weren't joking then?"

"What do you mean?"

"When you said they know about me already?"

"No I wasn't, and yes they do. From me they do, a lot. But since I've flagged you up and they've gone away to do their own checks, they probably know more about you now than I do."

Bill laughed crudely.

"So," he added, "is there anything juicy you want to tell me before I learn about it from my new buddies?"

"I wish," Maggie grinned, "I've been too busy to make time for anything like that. Jesus Bill, I haven't even dated in over a year. I'll be glad to have a life again to be honest, whatever it is."

"So do I call then?"

Maggie didn't speak but she just grinned at him. She rolled her glass around in her hand; he sipped his pint anxiously and waited. She knew how excited he was getting and so she made him wait some more.

"And what happens if you do?" she purred.

"Dinner in the short term, with a friend called Richard, then he'll set us up with formal interviews in their headquarters in due course."

"In due course?"

"Yeah, but soon. Within a week they reckon."

"And then will we be fast-tracked or something?"

"God no, far from it, there'll still be all the vetting and selection and so on. This just saves us all the initial discreet enquiries, that's all, and bouncing around from one department to another until we get in front of the right people."

"I see. Just to be careful I suppose?"

"Yeah. It's getting less hush-hush by the day they reckon, but it's still a bit of a maze for someone walking in off the street."

"I'll bet."

"This is more like if we'd called that number we were given by that guy at university, except now they've actually seen me in action as well so to speak."

"Yeah, you they have Bill. In action, under fire and under pressure. And running agents even..."

"Well, sort of..." he said self-consciously.

"Right, but they've seen you carrying out real contact intelligence is my point; whereas they haven't seen me do diddly squat in that sort of an environment."

"No, but they know you could. They know what I think, and they know we were both tagged as 'possibles' at uni'. And now they'll have checked your record in the City too, so that'll impress them I'm sure. But more than that, Maggie," he laughed, "they also know I refer to you as one of God's chosen people."

"Really?" she chuckled, "what on earth does that mean?"

"Well they think I'm a sound judge of character, poor fools, and they have a very high regard for my thoughts on people. That especially, that's sort of been my thing while I was working with them, and they know I'm certain you'll make a huge success of whatever you attempt in life." They exchanged serious glances.

"So I guess it just boils down to who's going to be the winner here? You and your bank manager, or me and the rest of mankind?"

"Us and *our* bank managers, Bill, not just me. You do know what we'd be giving up though, don't you? Potentially I mean. And now you've got Pam to think of too, don't forget. You've got a wife to support as well now."

"Oh I reckon I'll be able to make ends meet," he smiled, "me and Pam aren't cut out to be wealthy, and she knows how determined I am to do this."

"Hmm," Maggie pulled a seductive smile and made Bill wait for her response, "then I suppose for Pam's sake I'd better hold your hand... in case you fuck it all up."

"You sure?" Bill asked, suddenly serious.

"No I'm not sure, but I am decided, so don't say anything now to make me change my bloody mind."

They clinked their glasses, drained them and then ordered another round. For the next half an hour they shared more funny stories, finished-up their drinks and then made the call. Dinner with 'Richard' was arranged for the next evening, and true to Bill's word their interviews at MI5's Curzon Street offices and Gower Street HQ took place over the following week.

Bill had been right, they certainly weren't fast-tracked and their inductions in due course were suitably rigorous. But both were seen as excellent candidates, and so it simply took as long as it took. As long as it always took. For Bill it was just so much waiting, for Maggie it was a chance to make a little more hay while the sun was still shining; about a quarter of a million pounds' worth. And everything that followed, as they say, is now history.

So... now I've introduced you to Bill Wallace and Margaret Allinson, two people I would be privileged to work with later in my career, I'd best tell you the rest of the story. My story specifically, but theirs too later on. They joined the Security Service the same year that I was born – something they would remind me of often in later years – but they joined at the back-end of 1981, after a summer of riots, intrigue and bloodshed; whereas I was born back in the January, and without a care in the world.

Although they physically joined the Service and began their careers in London, that year in Northern Ireland had been an exceptionally busy one. Indeed Bill Wallace had still been serving there with the army until the July. The IRA Hunger Strike had run from March until its conclusion - with the death of the tenth hunger striker, Michael Devine, on the 20th of August – and so it had been a summer of bloody street battles, burning vehicles and major incidents. Thus for Wallace it had been a summer of hundred-hour weeks and mind-boggling intelligence collection and exploitation. And for Allinson, his accounts of all of that had been her deciding factor.

For Bill, once they were trained and deployed to a working section somewhere, it was going to be business as usual; and for Maggie... well, it was going to suit Maggie Allinson right down to the ground. The events of that year and the *other* Maggie's steely resolve – that of Maggie Thatcher, the Prime Minister – had effectively made her decision for her. Maggie Allinson was 'in'... lock, stock and barrel. She'd give it one hundred per cent for the next forty years, and she'd never have a day's regret.

Nor me, once I joined later on and caught up with them. So now, I suppose, I had better introduce myself...

What's in a Name?

I'm Neill Pádraig McCormac. I was born in Daisy Hill Hospital in Newry, South Armagh, and I was raised in the Derrybeg estate not a kilometre away. But back in 1981, in Northern Ireland, that was the border heartland of the Provisional IRA, and at the height of what became known as the Troubles. So it was a pretty cool place for a young fellah growing up. Scary as hell for my parents I now know, but an interesting place for a red-blooded young boy right enough.

I'm a Catholic of course, along with ninety per cent of Newry, but my faith – or lack of it – isn't really relevant to my story. Not really. For me it's just sort of there in the background, a drab and constant canvas over which everything else was daubed until, one day, it was all covered up. Now, in my thirties, there's none of that backdrop still visible at all, while the rest of my life's been splashed on several coats thick. But it's relevant to the story overall – me being Catholic I mean.

Think of this collection of short stories then as something like a diary. Not mine solely, but as a sort of journal nonetheless. Except it's not going to be completed day by day, but more story by story, year by year or memory by memory as the thoughts occur to me. And there'll be other people's stories in here too, where they're relevant or wherever I think you'll be interested. Or maybe just where I think you need to know something crucial to understand the bigger picture. And besides, it is a sort of bigger picture too... a sort of mini-history... of the Troubles in Northern Ireland, and of life in Newry and in South Armagh in particular during those crazy, crazy years.

And if you're familiar with the story of me chasing the IRA Cleanskin Michael McCann, then this'll help you to understand how my life gave me an advantage and why I can't let it go. Not yet, not as long as he's still out there somewhere and in a position to do unspeakable damage. But first I need to tell you about me and my family. Just enough to be able to understand the rest and to be able to grasp the 'me' I've become. If that's something a normal person could understand at all.

The first thing I need to tell you about is the whole thing with Aunt Úna. Most everything I ever learned about our family I learned from her; right from my earliest days now I think about it, but especially later on and in my teens. She was our mum's sister and two years younger, but she seemed so much smarter and more worldly-wise than our mum. Than everyone in fact.

We all thought so, all six of us kids, but mostly me I guess. I know I was the only one to ever say it out loud, and that was a bit of a showstopper at the time. But at least Aunt Úna laughed. She laughed at nearly everything I said and did, and of course the more she laughed the more I played up to it. Aye, we were close when I was just a kid. Still are close. Always will be, I'm sure.

So Aunt Úna would tell us all the things our mum and dad couldn't remember, or couldn't or wouldn't say; but there again, it felt like I was the only one of us kids who was ever really interested. Then once she reckoned I was old enough to really understand, she also provided most of the facts, much of the context and all of the truth. And then from time to time our mum or our dad – usually our mum – would try to fill-in the blanks. But only if asked. Forced really.

Dad was a quiet soul, still is. He's straight as the day is long and incapable of lying, so he never said much about anything. Life's hard when you can't lie, and so I always presumed the two were connected. Although once, I remember, when I'd just turned fourteen but I'd long been cocky and brash, I asked him what I thought was a crucial question.

"So how did all us McCormacs," I asked reproachfully, "go from being wealthy merchants down in the town there to just ordinary people in the Derrybeg?"

"What do you mean?" he said, wounded.

"In just four generations I mean?"

"We were never wealthy," he stuttered, "not really son, just comfortable is all. And not us anyway, it was years ago."

"But I thought we were back then? I thought our great grandpa had a store on Buttercrane Quay and a shop on Sugar Island? That's wealthy isn't it?"

My father looked at me long and hard for whole seconds without a word, then he looked for a moment as if he might cry. A sorrowful man-cry. At last he answered.

"Aye, he did, but they were hard-working people rather than wealthy, even then. No son, we were never that, not really... and it was complicated back then."

"Complicated?"

"Aye, it was."

"But so what happened?" I spat-out without any thought for his feelings. Kids seldom do, I know now.

Another long pause, and even closer to man-tears.

"Bad choices, son," he said quietly, but he clearly hadn't finished and so I waited as patiently as a fourteen-year-old can. "Bad choices and two World Wars, that's what happened."

"I don't understand."

16

"No son, you won't yet, but listen to me and don't ever forget what I'm saying. You can't stop all the wars, not even this one festering on here these past twenty-something years, but you'll always be in charge of your own choices. Make them count for something."

Those words have stayed with me always. And I think I've done a pretty good job. But what's more, just sometimes, I learned that you can have a major part in stopping a war as well.

So let's deal with my name first. That seems like the obvious place to start. My forenames are straight forward enough: Neill, because that was a brother my mother lost and coz that's what both my parents had decided I would be called if I was a boy; and then Pádraig after my father. But then there's my surname, McCormac, and its uncommon spelling. Its distant origins are undoubtedly Irish... or Viking apparently... but right about there any simple explanation grinds to a halt.

Under even the most cynical Gaelic microscope it's said to mean 'Son of Cormac', and in that form it most likely dates back to the south-westernmost of the ancient Irish provinces, Munster, in about the 5th Century AD. That's cool, and geographically at least that put us about as far from any marauding English (later British) that an ancient Irishman could get. But how then, you might ask, over the next fifteen hundred years it became twisted into its current Anglo-Americanised spelling and took root at the opposite corner of Ireland (which is *still* under British rule), is a story probably best skipped over. Well. Then sit back and sip a glass of something special as you read, because here's how deftly a fifteen-stone Irishman can skip.

Y'see, the more usual forms of its spelling, McCormack, MacCormack or McCormick, are to be found all over the island of Ireland, and even the variant *Mac*Cormac seems to crop up often in Great Britain; but our derivative... McCormac... could only be said to be popular in one place: the United States.

Well there's the first weird thing. It always seemed to me then that we, as a family, might have been every bit as unusual as our surname, and that maybe we were descendants of that rarest of all breeds of Irishman in the nineteenth century: the one who was sailing *to* Ireland *from* America, when just about everyone else was going the other way. And if true, the reasons for that back in the USA should probably be skipped over even more surely.

Whatever the reason, our collective knowledge as a family only seems to date back to about 1700; although family folklore has it that we were in fact descended not from the ancient kings of Munster, but from *Kormákr the skáld*, an Icelandic poet from the Viking Age. It's possible I suppose – I don't dislike lager, plenty of Vikings landed in Ireland, I reckon I'd be not too shabby at rape and pillage and it would certainly explain our flaxen skin and our steel-blue eyes - but it doesn't sit comfortably with my dislike of the cold. So no, I think I'm Irish right enough, and the fact that I prefer whiskey and Guinness to lager tells me that I'm probably onto something.

But way back in 1700 though, we know that our direct descendants in nineteenth century Newry had not yet arrived. We believe they were still farmers in County Louth, in the Province of Leinster, and from somewhere around the town of Faughart. Now if that's true then that probably complicates the origins of our name even more, because in the 3rd Century AD the Battle of Faughart was fought by *Cormac mac Airt*, one of the High Kings of Ireland, and the name is alleged to have lingered-on as a surname in later generations. So perhaps I'm even descended from royalty?

Whatever the truth, and truth is a relative term in Irish folklore, by 1800 our forebears had migrated a mere ten miles into County Down, into the Province of Ulster, and become merchants in Newry. Back then Newry was a bustling market town and later, after the opening of a ship canal to Carlingford Lough in 1769, it was also a busy inland port. One obvious interpretation then is that as far back as that we were forward-looking traders and entrepreneurs; but another explanation could be that we weren't welcome anywhere else. Fuck 'em.

The first McCormac ancestor we know about for sure was my great, great, great, great grandfather, Lorcán McCormac. He was born in 1800 and had, by 1841, risen to prominence as one of the senior Guardians of the Newry Workhouse. The Workhouse was at the time a beacon of success throughout Ireland - and the site less than a century later of the Daisy Hill Hospital where I was born - but in just five short years from that date came the potato famine, and at the same time there went his brother Patrick to Boston. Patrick's departure had been baffling, and it took place amid what were cautiously described as 'dubious circumstances'. Or, it always occurred to me that he might have been the dodgy and Americanised *McCormac* skulking-off back to America that had given us the spelling of our name? Aunt Úna certainly thought so, and she'd point to any Irishman in *The Gangs of New York* and say, 'There, I bet he's one of ours.'

She had a theory about Patrick, but there again she had a theory about most conundrums which usually proved to be right. She thinks his disappearance on a boat from Newry to Liverpool, and then on another from Liverpool to Boston, was in some way connected to the non-delivery of a huge consignment of potatoes to the Newry Workhouse; but for which, unfortunately, he'd already been paid. And she thinks that although it didn't reflect on his brother Lorcán directly, that it signalled a turn-around in his fortunes and began his gradual withdrawal from public life. There's certainly not been any prominent McCormacs since.

The next three generations worked hard instead to build a thriving business on Buttercrane Quay, and then later on at a small shop on Sugar Island as well. And by all accounts they were doing a grand job, until in July 1914 they were rudely interrupted by Emperor Franz Joseph I of Austria and by Kaiser Wilhelm II of Germany. They and countless millions of others that is.

Within weeks a single bullet fired in Sarajevo had plunged the whole of Europe into war – the bullet that lead directly to over seventeen million deaths and some twenty million wounded. And in just a few weeks more the conflict had spread right around the world. Right around the globe and deep into the heart of Newry. But therein lies another story.

What's in a Place?

When Patrick McCormac fled to Boston in 1846 he became, remarkably, the last in the male bloodline of our direct descendants to emigrate. Whilst during and after the Great Famine a fair number of McCormac daughters sailed away with their husbands to America, Canada, Australia or Great Britain, the only men to leave Newry in the next hundred years were those who went to fight in two World Wars. And predictably, there was a significant number of them.

Gerald McCormac, my great grandfather, was one of four brothers who enlisted into the Royal Irish Rifles in August 1914. But four years later he was the only one who returned. At least most of him did. He only suffered minor physical injuries – he was one of the lucky ones – but he was also gassed, shelled several times and left for dead on the battlefield twice. Unsurprisingly he suffered for the rest of his relatively short days from what society politely called shell-shock. Today we call it PTSD, and modern combat suicide rates amongst veterans have reached the twenty per cent mark. The fate of the four McCormac brothers was a similar ratio of death to survival to that suffered by his cousins, his uncles and a wretched number of his friends.

It sounds like a grand gesture and that he needn't have gone. It was, and he needn't, but he wasn't alone. None of them *need* have gone, because although the whole of Ireland was still under British rule back then, and while Home Rule and mounting Irish Republicanism were the topics of the day, conscription was never introduced into Ireland during World War I. And so, every single Irishman who fought for the British – about two hundred-thousand of them - did so as a volunteer.

There were of course reasons other than manliness and glory. In 1914 unemployment was pitifully high, the availability of housing was the exact opposite, and the potato famine was still a recent memory; so for many Irishmen enlistment was a seductive alternative to their miserable lives of abject poverty. Against that backdrop young men and boys - and a scarcely believable number of not-so-young men - were whipped-up into a frenzy of patriotic fervour in recruitment rallies in cities, towns and villages right across Ireland. Even die-hard Republicans who believed they'd be rewarded with their independence for helping Britain after the war was over, enlisted in droves into one of the eight fiercely-proud Irish regiments or into the Royal Navy. Plus for many there was that additional 'X' factor: the genetic inability of the Irish to walk away from a good fight anywhere.

At least two hundred-thousand Irishmen from Ireland itself - some historians say more - and another hundred-thousand from America, Canada, Australia, New Zealand and the far-flung corners of the British Empire, took the King's shilling and lined-up to fight the Hun. Newry proved no exception, and it boasted the highest number of recruits per head of the population of any town in Ireland. And so it also claimed a proportionate share of the forty to fifty thousand who never came home when it was over.

Gerald McCormac was one of the many who returned in name only. The rest of him was clearly still out there somewhere.

Left for dead on yet another battlefield and for the rest of time. His father, Fergus, nonetheless worked tirelessly to school what was left of him in the ways of the family business, but the effort involved in that and his grief at the death of his other three sons killed him within two years of Gerald's return. That was a double blow to thirty-year-old Gerald, because beginning in 1919 and for the next two years, he was about to need the sage counsel of his father more than he could ever have imagined.

After the formation of the Irish Volunteers in 1913, the already substantial groundswell of Irish Republicanism gathered momentum across much of the country virtually overnight. Its open meetings and drilling, and its barely concealed militarism, were most evident in the three southern provinces and in and around Dublin, but in Ulster they were a vulnerable minority to the Protestant Unionist establishment. Newry and South Armagh in general, nestled along what would soon become 'the border', were caught squarely between both worlds.

In 1916 and midway through the First World War, the ill-coordinated and ill-fated Easter Rising in Dublin had seemed a distant and misguided affair to most in Newry; and even less relevant to Gerald and his one surviving brother as they were being 'shell-shocked' in the trenches at the Battle of the Somme. They were amongst the fifty-five hundred casualties from the 36th Ulster Division killed or wounded on the first day. Just the first day mind... it eventually lasted ten months. And despite the anger and despair of most Catholics at the executions after the Rising's failure, Republicanism in and around Newry remained far more underground than in many other places further south. But it was there all the same; and when Gerald came home alone from the war at the end of 1918, he couldn't have returned to a more dangerous place or at a worse time.

Upon his return he was best described as simple, although the psychological damage he'd suffered was far more serious and deep-rooted than that. But he was tainted immediately by his previous associations and by the long memories of some within the RIC, the Royal Irish Constabulary. The cynical memories of often bigoted and sadistic men of his adolescent belligerence to all those in authority, spewed easily from mouth to mouth.

He'd been an able-bodied, bright and charismatic member of the GAA before the war, the Gaelic Athletic Association; and although his only reason then had been to play Gaelic Football alongside his many sporting friends, the GAA and several other organisations had taken on a far more subversive complexion while he'd been away fighting. In January of 1919 the Irish War of Independence began in earnest, and as drilling and protests gave way to acts of guerrilla-style warfare across Ireland, men like Gerald came more into the Crown Forces' crosshairs. The bitter irony was that no man had less to do with the war than he did, and no man was less able to take an active part - but it didn't matter, by then his card was well and truly marked.

To add to his unwarranted suspicion one of his closest friends as he'd been growing up had been Paddy Rankin, who had since become the stuff of myth and legend as the only Newry man to take part in the Easter Rising. The fact that Gerald was never seen in Rankin's company after his return from France merely confirmed to some that they must be meeting in secret, and that his 'shell-shock' was just an elaborate ruse. He was a trained and blooded soldier after all, and such men were known to be giving weapon and other military training to the would-be rebels. To some then, the apparent severity of his contrived lunacy was merely proof of his cunning and sophistication. Such was the absurdity of the times.

Despite his fragile mental state and his father's death from a heart attack in May 1920, Gerald himself became a father just weeks later with the birth of Peter, my grandfather. That bode ill for the family business though, and Gerald's mother and his wife were scarcely able to stop it spiralling into bankruptcy. A number of opportunist would-be buyers were poised to step in, but the pace of revolution was picking up in South Armagh and several events that year rendered it an irrelevance. The following month saw a major turning point when a bungled IRA attack on three RIC in Cullyhanna ended in the death of one police sergeant and one

IRA Volunteer. There'd been several deaths in Dundalk by then, but suddenly the killing had come home to roost in Newry. Gerald subsequently appeared in police records as having been at the Volunteer's funeral, whereas in fact he'd simply been in a suit and a black tie as a sign of respect and he'd been on his way to Mass.

Then in Newry in November 1920, John Kearney the Head Constable was shot dead by the IRA as he left church in Needham Street. By that time the infamous 'Black and Tans' and the even more dreaded 'Auxiliaries' had arrived to support the police and soldiers in the town, and reprisals against Gaelic halls, known Republicans and Catholic homes were swift and often brutal. The die was cast and the flames were fanned almost daily.

In December things got hotter still, quite literally for Gerald and the McCormac family business, after an audacious but bungled IRA attack on the police barracks in Camlough and the soldiers who were sent to reinforce them. There were still more reprisals against Catholics in response. Elements of the police, the military and the Special Constabulary burned the Sinn Féin Hall in Newry and a number of Catholic homes and premises in the town and in Camlough. Among them was *McCormac & Sons, Purveyors of Tobacco, Provisions, Wines & Spirits*, on Buttercrane Quay.

By then the destruction of the largest part of the business was the least of my great grandmother's problems. Despite Gerald having had a complete mental breakdown in January of 1921, her only surviving son was harassed alternately by the Crown Forces on suspicion of being a rebel and by the IRA for being a suspected informer. By the time of the Truce in July though, even that didn't matter; because in the May Gerald had been committed to the Armagh District Lunatic Asylum. He eventually died there fifteen years later, aged just forty-six. God Save the King.

So now, bring on the next generation… and the miserable fate of the Irish to be caught yet again in the thorny web of British affairs. By the time Gerald's son Peter cycled forty-something miles to Belfast to enlist in the Royal Air Force in September 1939, he was a Catholic citizen of the still relatively new Province of Northern Ireland, the family business was no more, and at nineteen he had been a working plumber for a full five years. With just a basic education he'd enlisted with the romantic notion of somehow flying fighter planes against the Germans, but he saw out the whole of World War II in the no less vital role of ground crew for the Hurricanes and Spitfires flying out of Biggin Hill in Kent. Hardly a glamourous role, but he'd been there… and a large part of him always wished he'd stayed in England after the war. And some in Newry sensed it.

Both my grandfathers served in the British forces in the Second World War, which irked some in the town still smarting from our own conflict and the subsequent partition of Ireland, but in comparison with any previous male McCormac, Grandpa Peter lived a relatively quiet life. His plumbing business supported a modest home in Dominic Street and my father, his middle son Pádraig, was born in 1951. My dad took over from him when he passed in 1987. I was six by then and I'd got to know my grandpa reasonably well. I miss him still. Then later on I got to know him even better, through the tales of my Aunt Úna.

And then that leaves my 'Da'. He's the quietest of them all by a country mile, but a damn good plumber by all accounts. And although he was never an action-man sort of a dad, or the life and soul of every party – my mum would never have let him be that – I reckon he was a damn good father too. He worked hard and for long hours and got our mother a three bedroomed house in the Derrybeg as soon as they married. He stayed out of politics, stayed out of trouble and stayed out of pubs. He fathered Éamon, his first of six kids, when he was twenty-two, and Eilís, his last, just ten years later. Then he stopped. They stopped. Quite conservative for a Catholic back then, but all in all he seemed a pretty good catch for our mum and a damn good dad for us. And despite his fervent Catholic upbringing and a house full of strong characters (and even stronger nationalist views), none of us kids ever did drugs, got pregnant out of wedlock or joined the Provisional IRA.

Well…

None of us actually joined that is, but there was a fair bit of flirting went on. Welcome to life in the Derrybeg.

What's in a Date?

Back in January 1981, according to my Aunt Úna years later, there was a good deal of anxiety in our family about on what day I'd be born. Doubtless my father knew all about it as well, but from then until now he's never said a word about it. He'd never discuss something as dark and superstitious as that with us kids. Never has, never will, never could - and Mum was superstitious enough for the both of them.

And even then Aunt Úna only told me of their fears when I was fifteen, and once she felt I was old enough to understand. The same week that she and I talked for the second time about me not going to Mass anymore. Come to think of it, Aunt Úna began to tell me a lot of things right about then - and she began to teach me even more than she told. If there was one person in my upbringing who more than any other kept me out of the Provos and led me safely through the doorway to life, it was her. George Kennedy, a schoolmate at a crucial time in my teens, comes a close second. Thank God, no, thank my lucky stars for them both.

Aunt Úna said ninety-nine percent of that family burden was borne by my mother, which struck me as unfair because she'd just borne me for nine months as well. And she'd carried that fear for far longer than she'd carried me. She'd hauled it around with her for eight long years by then, since the birth of her first child – I was her fifth - and precisely *what* she'd been dragging around was the fear of each successive offspring, and so now me, being born on the same day as some local terrorist atrocity. Just like all four of my older siblings had. To her it was a dreadful curse, and one that somehow had to be broken.

It was actually a bit deeper and darker than that though, just like she was. Life wasn't life if our mum wasn't staggering around under the weight of something she neither deserved nor could prevent, and despite the priest's many attempts to help her she'd always find some other great weight to heap upon her shoulders. So in many respects, Aunt Úna always reckoned, I was the first lucky break she ever got. I guess the largest part of me has tried to live that way ever since.

My brother Éamon was our mum's first born, in 1973 and when she was just eighteen. What should have been a joyous occasion still haunts her today, forty-four years later. Just minutes before his birth my mother heard the shot from a British Army soldier that killed twelve-year-old Kevin Heatley near his home in the Derrybeg. In fact, right in front of *our* home in the Derrybeg, and less than a kilometre from her bed in Daisy Hill Hospital where she was busy having Éamon. She knew then that she hadn't prayed enough, nor confessed her many sins often enough nor fully enough, and that she and Éamon would pay the price equally. She never told Dad, but she told her sister Úna exactly that.

If she needed further proof that her fears were well founded and that her sins were insurmountable, then it came in the days before she had my sister Maud in 1975. On July the 17th she thought that she'd gone into premature labour when she'd heard that four army bomb disposal experts had been killed defusing an IRA device not far from Newry. Four brave ATOs, the Ammunition Technical Officers based in nearby Bessbrook Mill, who would face such odds almost daily. She had a special place in her heart for those poor young men.

She prayed for them always, although she dare not tell a soul, and in her mind she saw them as the young fighter pilots of the Battle of Britain who'd soared daily to almost certain death to protect the thousands of civilians below from the carnage of the Luftwaffe. It wasn't a comparison the IRA would have appreciated, and so she shared that with no-one either; except of course with Úna, whose secret loathing for the Provos – the Provisional IRA – was at least as great as hers.

But she never shared that with the priests though. For you could never be really sure back then. And so she didn't share it through the correct channels with God either; the root cause of her curse, she always believed. Instead she held on to Maud until the world was ready, literally. She cried and prayed herself into a stupor that day and on many days after, so that she didn't have Maud until she could hold on no longer; on May the 31st, and five days after she'd been due. A new day, almost a new month you might think; but no, things didn't get any better for Mum's curse.

When our mum first cradled Maud to her breast in Daisy Hill Hospital, in the self-same bed in which she'd had Éamon, there was a terrible buzz about the place and a terrible churning in her stomach soon followed. As the story unfolded and the nurses whispered more often and more loudly, the whole horrible truth of Maud's birthday became clear. Crystal clear and starkly awful. At 1 am that morning there had been carnage on the road from Banbridge to Newry, and the hideous face of even the Troubles acquired a new and disgusting scar.

Three members of the Miami Showband, one of Ireland's best known cabaret groups at the time, had been taken from their minibus, lined-up at the side of the road and shot dead by so-called Loyalist gunmen from the Ulster Volunteer Force. To add further injury to insult, two of the UVF gunmen had been killed when the bomb they were planting on the minibus exploded prematurely. In callously real terms it was just another day in war-torn Northern Ireland, but to my mother it was so much more; and Maud would be two years-old before our mum would celebrate her birthday for the first time.

How could she 'celebrate anything at such a time and in such a place' she would say? And when in January '76 the boot was on the other foot - when IRA gunmen lined up eleven Protestant workers at the side of the road at Kingsmill and shot them - it was hard to argue with her. Ten died and one survived... but not before they'd shot him eighteen times.

Two years after Maud came Margaret, on the 19th of May 1977, and for the first time my mother dared to hope that it hadn't coincided with some local atrocity. It hadn't directly, not a bomb or a bullet anywhere in the town, but not that you'd have guessed from her misery by the end of the day. What poleaxed her that time, Aunt Úna told me, turned out to be every bit as bad. But instead of a violent death this time, it coincided with a simple announcement from the Garda Síochána, the Irish police just across the border in nearby Dundalk, that they had "reliable evidence" that the missing soldier, Captain Robert Nairac, was in fact dead. That was a dreadful blow to my mother, and she'd been hoping to hear the exact opposite. Bob Nairac had been a fervent Catholic who'd been missing in South Armagh for four days by then, and our mum had been praying for him every minute of every hour of every day.

Nairac had been an intelligence liaison officer working out of Bessbrook Mill, and the around-the-clock helicopter activity in and out of the base - and so over our home and the hospital since his abduction on the 14th - had been non-stop in the search for him. So too, according to Úna, had our mum's concern for the twenty-nine-year-old's safe return.

That night he had gone undercover to the Three Steps Inn in Dromintee, from where he'd been jumped in the car park and taken to a field in Ravensdale Forest just across the border in County Louth. History subsequently showed that his conduct *after* capture was exemplary – he never once admitted who or what he really was and, a Boxing Blue from Oxford, he nearly fought free twice before he was eventually overwhelmed and shot dead – but his actions before that night had as good as ensured he was living on borrowed time. The subsequent award of a posthumous George Cross did nothing to turn back his clock.

It was a terrible time to be a woman of conscience living in 'Bandit Country' South Armagh, and our mother felt suitably terrible. She'd been in a pit of depression for weeks anyway. She had barely gotten over the death of a man called Robert Mitchell not three months before; not because she had known him well – she had only known him in passing, but for years and as the friendly grocer on Merchants Quay – but because she considered him to be a gentleman and because of the manner of his death. There'd been forty-two other such deaths in those three months as well. There seemed to be no end in sight for the ordinary citizens of Newry, and no depths to which some in South Armagh wouldn't sink.

As well as being a friendly and popular sixty-nine-year-old grocer, Robert Mitchell had been a Justice of the Peace for over thirty years and a leading member of the Orange Order. That alone was enough to seal his fate. Back then, in Newry's dwindling Protestant population of just fifteen hundred out of more than twenty thousand, that made him a legitimate target for the men of hate. The two IRA gunmen who killed him with a single shot to the head at his house in Windsor Hill, had held his two elderly sisters for ninety minutes while they waited for him to return home. The youngest, Ada, was just seventy-two. Elizabeth, her rock and her soulmate, was eighty-nine.

And so our mother's torment continued. It afflicted her so much, Úna said, that after Margaret she seriously considered having no more children. And so there might have been no me! But our mum was a devout Catholic, remember, and my dad's got no rhythm at all... so...

When my next sister was born, Eilís in 1979, it was my father's turn to be traumatised. Not that it helped my mum get over her superstition at all. Eilís's was, on the face of it, the worst of all the birthdays in our family, but my mum was so concerned for our dad that day that she choked back her tears and stumbled through his nightmare with him. That at least was progress.

There'd been a fearful expectancy in the town for weeks by then: it was August 1979 and so ten years to the month since the Troubles had started in earnest. Something foul was in the wind, something big, but little did we know the horrific double-bill that was destined for Eilís's birthday. And to make matters worse at the end of March, the INLA, the Irish National Liberation Army, had assassinated an MP called Airey Neave with a car bomb as he left the House of Commons in London.

Neave had been a highly symbolic target. During World War II he'd been a decorated soldier, he'd been the first British officer to escape from Colditz Castle, and he finished the war as a member of MI9 facilitating the escape of many other captured servicemen or agents. He was also a lawyer and spoke fluent German, and so he took part in the Nuremburg Trials as well. By 1979 he was the Shadow Secretary of State for Northern Ireland and the campaign manager - and relentless champion - for the rising star of British politics, one Maggie Thatcher.

Had Neave survived until the *Iron Lady's* victorious general election just five weeks later, he would have become the Northern Ireland Secretary; a fact not lost on his INLA killers. They told Neave's biographer years after, 'He would have been very successful at that job. He would have brought the armed struggle to its knees.' It had been a terrorist coup of the first order, and everyone in Ireland sensed – no, they knew – that the Provisional IRA would have to go one better. They didn't have long to wait.

On the day Eilís was born my father had been rushing back to the hospital for the birth and he was returning from a random job of work in Rostrevor, ten miles along the coast from Newry. He'd just driven through the small harbour town of Warrenpoint - already stunned at the news on the car radio of the killing of seventy-nine-year-old Lord Louis Mountbatten in County Sligo earlier that day - when he witnessed the beginning of an equal atrocity in his own rear view mirror.

It was soon after 4.30 pm on the bright summer's afternoon of the 27th. Those whom Tommy McMahon of the South Armagh Brigade of the Provos had already killed that day stood at three: Earl Mountbatten, the last Viceroy of India; his fourteen-year-old grandson, Nicholas Knatchbull; and Paul Maxwell, a fifteen-year-old boatboy from Enniskillen thirty miles across the border. There were four others on Mountbatten's boat: the eighty-three-year-old Dowager Lady Brabourne, who died from her injuries the following day, and Nicholas Knatchbull's mother, father and twin brother. They survived the blast but suffered horrendous injuries. Just like my father.

As my dad left Warrenpoint he'd just passed a suspicious-looking hay trailer parked by the side of the road near Narrow Water Castle, and he was about two hundred metres ahead of a three-vehicle British Army convoy he'd seen approaching the roundabout on the edge of town. The trailer had worried him, and so as he pulled away from the convoy on the fast dual carriageway after the roundabout, something told him to watch-out for the soldiers in his rear-view mirror. Huh, as if *he* could do anything to help them in any way? He was right, he couldn't.

As he watched he saw - and soon after that he heard and then felt - the colossal explosion that destroyed the rear 4-ton truck and killed the first six soldiers from A Company 2 Para. The massive explosion caused by the three hundred-kilogram radio-controlled bomb hidden under the bales of hay. He skidded to a halt instantly, dazed, confused and frightened, and he abandoned his car where it was. Then he began to part-walk, part-stumble, part-run back towards the burning vehicles and the stricken soldiers to see what he could do to help.

He never got there.

About half way back to the scene of the ambush a number of shots rang out, to and from the far side of the Newry River he thought, just a hundred metres away and safely in the Republic of Ireland. Our father sensibly took cover, although guiltily he told Úna later, and watched, listened and later smelt the carnage and mayhem from a distance. It's a smell, he claims during unguarded moments, that he can still taste.

It was a good thing he stopped though, because twenty minutes later and after more troops, more Land Rovers and three helicopters arrived, the second bomb went off not a hundred metres from where he lay. An even bigger bomb this time, built into the gate house and the likely Incident Control Point for any subsequent follow-up. The Provos had done their homework, and they'd been spot on. That bomb killed another twelve soldiers, and what little will to live my father still had on the day.

Even years later he never really talked to us kids about that day. None of us. Not Éamon, his eldest, arguably his favourite and a plumber just like him, and not even me once he believed I'd joined the 'Home Office' and so had some personal role in combatting the IRA. Although he did break down to Úna just weeks before my birth, and her tearful account of it to me years later still sends chills down my spine.

He told her how after the second bomb he wanted to run forward even more, and to help somehow, but how instead he lay even lower in the grass and seemed even less able to move than before. He tried to describe the smoke and the cries and the explosions; and what he thought were more shots, but which might have been just the soldiers' rounds exploding from the searing heat. He described the firemen from the first bomb staggering through the smoke and the limbs and the carnage, and the Wessex helicopter limping away with a broken rotor from the second; and he described the cars pulling up near to him, and their occupants climbing out, crying, clenching their fists, and all the Halloween-like faces with their hands to their mouths.

He got over that day eventually, more fully than our mum ever did in some respects, but not entirely he didn't. Jees, he wasn't alone. No-one who lived in or around Newry or the border back then ever got over those days entirely. Not even twenty years after it all ground to an ignominious halt. And as for the hundreds of families who were ravaged by it all directly... well, they'll probably never get over it at all.

So imagine my mother's trepidation when it was my turn, and when she was expecting me towards the middle of January 1981. Could things get any worse, she wondered to her sister? It was another particularly violent time right across Northern Ireland, and Newry, as always, was in the thick of it.

The back-end of 1980 had seen an abortive IRA hunger strike, in Her Majesty's Prison Maze and later in the Armagh Women's Prison as well, but the next eight months of the new year – my year – were to see a hunger strike to the death of ten IRA Volunteers; and of course all the associated attacks, riots and bloodshed right across the Province that went with it.

Just like with Maud in '75 my mother held on to me in her womb for as long as she could, and prayed that I'd be born into a world of peace and reconciliation. As if. So when on January the 16th my due date coincided with the murder of a forty-two-year-old major in the Ulster Defence Regiment, shot dead by IRA gunmen at the Warrenpoint Customs Post where he worked, my mother didn't even acknowledge that 'my date' had been and gone. She just held on, prayed harder and sought another.

Then the clock began to tick and she really began to worry. With me four days overdue, the body of twenty-four-year-old Maurice Gilvarry was dumped on the border after his execution for being a tout. A suspected informer in other words. That haunted her especially, killings like that always did, just as they did any right-minded citizen who had ever been seen being civil or kind to one of the British soldiers.

Then the very next day, the 21st, the clock ticked even louder and still more bloodshed. She felt a twinge but she hung on again; because that day Sir Norman Stronge, an eighty-six-year-old widower and former MP and Speaker of the Stormont Parliament, was killed by the IRA at his home in nearby Tynan Abbey. The gunmen killed his son too, and before leaving they burned their mansion to the ground. Its charred and smoking ruins were still smouldering when I was born – thank God - in the early hours of the 22nd.

At least the 22nd was a brand new day, and remarkably not a single person was killed. Not just in Newry, but not anywhere in Northern Ireland. Not on *my* day. Such days were almost unheard of, and so at last my mother's cycle of innocent births and violent deaths was broken. And her curse, she dared let herself believe, had been broken too.

According to Aunt Úna that made me special, and I guess as a result I was the first of us kids that she took a closer than usual interest in; although she was the same with Eilís and Kieran, one younger than me and one older, over time. She wasn't into kids, but I was her test case, her first of three saved souls for whom she was determined to show us that there was a bright and cheerful life to be had beyond the depths of our mother's virtual cell. In fact, 'Beyond the flames of her private Catholic hell,' were her actual words. And in some strange and pagan sort of way, it seems to have worked.

No doubt as a reward to our family, from God our mum chose to believe, no-one was 'killed' by terrorists on Kieran's birthday either in 1983. That made two in a row and was cause for further celebration, although her definition of not-killed was lost on me as a teenager. No-one was killed directly was her point, said Úna, although the day Kieran was born one prison officer died of a heart attack... when thirty-eight IRA prisoners broke-out of The Maze prison. And surprise surprise, guess where the Provos took them to hide straight from the breakout? Less than half were captured on the day and four more were rounded-up over the next two days, but the other half were smuggled all the way back to safe houses in South Armagh and County Louth to re-join the fight. Still more bandits for Bandit Country... just what we needed.

Except that looking back maybe the IRA did kill him, the warder that is - the Coroner could never say for sure - when they stabbed him during the break-out with a prison chisel.

Hey, killed or died he was dead anyway, like countless others before him and after, and the IRA certainly hadn't done anything to enrich his life. My mother's curse was a myth of course, as was me being the offspring who had broken it, but the nonsense of that day - the birthday of her last-born - showed what we right-minded citizens were up against. There was no rhyme nor reason, there was certainly no justice, and it was just that sort of a war. Get on with it, or go under.

Militis, Athleta, Amicus

This next story ends in 1982, the year after I was born and so moving along with the plot, but it began five or more years before that. Sort of. I find it fascinating to reflect sometimes on what others were doing at crucial moments in my own life, and even more so from the time before I was born. Especially when later on it's someone whom you meet and somehow interact with, and so you're able to track your converging paths.

This is such a story. It partly concerns someone I didn't meet until 2010, professionally at least, the week before he retired from the British Army and when I was based back in Northern Ireland and working for MI5 in T8NI. His name was John Conway and he'd been pointed out to me by others in the Service. Once we met I wanted to discuss the whole of his time in the army, and we'd talk again in years to come, but what I specifically wanted to talk about in some detail was what someone had described to me as his 'Crossmaglen years': the four years in the late-1970s and early-80s that he'd looked after Cross' in particular, and then another couple of years in the '90s when he'd gone back to do it again. Apart from anything else I wanted to hear his thoughts on Crossmaglen, Newry and South Armagh in general as I'd been growing up there.

We met-up in London at someone else's suggestion and we spent the best part of two days together. I'm glad we did. I got to bounce a lot of ideas off him and we both learned a lot. I learned about people mostly, and the army's ways of doing things, but also about life in general and the often crucial role of human nature in an armed conflict. That sounds pretty obvious, seeing as all wars throughout time have been waged not by the terrain being fought for but by the men and women who wanted it, yet its simple truth seems lost on a frightening number of key decision makers and sophisticated intelligence organisations around the world. It's a discussion I've never forgotten.

And we discovered that we'd met once before as well... when he was on foot patrol near Cullaville in 1998 and when I was seventeen and looking for the same answers about the Troubles that he was. Yet there were two crucial differences between us: I was growing up in South Armagh as an indigenous local, he was viewed by most as an unwelcome intruder; and we were asking very different questions, yet in an effort to arrive at virtually the same place. But that's another story for later on.

This tale though concerns Conway and an army mate of his but from an entirely different regiment to his own, and their serendipitous and fateful meetings over a five-year period – the total time they knew each other. But most of all it concerns the warrior creed and the fickle finger of fate, which is why I think you should hear it. It's more of the human aspect of war.

Despite Conway's Irish-sounding surname he was English, born and raised, just like both of his parents who'd met and married in the Royal Air Force in World War II. But it would seem he wasn't just English. When he was twelve he'd been stood-up in class and singled out by his over-enthusiastic geography teacher, because he had what Mr Hannah had bluntly described as, 'the perfect example of a Celtic skull'. Hannah then kept him stood up at the front of the class for the next twenty minutes, and he gave over half of his lesson on Ancestry and Regional British Geography using the shape of young John's head. It was embarrassing for a twelve-year-old on everyone's first day in a brand new school, but not as crazy as it sounds; and on closer analysis it explained a lot about the lad, as he settled awkwardly into his new secondary school, into the first really serious phase of his life, and into the onset of puberty and machismo.

It explained among other things his love of rugby, his interest in Celtic music and art, and of all things Welsh, Irish and Cornish. He'd never really known why until then, but Mr Hannah, himself a Scot and an ardent natural historian, said that his prevalent genes were almost certainly from his two grandfathers. Who were they, Hannah asked? Conway's paternal grandfather was from Cardiff, the capital of Wales (and *his* forebears were likely Irish migrants to the fortified harbour town of Conwy on the North-Wellian coast), and his maternal grandfather, who later emigrated to Canada, was from somewhere around Dublin. Mr Hannah was clearly right.

John was chuffed once he knew, and once he was allowed to sit down and get over his embarrassment, but from that day on he always felt more Welsh and Irish than English. That never caused a major conflict to his way of thinking though. At the end of the day he could be all three, and so he remained throughout his lifetime proudly British, but suddenly he learned he could be something more as well. Something ancient, emblematic and profound. I can't help but wonder now, in 2017, how he feels about Brexit and the events of the 23rd of June last year, but I've not yet had the chance to ask him.

Back in March 1977 though, John had just finished his second Emergency Tour of Northern Ireland and he'd been in the

British Army since December 1974. He was still a Private in the 2nd Battalion the Parachute Regiment, and the following month he got married. He and his wife hadn't planned to, not yet at least - they'd met through athletics six years beforehand and they were simply enjoying life - but part of what made them take the plunge was where the battalion was going next. West Berlin, and for two whole years.

The move followed the disbandment of the 16th Parachute Brigade and it was an opportunity unlikely to be repeated for a para battalion; although 1 Para had just been there from '74 to '76 while they kept a low profile in Northern Ireland following Bloody Sunday. 2 Para's tour promised much, and it didn't fail to deliver. The first lucky break for John and his mates in the Medium Machine Gun Platoon was to be re-trained and re-roled for the Berlin tour. Their battalion was one of the few in the British Army who retained the MMG role as a platoon skill. Most had embedded their Sustained-Fire gun teams into the rifle companies, where their team skills inevitably became jaded and almost a secondary duty - but not in 2 Para's 'Machine Guns' they didn't.

The GPMG in the Sustained-Fire role, GPMGSF, involved tripod-mounting the gun and then pre-recording targets out to fifteen hundred metres – eighteen hundred in extremis – with the famed C2 Trilux sight; the same one as used back then by the 81mm Mortar. That meant that you could switch targets, even in total darkness, in a matter of seconds. But how many seconds? That was the issue to the guys in the Machine Guns.

To fire your fall-back doomsday option, the FPFT – the Final Protective Fire Task – probably at night, and by definition whilst being assaulted head-on and so maybe overrun, your colleagues in their trenches needed to have absolute confidence that 'the Guns' knew what they were doing. Most targets were obviously to the front and a bloody long way off, but firing the FPFT meant unlocking the guns, re-laying the C2 sight, then swinging the gun through ninety degrees to fire directly across the top of the trenches occupied by his own guys in the flanking rifle company. The aim was simply to cut down enemy soldiers assaulting them out in the open in the huge and conical beaten-zone of the gun, but it was always going to be a shit-load of fire and a damn close thing. Once unleashed at over eight hundred metres a second a bullet can't choose sides, and so at that time the only safe place to be was pressed firmly into the bottom of one's trench. The place *not* to be, was stood above it with bayonet ready!

So in 2 Para the Machine Guns stayed as a formed platoon and practised their skills together; day and night, week in and week out. If deployed in combat the gun teams would be detached to the companies as and when necessary, but the rest of the time they ate, drank and played, fought, fucked and slept as a platoon - and that meant they were a pretty tightly-knit bunch. When guys from the platoon clocked a target 'switch' by the Demonstration Platoon at the School of Infantry at twenty-nine seconds, the 2 Para gun teams had an average of twelve seconds and a 'record' of nine. And safely. They were pretty damn impressive.

It was one of the best platoons in what was one of the best battalions in the British Army, as witnessed by its amazing action against odds of three-to-one at Goose Green in the Falklands not long after. So, nobody was in a hurry to break-up a winning combination, but for their forthcoming tour in Berlin the battalion had a conundrum. As part of the Berlin Field Force 2 Para didn't need a Medium Machine Gun Platoon, but what it had to find immediately and for the next two years was an Assault Pioneer Platoon, or Assault Engineers as the Field Force called them. Step forward the Machine Guns. Gladly. For six months prior to their departure from Aldershot, and then for the first few months in situ under a team of instructors from 38 (Berlin) Field Squadron Royal Engineers, the platoon re-trained and qualified as B2 Combat Engineers. Bingo.

Life for an infantry soldier in West Berlin in the '70s was an exhausting maelstrom of highs and lows. Among the highs were the inter-unit and inter-national sport; the clubs, bars and cabarets; the restaurants, cafés and beer halls; the Grunewald Forest; the city's many lakes; then of course there were the *women* at the clubs, bars and cabarets, restaurants, cafés and beer halls... and just the excitement of Berlin itself and the buzz of living 'behind the wall'. And there was Charlottenburg, and Grotty Charlotty's! And to cap it all, for a soldier, there was recent Nazi history on every corner, and usually quite a few bullet holes too. Oh, and did I mention the sport?

There was a huge amount of seriously competitive sport, both within the Field Force itself and between the other Allied Nations. In the French sector of West Germany for example, just a couple of hours away, the French, who still had conscription, had a unit in which they concentrated any full international athletes during their national service. That meant whenever you played the French in Berlin, in John's case at rugby or on the track, you were likely to face a couple of *ringers* from out of town who often looked vaguely familiar. But it made for some cracking games.

Amongst the lows, however, was the unremitting grind of company, battalion or garrison-level duties; a far greater than usual ceremonial burden, each involving endless rehearsals in baking Central European sunshine or in the driving rain; and the frequent Brigade-level call-outs, the infamous 'Rocking Horse'. The Rocking Horse was the Field Force's periodic dress rehearsal for repelling a full-on Soviet invasion of the Allied sectors of Berlin. To hear John Conway talk about those was a treat in itself.

For such rehearsals a soldier was to report immediately to barracks and parade, usually in the middle of the night and often in sub-zero temperatures, carrying one hundred per cent of a bewildering kit-list of things he was going to need to kill the enemy. Weapons, a stipulated amount of ammunition and certain key equipment were obviously top of the list – and so that was the first thirty-five kilograms he was going to have to carry – but then the real nonsense began. His KFS (knife, fork and spoon) might *have* to be in his rear-left kidney pouch for example – God forbid, never his right – because in the right one, as well as his mess tins containing a twenty-four-hour ration-pack and brew-kit, would be his spare socks, shaving materials, spare boot laces and his foot powder. And so on.

Turning out with all the right stuff in all the right places for an actual Rocking Horse wasn't the problem of course; for most soldiers, but sadly not all. So to ensure that the Commanding Officer was never embarrassed at such a fun event by the Field Force Commander, the battalion held its own rehearsals several times a month. And to ensure that one's Company Commander wasn't similarly embarrassed by his own CO, the companies held several a week. If you were unlucky enough to be in a platoon where the Toms weren't trusted to get their shit together for themselves, you could be doing some sort of a rehearsal every night. But not in the Machine Guns – they were better than that.

The funniest of a number of stories John told me was that of the luckless new addition to the battalion who just happened to be from Liverpool. All *Scousers* tell a good joke, some just make you laugh as soon as they enter a room, and he was one of those. But sadly for him this was going to take place on the battalion parade square in front of seven hundred elite soldiers, and not just in some bar with a few of his mates.

He'd passed-off at Depot Para just a month before, then after a couple of weeks leave he'd arrived in Berlin and was put into D Company. This was his first week in battalion, and so his first unit-level pre-Rocking Horse crash-out. The Machine Guns were formed up next to D Company that night, and so John and his mates saw what followed first-hand.

2 Para had two Commanding Officers during the twenty-four months they were in Berlin. The first was finishing his three years as the CO and was well known to Private John Conway, as they were both members of the battalion's First XV rugby team. Such instant recognition was sometimes helpful to a young soldier

groping his way through the complexities of regimental life, sometimes not, but on this occasion it meant John had a bloody good idea of what was coming before it had even happened. He nudged his mates to warn them and they weren't disappointed. It was about 2 am on the parade square in Brooke Barracks, 2 Para's home in Berlin, and it was about three degrees centigrade below freezing. The breath of the seven hundred-odd soldiers was freezing as it left their mouths; their hands, feet and ears had gone that way some time ago.

One man in the whole of D Company had put on his green woollen combat gloves, when they should in fact have still been in the bottom right-hand corner of his left-hand utility pouch. No-one had told him that. No-one had told him either that in 2 Para, gloves weren't for actually wearing. Not unless some extremity or other had already broken-off from frostbite - and even that had to be confirmed by a Medical Officer. It was a bit like one's rifle-sling was to be packed – at the very bottom of the right-hand external pouch of your Bergen rucksack – but under no circumstances back then was it ever to be fitted to your rifle! That's what you had two hands for, carry the damn thing, and you had to be ready to fire in an instant. The fact that your fingers might be too frozen to fire accurately was lost on most Sergeant Majors - paras didn't wear gloves... babies in prams did, and they were called mittens.

So, the be-gloved but luckless soldier, the brand new 'Scouser' from Liverpool, was in the front rank and he caught the eagle eye of the CO in the first ten seconds.

"You!" barked the Colonel.

"Yes Sir," said the Scouser.

"You've got gloves on."

"Yes Sir."

"I'll deal with this now, Sir," said the Regimental Sergeant Major, hard on the CO's heels, "you move on."

"No you won't RSM, I've got this." The CO turned back to his now quivering victim. "*Why* have you got gloves on?"

"Because my hands were cold, Sir."

"Sir, move on *please*," the RSM tried again.

"RSM, Step back." The CO pulled him gently by the arm to show that he meant it.

"Who the hell told you?" the Colonel bellowed at the young soldier... meaning 'who told you it was time to wear gloves?'

"No-one, Sir," said the Scouser, thinking he was about to be commended in his first week for his initiative, "I could feel them getting cold."

No reward was forthcoming.

This time the RSM *and* the Company Commander took an arm each and steered the CO and his flapping jaw onwards and beyond the screaming of the Company Sergeant Major. The CSM simply stepped-in behind them and marched the young lad to jail until morning... a long-morning, spent on the Assault Course. It was a cracking start to his first week in battalion and the highlight of the Rocking Horse for the Machine Guns, but it proved that not all lessons are best learned the hard way.

The other Commanding Officer, for the record, for the second year in Berlin and for the bruising two-year Northern Ireland tour that followed, was the magnificent Colin Thompson. In John's opinion he was the best Chief of the General Staff the Army never had. Sadly he would die of natural causes just three years later, and so his star would never fully rise, because it was *his* splendid 2nd Battalion that Lt Col 'H' Jones VC, OBE, would soon lead to such glorious heights in the Falklands War.

Life for those in the Assault Engineer platoon was far more interesting and rewarding than for the rifle companies. Between duties and ceremonial commitments it wasn't unusual for the soldiers to work six weeks in a row before having a weekend off, and then the call-outs were on top of that. At least when the Assault Engineers crashed-out, instead of digging trenches and freezing in them for twenty-four to forty-eight hours in the Grunewald, they would scramble over the city's many bridges rigging-up dummy demolition charges; or they would ferry Chieftain tanks across the Havel on five-man heavy ferries. Best of all, they still got to be 'The Machine Guns' and they kept up their gun-skills whenever other training permitted.

But I digress, back to sport in Berlin and the other soldier from the other regiment, the main subject of this story. Brooke Barracks was one half of a Siamese-twin-affair in Spandau that was Brooke and Wavell Barracks built back to back. 2 Para was in Brooke, on Wilhelmstraße and built by the Nazis in 1936, and the older Wavell Barracks on Seeburger Straße was home to the Welsh Guards. The Welsh Guards, needless to say, were very much a rugby-playing battalion. And within the battalion, the premiere rugby company was Prince of Wales Company. Herein lies the real point of this story.

In no time at all the two units' rugby teams were at each other in domestic competitions and 2 Para's rugby improved immeasurably. Not once in two years did they manage to beat the Welsh – although they bettered the French on several occasions – but by the end of the two years, and in the year that 2 Para made it to the quarter-finals of the Army Cup, they held them to just six points. Quite an achievement. The real losers from this period of 2 Para rugby though were 3 Para, who were beaten 56-0 by their sister battalion in a resurrected Airborne Brigade *Warrior Trophy* that year in Sennelager. John Conway was a wing three-quarter, and so he scored a number of the tries that day. Bonus.

The real point of this story though is the friendship that grew between Conway and a number of the Welsh Guards, and the guys in the Prince of Wales Company in particular. Not only did they socialise together on occasion in and around the barracks, in the second year they trained and sometimes played together as well. The Welsh so dominated the rugby scene in Berlin that the Field Force's equivalent of a Combined Services select team, the President's XV, would be put together on an as-and-when basis to play visiting representative or touring sides. But it was pretty much run by *The Welsh*.

The team manager was a commissioned ex-ranker from the Welsh Guards, the coaches were taken from amongst the battalion's Senior NCOs and Warrant Officers - including the legendary 'Sledge', the Company Sergeant Major of Prince of Wales Company - and so were the vast majority of the fifteen players for any given game. And rightly so. But then in one game against Swansea just before the Welsh Guards left Berlin, three outsiders managed to break into the squad: the by-now Lance Corporal John Conway and an officer from 2 Para, and one 'Blue Job' from the Royal Air Force at RAF Gatow. Recognition at last, and from no less than *The Welsh*.

Both battalions were heading for Northern Ireland next: the Welsh Guards on a four-month Emergency Tour of South Armagh, and 2 Para for twenty months as the resident battalion in Ballykinler, County Down. To cut a long and complicated story very short, a number of soldiers with a proven ability to talk to people soon found themselves working in intelligence roles in South Armagh instead of directly with their battalion. One of them was John Conway, and for the next four years he would be responsible for the Provo stronghold of Crossmaglen.

Imagine his delight then, when late in 1979, he moved into the base for the last six weeks of the current Crossmaglen Company's remaining time there, to find that it wasn't simply men from the Welsh Guards but the whole of Prince of Wales Company to boot. He knew many of them as well as he did guys from his own battalion, including 'Sledge' and a number of good friends from their rugby days in Berlin. One mate in particular though was Clive Ellis, recently promoted sergeant and with whom he would not only soldier in Cross' for their remaining time there, but whom he would meet again just before he sailed for the Falklands nearly three years later.

Over the next four years Conway would see nearly thirty different cap badges from the Army and Royal Marines roulement through Crossmaglen - a fair cross section of the British armed forces at the time - but few would give him the satisfaction of that first tour. Many of the young Welshmen were raised as farmers, and blessed as they were with the exact opposite of a posh English accent they would engage in long and meandering chat-ups with all manner of people throughout the area. John of course was the ultimate beneficiary - in his efforts to win hearts and minds across what was harshly declared an 'Int Desert' - as was his office and the 3 Brigade HQ.

Those were exhilarating days across the board for the young paratrooper, just twenty-four years-old and with less than five years' service, and there was only one major cloud on his horizon back then. It was in his rear-view mirror sure enough, and so receding all the time, but it was no less dark for that. His sombre burden was that the reaction force that had deployed smack into the second bomb at Warrenpoint had been a combined platoon of the Drums and the one he'd served-in pretty much since he'd joined battalion, and which he'd left just months before: the Machine Guns. Lest we forget.

From about that time in South Armagh and right up until I met him in 2010, Conway would become universally known in his world as 'JC'. Indeed, some people he met in years to come only knew him as that and didn't know his real name. I had come across such a person in the Security Service before I even met Conway. It had amused me, and so when I met him I asked John why? His explanation was simplicity itself.

"Ah, well see back in 1979 there were three Johns in the office, all with the same cap-badge, and it got more than a little confusing at times."

"Go on," I urged.

"Well *Big John* was exactly that, big, *Little John* was five-feet-three, and I was bang in the middle, so *JC* it was. Has been ever since."

"Right, so it's not what I heard then."

"I don't know. What did you hear?"

"So it's nothing to do with being a Roman Catholic then? Not that sort of *JC*?"

"Hardly," he laughed, "I'm non-practicing. Very."

"Me too."

"Yeah, I know, but I'll tell you what Neill, in my case it might be to do with *him*... as in, 'Jesus Christ, what's he fucked-up now?' Now that I could believe."

From the short time I got to know JC, I doubt it... but then there's all the stories that I don't know.

So the next serendipitous part of this story is Conway meeting up with Clive Ellis during rehearsals for 5 Infantry Brigade's 1982 landings in the Falklands. They met, fittingly, in Sennybridge Training Area in the heart of South Wales. JC was detached from Northern Ireland with another 2 Para man, Mick, and they were in the process of transferring to the Intelligence Corps. They had made various unsuccessful attempts to re-join their battalion en route to the Falklands, whereupon an inspired and innovative Int Corps officer, John H-W, tried to get them there with the Corps instead. He didn't manage, but JC remains grateful to this day.

He had them attached to the 5 Brigade Int Section instead, which at the time and prior to the formal re-establishment of an airborne brigade at all, comprised ten members - only the section commander of which was a parachutist. At least JC and his mate would have made an officer and two Senior NCOs if a parachute drop proved necessary, but that too was not to be. In the event neither of the parachute battalions jumped anywhere – it was the onset of the South Atlantic winter - and when the staff tables were drawn up for a re-invasion by sea, JC and his mate were dropped-off the manifest once again. But not before the random meeting with Clive Ellis.

The two paras had been assisting with the running of a live-firing exercise and some survival training for the lucky members of the Int Section still listed to sail south. After a long day's live-firing - during which Mick had saved some plonker's life from a dropped hand-grenade - and during an informal range reconnaissance by a user-unit for the following day, John saw Clive Ellis striding towards him. They shook hands, bear-hugged, caught up with each other's news and then sat down for an hour or more over a brew and some half-eaten rations. Then they said their farewells, yet again, and both headed south - Ellis off to the South Atlantic and JC back to South Armagh.

John's glad, he told me in 2010, that he had that precious hour and that they shared a brew, and he's especially glad they got to talk a little rugby and catch up with some news; because the next he heard of Clive was in the early days of the fighting on East Falkland. The very early days, and before some of them had even managed to shake-off their sea-legs and put ashore. In fact, some never got to the beachhead at all.

On the 8th of June 1982, when the Royal Fleet Auxiliary *Sir Galahad* was bombed by the Argentinian Air Force in the unfortunately named *Port Pleasant*, Clive was one of forty-eight men who didn't make it and who perished in the searing heat below decks. Life can be cruel and they deserved a better war than that. Death can be even crueller, and Clive Ellis certainly did.

"But you know what?" JC said when we discussed those Crossmaglen years and all that followed. "At least he'll always be what he was back then and in Berlin."

"How do you mean?" I asked.

"Well, he'll always be what they used to call him then, 'young Clive Ellis'. A great guy, a good soldier and a hell of a rugby player. I bet that's a lot better than whatever they'll say about us in a few years' time... I reckon he'd have settled for that."

Aye, fair play to him. I obviously never got to meet Clive Ellis, but I reckon he would have at that.

Windows to the World

So, I wouldn't know anything about the next four or five years, being just a toddler, except for what I found out later from mum's scrapbooks and her photo-album. And of course from Aunt Úna. I was about twelve when she first really talked to me about the Troubles, and up until then they were something grown-ups would talk about in terms of staying alive, staying out of trouble and staying true to your faith. Whatever that meant.

Most families in the 1980s seemed to take videos of special occasions, even in the Derrybeg, but not us we didn't. Mum reckoned all the cheap cameras from around abouts were either stolen or from Jonesborough market, and so the same difference. Either way, buying such fancy goods was 'putting money into the wrong hands,' she said, and so she wouldn't entertain it. But I believe now she was also frightened of what horrors they might capture and replay forevermore, like natives would fear the cameras of the early explorers. In their case they were frightened that such contraptions would capture their souls, but I reckon our mum was terrified of what sins they might portray.

No, with her photo-album censorship was a cinch. She could select and keep only the best pictures. Only the happy, smiling and uncomplicated memories that would allow her to put her own spin on what had been going on that day, and nobody else was allowed to touch them except to look. That part I understood eventually - and despite the Troubles we did have many happy days - but Jesus, her scrapbooks, they were something else again.

She had nearly a dozen of them in the end, each one a big thick door-slab of a book that weighed a ton. They went from just before Éamon's birth right up until the millennium, and then not a single newspaper cutting after the 1st of January 2000. Nothing ever again. My mum was forty-five by then, and so I suppose she'd seen enough in her lifetime to have formed her opinion of the world; or maybe she just hoped the new millennium would tell a different tale.

As with everything as I grew up the scrapbooks required Aunt Úna's interpretation before they made any sense, but the stark images and the raw facts they conveyed pretty much spoke for themselves. Even with Aunt Úna's explanations I could never be sure as a teenager whether they were catalogues of all the evil in the world, journals of the Troubles in Northern Ireland, or simply an addendum to the bible to frighten us kids back onto the straight and narrow. For years they did the latter quite nicely; but for a while there, they nearly led me the other way. It must have been the same for my siblings I guess, but some of us turned back more fully than did others.

There was nothing in the scrapbook from around the time of my birth, not even any cheerful stuff - like President Reagan securing the release of the fifty-two American hostages held in Iran for over four hundred days - but there were two whole pages of photographs in her photo-album. That was hardly a surprise though, coz it had been me who'd broken her curse, remember?

But there were a bunch of things pasted-into the scrapbook from not long after. Weird and seemingly unrelated things for a young mother living in the global backwater of Newry, and all of which were dark and in some way sinister or disconcerting.

There's a newspaper cutting, for example, from when Bobby Sands became the first to go on hunger strike on the 1st of March 1981, but not a mention of him being elected as a Member of Parliament for Fermanagh and South Tyrone the following month. And then, more tellingly, there was nothing either from when he became the first of the ten prisoners to die in early-May. Yet there were several articles from a fortnight later, when five soldiers were killed in a Saracen armoured car on Chancellors Road; but I guess that's because my mother heard the bomb go off just a couple of kilometres from our house. Jesus, half of Newry heard it, and the single biggest piece of wreckage they found was the huge radiator blown over a house and the nearby railway bridge. Five men and an eleven-ton armoured personnel carrier, blown quite literally to bits.

Two months later there was a cutting about the soldier killed and two others injured in Glassdrumman, when the IRA ambushed their own would-be ambushers from the Bessbrook unit's Close Observation Platoon. I don't think it was even the soldier's death our mum was recording that time - it was just one of a dozen killings that month - I think it was the fact that the IRA gunmen fired hundreds of rounds from an M60 machine-gun into the derelict van the young men were concealed in. For some reason she could never explain to her sister, she found that especially sickening; just as she must have the two following attacks in London - the last two things she pasted-into that volume in the October.

In the first of them Lieutenant General Sir Steuart Pringle, Commandant General of the Royal Marines, lost a leg in a car bomb outside of his home in Dulwich; and in the second, a police bomb-disposal expert, Kenneth Howarth, lost even more. He lost his life defusing a device in the Wimpy Bar in Oxford Street of all places, and my mother lost a little more of the faith she clung to so desperately. There seemed to be no rhyme nor reason to the cuttings, just things that caught her eye, and despite the hundreds of attacks in South Armagh and across the Province in the months that followed, the next thing she pasted into a brand new scrapbook was in London as well. As a result, for years I thought my mother had some secret obsession with horses, such was the space she devoted to her next two entries, but later I realised their wanton slaughter simply touched a million raw nerves among the horse-loving and fundamentally peaceful folk of Ireland. This time she wasn't alone.

The Hyde Park and Regent's Park bombs in two separate attacks on the 20th of July 1982 left eleven soldiers dead and fifty people injured, but the most striking images right across the media was of the seven horses of the Blues and Royals laying bloody and broken in South Carriage Drive. Naturally one of those convicted of the bombings in due course came from Crossmaglen, and my mother's shame was complete. Then, at the start of 1983, as if the Provos hadn't miscalculated enough in recent months, they kidnapped and killed the magnificent racehorse *Shergar*. Now to the Irish, that was a *real* sin.

Shergar was a one-off. Not only was he Irish-bred and a spectacular horse, he'd won the 1981 Derby by the greatest margin that century. He'd endeared himself to a nation of horse lovers – no, a world of horse lovers – with his elegant stride, his lolloping tongue and the valiant white flare on his face and his four white 'socks'. He was a horse in a million, but to the IRA godfathers in South Armagh and their ilk he was ten million in one horse. He was worth a thousand times his weight in guns, bombs and bullets, and he was owned – or so they thought – by the multi-billionaire the Aga Khan.

There remain endless theories about who were the actual masked men who took Shergar at gunpoint from the Ballymany

Stud in County Kildare, but even at the time few doubted that the two million-pound ransom demand was on behalf of the Provos. That was their first mistake, and although the horse was insured for ten times that, the Aga Khan was just one of thirty-four people in the syndicate that owned him. Their second was miscalculating the immediate and universal revulsion at their actions and their consequences right across Ireland.

Scores of journalist's arrived overnight and picked their way through any clues and leads, while just about every known IRA haunt or safe-house on both sides of the border was raided and searched by the security forces. There were no signs of Shergar right enough, but there were significant discoveries of arms and ammunition and a number of key Provos were forced to go on-the-run. Within days the horse's captors realised there would be no ransom, and so he was not only worthless, he was proving to be a millstone of unbelievable weight. They couldn't sell him, they couldn't move him, and they knew beyond any doubt that they could no longer keep him, so they did the only other thing they were any good at – they killed him. And not with a humane killer or a single shot to the temple, but allegedly with a machine-gun and in the most bizarre, bungling and sickening of circumstances. Not their finest hour, and my mother traced every painful second of it in that year's scrapbook.

The rest of 1983 through her eyes was equally bizarre. There's not a mention of the April bombing of the US Embassy in Beirut, which killed sixty-three and injured many more, and yet there's a cutting about the sale of the first compact discs in the UK. There's not a mention of Margaret Thatcher's landslide re-election in the June – largely thanks to the sacrifice of Clive Ellis in the Falklands and others like him – but in the September she saved two unrelated pieces about Ronald Reagan making GPS available to civilians, and the existence of what thereafter would be known as the AIDS virus. I think she was a Reagan fan, hence his repeated appearances, but I was pleased to see in later years there was never a mention of John Conway or his cohorts. Not in Mum's scrapbooks at least.

According to Aunt Úna our mum never really understood AIDS or anything about it, except that it was to be feared and so it had made it into her scrapbook. It also made it into regular warnings throughout my teens, although they were seldom accompanied by eye contact and never by further discussion.

The IRA bombing of Harrods in December 1983 got a whole two-page spread of its own, at least half of which concerned thumb-nail bios of the six people killed and some of the ninety injured. That attack so disturbed her apparently that we took down our Christmas decorations, but by the following year so much else had happened that Santa was allowed back in.

Two short cuttings announced the start of 1984: the first concerned the attempted assassination of Gerry Adams by the UFF, the Ulster Freedom Fighters, and the second the successful assassination of a young policewoman, Yvonne Fletcher, shot dead by automatic fire from inside the Libyan Embassy in London. More about Libya and Gaddafi later, but Aunt Úna observed it was clearly going to be that sort of a year.

The middle of the year was dominated not by our mum's scrapbook, but by two whole pages of photographs in her album following President Ronald Reagan's visit to his ancestral home at Ballyporeen in County Tipperary. Then her infatuation became clearer: Reagan was Irish-Irish, like Jack Kennedy had been, and not Comically-Irish, like President Barack 'Paddy' Hussein Obama, during a visit to *his* ancestral home in County Offaly some years later. Of course, the fact that Reagan had also been a dashing, Brylcreemed B-movie star from the earliest days of her childhood might have also had something to do with it; and in 1960s Newry for a young girl and until the start of the Troubles, there was pretty much only the old Picturehouse to go to.

None of the family got to see Reagan – indeed no others were interested according to Aunt Úna – but one of his junior staffers, Patrick McCormac IV from Massachusetts, stayed-on in Ireland after the visit and sought us out in Newry instead. He was a direct descendant of the first Patrick McCormac, of 1846 fame and the missing potatoes, and he was keen to get back to his roots. Well he sure did that, and he got more into the swing of things in *The Old Place* than he'd bargained for.

He couldn't stay with us in the house - we only had three bedrooms; mum and dad in one, us three boys in the next and the three girls in the other – so he spent a couple of nights in a small hotel in the town and came to spend the next two evenings with us. Aunt Úna said he was going to spend a third evening there too, until two guys in balaclavas engaged him in a little diplomacy South Armagh-style as he left the Derrybeg at midnight. According to the shaken Bostonian's explanation to Úna before he left, their brief and one-sided discussion went something like this:

"So you must be the arse-kisser to that Thatcher-loving fuckwit Reagan."

"But..."

"Best you know your diplomatic status here in South Armagh is hereby revoked."

The second hooded gunman laughed.

"So you get your sorry arse out of Newry or we'll arrange the trip for you. One way, steerage of course, and no happy endings."

Then they left... and so did he, on the first train to Belfast in the morning. He spent his last night in Ireland in the Europa – then Europe's most-bombed hotel – and he's pretty much dined-out on the whole episode ever since. But the one thing he's never done is return.

Mum devoted several pages of her scrapbook to the Provisional IRA's attempt to blow-up Maggie Thatcher and her cabinet in the Brighton hotel bombing in the October. Although the Prime Minister survived, five of her colleagues or their spouses didn't and over thirty people were horribly injured.

Inevitably the *Iron Lady* opened the following session of their party conference the next morning bang on time at 9.30 am, and she subsequently turned the attack into a political and moral victory. But, just as Aunt Úna had predicted back in April, it had indeed been 'that sort of a year.'

Had anyone known about the four huge shipments of state-of-the-art weapons, high-grade plastic explosives and ammo to the Provisional IRA from Libya in '85 and '86, doubtless my mother would have had numerous cuttings about those too, but after the mortar attack on the police station in Newry in February '85 Aunt Úna says her heart wasn't in the scrapbooks for the rest of that year.

In addition to the nine RUC officers killed there were a further dozen injured and twenty-five civilians. Mum knew a number of them. And as for the truck the home-made hundred-kilogram Mk 10 'Barrack Buster' mortar bombs had been fired from, well, guess what, that had been hi-jacked in Crossmaglen earlier. Although she'd never sit and go through them with me as I grew up, my mother described her scrapbooks as 'Windows to the world'. But the sage of the family, Aunt Úna, always reckoned they were more like portals to her cell. A glimpse out – or in I suppose – at her fears. Where music CDs, Ronald Reagan's GPS and the AIDS virus fitted into that analogy I'm not sure, but the books themselves are fascinating to plough through to this day. If more than a little morbid. But more of them later I'm sure.

And when I look back at those years, and 1985 when I was four in particular, I try to compare my recollections with those of four-year-old Michael McCann at the moment he lost his mother in the UVF bombings in Dublin. It's something I do often lately.

And yet there is no comparison. How could there be? My earliest distinct memories are happy and from six years-old, of a loving and caring family – even if my mother tried to care for all humanity - whereas his are of a violent and abusive father who deserted him, and of his mother being blown to bits right in front of his young and trusting eyes. And as for his memories of the years that followed... well... they must be about as different from mine as heaven and hell. And I suppose that, more than anything else, is the difference between us.

That and our choices.

Poppies, Prayers and Purgatory

Not all of my youngest memories are good though. One of the most vivid from my primary school years was of a family road-trip to Enniskillen in 1987, just a couple of months before my seventh birthday. Or it was almost a family road trip, because Éamon and Maud skipped home that day and didn't come with us. In fact they *refused* to come with us, much to my parents' disgust. My parents were kind of low anyway – Grandpa Peter, my dad's father, hadn't long passed - and so we were all a bit weepy.

The road-trip started something bigger than I could get my head around at the time though, and our previously happy, cohesive and very Catholic family fractured and was never quite the same again. But I soon began to understand in later years, once I got to secondary school and amongst the bigger kids. Once I realised where I lived, who I was, and what was going on all around me. Once I realised there was a war on.

I say happy, and we were by and large, because us kids had always just played until then – or played up – and we'd seemed fundamentally different from our mum and dad and immune to mum's permanent state of anxiety and shame. I guess what I'm struggling to say is that life was simple and secure for us, until a growing awareness of a wider world rendered it something else. And for once Aunt Úna didn't have to explain it all, and I worked it out for myself. But I hadn't really fallen under her spell by then. She was just fun at that stage, whereas our mum was anything but.

I didn't understand it at the time, but our mum was best summed up by something Úna used to sing to her to tease her whenever she heard a certain song on the '60s programmes on the radio. I now know it was *"Poetry in Motion"*, by Johnny Tillotson from 1961, and that it had reached Number 1 in the UK charts, but to me back then it was a tongue-in-cheek song called *'Purgatory in Motion'* and I wasn't sure why it was so funny. Only Úna and the older kids laughed... my father sure as hell didn't.

Purgatory was a concept I couldn't even imagine until I was a teenager, much less understand, and once I did I also understood why my God-shaped hole remained unfilled. The earliest priest I remember, Father Byrne, used to tell me about my 'God-shaped hole' and how I should 'let God's splendour pour in and satisfy my every need', but for me that well stayed dry until I filled it with other things. Strong, caring and positive things, but not God. Humanitarian things, but not Christian. Tangible, practical things, but not in the least bit Catholic. I think being taught to fear God is what did it for me, and if I'd been instilled instead with the love of God we might have established a dialogue. Whatever.

The family trip to Enniskillen was on a Sunday in late-November, and its purpose was to secretly attend the re-staged Remembrance Parade from two weeks before. Secretly of course because we were Catholics, Catholics from the Derrybeg Estate at that, and the Poppy Day Parade was a very British thing. Very

Protestant, very Crown Forces, and very offensive to the IRA and all those under their spell; although Enniskillen was a two-hour drive from Newry and safely on the other side of the Province. But our mum and dad insisted we go as a sign of respect because of what had happened. Looking back, I see it was a sign of disgust.

It must have been the 22nd I suppose, because someone said it was the twenty-fourth anniversary of President Kennedy's assassination, and I reckon looking-back that it was the first time I really took on board anything about the Troubles at all. It was certainly the first time I ever understood there was something called Remembrance Sunday, and that there were other parades as big as the Anniversary of Internment. We didn't get out much in the Derrybeg, and if you waited long enough the Provos would bring the entertainment to you.

I certainly recall all the news programmes from the Sunday two weeks before though, and our mum rocking in her armchair and gently sobbing for most of the day. The Provos had planned to attack soldiers of the Ulster Defence Regiment who would be on parade, but the bomb they exploded close to the town's war memorial caught everyone but. The Provisionals killed eleven people that day, many were pensioners and all were Protestant, plus sixty-three injured. Thirteen of them were children.

As if the IRA's gross miscalculation could get any worse, a few hours later it called a radio station and said it had abandoned another hundred and fifty-pound device in nearby Tullyhommon when it had failed to detonate. Had that one gone off as well its likely victims would have included many of the Boys' and Girls' Brigades assembled for the Remembrance Service there. Army bomb-disposal officers defused it and traced the command wire back to a firing point across the border in the Republic of Ireland, but Sinn Féin struggled even harder to defuse the universal condemnation that followed.

In elections soon after the attack Sinn Féin lost four of its eight seats on the council and it wasn't until 2001 that its electoral support returned to its pre-1987 levels. And on the day after the bombing I can remember Aunt Úna telling the whole family about U2's scathing denunciation at a concert in Denver. She was still angry herself, and she told us all how Bono - the revered singer of the almost sacred Irish band - had screamed "fuck the revolution" to the audience and railed against all the armchair Republicans in America who gave money and support to the so-called cause.

I think that stunned me more than the images of the bombing on the television. It was the first time I'd ever heard the 'F' word said in our house - I'd heard it plenty in the street, and I'd even practiced it myself – and then the actual performance stunned me all over again when I watched it for the first time some years later. It was in the middle of *"Sunday Bloody Sunday"*, and it's one of those many moments in music that stops time.

There had been several hundred at the original parade on the 8th, but over seven thousand turned out for the re-staged event; including huge numbers of Catholics like us, and even Maggie Thatcher, the Prime Minister from London. I remember I kept asking, "If this is the day they shot President Kennedy, why would the Prime Minister come to Northern Ireland to get herself blown up?", and I remember Aunt Úna joking, "Sure, it wouldn't be the first time, I suppose she's over it."

But the other thing that stunned me that day was the blazing row between my parents and Éamon. He was not far-off fifteen at the time, and he'd begun to form his own opinions about the Troubles and all they entailed. Or at least the thugs around the Derrybeg had. Maud and he were inseparable back then and she was two years younger, so he was a potent role-model for her too.

When they refused to go with us to Enniskillen to pay our respects, the mother of all fights took-off until Éamon stormed out of the house and he took Maud with him. So we went without them in two cars, ours and Aunt Úna's, and she says we never really got them back after that. Oh, they didn't leave home or anything, but they became scathing about the Brits and the police, and they would take the Provos' side over every incident, major or minor, until the former Catholic solemnity of our family home-life was shattered forever.

With all that going on and with my newfound awareness, several things about me changed forever too. I started noticing things for myself, and although I never compared notes with my mum's scrapbooks at the time, when I've dipped back into them since I've found that she'd held onto pretty much the same images and events that I have in my mind. And that's when I started to watch the news. Any news, all news, and every day.

Aunt Úna says it was the same for her generation too, and all her earliest recollections were of the Vietnam War night after night, or of the Apollo space programme and the earliest days of the Troubles; but the news for the next year or so virtually shaped everything else in my life. And it was nearly all bad.

On the 29th of February the next year, 1988, a crazy sequence of events filled our TV screen and my seven-year-old thoughts for the next couple of months. On that day two local men, 'the two Brendans' they called them, were killed by their own bomb out by Creggan near Crossmaglen. That didn't mean so much to me when I saw it that night on the local news, but two things that fell out of it in the following days had a profound effect. The first was my mother thanking God for taking them – the only time, she told Aunt Úna, that she'd ever prayed for the death of someone else's sons – and the second was the sheer scale and spectacle of their funerals.

Moley and Burns were two of the most active members of the South Armagh Brigade, and their bombs had brought carnage and heartbreak to countless families over the years. Including ours... because although I didn't know it at the time, Burns was allegedly involved in the Warrenpoint bomb that so crushed my dad's heart. No surprise then that they were buried with full IRA military honours, and no less than Gerry Adams and Martin McGuinness were among the pallbearers. Several thousand attended their funerals in Cross' and Cullyhanna, and many of them walked the four miles along tiny country lanes behind Moley's coffin from his home in Dorsey to the church. These were potent images to a seven-year-old boy, whoever they were and whatever side they were on, and I knew then that someday I would have to play a role of my own. Nearly thirty years on I can look back and know I was right... but I can also count my blessings for good choices.

Then, just six days later, one of the most bizarre and sickening fortnights of the thirty-eight year Troubles began to unfold, and my already heightened curiosity burned ever more brightly. That flame would never really go out after that, and my naïve and passing interest became an obsessive fascination; but as I grew the winds of adolescence blew me first this way and then that. Maybe that's why, once I *knew* which way to go, I never looked back at all.

Things happened quickly then, and with brutal finality at every turn. On the 6th of March three IRA Volunteers, Mairéad Farrell, Daniel McCann and Seán Savage, were shot dead by the Special Air Service as they prepared an attack against British Forces in Gibraltar. There were many questions and from many quarters: Were they warned or were they not? Were they armed - the follow-up showed they weren't - and were they about to activate an actual device, or were they still involved in merely their final reconnaissance? But once the shooting was over and the panic and the screams had died down on Gibraltar's ancient streets, only one thing was really certain: three IRA terrorists had died so that eleven people might not, as in Enniskillen; or like the eighteen soldiers killed at Warrenpoint; or the thirty-four innocent civilians, mostly women, slaughtered by the UVF in Dublin and Monaghan in 1974. Even at seven I could do the maths for myself, and three versus many seemed like a good outcome.

But not many in the Derrybeg or across South Armagh would have arrived at the same sum as me.

Then at the Belfast funerals of the fallen three, in the Republican plot of Milltown Cemetery ten days later, Michael Stone, a lone-Protestant Volunteer from the Ulster Defence Association, attacked the mourners with grenades and two handguns. Miraculously Stone only killed three people that day, but he injured more than sixty and the chaos and madness of the moment was captured by television crews covering the funerals. And so again I was among the thousands of stunned viewers who watched right around the world that night.

Not to be outdone by the sheer lunacy of that day, the sadistic finger of fate intervened at one of the funerals that followed as well. Two British Army corporals from the Royal Signals, Derek Wood and David Howes - not covert operators but in plain clothes and driving an unmarked car - drove into the funeral procession on Andersonstown Road by mistake. It was one of their last mistakes; they made others in the few precious minutes that followed.

They were overwhelmed in seconds, hauled from their car, beaten, stabbed and brutalised before being shot dead and dumped on nearby waste ground. And once more the savagery was filmed by the media present for the march to Milltown Cemetery - and yet again I sat in a bewildering smog of shock, awe and disgust at the grotesque images on our television. There was certainly nothing simple about 'these Troubles', I quickly learned, but to me and the kids I played with in the Derrybeg, we had no shortage of graphic images for our cowboys and Indians. I was at an impressionable age, and I think I might have even come out of 1988 looking the wrong way but for a number of things.

The first was my eldest brother Éamon. He had become almost rabid in his support of the Provos, and Maud was still under his spell. The arguments at home became angry and vitriolic and the rest of us kids sided with our parents out of fear as much as anything else.

The second was that my mother insisted I be moved from St Patrick's Primary School on the edge of the Derrybeg, to St Colman's Christian Brothers' Primary on the other side of town. Even at seven years-old I wasn't sure God and I were on the same wavelength, and the thought of having to face the Brothers at school as well as in church filled me with dread. When I started there in the September many of my personal fears proved correct, but with hindsight it at least taught me about discipline, structure and hard work; and it probably got me away from the Derrybeg just in time.

The other two things that turned my gaze back to the right side of the tracks, came before my change of school and via the news yet again. And both, as usual, were provided by the Provisional IRA. The first was the six British Army soldiers blown-up in their minibus in Lisburn in June, after running in a marathon for charity; and the last was in the August, when the IRA killed eight soldiers and wounded twenty-eight with a roadside bomb that destroyed their coach near Ballygawley. It seemed that every time I became in any way attracted to the romantic notion of a united Ireland, the Provos would do something horrific to push me away again. So too would the soldiers in Newry on occasion, although they were more thoughtless or stupid than horrific, and so it became about observation and balance and judgement.

Thus I began my new life in my new school, 'old before my time' Aunt Úna always said, and I watched the news, played my games and looked forward to my eighth and latest birthday. Life was pretty good at seven I reckoned, if a little serious - and my glass was undeniably always half-full - although my God-shaped hole remained pitifully dry.

Boys Must Be Boys

The substance of my nightly news fix on the television hardly ever changed, only the names did. Of the seventy people killed in Northern Ireland in 1989 as a result of the Troubles, thirty-eight were civilians, fifteen were British Army and nine were in the Royal Ulster Constabulary. Two of the slain policemen were Chief Superintendent Harry Breen and Superintendent Bob Buchanan; followed, ambushed and killed just down the road from us on the border south of Newry. They were the highest ranking RUC officers killed by the IRA during the Troubles, and they had been returning from meeting their Garda counterparts in Dundalk. The final report concluded that the gunmen may have known they were coming from someone in the Garda station, although basic surveillance seems just as likely. But who could ever be sure? And so who could you trust? Still more bandits for Bandit Country?

A total of six terrorists were killed that year, three of which were Republicans and three were Loyalists. That was the only fair and equitable thing on offer, and sadly it was only a statistic. A further eleven Royal Marine bandsmen were killed by an IRA bomb in their barracks in England, and the total number of men, women and children maimed or injured in 1989 ran into the thousands as always. Republicans were responsible for fifty-seven of those deaths, Loyalists for nineteen, and the security forces for two. All in all, it was a fairly typical year for the Troubles... except it was an unusually quiet one. On the streets of Newry that is, and across the Province in general. Yet for our family it was anything but a quiet year, and for me it proved to be pivotal in any number of ways.

I settled into my new school surprisingly quickly. After eight years growing up in the Derrybeg I didn't suffer for long from bullying. Not from the other kids at least, but a few of the Brothers were another issue. And our smart, pressed, black uniforms afforded us a certain anonymity. I had to remove my blazer and tie before the final leg of my walk home though, unless I wanted to fight the older kids for every inch; and I learnt how to not be seen or be noticed and how to fight like fuck if I was. By my ninth birthday in January 1990 I was quite the little hard-case, although unlike most of my peers I would only confront trouble if and when it sought me out. The rest of the time I was still what Aunt Úna called 'bookish, polite and courteous'. But that was often enough to be able to keep my hand in.

At home I was quiet though, and ostensibly meek. I was being taunted in the street as a 'posh kid' and I think my parents started to believe it too. But Éamon's adolescent outbursts and his surly behaviour was the main reason for my timidity, and my fear that my mum and dad would think I was headed the same way was the other. It meant that even at that young age I developed two different personas for two very different worlds, and I could stroll unseen and unflappable from one to the other seemingly at will. That would serve me well in the years to come. It was such a good act at home though that it even fooled Úna, and she normally didn't miss a trick about anything.

She told my mum that I needed something more in my life to keep me from the clutches of the thugs around our estate, but which would toughen me up and make me a match for anything they could throw at me. More than that, she berated her older sister that I spent all my time at home around women and that I needed positive male role models as soon as possible. My dad was always at work and Éamon, who hated me anyway for being the son who'd 'broken our mum's curse', was hardly ever in; and so Maud, Margaret and Eílis were the only older siblings I had daily contact with. Add to that my mother and Aunt Úna herself, and my mum agreed. She even confided that she thought I was becoming soft, but she could see no easy solution. Good job they didn't know the truth, but I realise now they were right in other ways.

To compound things Maud was as surly and belligerent as her older brother, and when the two of them and our father were in the house together there were invariably bitter arguments. Kieran was two crucial years younger than me, and so not a natural playmate, but he was already my shadow and Úna was determined that we and Eílis would be led along a different path. Eílis was the youngest girl and thankfully she was under our spell, not Éamon's, and so Aunt Úna reckoned she had a plan.

With my parents' blessing and in her own spare time, Úna took it upon herself to introduce me and Kieran to the world of Gaelic Football. It was only at the junior level but Eílis would come along too and the three of us – her 'Three Musketeers' she called us – would travel in her car to games or to practice at every opportunity for the best part of a year. They were bad times and there were some bad areas, but she drove us anyway.

Dad drove of course, but cautiously and he was forever working; our mum never drove at all and Éamon couldn't afford a car, so it was Aunt Úna to the rescue as always. What I didn't know at the time though, was that our pretty thirty-three-year-old auntie was having a torrid affair with one of the players from the Culloville Blues. So she was putting in some pretty serious training of her own then, and Gaelic Football had become her current thing as well. She felt that Kieran and I would benefit from more positive male role models, and that the camaraderie and the rough and tumble of a tough contact sport would counteract all the oestrogen sloshing around at home. She also knew the years that were just around the corner, and she reckoned if we got the football-habit now we'd avoid falling off the road altogether in our teens. Smart lady. Shame she was never a mum of her own, but that wasn't her thing and lucky for us.

She reckoned that Eílis would benefit too just from being around us and other athletes, instead of thugs, and that any time spent with her two closest brothers would be money in the bank for later on. At the time we simply idolised Úna - the whole family did, less Éamon and Maud - but now I appreciate just how smart, perceptive and remarkable she really was. She may well have saved my life, she certainly had a lot to do with shaping it, but at the time she was just fun to be around. It must have been hard for our mum to watch though; but to be blunt she seemed glad of her sister's help, and it sure as hell worked for us kids.

The football worked a treat. Best of all I found I was good at it. I was big for my age and fast, and the rough and tumble of the Derrybeg and the walk home from school made the juniors' training seem like a bit of a cuddle. And in Gaelic there's not really full-on tackling, so I had that thrill to come once I discovered rugby later on. It got me into it though, and the confidence it gave me helped me at school too. I ran rings around the other kids in any small-sides games of Gaelic Kick we played, and in no time at all I was excelling in the classroom as well. By the end of my first year there I was the *boy most likely to*, and so at the start of the second I was one of the few in the Derrybeg looking forward to going back to school. So was Kieran, my younger brother, because come the September he was due to start at St Colman's too - but two years behind me of course.

Playing along with the Under-12s at Cullaville had its moments though, or rather the drive down through 'Cross did, and after a scary incident in May Aunt Úna started taking us to the Shane O'Neill's GAC in Camlough instead. We could only train there and have a bit of a kick around, no real games, but it filled the football gap now I'd got the bug (while my God-shaped hole remained a yawning chasm) and it was only five minutes from home as well. I never did find out though, and a grinning Úna no longer remembers, whether it meant a change of boyfriend for her or not. The switch to rugby in Dundalk two years later certainly did, but that's another story and a later time.

The scare on the way to Cullaville was when we saw a thirty-one-year-old British soldier blown-up and killed by a bomb at the side of the road. Actually saw it. It was shocking beyond description. The bomb had been hidden near a telegraph pole and the patrol commander from the Worcestershire and Sherwood Foresters was killed instantly. It was the first death I'd ever seen, and it was hardly peaceful and from natural causes. I guess some people never see anything like that at all.

His three colleagues were only lightly injured, as were the two civilians in the car right ahead of us. The locals were treated in a nearby house and the soldiers were taken away by helicopter, but we had to sit there for hours while they cleared up and while the police took statements. It's the only time I've ever seen Aunt Úna in deep shock, and one of the few times I've seen her cry; but we sat on a couch in someone's living room and she hugged and rocked us until she had no tears left.

As it happened later that year Camlough didn't turn out to be much safer. Late one night in October we were woken by the sound of an IRA 12.7 mm Russian heavy machine-gun smashing its rounds into the armoured Ford Sierra of two policeman just beyond Bessbrook. Armoured was a relative term against such a weapon, and the more than sixty rounds that destroyed the vehicle killed Constable Marshall behind the wheel.

That was one of the last three things I remember from the news that year: that brutal killing not a couple of pitches-lengths from where I played my football, and the road being closed the next day; and the other two, which were so remote and unusual as to stick in my mind always. Just as they were stuck in our mum's scrapbook: The IRA killings, both in Germany, of Heidi Hazell, the German-born wife of a British soldier whom the Provos had mistaken for a servicewoman from the Dortmund garrison; and that of an Indian-born corporal in the Royal Air Force.

It wasn't really the actual killings I remember – they were so far away and there'd been so many in my short lifetime – but the attack on the airman stood out for two reasons in particular: His name was Maheshkumar Islania, and I couldn't fathom what on earth someone in the Air Force in West Germany and with a name like that had to do with a united Ireland; and I understood even less why they also shot dead Nivruti, his six month-old daughter who was in the car with him.

And twenty-eight years later I still don't.

Fence Posts and Milestones

1991 for me got off to a great start. In anticipation of us ten-year-olds moving-up to secondary school the next year, the Brothers introduced form captains into the senior classes in preparation for the prefect system at the Abbey Christian Brothers' Grammar School. It was taken for granted I'd go there next and to be honest, despite all the religious studies, I was kind of happy with the idea. In most of the other classes their form captains had been selected by the teacher, but in ours Father McFall had just been teaching Greek history and so he said the democratic vote of the pupils should decide. Remarkably to me at the time, their pick was me.

I reckon now it was for a variety of reasons. The bullies were scared of me, the wimps felt protected by me, I was better than anyone else at sport and I was smart but not a show-off in lessons. Plus, I'd stood-up to the Brothers over a couple of issues and Father McFall had stood-up for me, and so I think the other boys reckoned I'd make a good union rep. It suited me just fine though, and it meant I was treated more like an adolescent than a kid. Best of all it meant I got to talk one-on-one with Father McFall a lot too, who I had decided was a sort of male Aunt Úna. Except I guess he had no love-life, whereas even at ten years-old I'd worked out that she had enough of a love-life for both of them.

I don't mean that in a shameful or a slutty way but she was single, attractive and had a good job, and so she enjoyed a vibrant social life. Her words, not mine, and back then I didn't really know what that entailed; but I doubt if many of her Catholic colleagues and so-called friends in Newry would have agreed though. I don't recall whether she ever had a boyfriend in Camlough or whether she was still seeing the guy from the Culloville Blues, but what I do remember is that a few months after my tenth birthday she started seeing a lawyer called Dermott McCracken, who played rugby for Dundalk. That was a fortuitous pairing and within a few months it was to bring about the next big change in my life. In a long and meandering sort of way it was to also get the whole family a month in Dublin as well, but that will require more of an explanation for sure.

It all started just before the Easter school holidays. It started as something trivial enough but then it grew arms and legs, some of which got broken. The church got involved because they knew my mother, the plumbers' union got involved because they knew my father, and the school got involved because of Father McFall. But then the IRA got involved, this time officially, because they thought they knew my brother, Éamon.

No-one knew Éamon back then, certainly he didn't know himself, and so that meant the police had to have a bite at the problem too because that was their job. Now in any normal environment that might have been true, but an organisation less qualified or able than the RUC to deal with trouble in the Derrybeg was hard to imagine. And so a trivial fist fight between a rag-taggle of pre-pubescent schoolboys became a scary and ugly situation that lasted for weeks. Months in fact.

The walk home from school normally took about half an hour, but it was longer since I had to walk with Kieran too. We'd usually head into town and cross the Margaret Square Bridge, head up Monaghan Street and then climb Clanrye Avenue all the way home past the football pitches at Jennings Park. But some days, like the day it all kicked-off, we'd cross the river at Sugar Island and head up Canal Street and the Armagh Road instead. On those days we'd skirt behind Chequer Hill and cross the playing fields into the Derrybeg at Killeavey Road. Nine times out of ten that was fine, but not on this day.

From the lightly-wooded rough ground to the west of Chequer Hill, we were shadowed by three boys a year older than me. I recognised one of them as Ed McClory, and I'd bested him in a fight on the edge of the Derrybeg a few months before, but I didn't know the other two at all. That was about to change.

They were the two youngest Magee boys from Mountain View Drive, and their oldest brother Declan was a twenty-year-old IRA wannabe. He would actually tell people he was in the Provos until the army or the police came along, but both the IRA and the RUC knew better. The only people who listened at all were a few local punks with the same delusional condition.

As Kieran and I aimed for the gap in the fence around the playing fields the three boys headed our way from the bushes and McClory shouted after us.

"Hey, posh cunt."

That was a new word and it stung. Not because of what it meant – I didn't know what it meant – but because it briefly gave him power over me. I knew it was hurtful, and it was obvious he knew something I didn't. That was bad and potent ju ju on the streets when you're just ten years-old, and in front of two other tough-looking boys it stung even more.

"Get t'fuck," was my only response and I pushed Kieran to walk ahead of me.

The three of them started to follow us and I told Kieran to stay closer. I knew I could take McClory easily, and that's why I presumed he'd come back with two mates, but my fear was that one of them would go for Kieran and so split us up. That's exactly what they did. As we got to the fence and started to climb, McClory and the biggest Magee ran up behind me and the third pulled Kieran back and onto the ground.

I wasn't waiting to see if I could beat all three in a fair fist fight, and so I yanked the fence-post I was already holding with all my young might and pulled it free. It wasn't a particularly sturdy affair, a wooden picket maybe four centimetres thick and no more than a metre long, but it was loose anyway and suddenly I was holding it and they were still coming. I swung it as hard as I could and caught McClory on the side of the head. He went down wailing and clutching his ear, and the biggest Magee froze where he was. The next few moments were a blur, but I knew I had to keep moving. I trampled the gap in the fence into a bigger gap with one stride and then I took a swing at the boy holding Kieran. I missed but he stepped-back, way back, and so I screamed at Kieran to get up and run through the gap.

"Go Kieran, get through and go home."

Kieran did exactly as I told him.

"You little fucker," the oldest Magee screamed, although I was a full inch taller than him and stronger built, but he seemed pretty sure of himself and he started to walk towards me.

McClory was back on his feet by now, part-crying part-swearing and with a river of blood streaming from his torn ear. The younger Magee took one look at Kieran sprinting towards our home in Derrybeg and so he did the same back towards his house in Mountain View.

I grabbed both school bags in my left hand and slowly backed towards the gap in the fence and crossed through. McClory and the bigger Magee followed but stayed just beyond the sweep of my fence-post.

"When we take that off you, you little wanker, we're gonna fucking kill you with it. Y'know that, don't you."

I didn't doubt it for a minute. I didn't say a word.

"You've ripped my fucking ear off you little cunt," McClory exaggerated with his new favourite word, "you bet we're gonna kill you."

I continued to walk backwards with my heart in my throat and my fence-post in my hand. Still I didn't say a word. There were several hundred metres to the far side of the playing fields and the safety of the Derrybeg, and I must have looked like a cornered insect retreating backwards in some lethal dance of death.

I wasn't sure what would happen if they both rushed me together, but with the fence-post I fancied my chances and I honestly thought I might have to kill them if they did. Or at least Magee. He looked like he meant business, and I wasn't worried about McClory except that now he was a mass of blood he actually looked quite scary. But that was just appearances, I knew.

Our infantile Mexican stand-off slowly backed its way across the playing fields, with me being goaded by a torrent of threats and swearing all the way. But neither boy ever came any closer, and I looked as determined as I could manage to use the fence post again if they did.

When we eventually got to the far side and the corner of Killeavey Road, we entered the next phase of our impasse and we were reinforced by four others: Éamon and Kieran were running down the road from our home, and the younger Magee and his brother Declan were striding across the playing fields behind McClory and the third brother. We all arrived on the corner of Killeavey Road at the same time. The shouting and the threats began anew and we were soon joined by half a dozen housewives from the 'Beg and a load of other kids.

One of the women attempted to give first aid to McClory's torn ear, while Éamon and Declan Magee made a beeline for each other. Kieran and I were safe by then, that I knew, but what I didn't know was what would happen next. Surely the grown-ups would take over, wouldn't they? I kept a hold of my fence-post and made my way to Éamon's side just in case.

"Put that down, for fuck's sake," he commanded. Éamon was eighteen, Declan Magee was twenty and bigger than he was. I hoped Éamon knew what he was doing but I did as I was told.

What followed was not for the ears of the mothers or the young kids present, but no-one actually laid a finger on anyone else. For the first time ever I was fiercely proud of my older brother and he didn't yield an inch. What they promised to do to each other in the coming days though was a different matter, as were the threats the younger Magees made against me at the same time. When it was done and the adults moved everyone on, we all went our separate ways. The Magees and the still bleeding McClory skulked away home towards Violet Hill, and us three McCormacs walked into the Derrybeg together. Éamon forbade us to tell our parents anything about it, but they found out that night anyway through neighbours and friends.

My mother went quiet, went to church and then went to bed. At least for once she never went to pieces. My father though became angry and railed against the Troubles – he knew it wasn't over – but for the first time in two years he praised Éamon and actually said he was proud of him. Éamon took his kudos dismissively and warned our dad to stay out of it, and so they finished up arguing again anyway.

Éamon said he'd deal with it if and when it became necessary, and he told Dad to not meddle in things he didn't fully understand. But Dad understood all too well, and he became morose for days. In fact, the whole family lived under a cloud for weeks, but no-one seemed sure when or if the storm would ever come. I wasn't back at school for another two weeks because of the Easter break, so that wasn't our parents' main concern; it was what might happen around the Derrybeg at night, and not to me and Kieran so much as to Éamon. Well nothing is what happened in the short term, as is often the case, and so I guess they all thought it had gone away; but then on August the 9th, straight after the Anniversary of Internment parade, history, bad blood and vengeance all came a'calling.

Declan Magee and two of his mates approached Éamon in Larkin's Bar that night. They all had a fair bit of drink taken and trouble was inevitable. Magee picked an argument and kicked-over the coals of their stand-off on the edge of the playing fields. He said the fence-post saga wasn't forgotten, and that younger kids than me in the past had taken a beating for anti-social behaviour. He never said so directly but he strongly implied formal IRA sanctions, and Éamon told him to go fuck himself. Good drills so far, but sadly he told him in front of a lot of other people and so face was lost. IRA or not, Magee wasn't the sort of guy to leave it at that.

Then Magee said the Provos were already angry with me for another reason. *Me*, and just ten years old; Éamon was furious. Éamon's usual red mist descended, and although he had little time for me in the normal run of things he demanded to know what the hell Magee was on about. Magee relished telling him, mostly for his own kudos and for the benefit of all the other drinkers.

Magee recounted how I'd made anti-IRA comments at school, when just before Easter I'd said that the late Collie Marks was a terrorist and he'd gotten what he asked for. On the 10th of April, twenty-nine-year-old Colm Marks had been shot dead by the RUC whilst carrying out a mortar attack on the police station in Downpatrick. Marks was originally from Kilkeel and Newry and there'd been a fair bit of talk about it in the town.

Éamon defended me immediately and laughed that a ten-year-old wouldn't know to say such a thing. God knows how Magee ever got to hear about it – or even worse, if the IRA had -

81

but he hadn't been wrong: that's exactly what I'd said, to a group of boys in the playground one lunchtime. I didn't really know what I was on about, but it had felt clever at the time. When Éamon told me what he'd said I denied it, but I worried myself sick for weeks that I'd be killed for my treason. And so did my parents and Aunt Úna, for no other reason than it had been said. Nothing, I learned in later years ever scared Aunt Úna, but the Provos were a sick and twisted law unto themselves, and so she knew how quickly things could turn.

Things didn't turn though, instead they festered away and happened slowly over time - but they happened sure enough. The last weekend in September, Magee and four thugs jumped Éamon on Main Avenue and beat him with a baseball bat. He gave a good account of himself and he escaped serious injury, but by the time they were done he was concussed and they'd broken his arm. Then the following weekend Declan Magee was picked-up on Francis Street, dragged screaming into an alley and knee-capped with a .38" revolver. The IRA had weighed-in after all.

The police got involved, as they had to, but that in the Derrybeg just invites a whole different shitstorm to rain down from unbelievable heights. It soon became clear that the Provos didn't appreciate Magee quoting them and claiming his false credentials, and a couple of them in the Derrybeg appreciated him meting out his own rough justice on their patch even less. But what wasn't lost on anyone was that it would appear that the IRA had thought more of Éamon's potential than of Magee's, and that just worried my parents even more.

The RUC made things worse through an ill judged and poorly executed attempt to recruit Éamon as a police informer – another easy way to die in South Armagh – and the local community waited anxiously for the other shoe to drop. It didn't though, thanks yet again to the street-sense of Aunt Úna and the sage advice of her lawyer boyfriend, Dermott, in Dundalk. And through his contacts to the Irish Rugby Football Union.

The Rugby World Cup was imminent, and in 1991 the hosts were the British Isles and France. It was only the second World Cup, it was the first time it had been held in the Northern Hemisphere, and three out of the four of Ireland's pool-stage games were to be played in Dublin. Úna's boyfriend said he could get tickets for all of them, and he suggested the whole family go there for the month while things in Newry cooled-off. The idea had actually come from a friend of his in the Garda and it wasn't a bad one. It might even have come through him from someone in the RUC in Newry, but no-one was ever going to admit to that.

No need. They just wanted it to happen. And once us kids found out, so did we.

Gods and Goalposts

Nearly a month in Dublin for the Rugby World cup. Genius. Aunt Úna put up half the money and our parents put up all the prayers. All that remained then was to convince Éamon and Maud to put up with the rest of us while the dust settled back home in Newry. Úna took care of that too.

For the rest of us kids it was like Christmas come early, and for me especially it meant I needn't worry about my execution for treason by the IRA at least until we all came back in November. Or in my particular case, I wondered, would it have been *murder* for treason? I was only ten after all, and all I'd done was speak my mind. Looking back, that was the first time I'd ever asked such a profound question – probably coz I would have been the victim – but it wouldn't be the last. Few of them have ever been answered.

Six of us left for Dublin in two cars, my dad's and Aunt Úna's, so we'd have transport all the time we were there. Éamon, Maud and our mum travelled down on the train so we'd have room for the bags in the cars, and we left on Friday the 4th of October. Ireland's first game was on the 6th. We stayed in a cheap B & B in Rathgar, arranged by the church at both ends, and my dad's union fixed it so he could have the month off on half pay. Father McFall knew everything that had happened and so he'd arranged for all of us kids to have the time off too. He was brilliant, and it was him who spoke to Margaret's and Eílis's schools as well. He'd been a rugby wing forward himself in his day, and he said he was only sorry he couldn't come with us. Éamon had left school two years before and Maud just that summer. We were set fair and ready, and I forgot all about my imaginary death sentence. For then at least.

The bed and breakfast was cheap, cheerful and homely, and whatever the priest in Newry had told Mrs Donnegan, the landlady, she treated us like royalty. And Jees, she fed us like horses. The food never stopped coming, and once she saw the ages of us kids she baked some sort of a cake pretty much every day. She knew nothing about rugby at first, but she packed us off for every match in good time and insisted on a pass-by-pass rundown from me and Aunt Úna after each game. Mum and Dad had a room to themselves and so did Aunt Úna. To the best of my knowledge, looking back, I don't think she shared it at all that month; but her and her lawyer boyfriend stayed in a hotel for a couple of the nights when he travelled down from Dundalk to see her. Us kids were three to a room in two rooms, the boys in one and the girls in the other. It felt like the holiday of a lifetime.

Éamon wasn't too bad that month and he was only an arsehole to me and Kieran twice the whole time. I think he'd had his shock in recent weeks, and he was just enjoying being away. We all were, and I couldn't get over being able to walk or drive everywhere without being stopped and checked by soldiers or seeing policemen without guns and flak vests. And for the first time in my life, we didn't hear a single gunshot or an explosion the whole time we were there.

It was so different it was like another world, and I had to keep telling myself that this was the Ireland that had fought a civil war and had staged the Easter Rising. I made the mistake of saying so to Éamon one night as we were going off to sleep, and he swiftly added that it had also had to fight the War of Independence too, and that over five hundred brave Volunteers had died getting rid of the Brits. That was one of the two times he threw a fit that month. The other was when I cheered for England against France.

I loved Dublin, still do, and I guess most of my best memories in life pretty much stem from around that time and the couple of years that followed. In fact, my best family memory ever came from that very trip, in a rowing boat on the River Liffey with Aunt Úna and Eílis; but I'll come back to that spellbinding image another time. In the next story maybe. We stayed pretty close to Rathgar and the city centre for the first week. We watched Ireland smash Zimbabwe 55-11 on the 6th, after which I was smitten. I knew I'd have to play this remarkable game as soon as I possibly could. Gaelic Football had been great fun and it had changed my life; but I couldn't wait to learn how to tackle full-on, to bring other boys down as they ran at full speed, and to run freely without limits and with a ball in my hands. My move up to grammar school the next year couldn't come soon enough.

Three days later we returned to see Ireland beat Japan 32-16, by exactly twice their score; but the open exciting play of the diminutive Japanese and two of their tries in particular inspired me still further. A couple of them didn't look much taller than me, although they were far stronger and faster of course, and I couldn't wait to play my first game. Dermott McCracken, Úna's boyfriend, pounced on my remarks and said he'd take me to Colts rugby in Dundalk as soon as we got back.

We didn't see Ireland's next game. They went down 24-15 to Scotland in Edinburgh, but they'd done enough to come second in their pool and that meant they'd play Australia in Dublin on the 20th. Knowing that was a probable outcome, and with eleven days to kill until the next game we could go to, Aunt Úna had suggested we explore more of the city and of County Dublin itself, and our mum and dad had agreed. What followed was a different road trip every day, and even Éamon and Maud got into the spirit of it all. Just being away from the North had made them entirely different people. For a while at least.

We went to Skerries; and then to Malahide Castle, where we learnt how it was home to the Talbot family for nearly eight hundred years and how fourteen members of the family had sat down to breakfast before the Battle of the Boyne only to perish before dinner. We went to the historic fishing village of Howth; we went to Dublin Castle, seat of the British Administration until partition in 1922; and of course to the infamous Kilmainham Gaol, where the leaders of the 1916 Easter Rising had been executed. And although there was no such thing back then as the Guinness Brewery tour, we all went to an exhibition in the city and saw the nine-thousand-year lease signed by Arthur Guinness in 1759.

On the other side of Dublin we drove into County Wicklow and visited the exquisite Powerscourt Estate; and we discovered the jewel in the southern rim of Dublin's crown, the small seaside village of Dalkey, with its award-winning pubs and restaurants and its warm and cheerful people. It was all grand sure enough, and Aunt Úna made sure it was all fun for us kids, but for a highly spirited boy of just ten, some of those places were a lot more impressive than others. Pretty much all I wanted to do was get back to Lansdowne Road for the rugby.

The last game we saw live was on the 20th, the Herculean battle between Ireland and the eventual World Cup winners, Australia. Ireland lost by a single point in the dying seconds and it was a fitting testament, Éamon mocked, to Irish history in general. At that he and Dad had the only real argument of the trip, but all I could think about was the game itself. Dermott offered to get us tickets for the following weekend too - his treat and to see New Zealand play Australia in the second semi-final - but our dad politely declined and said we all had to be getting back to Newry. Astonishingly I agreed, I had to be getting along to Dundalk Rugby Club to start playing, but my secret fear about my impending execution for treason began again almost immediately.

As it turned-out I needn't have worried, and the enormous contrast between the North and the South became starkly evident. In the three weeks we'd been away from Newry, the Provos had beaten Declan Magee again for continued anti-social behaviour and banished him from the town; and so I never heard another word about it. Not so poor Éamon though, who continued to be hounded by the RUC Special Branch until he complained to *An Phoblacht* – the *Republican News* – in the hope of having them leave him alone. Well they did and they didn't after that, sort of, but one way or another that saga would follow him forever.

As Christmas and New Year approached and 1991 came to a conclusion, I snuck-in to our mum's secret cupboard and took a look at her latest scrapbook. I wanted to see what was in it from when Éamon got his arm busted and Declan Magee was shot by the IRA. I felt guilty I suppose, but there was nothing. Not a thing, from well before Easter and until nearly the end of the year. It was as if none of it had ever happened, and maybe in the baffles of our mum's mind it never had.

There were only two things in it for the whole year in fact, and although they meant nothing to me at the time I would remember them and return to them once I was in MI5 and at the height of our operation against NEON; against the IRA Cleanskin who so nearly destroyed much of Central London, Michael McCann.

The first was a single, local newspaper cutting from the year before, from 1990, and it concerned Paul Hughes and Donna Maguire. Both were originally from Newry and they were two of the four Provos arrested in Belgium following the killing of two Australian tourists in Holland in the May. It was a bungled attack needless to say, and the two London-based lawyers were mistaken for off-duty British servicemen. It had been a "tragedy and a mistake," said an IRA spokesman; but their feeble statement was "twisted, too late and meaningless," said the Australian Prime Minister, Bob Hawke. Just how many bandits could such a tiny region produce?

The second thing though was an assortment of cuttings from different papers over several weeks, about the death of a twenty-six-year-old IRA man called Frank Ryan. He'd been killed in England in November, along with his eighteen-year-old accomplice, Patricia Black. They'd been blown-up by their own bomb as they'd attempted to plant it in North London, and it had taken three days to identify the bodies... because until then the authorities didn't even have a clue they existed.

Clean as a whistle, both of them, and it served as a reminder that Michael McCann was merely the one we thought we knew about. What about the ones we didn't, I wondered back in 2015, what about the ones still out there? And you know, two years later and with the rest of my Security Service career still ahead of me, it's something I wonder about all over again at the start of every day.

Miracle on the Liffey

Somewhere in the eleven eventful days between Ireland playing Japan and Australia, all nine of us climbed into three wooden boats and rowed around on the River Liffey for a couple of hours. Although it sounds now like a far-fetched exaggeration, they were the two precious hours that were to change the next ten years of my life. Maybe even the whole of it.

The man who hired the boats to us told us we were to go out with a maximum of four to a boat, and so our plan to take two boats with four in one and five in the other wasn't permitted. He watched us discuss our predicament with some amusement and after a short while he offered us three boats for the price of two. Or rather, he offered Aunt Úna that deal, and in a moment or two you'll understand why.

My dad rowed the first boat, and in with him was fourteen-year-old Margaret and our Kieran, aged eight. Éamon rowed the second. He was eighteen and so the man let him, although his arm was not long out of plaster and half-way around Maud had to take over because it ached so much. Our mum was in with them, but she sat terrified in the stern the whole time. And Aunt Úna rowed ours, with me and twelve-year-old Eílis as her crew. So we had the best fun by far. And, it turns out, the best view.

We also had the prettiest skipper, of that there wasn't a shadow of a doubt. The man even said so, several times. Aunt Úna was all in white - much to Éamon's disgust - out of solidarity with England, which was the only home nation playing in the World Cup that day. But I mean *all* in white! Her long fair hair fluttered in the wind or framed her smiling face, and below it she wore a tight-fitting white T-shirt with a plunging neckline. Below that she wore a short, white-cotton mini-skirt and white, leather, lace-up boots to the top of her calves. There were twenty eyelets on each boot... I counted every one of them several times.

She looked stunning, and I was suitably stunned, but she probably wasn't ideally dressed for the maritime duties she was about to perform. Her T-shirt's V-shaped neckline plunged just enough as she rowed to reveal the edges of a white lacy bra. I'd never noticed a bra at all before, not anyone's, and suddenly I was spellbound. She wore a pretty gold chain against her bare neck as well, but for some reason the bra held my attention more.

And then her mini-skirt, when she stood-up, stopped at the upper third of her thigh; but when she sat facing backwards to row, with Eílis in the bow and me sat in the stern and facing her, on just about every stroke of the mighty oars I could see that her knickers were radiant-white for good measure too. Father Byrne had always said that an angel would be all-in-white if and when we ever saw one, and for the first time in my sceptical Catholic lifetime I believed him unequivocally.

Úna had never rowed such a heavy boat before, she said, but she was such an all-round natural athlete that she picked it up much more quickly than Dad and Éamon did. Then once they'd got the rudiments of it weighed-off as well, she'd make sure she was rowing just that bit faster and just that bit cleaner through the water than they were. I found that impressive – I found everything about her that day impressive - and once again her grit and natural competitiveness had an unexpected spin-off for me. The more she glanced over her shoulder to check her bearings, and the harder she pulled on the oars, the more of her panties I got to see... and all the more often.

Whenever she'd look at me I would smile, blush and look away for a moment. Not a confident or a knowing smile, but an embarrassed, 'Don't worry Aunty, I'm having a good time,' sort of smile. Yet looking back on it later there's no doubt in my mind that she knew I was having a good time, and looking back on it *now* I've a fair idea that she knew why too. Whenever she looked around at the far bank or stared up at the passing buildings is when I got the best view it seemed - or maybe it was just how awkward it was to row and steer looking backwards - and then whenever she looked straight at me was when I saw the least. That was partly because she squeezed her legs together a bit more, then smiled at me, and mostly because I was too frightened and embarrassed to peep up her skirt whenever she was facing me. But then whenever she looked away again, I stared so much it hurt. Ached, would be a better word.

After a while I wanted her to look at me more often than she did to be honest, but she was looking everywhere else as well. I wanted her to see that I wasn't staring between her legs the *whole* time and that I was simply having fun by being with her; but more than anything I think I just wanted her attention... and *then* for her to look away again so I could stare some more. What had always been such a simple and uncomplicated relationship until then, suddenly became a pre-pubescent knot of guilt and shameful contradictions - but not enough to stop me looking I recall.

Spellbound hardly describes what I was that day, that and hopelessly in love with my auntie; but from that moment on my life would never be quite the same again. How on earth could it?

That was also the day when I knew once and for all that I didn't believe in God. What I was thinking was sinful beyond reckoning, and what I was starting to imagine was even worse; but I didn't give a damn about either. All it felt at the time was exciting. I had no intention of confessing any of it, not a single thought; it was simply fun, it was none of the priest's business, and I even allowed myself to believe that night that maybe Aunt Úna had in some way got a kick out of it too. Dream on Neill.

Of course, looking back now, I know that all she found it was amusing. More comical than enjoyable, and we've re-lived that moment many times since I got older. It was something of a milestone for her too, she told me, and it was the day she knew she'd never have to worry about whether I'd soon be interested in girls or not. When I think back to that day though, I forget that I was just ten - I felt so much bigger than that. And in Úna's defence, it was me peeping harmlessly at her that day, just a young boy being a boy - she didn't have much say in it - and I would be sixteen before she'd ever tease me about such things for real.

And then *boy* did she tease me.

What's in a Smile?

By the end of the World Cup and our three weeks in Dublin I was ten, nearly eleven, and hopelessly in love with my Aunt Úna. I'd always loved her of course, as you would a favourite auntie, but then I fell *in* love with her. Such was the power of fresh white cotton, I would learn in years to come. That and her unblinking love and support for as long as I could remember. It was just a boyhood crush I know now, but it was a crush that was to last a lifetime; and the only way to describe it back then was 'smitten'.

It wasn't because her and Dermott had come up with the idea of going to Dublin in the first place, or because she'd paid for nearly everything and bought us treats all the time – although that doubtless had a lot to do with it at such a venal age – it was simply because she'd become the brightest star in my universe. Every day with her in it was somehow full of fun and hope and wonder, whilst any day without seemed to flounder aimlessly towards bedtime. And then, after Dublin, bedtime became one of the times

I thought about her most. It would be another eighteen months before I fully discovered masturbation, and even longer before I wholly mastered it, but long before that my night-time thoughts and fantasies were more about Aunt Úna than anything or anyone else. Smitten indeed.

For some years she had been the iconic figure to whom I'd prayed for good fortune. My guru in life. Like the Buddhas that so fascinated me in the Chinese restaurant on Monaghan Street, she was an always-smiling face and an ever-present force for good. A source of wisdom, straight answers and achievable goals. She seemed so uncomplicated by comparison to any parent I knew. Faith was still a word with no meaning to me back then, and if anything filled Father Byrne's much vaunted God-shaped hole then she did; and so I worshipped her with the commensurate obedience and loyalty.

But after Dublin and our fateful boat trip on the Liffey, she began to fill my thoughts in other ways as well. Before Dublin I'd been enchanted by her eyes, her incredible smile and her charisma; but afterwards I simply became obsessed with anything and everything below her waist. Even the sight of her bare legs would plunge me into an almost hypnotic trance, and just the shape of her in jeans would cause me to follow her around like a lost puppy. Looking back now on 1992, my new school dominated my eleventh year, and through that and Dermott McCracken so did the discovery of rugby for a while; but family life for the longest time revolved around Aunt Úna's groin, and whenever she wasn't looking I couldn't take my eyes off it.

It wasn't truly sexual then of course - although I thought it was - but it was a physically numbing feeling nonetheless. A dull, debilitating ache when I couldn't be around her, so that I visited her in her home at every opportunity. Our mum didn't mind, and I'd usually take Eílis and Kieran with me, but they weren't looking at what I was. They'd play games or watch the TV until it was time to go home, whereas I would watch every movement and every twist and turn Aunt Úna made.

One of the highlights of being there was to simply sit behind her in the kitchen when she washed the dishes, and so stare uninterrupted for fifteen whole minutes as she bent over the sink. In jeans she was a goddess, and in anything less there was always that million to one chance that she'd drop something and bend thoughtlessly to pick it up. And after she'd washed-up it was then my happy duty to help her with the drying-up, so I got to stand right next to her and smell her perfume, maybe even feel her warmth. Sometimes our arms would even brush together, and so I'd feel the sheer voltage of her bare flesh.

Quite often we'd stay over - just the three of us, never Margaret or the others – and so we'd sleep in ad hoc beds and on sofas; but in all those times I never got to see her naked. I just dreamt I did. In just a towel was the least I ever saw her wearing, and that was quite often; although I once saw her in just her bra and panties and I thought I'd died and gone to heaven. Not least of all because rigor mortis seemed to set-in immediately.

Úna wore short dresses or mini-skirts a lot back then, and catching a glimpse of anything beneath them became like looking at Mum's scrapbooks: opportunities were rare and fraught with danger, but whenever the chance arose my pulse would quicken, my heart would be in my mouth and I would flit from image to image until the risk of discovery became too great. Despite the merest glimpses of her bra when she was rowing in Dublin, I don't think I realised she even had breasts for another year or two, and I would be nearly thirteen and masturbating hard for Ireland before they too became a part of my obsession; but chances to look up her skirt became the stars by which I charted my week. And a week without such a glimpse was pure misery.

Other things in life eventually came along to relieve my obsession. The thrill of the rugby club in Dundalk for example, and of moving rapidly from the Colts XV to the Youths because of my size. Or the pressure of studies, the torment of early-adolescence, and most days the sheer brutality of the Troubles... they all took my mind off it all for a while. As did moving up to the Abbey Grammar School in September '92; but then whenever I was alone with Aunt Úna again, I'd turn to mush. Or was it stone?

She was thirty-four back then and she looked like a young Cate Blanchett: kind of ordinary-looking, like the girl next door, but undeniably beautiful. And she seemed to ooze sexuality from every pore. Or at least that's what I thought, and as far as I could tell at that tender age so did every other man she came into contact with. Although they were obviously sisters, the contrasts between her and my mother were countless. In appearance they were close (but certainly not in the way they dressed) and Úna doted on our mum, but in terms of personality they might have come from the opposite poles of the earth.

Aunt Úna would be out of the door and doing things in the open air whenever she could, while my mum would never have left the house at all if she didn't have to. Úna would party hard when the opportunity arose, my mum hardly ever. The younger sister would pick her moment and speak her mind, our mum would brood for days but say nothing. But Aunt Úna's greatest joy was hiking the many hills and forests of her childhood; mostly alone, generally in good weather, but always as and whenever the mood took her - which was often. We were surrounded by such places and she was spoilt for choice, and to my delight from the age of twelve she would often take me with her.

Just to the east of Newry were the Mountains of Mourne, looming watchfully over the South Down coastline and capped at both ends by Rostrevor and Tollymore forests. Then right on our doorstep were Slieve Gullion, the hills above Carlingford Lough and the wonder of Ravensdale Forest, although all of those were be-devilled from time to time by the angry sweep of the Troubles. But, when time permitted and the urge was upon her, Úna would take several days at a time to walk the Hills of Donegal just three hours to the west - our mum might reluctantly take thirty minutes to walk into town. They looked alike sure enough, like twins almost, but there any similarity ended.

At twenty-one my mother had been married four years and she'd had two kids. The next wasn't far off. At the same time Úna was nineteen, single and planning to stay that way forever. She was just about to drop-out from university in Belfast after her first year because she didn't see the point in it all. No, that's not strictly true; in fact she'd seen through most of her peers, that was nearer the truth, and she'd been offered a good job in Newry without having to wait for her degree. That was the crux of it. Besides which, in 1976 Belfast was raging – it was the second heaviest year for casualties during the whole of the Troubles - and so it wasn't much of a place to be. Not for Úna at least, and so she'd decided to crack-on with life in Bandit Country instead.

Úna was the brightest of all of us, and at sixty I reckon she still is. She got nine 'O' Levels and two 'A's without really breaking into a sweat, after which she'd been ushered off to Queen's University by her parents without any real discussion about why or what next. According to Úna they'd ushered my mum off to have babies in a similarly collaborative fashion. But Úna quickly decided that uni' wasn't for her, and right about then she was offered a plum job with an insurance company in Newry through one of her teachers who agreed with her.

Oh, I can imagine what you're thinking, but he wasn't trying to get rid of her. Quite the opposite. He told her she was one of those he looked forward to seeing each day and he rated her highly, but he also knew her mind was made up and that she'd be a success at whatever she attempted. More than that, he'd said, he was pretty sure that academic qualifications wouldn't have much to do with it. Then he had sex with her - but not before she'd left uni' and moved back to Newry. 'He was a man of principle', she'd joked to me years later, 'and so he waited 'til I was fair game.'

The late-1970s in Northern Ireland was a good time to be in property insurance and personal injury compensation, and in no time at all Úna became good at what she did. Very good. And despite her loathing of the Provisional IRA – her hatred of any terrorists in fact - they indirectly afforded her a very comfortable lifestyle. By 1980 she'd set herself up in a nice home on Windsor Hill and had a decent car. Lucky boyfriends who got to stay the night were few and far between, carefully chosen and frequently moved-on. As she herself put it, her existence in Newry was 'full, fun and interesting,' and that, on the right side of the law back then, was a pretty rare trick to pull off. But there again she was a pretty rare woman.

And then of course, the following year, I came along. The special child who'd broken her sister's curse and who represented their hope for a better future for all of us. And so indirectly I gave Aunt Úna a whole new challenge in life. She and our mum teamed up to show me and Eílis that there was an amazing world to be enjoyed beyond the blood and the grime of South Armagh; but without having to move right away to some new and emotionally barren safe-haven.

Éamon and Maud were already lost causes in their eyes, and in my mum's they were also cursed by their birthdays don't forget. As was Margaret in some respects; but Margaret failed to be a part of their family within a family mostly because she never seemed to get on that well with Aunt Úna. Maybe Éamon's spell was stronger, they wondered? Or maybe it was genetic? But Aunt Úna's efforts with Margaret always seemed to come to nought.

'Families are what they are,' Úna once told me in my teens, 'and so sometimes,' she said philosophically, 'you're better off just getting on with it than trying to change them.' So, when Kieran arrived in 1983, also *curse-less* like me, then that gave the pair of them three new souls who could be saved, and on whom they could focus their not-inconsiderable efforts.

The rest, they decided, they would help whenever and as much as they could... Éamon, Maud and Margaret... but with us three at least they reckoned we'd be listening.

And as for me... well I'd be watching closely as well.

The Wolf of Poison Glen

In June 1993 Aunt Úna took me to the hills above Poison Glen in County Donegal. The glen itself is near to the village of Dunlewey, and the hills are those that make up the Derryveagh Mountains to the south-east, facing Mount Errigal or thereabouts. It was one of her favourite places for walking. It was all just hills, hard grass and hard graft for a twelve-year-old, but I was pretty fit and I didn't care – I just enjoyed being with her.

We set off from Newry at four on a Sunday morning and so we were parked-up and climbing by 7 am. It was already light of course, and had been since long before five. By nine we'd climbed as far as we were going to and so we stopped for a picnic breakfast and a flask of hot tea. As we sat and enjoyed the warm summer breeze, I didn't know which way to stare – at the amazing view around Poison Glen and Dunlewey Lough, and down onto the old ruined church... or straight ahead and at Aunt Úna whenever she wasn't looking?

Our vista as we sat and ate was one of billowing white clouds with grey grubby cuffs, and of bright blue gashes of sky; and our landscape was a vast quilt of tough and wiry grass like the stubble on God's chin. Aunt Úna on the other hand was equally magnificent in her walking shorts, sturdy hiking boots and a tight-fitting T-shirt. It might even have been the one she'd worn rowing on The Liffey. When she was sat on a rock with her legs stretched-out, like then, she was just a beautiful thing to behold; but when she was stood-up, or when I'd been hiking dutifully behind her, then she was simply mesmerising.

I was quite the budding athlete at school by then, and when I watched her as she moved she seemed to personify grace and strength and efficiency. She never once lost her balance, and whenever I'd look up her legs seemed firmly astride the world. She wore a small joggers' rucksack high-up on her shoulders whereby there was an uninterrupted view of her perfect backside; and tired or not, I could have followed her forever.

We chatted as we ate, another of the highlights for me, about anything and everything a twelve-year-old boy growing up in a virtual war zone could possibly want to know. And unlike my parents, of course - in fact just about any parents I reckon - she would provide meaningful answers. She'd said such walks would be the perfect place to talk about life and living, and as we sat looking-out that morning – about as far from the Troubles as we could get it seemed – I suddenly understood what she'd meant.

We'd had to convince my mum that it was OK for me to go with her on a Sunday, because there was something planned at the church that day; but we'd gone to Saturday Mass the night before and so she'd let me. That's me and Mum and the others had gone to Mass I mean, not Aunt Úna. She hadn't attended Mass since she'd left home eighteen years earlier; exactly half her lifetime ago, she pointed out. Inevitably I asked her when did she think I could stop going, and we discussed at length why I couldn't just yet and why respect for one's elders and deference to my parents' wishes were essential building bricks for the next crucial phases of my life. It was a conversation we'd have again five years later, and which next time would be both humorous and profound in her updated advice.

At something before ten we walked on for another hour or so and talked about all the things I might do in the future, and then we turned and started to head back down so we could be on the road again and stopping for a late lunch by three. About half-way down we came to rest at an ancient boulder and sat to finish-off our flask of tea.

It was a picturesque spot on such a barren hillside, and at some stage the mighty boulder must have tumbled down the slope behind us – maybe as recently as a million years ago – and come to rest forever where it was. The fast flowing stream now slewed around its base and then cascaded down the hillside as steeply as the goat-track ahead. The nearest goat was across the valley over a mile away, and the closest human beings couldn't even be seen. We nestled into the shade of the boulder and shared the rest of our tea. We were snuggled-in shoulder to shoulder, and to my delight our bare legs were touching. It was the closest we'd been all day, and once again I was transported to another place. There followed a moment's calm while neither of us spoke and even the wind seemed to hold its breath for a while. As we both gazed out across some of God's finest work – if it really had been his doing, she teased – the stream murmured contentedly until we were ready to move on.

As we reached the bottom of the hill and set off along the trail towards Poison Glen and Aunt Úna's car, there were two men walking towards us in playful conversation. One of them I guess was in his late-sixties, the other in his early-twenties, and each had a vague resemblance to the other. Close enough, I thought, to be grandfather and grandson; and it struck me that both seemed to feel a certain pride at being with the other.

Their strides as they climbed the track certainly had more about them than mere grit and determination. The young man had tough and rugged features and intense serious eyes, although the warmth between him and his elder was clear. He looked strong and fit, and the old man too had clearly been an athlete of some sort in years gone by; so that they both looked like men who in ancient times might have led thousands into battle without question. Like *Cormac mac Airt* maybe? Then my mind tumbled through a cast of ancient Gaelic kings and warriors, but for no reason I can explain other than maybe I was descended from archaic Irish royalty.

They both glanced briefly at me and smiled, but then the young man especially seized on Úna and stared at her frequently until they passed and began to climb the trail behind us. And why wouldn't he? After a short while both men turned to get another look, just as I also turned to take another peek at them. The older man greeted me with a wave and a laugh and as they turned away again I half returned it out of embarrassment.

"What are you waving at?" Úna asked with a grin.

"At those two men?"

"Why?

"Because they turned around and waved at me."

"Yeah, because you caught them," she chuckled, "but you know why they turned around don't you?"

She grinned again and I felt compelled to speak the truth. She was better at this stuff than any priest I'd ever been cornered-by in Confession.

"Yeah," I blushed, but I answered honestly, "they were looking at your legs."

Well... half honestly.

"Yeah, right, 'course they were," she chuckled, "they were looking at my bum more like."

She shot me a sideways glance and smiled. I didn't reply because I wasn't sure how to.

"And don't you go and be judging them now," she teased, "because I've caught you looking often enough."

I blushed again and still I said nothing, but I knew I'd been busted and so I didn't contradict her. Then she spoke for me, and so eased my discomfort with a typical mixture of wit, wisdom and telepathy.

"Yeah, you're busted alright," she laughed, "but that's OK, it's a compliment..." she glanced at me again as we strode along. "And it's kind of healthy at your age. I'd rather you look at my backside than theirs... unless that's why you turned around and waved..."

"No way! I wasn't..." I protested, horrified that she might even think that's why, but then I could tell from her laugh that she was just jacking me up.

There was a more mature edge to our banter and our conversations since Dublin two years before, and especially since all the trips to the rugby club in Dundalk, and so I enjoyed it when she teased me like a grown-up. It felt like she was always treating me as an equal, and that age was something you couldn't have until you'd acquired it - simple as that.

"Don't worry, I took a look at him too," she grinned. "The young fellah I mean. He was just fit is all. And sort of good looking," she winked. "I'll bet he plays rugby, whad'ya think?"

"Yeah, that's what I thought too," I lied to further deflect my embarrassment. I hadn't thought that at all though, I'd just turned round to be nosey.

We walked on in reflective silence for a while until Aunt Úna seemed to pluck a question out of nowhere.

"What do you think they were talking about?" she said without breaking stride.

"What?"

"What do you think they were talking about as they were approaching us? Didn't you hear them?"

"Er, not really, well some of it, but..."

"Aye, it was funny. Funny weird I mean."

"Why?"

"The old fellah had just said, 'Call yourself The Wolf, you're certainly no mountain goat.' Didn't you hear that bit?"

"Oh yeah, I did, I heard that... but I didn't really understand what he was on about."

"Right," she answered thoughtfully.

"But the young guy had just stumbled, hadn't he? That was why, wasn't it?"

"Yes, I saw that, but it was just an odd thing to say."

"Why?"

"Well, he didn't say 'call yourself *a* wolf', he said '*The* Wolf'... like I said, weird."

"But he was just teasing him, wasn't he?"

"Yeah, he was, and he stumbled because he'd been staring at my groin for the last thirty yards, but it was still weird."

"Oh..."

"Aye, he missed his footing," she laughed, "and he nearly went arse over tit."

I felt a sudden pang of guilt to go with my own discomfort, because Aunt Úna's precious groin is what I'd been staring at for most of the past two years.

"Oh, I didn't see that," I mumbled.

"No, but I did, and he was embarrassed because I'd seen him trip-up; not because of what the old boy had said to him."

"Got it," I lied.

"Bad form for a young buck, me seeing him trip an' all. Huh, tripped over his bloody tongue most likely," she laughed, "nothing to do with not being a mountain goat."

I laughed back but I didn't answer, I didn't know what to say again, and so we walked on and spoke of other things all the way back to the car. As we stopped and brushed-off the dust before climbing in, Úna drew my attention to the ugly looking clouds out over the North Atlantic. We'd timed our climb perfectly, she said, and within an hour or two she reckoned we'd have been washed-off the side of the mountain. I knew she was joking, but she wasn't exactly wrong. When the weather turns in the Hills of Donegal it turns with the speed and belligerence of a raging bull. Even on a warm summer's day in June. Within an hour or so of us driving away the black grubby cuffs of the clouds were rolled-up in anger, and the bright blue gashes of sky turned into slate-grey sheets of rain.

As we drove off I looked-up and wondered if the two men we'd laughed at would be OK? The old man and his proud-looking grandson. And I pictured them slip-sliding down the goat-track, the stubble on God's chin now slick with spittle and the soil heavy on their boots. But they'd both looked like they could look after themselves, and so I thought no more about them. Not for another twenty-five years, and until I saw their pictures in the Special Branch office in Wexford.

From there we drove to Letterkenny for lunch, and we stopped at an old pub with a sort of Children's Room affair out the back. But the landlord said we didn't have to stay in there, and he let us sit at a corner table in the main bar. Of course he did, I reckon he liked Aunt Úna's walking gear too. Aunt Úna drank pints of Guinness – only two of them mind, coz she was driving – and I drank Coke; although she let me sip her beer whenever no-one was looking. She always did that.

After lunch and on the drive all the way back to Newry, I slept the whole way. That hadn't been my plan – I didn't like to waste any time with Aunt Úna – but she'd done tuckered me out. Our first big expedition to Donegal had been a resounding success, and we'd do the same and many similar things again in the future. Eílis started to come with us for a few months – she was far more adventurous than Kieran – but then even she got bored and got into other things, until eventually it became just me and Aunt Úna again. My dad even came with us once, but *only* once, and he seemed to have a really good time; but he was so exhausted by the end of the day he never did it again either.

And to be honest I was glad. I loved my dad, and on other occasions I enjoyed spending time with him, but that way I didn't have to share my soulmate.

Ghost Train

My trip to Poison Glen with Aunt Úna couldn't have come at a better time. I was still an avid watcher of the news and just over a year before there had been an IRA attack south of Newry that caught not only the national headlines but also my hungry imagination. In fact, it caught the eye of just about every young boy of my age that heard about it anywhere in Ireland. Twelve months later BBC Northern Ireland had re-ignited my interest with a look-back documentary and its own analysis.

It was remarkably daring and sophisticated even for the South Armagh Brigade, who over the previous twenty years had become something of the trials-unit for the Provisional IRA everywhere. As a rule of thumb if a brigade anywhere else asked Northern Command for five hundred pounds of explosives for a bomb, they'd be given maybe three hundred and told where, when and exactly how to use it. Whereas if South Armagh asked for a thousand pounds, they'd be given twice that and left – quite literally - to their own devices. Such autonomy, skill and know-how was seldom squandered, and the attack on the Permanent Vehicle Checkpoint at Cloghoge, right on the border south of Newry near Killeen, was but one example. There were many.

At least a dozen men from the South Armagh Brigade, but maybe twice that number, had set up the complex and multi-phased operation on the evening of the 30th of April 1992. While four of them held a family hostage in Killeen and stole their JCB excavator, another team stole a large walk-through type Renault van from Dundalk. In the next few hours the rest of the Provos' pieces came together to carry out one of their most innovative attacks to date.

First the excavator was used to construct a ramp up to the side of the Belfast to Dublin railway line a couple of miles south of the border, and at the same time the stolen van was fitted with train wheels so that it could run on the rails. Next it was loaded with a thousand kilograms of HME, some twenty-two hundred pounds of high-grade Home Made Explosives. It was then lifted carefully onto the railway line by the excavator, facing north, a mile-long command wire was added to fire the device, and then the bomb was armed.

A number of IRA Volunteers provided road-blocks, look-outs and sentries to ensure they weren't interrupted at each location, including either side of the checkpoint on the A1 cross-border road to ensure no civilian traffic drove into the killing area. Those stopping traffic on the busy main road in the South were even dressed in Garda police uniforms. Once they were ready to go the van was set-off in first gear and the command wire was paid-out behind it as it headed north towards its target. It was nearly 2 am. Over a mile later it reached the area of the PVCP, callsign Romeo One-Five, the British Army checkpoint manned around the clock by police and soldiers from the Royal Regiment of Fusiliers, and at a point where the railway runs parallel to the road and just yards away.

Other soldiers, on rural foot patrol in pitch darkness near the railway, first heard the van, and then saw it, and so were able to warn the checkpoint that it was coming; but they were too far away to stop it. As it approached the structure, one of those in the PVCP, Fusilier Andrew Grundy, both gave the alarm and tried to disable the van with rifle fire. He was unsuccessful, but at least his warning had allowed his colleagues to get into hardened cover. At the same time an IRA Volunteer overlooking the checkpoint radioed those with the firing pack and told them that the bomb had reached its target. Then it was detonated. Fusilier Grundy was killed almost instantly, and his ten-ton reinforced look-out post was lifted off its foundations and dropped twelve metres away. Twenty-three of his colleagues were injured but survived and the PVCP was demolished. It was never replaced.

Aunt Úna and I discussed the attack obviously - the whole family did - both at the time and then again during our all-day pilgrimage to the Derryveagh Mountains one year later. I don't know why, but we did. Her disgust and condemnation were unequivocal both times; and although I didn't share my secret admiration for the ingenuity and audacity of those involved, I was pretty clear on how unimpressed she would have been if I'd tried.

In the months that followed I thought about it a lot. About everything. The whole right and wrong of it; the inevitability of it because of Ireland's long and bloody conflict with the English; and about the various merits of the various forces and fighters involved. It's hard to be Irish and not have a huge cast of Celtic heroes, and amongst those the greatest number are bound to be warriors of some era and cause or another. (Many of whom, by the way, had proudly worn the uniform of His or Her Majesty's Armed Forces in any number of 'British' wars.) But I always had Aunt Úna, the rest of my family and my own hard-earned principles to pull me back from the brink. Less, of course, Éamon and Maud.

Many in South Armagh were not so lucky. Indeed, many young boys my age right across a still war-torn, still obliquely oppressed and bitterly divided Northern Ireland as a whole. At that age it would have been easy to toy with the idea of joining *Fianna*, more properly known as Na Fianna Éireann, the Irish Nationalist youth movement, which in recent times had come to form a training cadre for full IRA membership at age sixteen.

111

And against such a backdrop it would have been easy to see eventual promotion to the senior organisation as a brave and righteous thing to do. A proudly Celtic and patriotic thing to do. In short, a very attractive thing to do. The life of every teenage boy is plagued with zits, depression and unbelievably bad days, and on any one of the latter I could have easily decided to become the next Brendan Moley or Brendan Burns... but for the common sense and integrity of Aunt Úna and others like her, and the relative security of my upbringing.

It was a turbulent, hormonal and bewildering period I would forget all about for many years; and then re-visit at the height of the search for the IRA Cleanskin Michael McCann. And it was a period for *him* during which I concluded that most of his life choices had already been made for him. Our parallel courses were obvious, and the serrated-edge of our teenage anger was common to all boys our age, but the most striking contrasts in our upbringing were thankfully clearer still. If I'm grateful now for those wonderful years under the spell of my 'Aunt' Úna, then I'm even more grateful that I never found myself under the wing of a Frank O'Neill or a Cahal Brady.

And although now, in 2017 there's still no God in my God-shaped hole, I've since dropped-in a pearl of gratitude or two and then moved on to all of life's next great conundrums. Life is where you're at, get on with it.

As One Door Closes...

As I hit thirteen, and after a year or more spent obsessing over Aunt Úna's groin, I started to become aware of the budding young groins of others nearer my own age. Or more to the point, I started to take an interest in girls who seemed more than a little interested in mine. Nothing much happened during that first year though; because despite a lot of brave talk to and from the girls I selected to help me learn my craft, none of us really knew what to do. We just made a great show of sounding like we did.

Abbey Grammar was an all-boys school of course, and so the only girls worthy of such an experiment were to be found at similar all-girls schools across town. The young ladies of St Mary's, just five minutes from my own school, proved to be enthusiastic cohorts, as did the some of the young Catholic rebels of Our Lady's Grammar School, conveniently on my way home when walking across the fields from the Armagh Road. All of the above looked quite cute in their uniforms, and it wasn't usually too difficult to split the boldest lambs from the rest of the flock. But bold or not, they invariably seemed as clueless and inept as was I.

Or if I really wanted a crash-course in what went where, there were a few willing guinea pigs my age or older to be found under the cover of darkness in the Derrybeg itself. But they also had their drawbacks; and I soon learned that pioneers in life are often forced to be hardy rather than choosy, and to take the rough with the smooth gratefully. But it was still more bluff and bluster than skill or expertise, and for the longest while looking the part became far more important than actually doing the deed.

And yet the time for the deed was rapidly approaching, much to my horror, and images of Aunt Úna in the rowing boat on the Liffey seldom left my mind.

The next couple of years were difficult because I was pulled in so many different directions (mostly by myself), and then add to that the dreaded spectres of AIDS, apprehension or conception – immaculate or otherwise – and my fourteen-year-old Catholic machinery became frozen with fear and anguish. And just being Catholic – whether practising or not – confounded my circumstances immeasurably.

Men's magazines weren't exactly in wide circulation at school and under the gaze of the Christian Brothers, and the first time I ever got to watch a porn VHS at a mate's home - when his parents were out for the evening and we found his father's stash - was more terrifying than it was revealing. One thing was certain though, neither of those things were ever going to happen in *my* home; even after Maud moved to Belfast in 1995 and so there was one less female in the house. But like all things in life, nothing worth having ever came without hard work... and so I persevered. I persevered so hard some days my hand nearly fell-off.

The first time I ever unsnapped a bra though, I was so pleased with myself I thought I'd re-discovered nuclear fission. And the exhilaration of then sliding my trembling hand inside the scarcely full young cup, felt like discovering Atlantis. Small steps, I constantly told myself... and small breasts too back then, but I was on the way at last. After a few weeks of such aimless groping

I thought I'd mastered breasts quite well, so then I looked for bigger and better specimens on which to practice my art. Eventually I could even feign an air of confidence and expertise that wasn't truly the case, but then, inevitably, came the almost debilitating challenge of knickers.

The first time I was actually confronted with a pair on a real live girlfriend and expected to remove them – or worse still, grope around inside them and know instinctively what I was meant to be looking for – I became paralysed with fear all over again. But not *petrified* you notice, and a full erection was something that eluded me for weeks whenever that new and scary boundary loomed once more in front of me. It was like someone had re-set the clock to zero and wiped all my points, and I had to build some sort of a score again from scratch. But once more, just like everything else in life that had scared me to date, it was a fear that I first concealed, then conquered, and finally mastered. After which it was all about one of my grandpa's favourite mantras - 'Practice makes perfect' - and about racking-up the hours.

Actually losing my virginity, when the time came, was a fairly unremarkable affair compared to the months-long build-up, except that it happened on the same evening that the IRA ended their ceasefire with the Docklands Bomb in London. But at the time I'd felt I had to go through with it, because it followed months of shame and apprehension about what it was exactly that I was expected to do. Time to find out I thought, and thank God I was with someone that night who seemed to know.

She was nearly two years older than me, and she was one of the more impatient guinea-pigs from the Derrybeg that wasn't prepared to wait for me to get all my stars in line before taking the plunge. In fact, it was she that took the plunge, deep inside my trousers and before I'd made my mind up, so that she frightened the shit out of me before we'd even began. I'd been alone in sneaky circumstances with quite a few girls by then, but they'd all been *good* girls I'd got to know from St Mary's or Our Lady's Grammar; and although they'd seemed as keen as me and far more confident, they had lacked the same moral fibre each time it had really come to the crunch as I had - and so the deal hadn't yet been clinched.

Not so, however, for fifteen-year-old Shaela Keane from Iveagh Crescent. She quite literally got a grip of it all and showed me not only the ropes, but told me which ones to pull, when and how hard. She wasn't the sort of girl I planned to see again – and certainly not in public and in places where I might be recognised – but I remain grateful to this day for her skill, her patience and her dogged determination; and I think she might have shaved a whole year or two off the entire process.

But my ordeal wasn't over yet... because that wasn't the only thing she'd shaved! And that – that and her painfully rolling a condom on me which she seemed to produce from nowhere – was the scariest part of the whole deal. The few pictures of naked women that I had seen, I'd studied closely and so I knew what to expect. Or so I thought, and pubic hair was definitely one of my reference points. And so, when I first saw Shaela's barren red-zone, I contemplated making a break for it for fear she was diseased. I never got the chance, thank God, and it was as she calmed me down and jacked me up that I realised I still had most of my learning yet to do.

Fuck! Such was progress. But at least I could say the word now without shame.

From my inauspicious christening with Shaela in, behind and below the bushes on the edge of the playing fields behind our house, I progressed over the spring and summer months to a variety of impromptu love nests and sparring partners. But it was late in the school holidays before I ever got to use a real bed; one balmy afternoon in late-August, when one of the Grammar School girls took me home 'to study' before school started again, and safe in the knowledge that her parents would be working.

They were 'professional people', her term not mine – one was a lawyer, the other a doctor – and so they were never home before seven, she announced. She was right, and so in the coming days we were often 'studying hard' until six-thirty. I saw quite a lot of her until Christmas, but then we fell out over presents and talk of a family Christmas dinner, and so that was that. It might have also had something to do with her mum catching us 'going at it' half way up their stairs, but it's hard to tell what really pisses-off adults at that age.

Luckily the mum was the doctor, not the lawyer, and seeing as we were both under age she didn't want the dad to know. She'd seemed particularly surprised and impressed that I was using a condom, so that's what saved me I reckon. I thought that was particularly good of her, not telling the dad, and if it had been several years later and I'd been more sure of myself, I reckon I would have done something about the undeniable glint in the mum's eye after she'd sent her daughter to her room. I saw it again months later, when we met in the street as I walked home from school, but alas she never invited me around for tea.

She nearly did, she actually said so, and I think some doctors become so familiar with the human body that they don't have the same boundaries as the rest of us, but she didn't want 'simple courtesy and a harmless cup of tea' to be misconstrued by her daughter. Yeah, right, or by her husband or the neighbours more like. She was the same age as Aunt Úna, which certainly had something to do with my sudden interest, and I learnt a lot from her about bantering even in those two brief encounters - and it struck me at the time that she should probably have been the lawyer and not her husband.

But that incident meant back to the bushes, the bike sheds and the bus shelters; and so in real terms, that for me meant either wait until the spring or find some more *nice girls* with professional parents. I'd become used to my creature comforts and I didn't intend to yield them so easily. In the end I did a bit of both, but through the *good girls* I befriended - good *bad* girls, thank God - I met several MILFs, another lawyer, a fairly senior police officer and a small-business owner. All of them might have been viewed as alien to most of the kids in the Derrybeg, and some of them even as the enemy, but I got on well with them all. Much to my surprise I found I liked professional people. What's more, the things they said and did reminded me of the seasoned candour of Aunt Úna, and of the existence of a world not beholding to the Troubles. And so, predictably, sometime around about then I decided to one day be one of them.

As my sixteenth birthday approached and the milestone of losing my virginity became harder to see in my rear view mirror, I seized a random moment to take a look at my mum's scrapbooks for the past couple of years. I'd been too busy until then growing up and too confused by it all to take time out, and there had seemed to be so much to cram into those mid-teen years that it hadn't even occurred to me to look. What I found shocked me for the first time since I was ten, with regard to her scrapbooks that is, because it was almost as if she'd given up keeping them. She was slowly closing her windows to the world, it seemed, and so I hoped she wasn't giving up on life too.

Maybe my mum had been worried about us kids for those same few years, or maybe she'd been worried about something else, but she'd only used-up one book and she only had fourteen raggedy newspaper cuttings for the whole of the four years from 1993 to '96. There were hundreds of other incidents she might have included, but no, it was as if she'd censored herself. Or maybe she was just in denial – desperate for the diminishing Troubles to bypass Éamon completely, or for the Provisional's 1994 ceasefire to hold forever. Either way her heart, I reckoned, clearly wasn't in it anymore – or maybe it was just broken – and I was more surprised at the things she left out than by what she put in.

Plus, I also had a new awareness of the Troubles through the discussions I had with Father Kennett at school, and so I was looking through a new and inquisitive lens. Apart from teaching history, which he did with great passion and seemingly endless knowledge, he was our rugby coach and so I spent a great deal of time with him. He didn't skirt around issues and neither did he shirk the hard questions, so we talked daily about all manner of things and their implications. As a result, even I could remember a handful of things that had happened but which hadn't made it into Mum's scrapbook. Or maybe that was it, I suddenly worried? Maybe my mum remembered them rather too well.

And then it was like she stopped looking for things at all after the Provos eventually broke their seventeen-month-long ceasefire at the start of 1996, and I know with hindsight that she didn't start-up again until the following year. And by then there was a huge gap. She'd cut out a piece about one massive bomb in London, for example, but then there was nothing about the enormous bomb that demolished the centre of Manchester in June. Yet she'd been to Manchester and had friends there, that one was personal, and it had shaken her profoundly.

Nor was there a mention of the bomb that the Provos managed to get right inside of Thiepval Barracks in the October. That's where HQNI was, the British Army's Headquarters for the whole of Northern Ireland, and Aunt Úna and I talked about that for hours. My mum had sat and listened to us, yet not a mention in her book. But what *was* in the scrapbook was still interesting right enough, and there were things I'd missed or forgotten. I was in the house on my own for a couple of hours, and so I sat down with a mug of tea and read them all:

In January 1993 a total of seven-point-four million dollars were stolen from the Brink's Armored Car Depot in Rochester, New Jersey, in America; and four men were accused: Samuel Millar, Father Patrick Maloney, former Rochester Police officer Thomas O'Connor, and Charles McCormick. All had links to the Provisional IRA, or what the newspapers had started calling *PIRA*.

In March PIRA exploded two small bombs in waste bins outside shops and businesses in Warrington town centre, in the north of England. Jonathan Bell, three years-old, and twelve-year-old Tim Parry were killed. That's why to this day you'll not find waste bins in public places across much of the UK. Jonathan Bell had been in town with his babysitter shopping for a Mother's Day card, and over fifty other people were injured.

In April the Provos detonated a huge truck bomb in Bishopsgate, in the heart of London's financial district, which killed a photo-journalist, injured forty-four people and caused over a billion pounds' worth of damage. It was the second such bombing aimed at London's financial infrastructure in the past twelve months.

On the 23rd of October PIRA killed ten people, including their own Volunteer when his device exploded prematurely, with a bomb at a fish shop on the Loyalist Shankill Road in Belfast. The operation was a failure at several levels and was based on flawed intelligence. Eight of those killed were simply Protestant civilians.

A week later the Loyalist Ulster Defence Association, the UDA, acting under their cover name of the Ulster Freedom Fighters, the UFF, shot and killed eight people in a bar in Greysteel in revenge. Greysteel was an all-Catholic village in County Derry. A further thirteen people were injured.

On the 15th of December the British Prime Minister, John Major, and the Irish Taoiseach, Albert Reynolds, issued their joint Downing Street Declaration on the future of Northern Ireland...

But then in response, on December the 29th, the Provos announced that they would 'fight on against the British presence in Northern Ireland' in their New Year Message.

On the 2nd of June 1994, a Chinook helicopter, carrying twenty-five of Northern Ireland's most senior British intelligence officers, crashed into the Mull of Kintyre in Scotland. All twenty-five were killed, from MI5, the RUC and the British Army, as were all four crew from the Royal Air Force.

On the 31st of August the Provisional IRA announced a 'Complete cessation of military operations', its first ceasefire for nearly twenty years.

On the 13th of October, just six weeks after PIRA's historic statement, the Loyalist paramilitary groups announced a similar ceasefire. Beside that newspaper cutting my mother had even dared to write, 'Peace at last? In the name of the Father, the Son and the Holy Ghost, and for the Love of Mary, *please* let it be so!'

In March 1995 the Northern Ireland Secretary, Sir Patrick Mayhew, set out the conditions for Sinn Féin, the political wing of the IRA, to join all-party talks; including the phrase 'the actual de-commissioning of some arms'. That statement so worried some of the rank and file of the Provisional IRA that Gerry Adams, Sinn

Féin President and an oft-alleged IRA leader since the early-70s, was forced to reassure PIRA that its role was not yet over...

And then in August Adams told a rally in Belfast that "the IRA haven't gone away, you know." Surprisingly, there was no comment written beside *that* cutting from my mother, but I remember her despair and her weeks-long depression clearly.

In January 1996, US Senator George Mitchell gave his name to the six principles finally agreed by the British and Irish governments, and by all the political parties in Northern Ireland seeking a place at the talks. Gerry Adams and Sinn Féin accepted them, but they were strongly criticised by hard-line Republicans. As a result, there were a number of resignations from the party and widespread concerns that the IRA's sixteen-months-long ceasefire might collapse – or be deliberately broken. Not least amongst those concerns were those of my mother.

And then on the 9th of February – and fittingly my mum's last cutting in that scrapbook - she and the world got their answer, when the Provisional IRA detonated a three thousand-pound bomb at Canary Wharf in the financial centre of London's Docklands. Unsurprisingly it was the work of yet more bandits from South Armagh, and it caused two deaths, over a hundred injuries and millions of pounds' worth of damage. More to the point, it ended the ceasefire, caused the Peace Process to flounder yet again, and coincided with me losing my virginity and most of my remaining inhibitions... somewhere in amongst the bushes between Violet Hill Avenue and Chequer Hill. God damn the Provos, and God bless Shaela Keane and several others like her.

I don't know what else to tell you... except that as one door closes another invariably opens, and as I tumbled through my latest doorway I was able at last to put puberty, virginity and delinquency safely behind me. The trick, I have learned since, is to collect your thoughts, step boldly through, then see what's on the other side. You don't know until you try, and the only real failure is not making the effort in the first place. But quite often you may not even have a choice. Like Michael McCann, I suspect.

Pride and Pocket

So, as I keep mentioning it in passing anyway, I reckon it's time to tell you a bit more about the IRA's various attempts to break the bank or to cut off the head of the proverbial British viper. And I know all this not from being in MI5 twenty years later, but pretty much from being 'born middle-aged', as Aunt Úna puts it, and from my thirst for knowledge at the time.

Thus, in real terms... that means from being a nosey little sod in Mum's scrapbooks; from watching the news; from reading the papers; from books and magazines; from the BBC's world-renowned documentaries and from the best of Ulster TV and RTÉ; and from endless discussions with Dermott McCracken, with Father Kennett, with an old World War II veteran I used to talk to on the way home from school, and with Aunt Úna herself – who through her numerous work contacts and just through being interested, seemed remarkably well-informed about pretty much everything. Especially some little-known-about but astronomical insurance claims arising from London in the 1990s.

So here we go then. It's quite a story. When the Provisional IRA detonated its huge bomb at Canary Wharf in February 1996, it was neither the first nor the last of its multi-million-pound attacks. It was but the latest of a determined strategy designed to wear the British government down through energy-sapping body blows to its pride and pocket. If they couldn't bring the people of Britain to their knees, nor their government ministers, then they'd damn well try the treasury. And it damn well nearly worked.

In the past twenty years the IRA had tried all manner of guerrilla tactics in the UK and across Europe. An army colonel had been shot dead whilst running through the woods in Germany, British barracks had been bombed, shot-at and mortared, and servicemen and occasionally their families had been attacked and killed outside of Ireland and the UK in Holland and Germany. Even Australian tourists had been caught up in it all, simply because they looked like off-duty British soldiers. Were it not for the SAS operation to stop them, there would doubtless have been bloody carnage in Gibraltar too; and there had been literally thousands of bombs against commercial targets since the start of the Troubles. Imagine, say, four or five attacks like the Boston Marathon Bomb per week, but *every* week and for over thirty years. And most, of course, were much worse than that. Much worse.

As far back as in 1990 thought had been given by the Provisional IRA to attacking London's financial infrastructure, and in July of that year a large bomb at the London Stock Exchange caused massive damage but no injuries. But significantly, not enough damage to achieve its aim. So then, just six months later, they embarked on a new phase of targeted bombings and set-out to take the war against Her Majesty's Government to the next level. To a gargantuan level. New and carefully selected personnel, a new plan, a new ethos and a whole new level of targeting, brought about whole new levels of damage, cost and concern. And every single bomb had the capacity to kill of course, which despite carefully coded warnings they did with sickening regularity.

At about the time of the Stock Exchange bomb, and maybe even prompted by its relative failure, the Army Council of the

Provisional IRA authorised a mortar-bomb attack against Maggie Thatcher at her residence at 10 Downing Street. Their aim was simply to kill her, and as many of her senior cabinet ministers as they could catch in one place; and so they sent two senior IRA members as SMEs, as Subject Matter Experts, to London to plan and prepare. One was from South Armagh and was an expert on the conduct of mortar attacks, the other was from Belfast and was an authority on their manufacture.

Next a mainland ASU, an Active Service Unit operating in England, bought a Ford Transit van, hid it in a rented garage, and then started to prepare it and the mortars for use on the day. They cut away a section of the van's roof and replaced it with a cosmetic patch, by which the tubes would be concealed but *through* which they would fire, and then loaded the bombs into place. Each one was over a metre long, weighed sixty kilograms and contained twenty kilograms of Semtex plastic explosive. Then the SMEs returned to Ireland to avoid the risk of capture before, during or after the attack, and the ASU awaited its opportunity.

That November, however, Maggie Thatcher resigned from office after a short but decisive Tory campaign to unseat her as Prime Minister, and so PIRA's Army Council were forced to review their options. They decided to attack her successor anyway, John Major, and revisited their intention to do so during a cabinet meeting if at all possible. On the 7th of February 1991 they got their chance. Whilst Major met with his War Cabinet and other senior intelligence and military personnel over the conduct of the Gulf War, the ASU moved the baseplate into place in the heart of government and during a flurry of snow.

The driver parked it at the junction of Whitehall and Horse Guards Avenue, about two hundred metres from Number 10, activated the firing mechanism and then left the area on the back of a motorbike. A few minutes later the three mortar bombs were launched, and a small explosive charge in the van - designed to destroy any forensic evidence - set it on fire. Two of the bombs fell close but not close enough, and the third fell in the back garden of Number 10 and did significant damage to the rear of the building.

Not though, to the cabinet members inside. Straight after the attack John Major is famously reported to have said, "I think we had better start again, somewhere else." The room was vacated, the meeting was re-convened minutes later in the Cabinet Office Briefing Rooms, known as COBRA, and the noble white swan of Her Majesty's Government swum calmly by... but defiant and unflappable or not, the Provisionals had made their point and the Army Council re-convened to plan its next audacious attack.

In an IRA statement from Dublin the organisation said, "Let the British government understand that, while Nationalist people in the six counties are forced to live under British rule, then the British Cabinet will be forced to meet in bunkers." In a separate statement, the head of the explosives section of the Met Police's Anti-Terrorist Branch went further, when he said that the attack was '...a remarkably good aim if you consider that the bomb was fired from two hundred and fifty yards with no direct line of sight. Technically, it was quite brilliant and I'm sure that many army crews, if given a similar task, would be very pleased to drop a bomb that close. You've got to park the launch vehicle in an area which is guarded by armed men and you've got less than a minute to do it. I was very, very surprised at how good it was. If the angle of fire had been moved about five or ten degrees, then those bombs would have actually impacted on Number 10.'

Trust me, they impacted on the national agencies and on more than a few in the government anyway!

London didn't have long to wait to see what PIRA would do next. On the 10th of April 1992 they detonated a one-ton truck-bomb outside of the Baltic Exchange, one of the key locations at the time of the City of London's financial sector. Despite warnings it killed Paul Butt, a twenty-nine-year-old Exchange employee; Thomas Casey, a forty-nine-year-old doorman; and fifteen-year-old Danielle Carter. It also injured another ninety-one people, and estimates in 1992 put the damage at eight hundred-million pounds - which was, at that time, two hundred-million pounds more than the cost of the ten thousand or more explosions during the Northern Ireland Troubles thus far. The IRA had made its point yet again.

There was then a seemingly relentless campaign of lesser devices - some of which killed though, and many of which caused casualties - over the next twelve months. By April 1992 there had been at least a dozen such devices set off across the city since the start of that year, and over thirty during the previous twelve months. But then on the 24th of April came the next big one. The IRA had a new strategy and they were on a roll.

Back in March an Iveco tipper truck had been stolen in Staffordshire, in the English Midlands, and the Provos showed their ingenuity yet again when a one-ton bomb made in South Armagh was smuggled into the country under a layer of bitumen. Then on the day of the attack members of a PIRA ASU drove it into Bishopsgate, a major thoroughfare through London's financial sector. They parked the truck outside of the Hong Kong and Shanghai Bank, activated the arming mechanism and left the area by car. A number of telephone warnings were then given by a caller using a recognised codeword from a callbox back in Ireland, and guess where?... in Forkhill, South Armagh.

When the bomb exploded it damaged buildings over five hundred metres away and the cost of repairs was estimated at the time to be at least one billion pounds. Over a million and a half square feet of office space was affected, and there was over five hundred tons of broken glass. More to the point, and despite the warnings, a photo-journalist Ed Henty was killed and forty-four people were injured. Civilian casualties would doubtless have been higher had it not been a Saturday morning.

There were some positive outcomes as well though: in the aftermath authorities introduced a 'ring of steel' of physical security measures; and the Disaster Recovery Plans agreed and instigated by most of the companies in the area following the bomb, saved countless billions in lost revenue following the 9/11 attacks in New York less than a decade later.

And the actual explosive power of the Bishopsgate bomb? It was equivalent to one thousand and two hundred kilograms of TNT... a little over twenty-six hundred pounds of high explosives.

Next, a new and equally devastating tactic. In December 1993 a cascade of coded bomb warnings from the IRA served to close or paralyse forty mainland railway stations and huge swathes of the London Underground. Although not injured, over three hundred and fifty thousand commuters were affected and the capital's economy lost an estimated thirty-four million pounds. At one point, and at the height of the city's morning rush-hour, the London Underground had to evacuate no less than sixty thousand people - commuters, tourists, traders, residents and countless others - from a hundred tube stations in just fifteen minutes. And this time, not an actual bomb went off anywhere. PIRA had made yet another point.

They would similarly take the piss just sixteen months later, when a number of PIRA bomb warnings and two actual explosions on an electricity pylon near the M6 Motorway disrupted traffic throughout southern England and the Midlands. In the London area alone both Heathrow Airport and the M25 Motorway were closed, and a transport spokesman estimated that there was at least another thirty million pounds in lost revenue.

Heathrow, God bless it, had been in the news before that and even deeper in trouble. Between the 9th and the 13th of March 1994, the Provisional IRA carried out three separate stand-off mortar attacks on one of the world's biggest and busiest airports. On the 9th they launched four bombs from a car at the Excelsior Hotel, which landed on or near the northern runway; on the 11th four more bombs launched from waste ground impacted on an aircraft parking area near Terminal 4; and on the 13th, five bombs landed in the vicinity of Terminal 4 itself. Despite the highly successful, highly complex and constantly evolving security within the airport's massive footprint, PIRA had simply moved its point of attack hundreds of metres into Heathrow's hinterland and created a tactic that was virtually impossible to prevent.

Then, on the 9th of February 1996 – the evening of my very own big bang beneath the bushes at Our Lady's Grammar School in Newry – they carried out the Canary Wharf bomb, in the Docklands financial district of London. Yet another colossal truck bomb had been planned, constructed, deployed and detonated by members of the South Armagh Brigade into the heart of England's capital. This time it contained no less than fourteen hundred kilograms of HME - over three thousand pounds of PIRA's tried and tested fertiliser-based explosives – which had been packed into secret compartments in a flatbed lorry disguised to look like a tow truck. And that was the bomb that signalled the end of the seventeen-month-old ceasefire.

The actual attack of course had been planned for weeks or months, and throughout the ceasefire the Provos had continued to gather intelligence, plan and prepare, acquire and stockpile weapons, and manufacture more of its high-grade home-made explosives. But then, with the Peace Process stalled and not going their way, they chose to use it. On the 7th of February, two days before the attack, both the truck and the bomb were moved from South Armagh to Scotland via the Larne-Stranraer ferry. From there it was driven over three hundred miles to a location in East London, where it was made ready, a mercury tilt-switch anti-handling device was added to make it more difficult to defuse, and finally it was driven into place.

The detonation itself was devastating, and the blast was both felt and heard right across the city. It physically shook Canary Wharf Tower and left a crater ten metres wide and three metres deep. The head of the Metropolitan Police Force's Anti-Terrorist unit described it as, "a scene of utter devastation," and, "...like a scene from the apocalypse". Just the blast cost insurers a hundred and seventy million pounds and, despite several IRA warnings, over a hundred people were injured and two men in a newsagent's who were closing-up but didn't leave quickly enough were killed instantly. Twenty-nine-year-old shop owner, Inam Bashir, and his thirty-one-year-old employee, John Jeffries, were reportedly blown through two walls and then buried by rubble.

Just as the Peace Process, for the time being at least, was blown through three countries and buried by red tape. But unlike Bashir and Jeffries... it was never pronounced dead.

R.S.V.P.

In my own tiny world only three momentous things happened in 1997. My brother Éamon got married in Belfast; then there was something that fell out of that directly; and I saw a soldier shot dead right in front of my eyes. The last British soldier ever to be killed by the Provos during the Troubles as it turns out, but none of us knew that at the time. He was just the latest back then, and of course there had been hundreds before him - and so we didn't know he was the last. We certainly daren't have guessed.

Oh yeah, maybe four things, because then right at the end of the year I met a boy two years older than me called Tommy Bray. He was an interesting character and we got on right away, but I had no idea how interesting, or of the significance of meeting him, until years later. Until now in fact, in 2017, and more than a year after Michael McCann's failed attack on the BT Tower.

In my mum's photo-album there was pretty much only Éamon's wedding. That was the only real show in town for her. But her scrapbook from that period was speckled with largely unrelated world and home events. Those from home were the worst, although for once there were more good things than bad, but the first item of the year took place so close that she saw it happen. Me and her both. That sent my mum back indoors for a month or two, whereas it sent me into shock. At first at least. But then it sent me into a rage that probably put me on the straight and narrow once and for all.

With Father Kennett berating the terrorists by day at school, and then my parents and Aunt Úna the rest of the time, I was starting to see the world for what it really was and the mindless violence for what it wasn't. It wasn't the answer, of that much I was sure, and the more I thought about it the more I realised that it never could be.

On the 12th of February 1997, Lance Bombardier Stephen Restorick of the Royal Artillery was shot dead just up the road in Bessbrook village. Just minutes and a few hundred metres from his home-from-home in the old mill there. He became the latest British soldier to be cut down – cut in half almost - by one of the IRA's dreaded Barrett rifles; a nearly five-feet long anti-materiel weapon that can fire a .50" armour-piercing round accurately out to eighteen hundred metres. Very accurately.

I say the latest, because in the past five years nine soldiers had been killed across the region by the sniper teams in South Armagh; and although that wasn't a large number in the great scheme of things, that weapon, and the sniper attacks in general, had a more crushing effect on the morale of the soldiers patrolling South Armagh than any other tactic throughout the Troubles.

Five years later at university I would produce a three hundred-and-sixty-page dissertation on the dreaded Barretts and how they found their way to Northern Ireland from America, some of them during the 1994-96 ceasefire no less. But I think it was actually thoughts about Stephen Restorick that led me to do that. About watching him laughing and joking with a woman one minute, and then poleaxed by the enormous kinetic energy of the round the next. He'd just stopped her in a routine VCP, a Vehicle Check Point, and he'd literally just handed her driving licence back through her window. Then *'Wallop'*... he was no more. I think the woman was injured too by the same round, although it wasn't mentioned in mum's newspaper cutting and the news said she recovered. Not so the soldier - or his family I would guess, once they realised he'd been killed so close to the end of the Troubles.

On reflection I reckon I was drawn to write that paper at the human level - not at the technical, para-military or even at the political level - and by the fact that the first British soldier killed by the IRA in the Troubles had also been in the Royal Artillery; Gunner Robert Curtiss, back in February 1971. And so there seemed to be a certain inevitability to it all; a sort of cosmic symmetry that somehow had to play-out before it all could end. Or maybe it's simply because I watched him die. I like to think though it's mostly because by then I knew I wanted to have something to do with stopping it from ever happening again.

Whatever, but write it I knew I must. Either way, the rest of the cuttings weren't nearly so harrowing; but there again, they weren't nearly so personal.

In March the President of Ireland, Mary Robinson, met Pope John Paul II in the Vatican. That was huge to my mother, but I don't think I even noticed at the time. Then in July the Irish Taoiseach, Bertie Ahern, met British Prime Minister, Tony Blair, for the first time; there were Nationalist riots and gun battles in Newry and across Northern Ireland, when the Unionist Orange Order were allowed to march through a Catholic area in Portadown; and the Provisional IRA instituted a second ceasefire. We didn't hold our breath for its success, I remember. Also in July the UK handed Hong Kong back to the Chinese after a hundred and fifty years of British rule – a fact not lost on the IRA or its political wing, Sinn Féin; and then two weeks after Éamon's wedding, on the 31st of August, Lady Di' was killed in a car crash in Paris.

The cuttings continued, so I made myself toast and a mug of tea and so did I.

In October substantial all-party talks began in Northern Ireland; a majority of those at an IRA General Army Convention supported the ceasefire; and, as a result, the next month the

Provos' Quartermaster General, Mickey McKevitt, formed and led a breakaway movement called *Óglaigh na hÉireann*, soon to be dubbed the *Real IRA*. Then, in the November, Mary McAleese succeeded Mary Robinson as President of Ireland, the first time in world history that one woman had succeeded another as an elected head of state.

Some of the cuttings were fascinating, some not so much so; but some were things I hadn't known at all, so I made a fresh mug of tea and finished reading.

Finally, in the December, a man called Billy Wright was assassinated under the noses of the warders in the Maze Prison. Wright had been the leader of the LVF, the Loyalist Volunteer Force, and he'd been shot dead by fellow prisoners from the Irish National Liberation Army, the INLA. The same INLA, of course, that hadn't declared a ceasefire, and so the Peace Process trundled on regardless; but it wasn't lost on anyone that despite the new and hopeful atmosphere, Northern Ireland's madness continued.

There were other major or minor distractions in my life that year too, but despite those it still flourished at what felt like a whirlwind pace. In July, for example, Aunt Úna took me and Kieran to stay in the village of Curracloe in County Wexford for a few days, to watch from a distance as they filmed the D-Day landing scenes from the movie *Saving Private Ryan*. And then late in the year and at just sixteen years-old - almost seventeen though - I was asked to play for the Dundalk 1st XV in an ad hoc touring side against Blackrock College near Dublin.

Momentous stuff, all of it, but that brings me full circle and back to the other two things that stood out in that year, and so to my next story. Éamon's wedding, and the life changing event that fell out of it.

Two years earlier Maud had met and married a Belfast man called Ronan Kelly from the Ballymurphy, a hard Republican housing estate in West Belfast. Although they'd first met in Newry she'd left home and moved to the capital at the start of that year, aged twenty and so she could be a hairdresser 'in the big city'. If that's how she'd felt, said our mum and dad, then they would have wanted her to move to Dublin instead and they would have helped her to set-up there... there were no signs of the Troubles in Dublin. She'd gone to Belfast anyway, and as soon as she married Kelly they realised why.

Éamon had missed her terribly to start with, and suddenly he was the only real Nationalist left in the house. Certainly he was the only blinded and outspoken one who shot from the hip always and never wanted to see both sides. So he'd gone to stay with Maud whenever he could, and by the end of 1996 he'd visited often enough to be engaged to Kelly's sister, Clodagh. In August of the following year they married.

The ceremony was in St Teresa's on the Glen Road, and the reception afterwards was in the infamous Europa Hotel in the heart of the city. We, of course, were all invited.

Flat Shoes and High Hopes

The wedding was as weddings are, although the Kellys seemed a particularly insular bunch who didn't get on readily with any of us from Newry. At the wedding itself it didn't seem like they even tried, although I always reckoned it was because they knew of the tensions between Éamon and Maud and the rest of us. But the reception was different. It was a pretty raucous affair, and the drink loosened them all up quite nicely. Too much for my parents' liking, and even Aunt Úna kept way more on the fringes of things than was normal for her.

The Kellys weren't an IRA family per se, but they were certainly that way inclined and we had doubts about Ronan's elder brother, Conor. A Garda former boyfriend of Úna's had run a check on him when he'd set a pattern as a border-crosser for a while, and although his business in the South had been legitimate the check had come back from the RUC in Belfast to show that he was traced as a fringe member of the Provos in the Ballymurphy. But there again... if you believed the RUC checks on Catholics from certain periods of the Troubles, then *everyone* in the 'Murph was a member of the IRA. It was a bit like the Belfast equivalent of Crossmaglen, and it certainly had its fair share of urban bandits.

We as a family had got three rooms in the Europa. Even Aunt Úna shared for once, with Eílis who was by then eighteen. Úna usually liked the freedom and the privacy of having her own room, but she didn't want Eílis being on her own. My mum and Margaret shared another, and Da, Kieran and I were in the third. All of us guys wore suits, and mine was brand new for the wedding because I was growing and filling-out so fast. All the women, unsurprisingly, were dolled-up to the nines, and Aunt Úna especially looked like someone from the set of a Bond movie.

She wore a black, sequinned cocktail dress to just above the knee – to go with the men's dark suits she'd said – the neckline of which was V-wired, strapless and so bra-less as well. It was all very tasteful and nothing was on show, but her bare shoulders, beautifully styled hair and her subtle makeup all combined to conjure up quite the picture. I seldom saw Úna wearing lipstick, so the deep, red, glossy brand she wore for the reception was mesmerising. I could scarcely imagine what she was wearing under her dress, and it had been several years since I'd spend ages trying to sneak a peek to find out. Guess I'd grown-up after all.

As the evening wore on and the fun of drunken relatives wore off, I walked out the front of the hotel and stood looking across Great Victoria Street at the Crown Bar just fifty metres away. Often described as a world-renown masterpiece of pub architecture, and always listed amongst Belfast's top places to see, I longed for the day when I could stroll in and see for myself. I had an inkling by then I'd probably go to university in Belfast, and so I knew I had less than two years to wait.

I'd heard a lot about the Crown and so it was just one of those things I had to do. One of those places I had to see for myself once I turned eighteen. I knew that many of Belfast's greatest buildings hadn't fared well during the 20th Century - be it from the Blitz in 1941, the redevelopment blight of the 1960s and '70s, or during the terrorist bombing campaigns of the Troubles - but I also knew the Crown was one of those that had made it, and that it was probably the finest example of an old Victorian Gin Palace anywhere in the world.

Despite its intricate tiling, woodwork and stained-glass windows - thanks to the many Italian immigrants who'd worked on it after hours – it was a pretty ordinary-looking building from where I stood; but its splendour, I guessed, would only be realised once you entered and immersed yourself within. As I stood on the opposite pavement and pondered its likely secrets, it became a metaphor for life and I couldn't wait to burst in.

Before I could begin to mull over that journey too deeply, Aunt Úna slid up behind me, snuck her maternal arms around my waist and gently squeezed. My sixteen-and-three-quarter-year–old frame was a full two inches taller than her by then, less maybe with the high heels she'd worn for the wedding, and she nestled her head onto my shoulders. It was far too warm for a coat and so I could feel her ample breasts pressing against my back. Yet more dreams of a future still temptingly just beyond my reach.

"Found you," she said.

"Hi Aunt Úna."

"Penny?"

"What?"

"Penny. For your thoughts. You alright?"

"Aye, I'm fine."

"Really?"

"Really."

"You've seemed a little quiet this evening."

"Huh," I scoffed, "it's pretty easy to seem quiet around the Kellys, don't you think?"

"Yeah," she laughed into my back, "they are pretty fucking obnoxious, but is that all it is?" Úna hardly ever swore, but when she did it was usually funny and it went straight to the heart of the matter like an arrow.

"Aye, honestly. Just thoughtful is all."

She paused and weighed my words.

"Thinking about what...?" she squeezed again.

"All sorts. Honest. But it's all good.

"I hope so." She paused. "So give me an example."

I pondered for a moment. I could never not do what she asked, and then I spoke softly and truthfully.

"It's just with Éamon leaving an' all, well... y'know. Now I'm the oldest boy, and I'll be leaving too in a couple of years... it's all just a bit of a crossroads I suppose."

"But you're not thinking of staying I hope?"

"God no. No, I'm moving on in a couple of years, get on with things, you watch me..."

She squeezed a little harder and I felt the smile on her cheek as it pressed into my back.

"It's just tomorrow's the start of the new order," I continued, "and well, y'know... none of us really knows what that's going to be, do we?"

"No-one ever does," she murmured gently, "but are you worried about Éamon in Belfast an' all?"

I thought for a moment.

"No, not at all, he's totally in charge of his life now, same as Maud, and it's up to them who they run around with up here."

"Exactly. But... are you worried about him running around with the IRA?" she asked astutely.

I thought again.

"No, not anymore, but I know my mum and dad are. Nope, you know what, if he's not got sucked into it all in Newry then I reckon he's even more likely to become just an armchair Provo up here in Belfast."

She laughed.

"But Jees, they're all so bloody tribal," I continued, "Frig, what about Maud's husband? Arsehole or what?"

"Aye," Úna laughed, "and like South Armagh isn't tribal? Is that what you're saying?"

I didn't answer, I just laughed back and she slid around to stand beside me.

"Hey, look at me," she grinned. I did as she said.

"What?"

"Just checking you're OK. You sounded so serious then."

"I'm fine."

"So grown up..."

She studied me for a while to see if she agreed.

"Oh my God Neill," she chuckled, "when did you get so friggin' old all of a sudden? Hark at you."

"Yeah, I guess..." I smiled.

"Is that me I wonder, am I a bad influence? Or is that just the way you really are?"

"Hey, I'm a good pupil," I laughed.

"Right," she smiled, "but then maybe I shouldn't be such a good teacher. Maybe I need to let you be more of a kid for a while longer. You can't go around twice y'know."

"Huh, not for me you needn't. I like being treated like a real person. Bring it on."

She looked at me sideways for a while – a long while it seemed – and then hugged me into her side.

"What were you staring at?" she chirped.

"The Crown Bar and Liquor Saloon," I read aloud from the lettering on its flamboyant façade.

"And?"

"Well I know it's famous."

"Aye, 'tis. But how do you know about that place?"

"Oh, it gets mentioned on the news an' all, and I've read about it a few times."

"And what about it?"

"Heard it's a bit special, that's all."

"Yeah, it is," she stared towards it as I had done. "It looks spectacular inside," she added, as though she was worried I'd be disappointed by my first impression of the outside. "And then there's the most amazing bar area, and booths all down the other side of the room..."

"Aye, that's what I'd heard."

She stared at me again.

"Do you want to see it?"

"What?" I looked at her.

"Do you want to go inside and see it?"

"I can't."

"You can with me."

"But I'm not old enough."

"Yes you are, you're sixteen. You're allowed in, you're just not allowed up to the bar."

"Or to drink."

"Yeah, that too, but I'm pretty sure we can get around that bit, right?" She grabbed my arm and got ready to cross the busy four-lane road. "You look twenty-something in that suit, and it's never stopped us when we've been hiking this past year. Leave that bit to me."

"You're the boss," I said with a grin. "Get me into trouble why don't you." She laughed hard and moved me to the kerbside to wait for a gap.

We picked our moment and trotted across the road in between the traffic. Then we slipped chuckling into the bar. It was packed, and the vast majority of the revellers were men, but other than to take a good look at Úna in her party frock no-one paid us the slightest heed. There wasn't a hope in hell of getting into one of the booths and so Úna set us up at the street-end of the long bar, courtesy of a guy at the counter who had to pull his tongue back in to make room for her.

I was too nervous to take it all in initially, but Úna soon snapped me out of that when she gave me a ten-pound-note and told me to order. I didn't argue, I daren't, and so I turned confidently towards the bar, pulled her closer to emphasise my height and waited for a barman to come over to us. I realised what she'd said about me wearing a suit, with my collar open and my silk tie fashionably loosened, and when the barman approached he served me without a second glance.

I ordered a pint of Guinness and a vodka and tonic as I'd been told, and it took me a moment to realise the Guinness was for me. Úna took her drink, backed into a space in the crowd and then grinned an impish smile for me to follow. I picked up my beer and did as she said.

"Now then," she leaned-in and whispered over the din, "come and stand next to me, enjoy your beer and look like you've got every right to be here."

"If you say so."

"I do, and..." she leaned-in even closer, "then you watch how jealous all these fellahs are of you coz I'm only wearing half a dress. Enjoy the moment."

With that she backed away grinning broadly and bade me to follow her further into the heart of the bar.

We couldn't really talk much for the next fifteen minutes, it was all too noisy, but we had a fragmented conversation about the wedding and Éamon's new in-laws – 'outlaws' she joked - until we'd both finished our drinks. Then she said we should be getting back to the reception. Soon we were outside and waiting for a gap in the traffic again.

"So are we going back now?" I asked forlornly.

"Yes," she scanned me, "Why? Don't you want to?"

"Not really."

"No, me neither," she laughed, "but we should I suppose. Well, in a while at least."

I didn't answer but I shot her a hopeful glance. I think with hindsight she may have misread it, but either way it put the rest of our time away from the reception on a whole new footing. There was even a pun in there somewhere a few minutes later.

"Come with me," she grabbed my elbow and strode into a gap in the traffic. "I'm getting out of these heels before we go back in. I'm gonna get blisters and break my bloody neck if I don't."

We got half way across the road and then waited for a gap to cross the rest.

"Say that again," I laughed, "are you going back into the party barefoot?" In the normal run of things she was barefoot nearly all of the time.

"Wish I could," she grinned, "but I've got some cute little flat shoes I packed for when these got too much; and that was about two hours ago."

"I'll change them for you," I offered boldly.

"Yeah, I bet you would," she shot me a mischievous glance and chuckled, "I bet you'd like me to put my foot up into your lap in this dress. Dirty little sod."

"Hey, not so little you were just saying. And you see me playing rugby often enough."

"Aye, but I got the rest right, didn't I."

With that, and before I could answer, she giggled and darted between a bus and a couple of cars. I followed. She leapt onto the far pavement and very nearly toppled, as she'd predicted. I caught up with her and we both stood laughing for a while.

"See, nearly broke my neck after all," she laughed.

"Aye, well you nearly broke your ankle right enough."

"Come on then. Come and change them for me," she said grinning. "Otherwise you might *have* to carry me back in."

I didn't say anything. I was suddenly speechless, and so we walked chuckling to the lifts and selected her floor. We had a long wait and after a while she glanced at me with a quizzical look and then spoke.

"Jesus Neill, I don't know anymore."

"Know what?" I asked.

"Between you and me I mean. It's all so strange these days. You're such a young man now, really, I have trouble remembering what else you are."

"What do you mean?"

"I mean that you're my sister's little boy, that's what."

"Oh," I mumbled.

"Jees... I used to change your nappies."

"Don't remind me," I attempted to sound witty and confident, "but you'll not be needing to do that anymore."

"No, not that at least," she laughed. "Reckon I'd get a shock now if I did though, right?"

This time it felt like it was her who was nervously attempting humour. The lift arrived and we got in. We stood on opposite sides with our backs against the mirrored glass. I don't know why, but a sort of infectious chuckling broke out again. Úna smiled the whole time and at one point she stepped towards me and then stopped. I thought for a moment she was going to kiss me – I sure hoped so – and then I thought she was going to speak. But in the end she did neither. Could this be *the* moment, I dared to hope again? Images from the River Liffey filled my mind's eye.

Before that question could be resolved the lift stopped at her floor. The doors opened, she giggled and then led the way to her room. Once inside she dead-locked it – so Eílis couldn't enter I presumed – and then my hopes really soared. She told me to sit on the end of her bed while she rummaged in her suitcase for her flat shoes. I dared to hope for a third time!

Once she'd found them she walked slowly back towards me and put one of her high-heeled feet gently in my lap. Even through her shoes she must have felt my erection instantly, but she didn't show it in any way.

"So, interesting... you reckon you're going to remove these for me. Is that right?"

"If you like," I murmured with a trembling voice.

Although I'd lost my virginity almost two years before, suddenly I didn't feel nearly so grown up.

"So remove it," she purred.

"Change them for you, I said." God knows why I said that. It sounded so lame and I was almost whining. Thank God she virtually ignored me.

"So you did," she smiled, "but you've got to take these off before you can put the others on, true?"

143

"True," I mumbled.

I unbuckled the fine leather strap and removed her shoe. Holding the back of her calf as I did so felt amazing, and I could see the top of one stocking and a suspender strap but no more. I became even harder in an instant.

Then Úna put her suddenly naked foot down and replaced it with the other, but this time as she did so she hitched-up her dress ever so slightly to make it easier. That meant I could see both stocking tops and just the tiniest glimpse of her panties too. She saw me looking – she couldn't help but see me looking - and it was clearly what she'd intended. I tried not to show I was trembling as I unbuckled the second shoe.

As I removed it and held the back of her calf as before, she lifted her dress a little higher and replaced her stockinged foot back on my groin. In case I was in any doubt about what she was doing, she gently teased me through my trousers with her toes. It was time for silence thank God, and as I struggled to think of something to say she just smiled down at me with the tenderest smile I'd ever seen her wear.

Was it the booze, I panicked for a moment? Was it because it was a family wedding and someone always got laid? Úna herself had joked to me about just that at the start of the day, and had that been a hint I wondered? Or was it because I had come of age and at last the inevitable was about to happen?

Empty God-shaped hole or not, for a moment I almost prayed that it was the latter. I was stunned into silence I know, but if I was frightened about anything it was at the terrifying thought that that moment might never happen again.

And I was right.

I was right to be frightened of that, just as I was wrong to be thinking what I was, and in that instant I saw the self-same thoughts in Úna's conflicted eyes.

She gently slid her foot from my groin and lowered it to the ground. Her dress dropped too and suddenly she was decent again. I'd preferred indecent better, but in my heart I knew that the moment had passed. Before I could worry what to say or do next, Úna said it for me.

"Oh my God Neill..." she stepped towards me and cradled my head softly into her lap. She smelt wonderful. "You know what nearly just happened here, don't you?"

I couldn't speak, so I didn't even try.

"It's been building for months, I know," she said quietly, "and I can't believe we nearly let it happen...." She cradled my head still further, and I could tell she didn't want me to look up at her just yet. I said nothing.

"There's not a doubt in my mind it would have been wonderful," she continued gently, "truly wonderful, but I'm even more certain that in time it would have spoiled what we have and hurt us both."

I slowly pulled my head back and tried to look up at her. She stepped back slightly and gazed down at me tenderly. There were tears in her eyes.

"We're so close Neill... so special..."

"Wouldn't it make us closer?" I croaked hopefully.

"No," she smiled, and her voice trembled ever so slightly, "not closer, I don't think that's even possible."

"But..." I offered. That's all that came out. I didn't even know 'but what', and so I fell quiet again.

"Like I said," she continued, "it *would* have been wonderful I'm sure, maybe even for a month or two... Jesus Neill, maybe even for a year or two..."

"But...?" I mumbled again. This time it was very definitely a question.

"But then it would have gnawed away at us over time," she said tenderly, "until there was none of the old you and me left. Trust me. And then your mum and dad would have seen..."

"They'd never know. We'd never tell them surely?"

"Oh but they would have. They wouldn't need telling. We'd know, even if they didn't – every time we looked at them – and then one day we'd know they knew too. And then we could *never* tell them. That would be the worst moment of all."

For the first time ever I wished my Aunt Úna wasn't so wise and so thoughtful. And so damn faithful. She'd always been all three to me, and she'd saved my life through such fidelity – of that I was sure – so I couldn't now be surprised that she was doing the same for my mum. For my mum, and herself, and for me.

"Oh Neill, stand up here and hug me for God's sake. Stand up and hold me close."

I did as she asked, and as she put her arms around me and put her cheek on my shoulder the sudden anger ebbed from my body. She held me tight for long seconds.

"Neill, Neill, Neill..." she whispered slowly into my neck, "so close... so close... but thank God..."

She eased away from me slightly and looked up at me. There were still tears in her eyes but her usual joyful smile had returned. Her winning smile, so positive, so bright and cheerful... and to my dismay, so resolute... and in that instant I knew her good voices had won.

"Kiss me," she smiled, "but no tongues, seriously," she laughed tearfully. "I'm hanging on by a thread here, but you know I'm right."

For the first time ever I didn't do what she'd asked. I was frozen to the spot and fighting tears myself. She sniffed, smiled and then reached up to me and kissed me herself. It was a long, but not deep, and very tender kiss full on my lips. For the first time ever. And no tongues, as she'd made clear. When she stopped, she leant back in my arms, smiled her most beautiful smile and then kissed me again... but this time just the merest peck on the lips. Then she pulled me in close and hugged me as though her life depended on it. I liked to think later that night that maybe, for one fleeting moment, it had.

"Come on," she whispered, "let me get these shoes on and then we should get back."

We moved across the bedroom in embarrassed silence and I dreaded stepping outside. She sensed it – hell, she probably even felt it herself – so that she stopped at the door, held my hand and looked me straight in the eye. Another beautiful smile but this time no tears.

"Listen, I'm glad we kissed like that Neill. Honestly," she squeezed my hand, "and please know how precious this moment is. You know how much I love you, and now you know that a part of me wants to love you that way too..."

"Me too," I said feebly.

"But I guess we'll both just have to imagine the rest, and I think it would have been just as special as we are..." She leaned-in close and kissed me gently on the lips again. "But this way, we can stay as special as this forever. Do you understand?"

I nodded and attempted a smile, but I didn't really.

"And *this* way..." she broke into a wicked grin that always told me a joke was coming, "we don't have to get all the signs off my little black dress that would have told the whole world I'd just jumped my nephew."

There! Typically Úna. She'd killed-off all possible taboos in one simple joke, and focussed my thoughts on our discreet return to the world outside our door. And of course my broken heart and how much she loved me.

I didn't know if 'jumping me' would still have been my preference, but it would indeed have been as wrong as a wrong thing could be; and so with one smile and a handful of words, she'd banished all guilt and dignified what had just happened before we'd even left the room. My oracle, my very own guru in life, had shown me triumph in defeat, and with honour, yet again.

Our return to the reception hall was pure Úna too. There was more laughter on the way to the lift – but in a different tone and with a warmth that promised more – and when the door closed one more gentle kiss told me to be happy and that all would be well in time. Just before the door opened she held my hand and kept holding it.

"Right, let's go and have some fun, and Neill..." she smiled deep into my eyes, "just be your normal self and follow my lead. We've always been close, remember. Now we're closer than ever, and no guilt to ruin it for us."

We left the lift, walked through the hotel and re-entered the hall together, still holding hands. Nothing could have looked more natural. When we got back into the hall the family were spread to the four corners anyway. The bride and groom were doing the rounds; Maud and her husband were going around with them; Margaret was dancing with the photographer, who was a friend of the groom's. I didn't have a clue where Eílis and Kieran were, and Dad was swapping pints and stories with a Kelly uncle who was a plumber in Belfast. They at least seemed to be getting on famously, and it meant we had at least one new relative who we could look forward to seeing again. My mum was sat quietly at our table eating fruit and sipping Champagne.

"You've changed your shoes," Mum said to Úna as we approached. "Wish I'd thought of that. And you found Neill. I reckoned he'd found himself some crusty-old professor to talk to in the lounge or somesuch."

"No, nothing so boring," Úna replied confidently, "he just took me across the road for a drink."

"He did what?" my mum exclaimed.

"Yep, he sure did. I saw him outside staring across the road at the Crown Bar, so we went over there and he bought me a drink at the bar."

"Oh my God," my mum laughed, "what with?"

"Oh, I gave him the money, but he stood there OK, with me right next to him, and he ordered a pint and a vodka and tonic... and the barman didn't even bat an eyelid."

"For goodness sake Úna," Mum laughed again, "you'll get him arrested, but I know what you mean. Look at him, he looks quite the part in that suit, doesn't he."

"He does," Úna took my arm and pulled me in close, "and with me in this dress he was the envy of every man in there; and he carried it off like a natural."

"You two..." my mother shook her head smiling, a warm and sincere smile, "what on earth will you two get up to next I wonder? But he's not exactly that chicken-legged little boy you used to drag around with you, is he?"

"No he is not," Úna said proudly, and she pulled me even closer and gave me a genuine peck on the cheek. "Reckon we've created quite the catch here, don't you Mary? And some lucky girl in a few years' time is going to reap the benefits of all our hard work. Whad'ya think?"

"I think you're absolutely right," Mum beamed with pride, "quite the young man indeed, but don't be wishing any more weddings on us for a while." She rolled her eyes.

"Yeah, exactly," Úna laughed.

"No, let this one get on with all his studies and his sport for a while," Mum continued philosophically, "and give him his space to go off and learn about life for a bit."

"Precisely," Úna pulled me in close again, held me for a second and then slowly released me, "and now he's taller than me and can carry it off in a Belfast pub no less, I reckon I'll be able to help him out with some of that."

"Aye, I know you will," Mum smiled thoughtfully, "and with my blessing, but you just keep him safe is all. If you promise me one thing Úna, promise me that. Guide him safely through the terrors of that place where we live and I'll be in your debt forever."

"Jees you two," I objected, "I'm stood right here you know. I can hear you... and I don't need any minder."

"Well, I sure hope so," said my mum.

"I will, I promise," Úna smiled sincerely, "but you watch big sister, it's him that'll be showing me a thing or two before too long. We've got ourselves quite a special young man here. Very special indeed, and I'm proud to be one of the people in his life he's not afraid to say he loves."

Indeed.

Europa, Euphoria, Utopia

Life after 'the Europa' was a very different beast indeed. Just about every aspect of it seemed easier, more assured and eminently more productive. The early onset of puberty a couple of years earlier had made me far more confident at school in the first place, but Úna's discreet acknowledgment of my newfound virility boosted my self-esteem way beyond that. Apart from the normal earthly pleasure of any time we spent together, her clear endorsement of my looming manhood after that weekend gave me confidence and self-respect beyond measure.

Such occasions were all discreet and sensible – when I would visit her at home for dinner, or when we'd walk the hills or take trips away together – but the nights I stayed over at her house then became precious beyond measure. Eílis and Kieran hardly ever stayed as well by that time, and I resented them bitterly when they did, but both Úna and I were magnanimous if they asked and we were careful to never give the slightest hint that there had nearly been more. That there was more – albeit platonic. It required patience and maturity I never knew I had, and I learned quickly how to deal with crushing disappointment one moment and then how to bounce back with cheerful optimism the next day - but they were invaluable lessons for life and I banked them all.

It was late-summer when I began to fully unwind into the new boundaries of my relationship with Aunt Úna. We never once mentioned what had happened, but neither did we hide it from each other and it was there in the room with us always. Like a trophy. There was never a hint of shame though, indeed there was always a clear sense of pride and affection, and only the two of us ever knew why we laughed so much in each other's company. My mum knew though, I reckon... something... maybe... but then she was so comfortable with it all as I grew even stronger, that she must have also *known* it was platonic; and that's when I knew Úna had been right to stop us when she did, and that both my parents would have known the truth if we hadn't. But as I've said so many times before – clever lady.

Before the next school year began again in the September, for example, Aunt Úna took me once more to Donegal, prompted by the forecast of exceptionally warm weather and by the need to be alone. I think she knew that one year further on, I'd be even further down the road to manhood and even less under her tender wing. We climbed again at dawn, we shared breakfast and hot tea as we had the last time, and we stopped for a far longer and more intimate pub lunch than ever before; but in between, and at the top of our climb, we lay under the warm sun and discussed things I'd never shared with anyone.

I can scarcely begin to describe the sheer joy of the twelve months that followed Éamon's wedding, or of the warm and cosy intimacy of the next seven years until I joined MI5; but suffice it to say that it changed my life profoundly, and we remain as close today - although sadly never lovers - as we were back then in the Derryveagh Mountains and on top of the world.

Rugby was once again the next big thing on my plate, and even that thrill was enhanced by my near-miss with Úna. Despite driving me everywhere still, she'd always treated me like a grown-up; but after Éamon's wedding she treated me virtually as an equal. Especially in front of others. I knew by then that I'd never share her bed, although my willpower wouldn't have been nearly as strong as hers, but for the longest while I was happy and I sought no change. And then when I did start dating seriously, or simply going with older women because that soon became my preference (about Úna's age strangely enough), she remained the most valued source of counsel in my life. She even taught me a few tricks of the trade, but sadly she never showed me as well.

And then the year finished with a bang anyway, although not the one I'd dreamed of for so long. In the December, me and another boy from Abbey Grammar played for Dundalk 1st XV, for their full senior side. The other boy was a back row forward named George Kennedy, who lived in Dundalk but attended my school across the border in Newry. We'd actually known each other through playing Gaelic-Kick and junior football since we were twelve, and so Úna knew him too, but we'd not become mates of any sort until secondary school. And not close mates at that, until after the Dundalk game.

Despite being from the South and growing up in Dundalk, George was passionately pro-British and anti-Republican. I was neither of those things in my early-teens and for me the jury on a united Ireland was still very definitely out. So we weren't natural playmates until there was a reason to be. We were both big for our age and at sixteen George had begun to fill-out at an alarming rate. That made him kind of a rival when it came to sporting prowess at school. Plus, when we'd both started at Abbey Grammar in '93, he'd already been playing rugby for three years, so I resented that even more. But we both played in the school's 1st XV, and we both played for Dundalk in the Under 18s (although by age we should have played for the Under 17s), and after the Blackrock game we were both jointly the two youngest players to ever run-out as starters for the club's 1st XV. We even got a tankard each to mark the game. That had been because of absences through injury for both of us rather than straight forward selection, but no matter; despite that, suddenly we had a reason to become closer than usual mates. And in pretty quick-time we did.

At school level I'd started in Year 7 as a winger, based more on my speed than my size. Father Kennett was a brilliant coach who'd played once in his university days for Ireland Under 20s, and by Year 8 he'd moved me to outside-centre. I respected him, like Father McFall before him, and so that was good enough for me. The next year and as I bulked-up still further he moved me once again to inside-centre; and then in Year 10 he went the whole hog and moved me into the pack at flanker.

That resonated with me. The best Irish try I'd seen in the whole of the 1991 World Cup had been scored by a flanker, by Gordon Hamilton in the quarter-final we'd watched in Dublin against Australia. So that suited me just fine. Dermott McCracken was especially pleased, because that's the position he played for Dundalk; as was Father McFall back at St Colman's when I told him, coz he'd been a flanker too.

I was fast for a flanker and getting bigger by the day, and I loved tackling even more than scoring; so for me the game seemed pretty straightforward. Kennedy on the other hand had always played in the forwards, and he'd gone from hooker, to flanker to Number 8 and that's where he played for the school 1st XV at the time of the Dundalk game. He had a similarly direct style of play, and George with the ball and in full flight was a dangerous thing to have to stop for someone of any age.

It was Dundalk's 120th Anniversary season, and so they played a whole host of clubs and representative sides on both sides of the border. In the world of rugby, unlike in the game of football, neither the border nor the Troubles had ever existed; and so you aspired to play for Ireland, simple as that. There was no North or South for the oval ball, and there was only the one green jersey, and even at the height of the Troubles someone hallowed enough to wear it would have been feted pretty much anywhere.

For the important away game to Blackrock College near Dublin, however, two of Dundalk's regular 1st XV players weren't available - and so they asked George to play at flanker and me at Number 12, my old position of inside-centre. Úna was there to watch of course, and after the game she treated me to a night in the not-long-opened Clontarf Castle Hotel in Dublin. Mum and dad thought that was cute of her and made me promise to say thank you, although my mum actually thought it was so she wouldn't have to see the state of me drunk after the game. If only I could have thanked her as I'd wished.

George and I both had a good game and we held-up well against the fully-grown men playing all around us, but it was an education for sure. George and I even linked-up once for a score, when I was able to slip the ball to him on a charge as he crossed the line from about two yards out. But we were beaten handsomely, and the young star of the opposing side gave me a lesson in ferociousness, tackling and humility I've never forgotten. Along with me and George we were the three youngest players on the pitch, and it was my bad luck that he was my opposing-centre. His name was Tommy Bray.

Teenagers or not we were able to sup pints after the match, and George and I hooked-up with Bray in the clubroom over a plate of Irish stew. He was an amazing character, and as fearsome as he'd looked on the pitch his deep, sparkling brown eyes in the bar drew us into a funny conversation within moments. He was fully bi-lingual – the first such beast I'd ever met, unless you count the priests and their incessant Latin - and he'd spent as much time living in France as in Drogheda, from where his father served as a High Court Judge. His mother was French, from Lyon, and he'd lived there for six years from when he was nine and when his father was working with Interpol.

We never saw Tommy Bray again as teenagers, more's the pity, although George and I became the best of mates after that weekend and we ran out for Dundalk on several other occasions after that as well. We were even singled-out and stood-up by the headmaster in Assembly the following Monday, so we could be applauded by the whole school, Father Kennett's doing, for playing in the full adult side at Dundalk and so for representing Abbey Grammar so well. But I saw Tommy Bray again. We both did in fact. And once we'd met up once more, years later, I saw a lot of him and in the most intriguing of circumstances.

Call it fate, just like JC and Clive Ellis would have.

Where the Hell's Main Street?

My seventeenth birthday saw me behind the wheel of a car for the first time. Well, not for the very first time, but for the first time on a public road, all legal, with 'L' Plates on and getting ready to drive somewhere. I was taking the first of five one-hour lessons my parents had bought me for my birthday, and they'd already booked a driving test for three months later in the hope that I picked it up quickly enough.

It had been my dad's idea for once, and with no help or suggestions from Úna or from anyone else; although he'd then asked her in secret to take me out for extra practice before my test and whenever he couldn't make it because of work. She'd been only too pleased to oblige, and I'd been only too happy for yet more one-on-one time. It was still early days, but life at seventeen was looking pretty damn good.

My driving instructor had to stick to the roads in Northern Ireland of course, because of his insurance cover when driving with a student; but when we put the 'L' Plates on Úna's car, or when I went out with my dad, we could pretty much drive all over Counties Armagh, Down Monaghan and Louth; and so we did. With Úna I went to Armagh itself, to Carrickmacross, Banbridge, Monaghan and right along the coast to Newcastle. And of course she'd let me drive to Dundalk and back for rugby matches or just for training. And then with both of them I also got to drive out to Kilkeel, Hilltown, Rathfriland, Poyntzpass, Markethill and Keady. Notwithstanding the so-called ceasefire, for some reason neither of them would let me drive to Forkhill or Crossmaglen. Not back then, anyway.

We even had to abandon one drive, the one and only time my father let me drive all the way to Armagh and back, because it was the day in March the Real IRA fired five mortar bombs at the RUC station there. The Real IRA were one of two dissident groups then vying for ascendancy, and the other group, the Continuity IRA, had been around but not doing much since the Provos' first ceasefire in '94. But neither so-called organisation was even a shadow of the Provos or their capabilities and expertise – as they were soon to demonstrate.

The 'Conts', as they became known at my school (which is especially funny if said with a broad Newry accent), got a lot busier during 1998, but for South Armagh and thereabouts it was the Real IRA that got a good toe-hold; as witnessed by the next mortar attack they carried out, against the Brit base in Forkhill on the 24th of March. The attacks weren't often in Newry anymore, although they weren't that far away, but it still didn't feel much like peace had broken out just yet.

My first three proper lessons went well, and so my two 'additional-instructors' set about polishing whatever they could whenever they could. Hill-starts in Barcroft Park could make your eyes water, and so both worked hard to get them perfect. True to his word my dad took me out whenever he could manage; and so patient and methodical was he, he turned out to be an even better teacher than Úna. Me and my dad were closer by the time of my driving test than we'd ever been. It felt good and that was an unexpected bonus.

The test too went well, and I passed first time; although my examiner, a woman, gave me a second go at parallel parking after an irate van driver kind of fucked up my first attempt. She was amazing, and not only did she give me another chance, she leapt out of the car in a flash, threw her clipboard on her seat and tore into the driver like a madwoman. She used a few words I'd not even heard in the Derrybeg – I think she made them up – and afterwards the driver got back into his cab and slunk away at about twenty miles-an-hour. My examiner got back into our car, calm as you like, and said, "Sorry about that Mr McCormac, but rudeness on the open road should be punished. Now collect your thoughts and let's try that again. I'm pretty sure you're better and safer than that van driver already."

Life after my driving test felt like a brave new world, although I was some years off affording my own car of course. Úna told me one evening she'd love to buy me one – maybe once I got to university, she added – but that was a whole lot more indicative of something more than either of us felt was wise. We were in danger sometimes, we agreed, of people thinking we were having an affair even though we weren't. I offered to make an honest auntie of her by going through with it, then it wouldn't matter, but she continued to remain sensible and honest for the pair of us... so just more banter and sadly nothing more. She said I was a trier though; she gave me that at least.

May turned into June, and then July into August, and as the weather improved and the days got longer so did many of the journeys we'd take with me behind the wheel. And then in the middle of the month Úna and I had something special planned. We were going to climb Mount Errigal, take a picnic lunch in Poison Glen, and then stay in the spectacular Mount Errigal Hotel. It was to be my longest drive to date, her treat, and it was supposedly to celebrate me having a driving licence; but we of course had other things to remember.

It was the first anniversary of Éamon's wedding, and so the start of our affair that never was. But marking silly little things like that, and celebrating them rather than fretting about them, was part of the private fun we had. Éamon had been married on Saturday the 16th of August 1997, and so he'd planned to celebrate on the 16th, naturally, the Sunday; but *we* had planned a night in a Donegal hotel for the Saturday, the 15th of August, exactly one year later. She was even going to try to get me laid, she promised, and she said it with a twinkle in her eye that suggested she'd already arranged it with a girlfriend of hers. It was all a bit of fun and a great idea... but it fell on a bad day. A sadly dreadful day. And by the end of it, it had proved to be one of *the* most dreadful days of the whole thirty-year Troubles thus far.

It was the day of the Omagh bomb.

We never did get our night in the Mount Errigal Hotel, although we'd climbed, walked and lunched as we had planned; but we'd driven through Omagh to get to Poison Glen only that morning, and when we heard the news at about 4 pm we knew we had to go back there. We didn't know why, there was nothing we could do, but we knew we had to share Omagh's dreadful moment, and its grief, and then we knew we would go straight home.

That morning we'd left Newry a little later than usual for a drive to Donegal, at about 4.30 am, and so we passed through Omagh about an hour later, at a little after half-five. The streets were virtually deserted and although it would be a busy Saturday of shopping later on, not even the traders were up and about yet. Because of that we turned off the main A5 and actually went through the town centre rather than bypass it.

That was normal for Úna, especially when she wasn't driving so she could have a good look around, and she would never bypass one of Ireland's historic market towns if she could drive through it without the blight of traffic. And I didn't mind, I would have driven for ever back then; and besides, any chance to drive her two-year-old Volvo 850 was a treat in itself. It was a 2.5 litre diesel-turbo estate, and the nicest car I would get to drive for the next ten years or more.

We turned north off the roundabout just before the Drumragh River and went two more roundabouts and up past Omagh High School. We both knew it, and I'd played rugby there not six months before. It was a mixed school, and prompted by Úna I remembered it especially well. There was one pretty little sixth-former in particular she thought I should be trying to see again, but until then I'd done nothing about it. Then we turned left onto Campsie Road and drove its full length; straight through the centre of town and past where it turned into Market Street, then High Street, and later John Street. It sounds confusing, but it's just one long straight road through the centre of town. The road the Real IRA would later call Main Street.

When we popped out on the other side of town via John Street and James Street, we arrived back at the main A5, the Great Northern Road, and then continued on our way to Strabane to cross the border. From there we carried on to Letterkenny to drop-off our bags at our hotel on the way through. We did that at about 6.30 am, and because they were serving breakfast we stopped and had a slap-up fry before carrying on. We were having quite the day already, and it hadn't really started yet.

The unscheduled stop for breakfast meant we didn't start climbing Errigal until eight, but we took our time and crammed everything into the day that we'd planned to. Then, as we were driving back towards Letterkenny at about four, we caught the news on the car radio. We would have caught it on any channel... because there was little else for days.

Just fifty minutes earlier the Real IRA had set-off a five hundred-pound car bomb in Lower Market Street, Omagh, and killed twenty-one people. Another eight had died on the way to hospital. One of them had been a mother pregnant with twins, another a Mormon teenager. Some were Catholic, some Protestant, many were visitors to the town, but all were innocent bystanders enjoying the newfound freedom of the Provisional IRA's ceasefire.

The roll of horror went on. Six of them were children, another six were teenagers. Two of them were visitors from Spain, and yet others were tourists on a day trip from across the border. And although we'd missed the bomb by a full nine and a half hours, we'd passed that very spot and driven along the same street just that morning. We knew that under different circumstances we could have been amongst those killed; or simply among the three hundred or so injured, some of them terribly. *Grotesquely* seems to be a better word, and of course, permanently.

Úna had one of the early mobile phones and we eventually managed to call home to tell them we were alright. They knew Omagh was bang on our route and they couldn't have known where we were at the time. Sure enough they'd been worried sick, and Mum had felt sure Una would have stopped-off at the shops there for something. Then we headed to Omagh itself to see what we could do. Nothing, is what we could do... not a thing.

The bomb was as bombs are, and the real tragedy of the attack was not how lethal it was but how farcical. Of how people were effectively herded towards it and not away from it, and of how the Real IRA showed just how dis-organised an organisation they were.

Two days before the bombing the car, a maroon Vauxhall Cavalier so famously captured on film by one of those killed, was stolen from Carrickmacross in County Monaghan. Its Southern Irish plates were removed, new Northern Irish plates were put on, and then it was fitted with its two hundred and thirty-kilogram bomb. On the day of the attack it was driven across the border soon after 2 pm and parked in the busy town centre. The two men who placed it couldn't find a parking space near their intended target, the town's courthouse at the top of the High Street, so they parked it wherever they could, in Lower Market Street, and walked away.

Not long afterwards three telephone warnings were made by the Real IRA, using the same codeword that they'd used during a previous bomb attack in Banbridge two weeks earlier.

The first call was to Ulster Television at 2.32 pm and said, "There's a bomb, courthouse, Omagh, Main Street, five hundred pounds, explosion thirty minutes." Omagh doesn't have a Main

Street... and the courthouse is at the junction of High Street and George's Street. And so the confusion began.

One minute later a second call said, "Martha Pope (RIRA's codeword), bomb, Omagh town, fifteen minutes." Was it fifteen minutes or thirty? And was one message more up to date than the last? The confusion continued.

And then a minute later again a third call was made, to the Samaritans' office in Coleraine, stating that a 'bomb would go off on the main street about two hundred yards from the courthouse'. Coleraine is over fifty miles and a dozen towns and villages from Omagh. The picture didn't get any clearer.

It was a Saturday remember, a busy shopping day, and the town was packed as usual. And Market Street/High Street/John Street was the most packed. Not only had the courthouse been mentioned in two out of the three calls, with the exception of the police station it was the most obvious target for terrorist attack anywhere in Omagh. It made as much sense as anything that day and so people believed it.

All of the calls were passed to the bewildered RUC on the ground, who working off their latest information placed a cordon across the junction of High Street and Market Street by Scarffe's Entry. Then they began to evacuate buildings and to move people down the hill and away from the courthouse... and so *towards* where the bomb had actually been left, some four hundred metres away from the courts.

"Where the fucking hell's Main Street?" one policeman frantically screamed to officers who knew the town better.

"We haven't got one," came the answer, as they herded people ever closer to the bomb.

"But they must mean here," screamed a third, "the High Street... this is it..."

"Aye, I guess," said the first, "then just keep the courthouse to your back and keep people moving... there's conflicting warnings of how long we've got."

Within seconds the deafening *boom* of the colossal blast drowned-out all other sound, and what one survivor described as an 'eeriness, a darkness that had just come over the place' enveloped everything. The same survivor talked also of 'screams' and 'bits of bodies, limbs or something' scattered all around.

That was virtually the scene that Úna and I found when we arrived at five-forty, although the actual explosion had been two and a half hours ago by then. Not so the carnage, shock and bewilderment though; they were still very, very current. There were people milling about everywhere, in amongst the rubble and up and down the street, and clearly there was still much to do; but thank God there was no more screaming or crying or wailing. I would have struggled with that. There was simply a quiet determination to keep working, and a mass of vacant and exhausted expressions. Nearly everyone we saw had blood on them – some were covered – although it had been over an hour since the last casualties had been taken away.

Although we couldn't even get close to the seat of the explosion, smoke was still rising above the roof tops and the view down the length of Market Street looked like war-time pictures of Berlin after it fell to the Russians. So did the faces of people we passed. The best thing we could do to help, we were told by those on the cordon, was to go to the hospital to give blood; and so that's what we did. Then we went home.

And very unusually we went home in silence. All the way, and for nearly two hours; down through Ballygawley and Aughnacloy, through Caledon, Armagh and Markethill, and then on into Newry. As to be expected there were police road blocks and checkpoints all the way, but other than to answer their questions we never said a word. There were no words.

Úna still let me drive, she asked me to in fact, but after the first few road blocks she took over to avoid having to explain all the time who we were and why I was driving. But our discreet celebration of our non-affair was never mentioned. Ever.

Not that year nor any other.

What's in a Secret?

The next significant drive I took with Úna was about a month later, to and from Carrickmacross to play Gaelic Football. It had been over a year since I'd played footy, and I'd been asked to make up the numbers by one of the men I still knew from my Culloville Blues days. He'd more recently seen me playing rugby in Dundalk, and he'd asked me to help out. 'Twas a 'special game' he'd said, a 'local derby', and against boys and fellahs I'd know from before. I'd agreed straight away to show off my new skills, but it turned out to be not that special a game after all.

Now, years later, the drive comes to mind far more readily than the game, because of two conversations we had on the way home. One was funny and will always spring to mind, between just me and Úna; and the other was funny too in places, but it's because it was an intriguing three-way discussion between me, Úna and a soldier who stopped us in a road block. That will always come to mind now too, now I'm in the Security Service and have a vested interest, but for entirely different reasons.

At the time it was just an annoyance at first, being stopped by the Brits I mean, and then it turned into an amusing bit of banter with some poor guy who was simply doing his job. But with hindsight, and with a few hints from Úna at the time, I realise now that it was a special job and it had been quite the chat-up. Plus I've met the guy again since, and now I count him amongst my friends. But first the funny conversation with Úna.

With my eighteenth birthday just three months away and with my increasingly independent outlook on life, I decided to run something past her before dropping it on my mother and so maybe hurting her. I asked Úna when did she think I could stop going to Saturday Mass? We'd just pulled away from the Emmets clubhouse and we were heading away from Carrick' on the 'Blayney Road and the N2 heading north. Despite a monster dead-leg from the game and a gash above one eye, I was driving. The eye hadn't had stitches, although it probably should have, and a butterfly closure and some Steri-Strip held it all together quite nicely. Between me and Dermott, who was still her boyfriend, Úna had become quite expert at those.

After a few hundred metres I turned east onto the winding country lane that led to Donaghmoyne and then on up to the border just below Cullaville. It was a more testing drive for me than just main roads, and it soon became all blackthorn hedges, overhanging trees and big old dry-stone walls. 'Twas fun in other words, as well as good practice. This was the part of Monaghan, Louth and South Armagh that I loved so much, and so I was enjoying my drive in Úna's big Volvo; but even without the Troubles it had always been Bandit Country. There's an old folk song that goes, *'From Carrick' up to Crossmaglen, there's far more rogues than honest men,'* and that wee ditty preceded the Easter Rising, the border and the Troubles by more than a hundred years. But both the day and the drive were proving to be great craic, Úna was still laughing at my injuries, and we were both in good spirits. Now was the time to ask, I judged.

"So listen," I used my nephew-to-Aunt Úna voice (although I no longer called her aunt or auntie at her own request), "There's something I've been wanting to ask you for ages. Y'know, for your advice sort of thing."

"Go on," she shot me a glance as I drove.

"There'll never be a right time to ask my mum, I know, but when do you think I'll be able to stop going to Saturday Mass?"

It was a question we'd discussed at length when I was twelve, and then I'd asked it again at fifteen but we'd not really got around to finishing the conversation; and this time I was bound and determined to get an answer.

"Oh Christ Neill," she laughed, "that one again. Look, you see there's two answers to that question, and then two parts to the real answer, so you'd better keep your mind on the road if you really want my opinion."

"I do."

"OK then, but the first thing is you're asking the wrong person. You know my thoughts on this. Of course you should stop if you're sure, but that's why I haven't been to Mass for the last twenty-something years myself."

"But? I can hear there's a 'but'."

"But... the two parts to the real question are this: there's what you should do for you, and you're old enough now to decide for yourself and be right; and then there's how much it will hurt your mum. That's actually two different questions."

"I know," I said guiltily. "So answer the *me* part first, and then I need to know what you think about Mum. You especially."

"Stop going if you're sure." She glanced at me and I was nodding as I drove. "But then let's talk about how and when you break it to your mother. You know your dad will be fine, and half the time he only goes to please your mum anyway. Like I did 'til I was your age."

"So what about Mum then?"

"Well, I'll tell you what I think, and then it's got to be your own decision – hurt and all – but the best way I can explain it is to tell you a funny story about a friend of mine who was going through the same thing when he was about your age."

"A friend?"

"Yeah, but it was the same question."

"Go on," I said enthusiastically. All of Úna's stories were interesting and most were entertaining, so I had no reason to believe that this would be any different.

"Well a boy called Willie Carroll was always a really good friend of mine, from the age of about ten or so. He lived not far from us and we were at the same primary school, but we just got on well. Always."

"What, like a boyfriend you mean?"

"No, quite the opposite, just like a best mate or a brother. In fact, he was gay, and that's part of the story, but this was back when that wasn't an easy thing to be; and around here back then... y'know, the late-60s, that could even be a dangerous thing to be."

"Right."

"So Willie and I were talking one day when we were about fourteen, and I think he was starting to worry that I'd make a pass at him or something. We both knew we were very close, and we were just at that fondling age..."

"Yeah, I get it," I blushed.

"So he looks all shy and embarrassed and he says he's got something to tell me, and I beat him to it and said, 'You're gay, right?' 'How do you know that?' he exclaims, and we chat and I tell him I've sort of always known. And so then we're closer than ever and he's happy, coz he's got it off his chest... and to me especially, coz he'd felt pressured as a boy..."

"Got it, but I don't get the connection to Mass an' all, unless there's something about Confession coming-up?"

"No. Well, here it is and you'll see, and Confession's got nothing to do with it. Back then, when we were fourteen, I'd asked him if he'd told his mother. I knew her pretty well I thought; I was always 'round there supping tea and eating her cakes and things, and I really liked and respected her. I reckoned she was a shrewd judge of everything in life, and I sort of looked up to her as wise counsel and a second mum."

"Sort of like you are to me?" I asked without thinking. She looked across at me warmly and smiled, then put her hand on my knee as I drove.

"Yes, just like us," she beamed, and then carried on with her tale. "Well we talked about it for hours and in a nutshell he said he could *never* tell his mum, he thought it would destroy her. I told him I didn't agree, and I reckoned she was a lot more broad-minded and worldly wise than he believed, but he couldn't see it."

"So what happened?"

"Nothing then, and not for a couple of years, but then when we were sixteen or seventeen, just a wee bit younger than you are now, we had another conversation. And he was cracking up so he couldn't speak, he thought it was so funny."

"What was?"

"Well, he'd plucked up the courage and sat his mum down to tell her, but he thought he'd soften the blow by telling her he wanted to stop going to Mass too."

"Jesus. Soften the blow or double it?"

"Aye," Úna laughed, "well that's just it. She sat and heard him out without a word, he says, and then she just sat and stared at the crucifix on the wall for the longest while. And then she spoke... slowly and very calmly... and she said something like, 'Well Willie, that's a lot to take in all at once, but if you're gay then you're gay and God must have a reason. But you know he'll always love you, and you know that I will too, just as much as now and forevermore. But now you listen to me for a minute... oh dear, oh dear... you stopping going to Mass now... well that's serious!

That's a whole different matter, and that's quite a serious thing you're suggestin'."

Úna was laughing as she finished the story and I joined her, genuinely, but then I gradually fell silent as I drove on and thought about the precise meaning for me.

"So, what are you saying?" I said after a while. "Are you saying I shouldn't tell her?"

"No, not at all," she was still chuckling about Willie, "but just know she's going to think it's 'quite a serious thing you're suggesting', same as Willie's mum maybe."

"Right, but only to her though. Not to me."

"Correct, not to me either, but it is to your mum, and that's what you wanted me to comment on."

"Oh God, I just don't think I can keep doing this, is all. I've never really believed, and well..."

"Yep, I get it, and that's me and the decision I made all those years ago. And for you Neill, you're right."

"How did Mum take it when you stopped going? I presume you used to go together?"

"Yes, always, and the other kids too; but we were the two oldest, so it was only really between me and her."

"And so how'd she take it?"

"Surprisingly well."

"Really?"

She looked across at me as I slowed coming down a wee hill and stopped to negotiate the crossroads at Corcullionglish. She studied me hard for a moment, and then carried on speaking.

"But I was so independent by then," she said, "I think she'd been expecting it. A bit like you've become this past year or so."

My turn to stare at her.

"So do you think she's expecting it from me too? You think she'd take it the same way with me?"

She didn't answer immediately, so I pulled away from the crossroads but she kept looking at me.

"Yes I do," she smiled tenderly, "aye, I reckon. And yes, I think she's probably been expecting it for some time."

Then she looked ahead at the road and smiled a contented sort of smile of a proud auntie.

"But she's never said so, has she?" I asked. "To you I mean, in private?"

"No, not about that she hasn't." She glanced across at me as though there were other secrets they'd discussed, but I didn't pursue it. "But it's hard for a mum, remember, to watch a son reach that age when he's *really* his own person – a son especially - and to know he's going to be leaving home soon..."

"Aye, I guess."

We drove-on in silence for a while and Úna knew I'd decided, but I did us both the favour of not checking with her once again. She'd given her advice, and that was all I'd asked - and I'd made my decision, and that was all she expected. To discuss it further wouldn't have been doing right by either of us. And so we didn't. Instead I drove the half a mile or so to the border in cheerful conversation about something else... and to our second funny story.

Handle With Flair

I drove on through Corcullionglish and started the long and gentle descent into the Fane valley. Then as we snaked our way down, around and under the old railway arch I got the tingle that I always felt on that stretch of road; that shifty, ghostly, leafy lane that dissected the old railway cutting and where scores of IRA had trained over the previous quarter of a century. More than one huge gun battle with the British Army had been spawned there, when a training camp of twenty to thirty Provos had crept up onto the high ground overlooking the border, and then tested their guns and their newfound skills on a Brit patrol in Cullaville. Not so that day, thank God, and for one brief moment I reflected that the latest Provie ceasefire and the Good Friday Agreement might truly amount to something. And as for the Dissidents? Well who the hell really knew?

CIRA, the Continuity IRA, had claimed an attack against the RUC on Moy Road on the 4th of September, but the police couldn't even confirm it had taken place. Methinks the claim didst proceed the attack, and then for whatever reason the deed itself had never even happened. That was about par for the course for CIRA at that stage. And RIRA, the Real IRA, well they'd suspended all military operations three days after the debacle in Omagh while they got their act together. Shit, that was going to take them a while. Then sure enough, three weeks later and on the 7th of September, they converted that to an actual ceasefire; but no-one believed it would last, and few even believed it was real. Time, as they said, would tell – but while we were waiting to find out, South Armagh continued to be where they operated from.

I drove on another hundred metres and knew that the River Fane now wound its way parallel to the road but behind the trees and the bushes away to my right. The road led me down to the ruins of Kingham's Mill and the sometime Customs Post just inside the Republic of Ireland, and to the bridge that was the border crossing itself. The old mill had long since been overtaken by progress, by weeds and by time; and whenever the Customs had tried setting up there, they'd invariably been overtaken by the Provos. Eventually they'd given up. Now only leprechauns and the odd fisherman took shelter there.

Then I got a wee shock. As we swept over the old stone bridge and so back into the North, I caught my breath as we rounded a blind bend and ran smack into a Brit roadblock by Annaghgad Road. The infamous Annaghgad Road, where a twelve-man IRA patrol with rifles and an M-60 machine gun had tried to bring-down a British Army spotter plane that flew low over the top of them to get photos. I could only see four of the Brits, but experience told me there were at least another eight hidden in the bushes somewhere. Certainly that close to the border there would have been. And a policeman or two I was sure.

My native dread of being arrested or harassed for some reason – often for no reason, history would argue – subsided quickly though; partly because I was with Úna, but mostly because I was in her car – and so I knew it would be legal, roadworthy, fully-insured, and not actually my problem. The soldier in the middle of the road waved me courteously to the side of the lane, where there was another car already pulled-in in front of me. As I stopped the other car was moved on.

The soldier who pulled-me-over looked older than they usually did, and he smiled a thumbs-up through my windscreen at where I'd parked; so maybe this one was going to be OK, I hoped. I glanced across at Úna, who looked calm enough for both of us, so then I powered-down my window and got ready to hand over my embarrassingly virginal driver's licence. He stepped towards me and took it with a smile.

"Thank you, young fellah. Wow, you look like you've been in the wars?"

I'd forgotten all about my gashed eye and Una's handy-work with Steri-Strips and plasters.

"Och, no," I put a hand to the big scab on my eyebrow, "I've just been playing football."

"Gaelic I presume?" and he pointed a thumb back over his shoulder towards Culloville Park not a hundred metres behind the trees. "So was there a game today? I'd have tried to watch a bit of it if I'd known."

"No, not here there wasn't," I mumbled uncertainly, "we were in Carrick'. We're just on our way home."

He stooped down lower, glanced in the car at Úna and acknowledged her with a nod.

"Afternoon ma'am," he said. Úna just nodded and smiled back in silence.

"Tough game by the looks of it?" he smiled at me.

"Aye, sort of," I said sheepishly.

"Did you win?"

"Aye, we did."

"Really," he chuckled and looked at my eye again, "so what does the other guy look like I wonder? How's the losers?"

Both Úna and I laughed, and once the soldier saw we weren't going to be anti-Brit he joined in as well.

"Ah, well, it wasn't another guy as such," I said lamely, "it was just a stray knee sort'a thing."

"Oh," he shrugged, "pumping knees'll get you every time if you don't see them coming." I just nodded my agreement.

"So going home you say?" he looked at my driving licence, "to this address here?"

"Aye."

"In the Derrybeg?"

"Aye."

"Main Avenue?"

"Aye, 'tis."

"Wow, Derrybeg, Carrickmacross, Crossmaglen," he rolled his eyes, "you sure get to visit all the best places."

He was teasing, and it had been funny the way he'd said it. I laughed an embarrassed sort of laugh, but before I could say anything Úna joshed him back from the far side of the car.

"Who said anything about Crossmaglen?" she grinned. "We might not be going to Cross', or do you think that's where we've come from?"

He didn't answer instantly, so she joshed him some more.

"So do you think we're a pair of bandits maybe?"

"No ma'am," he smiled and leaned-in again, "I don't, and you might not be going to Cross', but that's the quickest way back to Newry, isn't it?"

"Maybe," she smiled at him.

"And besides," he teased her back, "how do you know I don't already know you were in Cross' earlier today? Before you went to Carrick'?"

Úna matched his cheeky expression.

"And you can tell that, can you?" she said sassily, "with all your radios and your computers an' all?"

"Yes, I could," he laughed, "if I wanted to I could. But I was bluffing. No need now," he grinned, "you just told me."

All three of us laughed again.

"So young fellah," the soldier studied my licence again and directed his next question to me, "please tell me this isn't *your* car, because if it is I'm definitely in the wrong business."

More chuckles from me and Úna.

In September 1998 I was a burly seventeen-year-old, but I reckon I looked my age and not a day more. Úna, however, was a still pretty forty-one and could have passed easily for thirty-four. That would have still made her twice my age, and I could see the cogs turning behind his deep brown eyes as he waited for my explanation. 'If only' I was her lover, I wished... but I sure as hell didn't say it.

"No it's mine," Úna said before he even asked a follow-up question, and she leant across and passed him her driving licence as well. It was a lot more tattered than mine. "I'm his auntie."

"Lucky Neill," he smiled at both of us in turn, and then he studied her licence without saying anything. I think he was listening to something coming over his radio earpiece at the same time. He took it all in though, her details, and after a while he made just one comment as he passed hers back with a 'Thank you'.

"Windsor Hill," he said, "nice."

But he held on to my licence and he clearly wanted us to stay and chat some more.

"So not long passed your test then, Neill, from the look of your licence," the soldier said, "but I see you've been old enough to drive since January...?"

It was obviously a question, so I glanced across at Úna and when she nodded all was OK I answered him.

"Aye, I passed first time," I said proudly, "but I didn't take my test 'til after Easter. There was a big-old waiting list."

"First time, hey, good job," he smiled, "took me two goes...
but in my defence that's partly because I never had a lesson until
after my test."

"After?" I queried, not believing him.

"Yeah, after. How's that for over confident?"

"How so?" I asked.

"Well, I'd done a lot of driving on private roads by the time
I was seventeen, and a fair bit more than I should have done on
public roads too," he grinned. "And so I thought I could drive."

"But you couldn't," I offered.

"Oh no, I could drive alright. I knew how to drive well
enough, but I obviously didn't have a clue how to pass the test. Big
difference," he laughed.

"So did you have lessons then?" I asked.

"A lesson. Yes I did, just one. Yup, and then I sailed through
the next test."

"Jees, just one?" I was genuinely impressed, I thought I
was a quick learner, but I'd needed every one of my five lessons;
and it must have showed, because then he became even friendlier.

"But you wouldn't be doing that around here though," the
soldier shrugged, "am I right? Too many police around, and with
a name like McCormac and living in the Derrybeg, you wouldn't
get too many second chances I don't suppose."

"No, I guess," I said timidly.

"That's pretty perceptive," Úna remarked dryly from deep
inside the car. "And very honest."

He just smiled at her, but he didn't comment.

"So do you not get on with your police friends then?" she
followed-up inquisitively.

The soldier got a little lower in my window to be able to
answer her. As he did so he lowered his rifle from its sort of 'ready'
position - held across his front with his right hand on the pistol
grip - to a more relaxed posture with it hanging down by his side.

He never lifted it up again after that, until he let us go twenty minutes later.

"Quite the opposite, ma'am, I do," he said to Úna with a smile, "most of them anyway, but that's just life – I don't get along with all of my own guys either. No, it's just they're looking for different things to us, aren't they."

"Like what?" said Úna.

"Well, y'know better than I do how it goes: bald tires; no insurance; smuggled pigs; bandits..."

Úna laughed.

"...or not even bandits," he continued, "just maybe people they've met before and fallen out with, and... well, then it's just human nature I suppose."

"Aye, 'tis that," she nodded, "and occasionally it's a bit of *in*human nature as well."

"Yeah, I'm sure, and for which I apologise..."

"Hey, it's not your fault, and at least you seem to know it..."

"No, but on behalf of the system I mean..."

"You mean there is one?" she teased.

"Some days," he chuckled, "when we're in charge and not them... but see, if this ceasefire is the real thing... who knows? Maybe you'll get to drive around here without all of this one day? Without us and our blackened faces."

"Hey," Úna shrugged, "we've got nothing against you boys when you behave, it's just you shouldn't have to be here in the first place, right? And with a bit of luck, like you say, maybe soon you won't have to be."

"Hear hear," said the Brit, "so let's hope this time it all holds and they mean it."

Úna pursed her lips into a hopeful-looking shrug and nodded. Then it morphed into a smile.

"So what do *you* think?" she asked the soldier.

"What, about the ceasefire?"

"Aye."

"Oh I think they mean it. This time. But it's far easier said than done, so there's a lot of moving parts to tie down before we can all pack up and go home I reckon."

"Aye," Úna nodded her agreement.

"And then of course there's the Dissidents," he continued, "we'll have to wait and see where all that leads to as well. But hey, they're not the Provos, that's for sure; and so hopefully they'll burn themselves out and give it all up at some stage."

"Hope so," she answered, "but a fair few of 'em are former Provos, don't you think?"

"I don't know," he said, "what do you think?"

Úna just smiled, but she didn't answer. For a moment I glanced backwards and forwards between them both, but after a while he smiled too and then continued.

"No, of course, I shouldn't have asked you that. You're from Newry and you wouldn't know," he grinned, "but I reckon you're right about a few of them from around here sure enough."

"Aye, well, fuckwits all of 'em," she said boldly, "and hopefully the more sensible ones will prevail."

"Let's hope," the soldier said, and he seemed to study Úna closely for a moment before speaking again.

"I've got another question for you though, Miss Brennan. Sorry, was that correct? Is that your name?" It had been on her driving licence.

"Yes, but you can call me Úna. Miss Brennan makes me sound like a librarian or something."

"Thank you, Úna it is, and for the record I've known some very attractive librarians..." he smiled – she smiled back – "but it's actually a question for either of you I suppose."

"Go on," she said.

"The wee stone bridge back there, that crosses the border. Does it have a name?"

"I don't know," Úna replied truthfully. "Maybe, but you'd have to ask a local."

"Yeah, of course," he chuckled, "but they're not too free with their answers around here."

"No, I suppose not," Úna laughed.

"It's Art Hamill Bridge," I piped-up out of nowhere.

"Is it? So it's not Kingham's Bridge then?" the Brit asked. "After the old mill on the Monaghan side?"

"No, Art Hamill Bridge," I confirmed.

They both looked at me together.

"How on earth do you know that?" Úna chuckled.

"From some of the guys in the Blues," I said. "They always call it that whenever they mention it."

"Y'know, I think he's right," said the Brit, "it rings a bell, so I must have heard it somewhere before."

"So who's Art Hamill then?" Úna asked.

"Now that I don't know," I said, "but I'm pretty sure you mean who *was* he, not who *is* he?"

"Smart-arse," Úna laughed.

If the Brit knew better he wasn't about to say, but he was too busy smiling at us two.

"Huh," Úna shrugged, "Well done you."

"Well done why?"

"For speaking up," she smiled.

"So do you play for Culloville?" the Brit asked.

"Used to, when I was eight or nine."

"Oh wow, so what about now?" he asked. "Who were you playing for today?"

"For them again," I said, "but just as a one-off. I played for Camlough after that for a year or two because it was closer to home; but I don't really play footy at all anymore, I play rugby now so I've no time for both."

"Really? That's my game. Or at least it used to be," he said enthusiastically, "so who do you play for around here? A school side I suppose?"

"Yes, Abbey Grammar..."

"Cool. That's the Christian Brothers' grammar, isn't it?"

"Yes."

"Up by Courtenay Hill there? In Newry."

"Yeah, that's it."

"Nice school," said the Brit. "Good rugby school I hear."

"But he plays for Dundalk too," said Úna.

"Good man." He studied my driving licence again. "What, in the Under 18s?"

"No," she added proudly, "usually for the Under 20s, and a fair few games for the adult sides whenever they ask him."

"God, you're kidding... mind, he looks big enough."

"He's run out for the First XV before now," she beamed, "a couple of times in fact. And then a few times for the Seconds."

"Hey, well done again. That's huge. What position?"

"Flanker, but I played centre for the Firsts."

"Right. I can see it."

"Where did you play?" I asked him. I couldn't really see his physique under his uniform and his flak jacket.

"Back three, but wing-three-quarter mostly. Or at outside centre once in a while."

"Cool," I said, "I started at wing, then played in the centre for a year, outside and inside, but then my coach moved me all the way into the pack in the end."

"Why? Were you getting slower," he laughed, "or do you just like tackling?"

"Love tackling," I beamed.

"Hence the gashed eye," Úna joked, "loves tackling even when it's not really a part of the game, like in football."

We all laughed.

"So what do you call it?" Úna asked in the brief silence that followed. "You guys must have a name for it?"

"What? The bridge?" said the Brit.

"Yeah. If you didn't know its name..." she clearly thought that really he did, "what do you guys call it?"

181

"Huh," he chuckled, "H32(A)."

"Hotel what?" she looked bemused.

"Hotel Thirty-Two Alpha," he grinned broadly. "Meaning police division 'H', border crossing point thirty-two, and the 'A' in brackets stands for Approved."

"Right," she said, still smiling but a little bemused, "should you be telling me all that?"

"Why not?" he laughed.

"Well isn't it a secret or something?"

"Hardly, what are you going to do? Sell the names of the border crossings to the Russians?"

"No," she laughed, a real belly laugh, "so is that how you name them all, right along the border? Or rather number them, I suppose?"

"Yeah, pretty much. Like, er, let me think... are you familiar with the Concession Road?" he pointed a thumb back over his shoulder to Cullaville just up the hill.

"The main Dundalk to 'Blayney road you mean?"

"Yes."

"Yeah, go on."

"Well, the Dundalk end of that is border crossing point Hotel Twenty-Nine (Charlie), and this time the 'C' in brackets stands for Concession..."

"Coz it's the Concession Road?" she asked.

"Exactly, and the other end, the Castleblayney end, is Hotel Thirty-Three Charlie, as in H33(C)."

"Got it," she grinned, "I think. So then there's two others somewhere, H30 and H31, between the Dundalk end of the Concession Road and Art What's-his-name's Bridge here at Hotel Thirty-Two Alpha?"

"You have got it. Your auntie's quick, Neill. Very."

Úna grinned broadly, but she hadn't finished with him yet.

"But so what about all the *un*approved crossings? There must be loads of them," she asked astutely. Like those two maybe."

"Yeah, there are, but so they're just plain-old numbers, and nothing in brackets…"

"So not 'Approved' then?"

"Exactly, and technically no-one should be using them to cross the border at all."

"Got it."

"But then out of the kindness of our cold Brit hearts," he grinned, "we just leave those wide open so you can all use them whenever you like."

"And people do I suppose?" Úna asked playfully.

"Oh they do that," the soldier smiled, "day in and day out. Like Hotel Twenty-Five, for example."

"Where's that?" she took the bait.

"Slab Murphy's farm."

"Oh," she paused sheepishly, "I guess they come and go across that one pretty much as they like then?"

"Yeah, pretty much," he grinned broadly, "usually twelve at a time." Úna laughed hard. "But I don't suppose you know too many people around here though, do you?"

"No, not so many," Úna said, "and definitely not him. Just a few people through Neill and his sport, and one or two over the years through business."

"Which is what, if you don't mind me asking?"

"Insurance."

"Claims?"

"Sometimes, but brokerage, advice on policies, claims examiner for a while, and so on, and a lot of other things too; but yeah, it's been pretty profitable during the Troubles if that's what you were wondering."

"Yeah, I'm sure it has around here," he smiled, "hence this nice car I suppose?"

"Yep, it's kept me in makeup, put it that way."

At that point another soldier walked across and passed our Brit a page torn out of a notebook.

"Excuse me," he said as he studied it, then he nodded to the other young soldier and turned back to Úna and me. Before he could speak again Úna had beaten him to it.

"So aren't you going to search us?" she asked playfully. Then she realised what she'd said and giggled.

"With pleasure," he laughed, "but I wasn't going to."

"I don't mean me personally," she laughed back, "I know you're not allowed to search women." He smiled. "I meant search my car. Our car."

"No," he grinned, "I'm not."

"Really?"

"Really."

"Why?" she persisted.

"Ceasefire. The war's over, remember."

Úna just laughed and looked up the road at the other soldiers. The RUC man had come on the scene by then, but the others were clearly keeping him away from our car and keeping him talking fifty metres away.

"So what was that your colleague passed you?" Úna asked boldly. "It was obviously about us."

"Why do you say that?" the soldier grinned.

"Oh, just his body language, and the way he looked at us before he gave it to you."

"Huh, smart lady. You really *are* quick."

They both grinned broadly at each other.

"So was it?" she asked again.

"Yes," the Brit nodded, "he was pointing out that you were in Omagh on the day of the bomb."

We were both shocked by his honesty, and a little impressed I think. His attitude hadn't changed at all; he was still just chatting, but he'd just come straight out with it and told us what it said. Like friends over coffee.

"Or at least your car was," he added, "that might not be the same thing of course. Twice in fact," he looked at the note again, "a couple of sightings in the morning, and then loads after the bomb and all the way back to Newry that night."

Úna was nodding.

"Yes, we were both there," she said with equal honesty, "and that was a dreadful, dreadful day."

"What just you two?" he asked, a little surprised.

"Yes, we'd driven to the Derryveagh Mountains for the day, and so that's on the way. We do it quite often."

"Right, got it. So what did you do? Cross the border at Strabane and up through Letterkenny?" he asked.

"Yes."

He paused for a moment and studied Úna's eyes, as though deciding at a fork in the road.

"So you two seem pretty inseparable?" he smiled.

"We are pretty much," Úna said, "Neill's my sister's boy, and well... we've always been close."

"Like I said," the Brit smiled back, "lucky Neill." He clearly wanted to ask more, but he didn't.

"And then what," he continued, "you just drove back into town that day and found it all blown to hell?"

"No," she said, "we heard it on the car radio and so just kept driving 'til we got there. It was awful."

"Yeah, it was indeed."

"Were you there?" Úna asked him.

"No, I was on patrol around here as usual, so we heard about it on our radios too... but I can imagine."

"I suppose you've seen things like it before though?"

"Yes. Yes unfortunately I have."

"We tried to help," I said, "but we couldn't get near and there were hundreds helping already."

"Did either of you know anyone?" the Brit asked.

"No," Úna said shamefully, as though everyone deserved to have known at least one person there.

"Well..." said the Brit, "small mercies."

"But we gave blood," I piped-up.

"You did?"

"Aye, when we couldn't help in the rubble an' all, a young policewoman suggested we should go to the hospital and give blood, so we did. Both of us."

"Huh, well," the Brit smiled, "I've got to say, having got to know you both a little bit, I'm not surprised. Not surprised at all. Well done to both of you."

"Aye, well, just doing our bit," said Úna.

"But I guess you know you've probably saved a life or two," he added, "and as I'm sure you also know, there were people from all-over got caught up in that thing, not just locals."

I took it from that that he meant Protestants as well as Catholics, but none of us commented further. The Brit nodded thoughtfully and then handed back my driver's licence. For an instant I held my breath, as the shot that killed Stephen Restorick in exactly the same situation ricocheted once more around my mind. Although one whole sniper team had been caught by the SAS the year before, and although the Provos' ceasefire appeared to be the real thing, I guessed those monster Barrett rifles were still out there somewhere and we were in the middle of what was still Real IRA country.

"Well it's been good talking to you both," the Brit said, and it snapped my thoughts back to the here and now. "But best I get you on your way."

"Oh, we're in no hurry," Úna replied, "you just do what you've got to do and then we'll be off, but there's no great rush on our account." I think actually she was enjoying herself.

"Good, but I'm done ma'am, and I've kept you here long enough. Don't want to get any tongues wagging."

"Aye, I suppose you're right." She instinctively looked over her shoulder and then scanned the road ahead. "So you're happy that we're not bandits then?" she teased him.

"Yeah, I'm pretty sure of that much," he smiled, "and I've got to say, quite the opposite I would have said. In fact, it's been a pleasure to meet you both, seriously. And just talking to you."

"Likewise," Úna smiled.

"Yours must be quite the family, and if there's more like you two knocking around South Armagh then this just might end for the best after all."

"Appreciated," Úna smiled and nodded.

"Is that it then?" I asked. "Can we go?"

"Yes, you can indeed," the Brit smiled, "and who knows... I might see you both out and about somewhere else another time."

"Aye, maybe," said Úna.

"Stay safe," he said, and he pointed to my swollen eye, "and you be careful driving home young Neill. No more collisions today, special passenger on board, remember."

We all laughed.

Then he gave a little wave, backed slowly away from my door, and took full control of his rifle once more.

As we pulled away and headed up the lane to Cullaville crossroads, I watched him in my mirrors - and then his colleagues - until I couldn't see them anymore. No snipers today, I thought, and I stopped to negotiate the busy junction. Then I turned to Úna to see what she'd made of it all.

And as usual, she'd made far more of it than I had.

Great Oaks...

"So what was the craic with him then?" Úna said as I pulled away. "What did you make of that?"

"Och, he seemed like a nice enough fellah," I said.

"Aye, he did, and he probably is," she smiled, "but you be careful of being too friendly with the likes of him."

"Why, didn't you believe him?"

"No, it's not that. I think he was straight enough with us all right, it's just you'd always be having to watch where a bit of craic like that was leading."

"What do you mean?"

"Well... how old do you think he was?"

"What?"

"He was no young soldier, was he? So go on, how old do you think he was?"

"Oh I don't know, forty-something maybe."

"Right. And how many Brits do you see on the road who are nearer fifty than twenty?"

"Oh, I've seen quite a few…"

"Yeah, but they're all Irish. Think about it. They're all in the Ulster Defence Regiment or policemen, but how many British soldiers do you see stopping cars like that?"

"Yeah, I suppose, but what are you getting at?"

"Oh, I don't know, nothing really." But she was. "He's got a job to do and I wish him no harm, but it's not something I'd want to see you getting sucked into."

"What, joining the army you mean?"

"No, joining his band of brothers instead."

"I'm not with you…"

"Well you just describe him to me. Go on. What did you notice about him?"

"Nothing in particular," I said truthfully.

"No, I mean tell me all about him."

"Well, like I said, he seemed like a nice enough fellah; and maybe that was *because* he was older," I suggested, "and not in spite of it."

"No, I mean describe him physically. Exactly what did you see when he was chatting to you?"

"Um, well… his blackened face obviously, and his radio an' all, but he looked just the same as the others except his age. I'm not sure what you're getting at?"

"What about his hair?"

"What about it?"

"Didn't you reckon that was a bit long for a soldier?"

"Aye, I suppose…"

"And had he shaved do you reckon?"

"No, I guess not, there was a bit of a stubble thing going on there I guess; but hey, I just thought he'd been out patrolling for a day or two."

"Aye, maybe," she smiled, "but I reckon Brits that age are usually holding briefings, or maybe holding a pen somewhere, but not out patrolling and holding a rifle."

"So what are you saying? He's too old to be SAS surely? Is that what you're saying?"

"No, but there's others like them don't forget, and I reckon it's his job to have you think he's a nice fellah."

"Oh OK, now I know what you're getting at," I nodded, "but I mean he seemed like a *really* nice fellah. You know, for real I mean. Not just coz he was doing a chat-up on us."

"Well so long as you know that's what it was."

"But I thought you and mum kind of supported those guys?" I looked at her as I drove. "Y'know, wished more people would help them out an' all. You've always felt sorry for them whenever we've discussed them in the past."

"I do... still do," she cocked her head, "and I'm not so naïve as to think it's all going to go away even if the Provos do. And what's more, I wish I had the courage of my convictions to try to help him. But that door needs to stay firmly closed to you Neill."

"Why? Why to me?"

"It's different for you. You'll be out of here to uni' in a year or two, and good riddance to bad places, so don't be talking to him again if you see him before you go. Or anyone like him."

"But that was harmless enough, surely? And it was sort of interesting, don't you think?"

"Yeah, and talking to him once like that is, but for God's sake don't be seen talking to him twice."

"I suppose. Aye, I understand. But if that's what he is, it's not like some of the stunts the Special Branch pulled on Éamon though, is it? Y'know, backing him in a corner sort of thing."

"No, he's not that at least."

"And it's not like he kept pumping us for information or suchlike. He didn't even ask us anything."

"Really?" she chuckled, "well I'm glad you think so."

"But he didn't, did he?"

"No, he didn't ask us much, I'll give you that, but he learnt plenty, trust me. Just from chatting with us. It'll be quite the report he writes on us two, you can be sure of that."

We drove in silence for a minute or two, then as we entered Crossmaglen, snaked around top end of The Square and headed out onto the Newry Road, she cracked a bit of humour to lighten the atmosphere.

"Just so long as he writes I looked young for my age, then he'll be good with me."

"Well he liked flirting with you, that much was obvious."

"Really? I thought it was me leading him on..."

"Aye, you were, so he can't have been that dangerous."

We both laughed, but she hadn't finished. I knew that. In the heavy silence that followed she put her hand on my knee and gave it a squeeze.

"Look, if you want to make a difference," she said, "then join something, join the police or suchlike, and get these fuckers that way... but up in Belfast or somewhere, and not around here."

"The police?" I chuckled, "what, like the guys we were just on about chasing Éamon? Hardly."

Úna didn't answer at first, she merely glanced across at me and conceded the point, but then as we drove on she weighed her response and then delivered it.

"But they're not all like that. Some of 'em are smart, really smart and doing an important job. Look, go to uni' first Neill, then do it; or even take it to the next level, do it in London and at the national level. Join the Met Police and work in the Anti-Terrorist Branch or something, but don't ever be telling anyone around here if you do. Not even your mum and dad. Just go and do it."

"What about you?"

"Not even me," she glanced at me, "although I know what's in your heart and so I reckon I'd know if you did. But you know

191

what? If that's what you decide to do, you know how proud I'd be of you. So just go off and do it if that's how you feel."

That brief discussion had a far more profound effect on my future than Úna probably ever realised. Certainly far more than I ever told her. That and the brief chat-up with the Brit near the border. That Brit, by the way, in case you haven't realised it yet, was forty-three years-old at the time and he was known to all the other blackened faces in the road that day as 'JC'. He was the John Conway I told you about a dozen or so stories ago. And when we met twelve years later in London, he'd done his homework and he knew it was me he'd stopped before we even shook hands.

We both recognised each other, but unlike him I wasn't sure where from. Not straight away. No blackened face that time, you see. But he'd suspected when he'd first ever heard my name and my background from an MI5 colleague, that I might be the same Neill McCormac from the Derrybeg that he'd pulled-in that day above Art Hamill Bridge. Aye, and his wily auntie. And as soon as he saw me he knew he was right.

We cleared that up in the first two minutes, and as soon as I got over the shock we re-lived that meeting before we did anything else. He couldn't remember Úna's name off the top of his head, but once I reminded him we spent the next fifteen minutes talking about just her. He clearly had a bit of a soft spot for her and how she handled herself that day, and so we had that much in common from the outset. As we talked over the next two days I learned we had so much more as well.

Inevitably, because by then I was an agent handler too, I asked did he think that we'd had any source potential when he'd stopped us that day. His response surprised me, but it also cleared up a lot of things that had crossed my desk in recent years.

"In a place like Cross' anyone who'll even speak to you has some sort of potential, but that's just the first tick in the box; and then there's all the other ticks you already know about. Some of those can take ages to get, and some, as you well know, you may never achieve at all. Never say never, and leave the door ajar by all means, but then move on."

"So what about us? Did you not like the look of us at all?"

"Well, your Aunt Úna might have been useful in earlier times, depending on who or what in Newry she knew and how far she was prepared to go out on a limb, but you were too young in my mind and so it was just a bit of good craic with you two. And then, once I'd had a closer look at you both after that patrol, well that's when I knew we should leave well alone."

"Really, but I was nearly eighteen," I must have sounded a little hurt, "and weren't you tempted to see if I could get closer to the Dissidents or something?"

"Not for an instant. Maybe ten years before that, in 1988 say, or in 1978 for sure, I'd have bitten your arm off probably, but not by then. And us especially, the Army, I had strong thoughts on all that by then."

"Go on," I said, fascinated.

"Well I reckoned we'd be out of there within ten years, even back then. Of course, we all *hoped* the ceasefire would hold rather than believed it, but even if it hadn't, we knew the Provos couldn't balance the books anymore; we knew the leadership were hell bent on peace and meant it; and we knew the whole thing was withering on the vine, even before 9/11 pissed-off all the American fundraisers and geed it all up a bit."

"But what about the Dissidents?"

"Well it was early days for them right enough, but they clearly weren't going to be the A-Team that PIRA had been. And they couldn't be: the whole backdrop to society had changed and they didn't have those thirty years to grow and a following to take them forward. There were never dustbin lids banging all over Belfast for the Dissidents, right?"

"Right."

"CIRA hadn't amounted to much in their first four years; and although RIRA were looking like they'd be more of a handful, we just had to trust that they'd become the mavericks they did over time and that not too many people would get killed in the meantime. But hey, that was always going to be for the police and the Service to sort out after we'd gone. Even one nut with a gun can do a lot of damage, ask the FBI."

"Yeah, right," I laughed, "but you say you reckoned you'd all be out of there within ten years? What if you'd been wrong?"

"Ah, well, then we'd still be there and I'd be looking up seventeen-year-old Gaelic Footballers again..."

I laughed.

"And I'd certainly be looking-up your Aunt Úna," he smiled cheekily, "but I wasn't wrong, was I? It was obvious the Service would have the lead; I knew the RUC - PSNI as it became - would be the new point patrol; and I was pretty sure that the Army, and so army handlers, would be done and out of there before the next generation even cut its teeth."

"Yeah, I see. So no more recruiting?"

"No, quite the opposite, but only those who were already in a good position and who were going to make the cut if it came time to hand them over to a sister organisation. Hey, just my thoughts, but I felt them pretty strongly back then. I reckoned the worst thing we could do was bust our balls recruiting new people just in time to tell them it was all over and we were handing them over to someone else; and I reckoned the writing was on the wall even then."

"And so I wouldn't have made the cut?"

"Clearly not," he laughed, "I mean, look whose side you're on now. No, you were one of the good guys – and I could see that in you even then."

"But what about in 2001?" I smiled.

"Ah, with Eric Lawrence you mean? That's different. Very. Everything had changed by then, not least of all you and your circumstances; but there at the roadside in '98? No way. No, I reckoned you were safely out of bounds."

"Sensibly out of bounds."

"Exactly."

We both laughed. Captain Eric Lawrence and my dealings with Headquarters Northern Ireland is a whole separate story I'll tell you about shortly.

"And not Úna either? Would she have made the cut?" I toyed with him a little, and played on his obvious attraction to her.

"No," he smiled, "neither of you would have, and there was nothing in all the checks I did that suggested otherwise. So why fuck with good people who were absolutely nothing to do with it all already? Shame though, you two were fun is my recollection."

"Aye, we felt the same... although I think Úna was a bit frightened by your stubble," I teased. "She liked you, I could tell, but she thought your bit of stubble spelled danger."

"Yeah, she would. She was one sharp lady alright, I can remember that much..."

"She still is."

"But that little bit of stubble used to save me hours of small talk some days."

"Aye, I'm sure," I chuckled, but as we carried on talking I couldn't help but recall the shock I'd felt driving around that blind bend that day, and seeing JC in the middle of the road and his mates in cover nearby. For me it was a shock that soon passed, and despite the Republican propaganda of the day I knew that the worst that could happen to me was that I'd be fucked around by some arsehole in a road-block for half an hour.

But then I imagined how JC and those like him must have felt, when they occasionally drove covertly around the same leafy lanes and blind bends; because if he'd come across a Provo in the road, who in that part of the world would also have been part of a twelve-man patrol, armed with Armalites and an M60 machine-gun as standard, his shock would have been real and physical, and his life-expectancy a matter of minutes. 'Twas a sobering thought, which I'm glad I hadn't had on the day I applied to join the Service.

As we slowly sipped pints of bitter and chased them with a whiskey, we went on to discuss all manner of things, people and places, and the next two days flew past. A lot had happened in the twelve years since that checkpoint in Cullaville, and to Conway especially, but by the time we parted I reckoned he had the same cheerful and positive outlook as the man in his stories from Berlin thirty-something years earlier.

He'd lost his wife of twenty-nine years for one thing, in a flying accident on the other side of the world; but despite that his kids had grown up to be good people, he'd not long met and married his second wife, an American, and he still reckoned he was 'one of the luckiest men alive'. That's another valuable lesson I've never forgotten, and it's a pot of resolve I've scooped from many times since.

"I reckon the true measure of a man's life," he'd told me, "is how he deals with all his bad stuff. Your good stuff is easy to deal with - although a lot of people seem to struggle with that too," he chuckled, "but we all have bad stuff happen in our lives, and I reckon how a person copes with that, and how he gets on with life afterwards without saddening and demoralising everyone around him, is how they mark your card."

I was pretty clear on his views on religion, so I never asked who 'they' were exactly, but I got his meaning. He went on to explain why, despite his loss, he felt so 'lucky'.

"I've always reckoned if we could drag all our bad stuff along to a car boot sale somewhere, and pile it all up on our stall, then if we took a walk around and checked out everyone else's bad stuff for comparison, well I reckon most of us at the end of the day would be glad to just slink away with what we'd brought."

"Jesus, I know what you're saying, but..."

"Look Neill, I've been fortunate enough to know not one, but two of the most remarkable and crazy women you could ever imagine; and on opposite sides of the planet at that. And we didn't just become lovers or mere friends or something, I finished up married to both of them."

He smiled, downed his whiskey and looked me in the eye – as if it was a challenge to fault his argument.

"So tell me," he said, "notwithstanding all the bad stuff that makes up a life... how can a guy get much luckier than that?"

I can work with that.

My Grandpa Peter had a favourite saying, one of many in fact, which he'd learned from someone who'd impressed him in the years after World War II. The young man he'd met had joined the British Army *after* the war, and he'd served in Palestine and was about to ship-out to the war in Korea. I can't remember much else my grandpa said about him, except he'd done a plumbing job for him just across the border in Hackballscross and that he reckoned he was a 'giant of a man in every way'. That and the saying itself, of course, which is one of those hand-me-down tenets I still live by today....

'Life is where you're at, get on with it'... and whenever I think of JC, I can almost hear him saying it too.

Sticks and Stones...

"Hey, posh cunt," Fin Magee began his unsolicited derision exactly as Ed McClory had eight years earlier. I was once again crossing the playing fields to go home after school. But a lot had changed since then.

'Oh hell no,' I thought. I was by then just turned eighteen, I was in my last year as a Sixth Former at Abbey Grammar, and I was about to trial for the Ireland Under 19s rugby squad. In addition to that I'd been boxing for nearly a year to improve my all-round fitness and my reactions. Fin might have just turned twenty, and he was the bigger of the two youngest Magee boys... but what on earth was he thinking?

Unlike eight years before three things were fundamentally different: I was on my own and so I didn't have Kieran to worry about; Magee was with two guys I'd never seen before; and I didn't have a fence-post in my hand. So, whatever I did next I'd only be able to use my fists, my feet, my head and my elbows... I drew a line at biting... and I intended to use them all if it came to it. They were about twenty metres away and ambling slowly towards me.

"So where's your big tout brother these days?" Magee continued. "Run away to Belfast is what I'd heard?"

I ignored his words but I stopped in my tracks and put my schoolbag down. Magee looked sorry he'd spoken for a split second, but then he recovered his bravado and carried on slowly towards me flanked by his two cronies. When I took my blazer off as well and dropped it on top of my bag, he stopped once again. The gap now was down to about two metres. He'd made a big mistake – I'd just decided – but he clearly hadn't realised yet.

I already had my sleeves rolled up – I always did. I knew I couldn't back-down, he'd dog me forever if I did, and so I stayed where I was but went on the offensive. If they were serious, they'd close the gap, and if they weren't then I knew I had to have at least the last word. My instinct was that I needed to have more.

"Éamon's no tout, and you know it," I growled, "and unless you want to get your fucking kneecap blown away like your brother did, you should watch what lying shit you come out with. Where's he hiding these days anyway?"

"Yeah, right," he sneered, "there's a ceasefire now don't forget, and like you had any pull with the Provos anyway."

He laughed at his own joke and his two mates joined in pathetically.

"Besides," he continued, "I thought you and Éamon didn't get on with each other? Seeing as you're the goody-two-shoes posh-twat of the family, and he's the black sheep..."

"Well he's still my brother, put it that way," I replied calmly, "and it's none of your fucking business. And so that's the only two reasons I need."

"To do what?" he scoffed.

I took three strong paces towards him to close the gap, and as he raised his hands to grab me and opened his mouth to speak,

I drove a vicious punch through his feeble guard and hit him full in the face. He was felled backwards immediately, his nose split open – and broken I later learned – and blood streamed from his lip where a tooth had come through it. The hole in his lip shocked him for a second time, and he floundered aimlessly on the ground for a moment while he pawed at it.

Next came the other two. They had both been as surprised as Magee, but they soon recovered and launched themselves at me from either side. They tried to smother me rather than lash out – their bad - and so I punched accurately and made space rather than be hemmed-in and overwhelmed. I caught one with a strong blow to the side of the face and kicked the legs out from under the other. That bought me a moment to kick Magee hard in the ribs as he struggled to get up. I turned and stamped hard on the knee of the other kid on the ground, and then waded into the third, still on his feet, with a flurry of blows that forced him backwards and to cover his head to protect himself.

He'd had enough and he said so. Magee's biggest friend, who couldn't even stand because of whatever I'd done to his knee, stayed on the ground gritting his teeth and cussing with pain. I stamped on it again to make sure, and his cussing became actual tears. That left Magee himself. As I walked towards him he tried to get up yet again – which surprised me, because I'd always reckoned he was a bully and a coward rather than an actual fighter – so I took a run-up and kicked him even harder in the side as he got to his knees. He dropped like a stone and curled groaning into a ball. The third kid hovered uncertainly some yards away, but he came no closer and didn't say a thing.

"Are we fucking done here?" I screamed at Magee on the ground, but I looked at the standing kid as I did so. Shouting so hard had made my voice rise, and I wished it hadn't sounded so girly. I countered quickly and hoped they hadn't noticed.

"Coz if we're not, you three are headed for Daisy Hill..." the hospital not half a mile away, and to which Magee's mum took him later anyway. There was no answer from any of them, and so I had my final say after all.

"Listen you pieces of shit, I'm not a posh cunt and Éamon's not a tout; but if you ever want to go over any of this again, just say the word."

I picked up my blazer, my bag, and a feeling of smug invincibility, and then I slowly walked away. It was good to be walking, that way they couldn't see how much I was trembling.

It was a long way across the playing fields, but within seconds I enjoyed every metre of it. A few others had watched it all from a distance, including several adults, and I walked through the middle of them without a word. There were good people in the Derrybeg too, the vast majority of them in fact, and I like to think I made their day as much as mine. A year later I was at uni' in Belfast, and so pretty much done with the 'Beg for good, but on reflection that was the last time I was ever hassled by anyone in Newry period. It hadn't exactly been dealt with in accordance with the Marquess of Queensberry's Rules, I chuckled aloud with delayed shock, but it had been quick and effective. Job done.

There wasn't a peep from the Magees or the other boys' families, nor from the police nor anyone else. I didn't tell anyone at home – why worry them – and so I carried on as though nothing had happened. Amazingly all I had was grazed knuckles and a swollen eye... one of them must have got a punch in after all, although I don't remember it... and nobody at home even noticed. I always looked like that from rugby training.

The next day though, my dad heard from a neighbour that I'd been in a fight and that Fin Magee had got a broken nose, three cracked ribs and lost two teeth. Both his nose and lip had needed stitches and his face was swollen like a blowfish. When dad next saw me all he said was, 'Are you OK?' And when I said that I was fine and it had been about Éamon, he simply put a hand on my shoulder and said, 'Well done son, these things are better dealt with than left hanging.'

My father was a master of understatement, always, and I didn't know which of us was more proud of the other. It was a good feeling and a good outcome, and so we both just left it at that. Except that evening he took me out for my first legal pint with just the two of us. It was the best tasting pint I've ever had, and a feeling I'll never forget.

George Kennedy on the other hand was furious when I told him about it. He wanted to go and find them straight after school so he could add his two penn'orth, but really he was just pissed he'd missed all the fun. Within the year I'd be at his side and so able to help him out in a similar situation in Dundalk, so after that he felt better and exonerated of his untimely absence.

My dad never told our mum at all though, nor even Úna, and so for the first time ever neither did I. Although, predictably, Úna found out months later of her own accord. Nothing escaped her forever. She learned all about the fight and Magee's hospital treatment at work, not at home, and so the next time she saw me she pulled me to one side and confirmed what she'd heard. After I'd told her she didn't say a word. Instead she smiled proudly, gently shook her head and simply stroked my cheek.

That's when I *really* knew I was ready to face the world.

Unchained Melody

The second half of 1999 was a cyclone of adolescent highs and lows. It proved to be a period of soaring achievements and bitter disappointments; of bizarre Bohemian conquests and failed romances; and of relentless sport, endless studies and crucial exams. And for the first time in the two years since we became good mates at the Blackrock College game, I spent more time in the company of George Kennedy than with Úna. *More* time though, not *better* time, and she remained my go-to counsel and primary bolt-hole whenever I was especially low or particularly high. The rest of the time I just lumbered on, as teenagers do, and although I never really noticed that she wasn't there... funny old thing... whenever I looked up and I needed her, she always was.

In the spring I tried-out for the Ireland Under 20s, but I wasn't selected; quite simply because I wasn't good enough. I was good, very good, but at flanker there were three other guys much better. Simple as that. I played well in the final trial, but I reckon I placed too much emphasis on my tackling game. That's all well and good if you never miss a tackle, but I missed one in the last ten minutes in such spectacular fashion that I think I made up the selectors' minds for them. The opposing full back had scuttled back to his own touchline to gather up a long kick, just as I was in full flow and charging down the same wing. Bingo, and I lined-him-up from a full twenty metres out to nail him! He gathered the boggling ball with difficulty, weighed up his options and regained his balance to kick for touch in one graceful movement. Speed and strength over grace and finesse, I thought, and so I found an extra gear from somewhere and bore down on him even harder. Everything was perfect... I was flat out and closing fast, he was stood right in front of the main stand – and so the selectors – and my rib-crushing crash-tackle before he could get his kick away was going to be the hit of the decade.

And it would have been, except that as I launched myself into the horizontal, he deftly stepped to one side... and so I sailed past without even touching him, and all I collected were two arms full of air and a face full of mud. Well, I'd certainly made sure the selectors had noticed me at least, and as I got to my feet and caught up with the play I saw that they were both applauding and laughing with equal vigour. The laughter, however, lasted longer.

But life's where you're at, remember, get on with it, and that weekend put my rugby in perspective at just the right time for me to give an extra ten per cent to my academic studies. A tiny part of me was glad in fact, because George hadn't even made it to the trials. He should have in my opinion, and he'd become a giant of a second row in the past twelve months, but his latest sudden growth spurt had been at the expense of his speed and agility, and the rest of his body hadn't yet re-calibrated.

Yet there were two joint projects that we did undertake that summer: one was a Goth-looking barmaid in Dundalk, and the other was our applications for Queen's University Belfast in the

September. We were accepted into both, and so we tackled both together - as best mates do. Both demanded exceptionally hard work and application, and so we applied ourselves in that spirit. Neither seemed disappointed when we were done.

Our Goth episode – we nicknamed her *Enya Slitherhands* - was a fairly typical occurrence for that spring and summer. George and I became pretty much inseparable, and most evenings after school he'd come home with me to the Derrybeg to study (I think he was still secretly hoping to run into Fin Magee), or we'd go into Dundalk by train and to his home instead. Quite often we'd stay over and go to school from each other's home, and so just as often that would involve a 'quick pint' before bed. We kidded ourselves we were working on our social stamina for university, but the truth was we were just enjoying each other's company. So, it would seem, were a lot of other people.

Mostly through the rugby club, although it carried on at university once we got there, George and I became quite the pub cabaret act. George, who was the Southerner after all, was as fiercely pro-Royalist and pro-Brit establishment as ever; and I, from the North (although I'd become deeply anti-terrorist since the Omagh bomb), still argued on occasion for a united Ireland and for full Irish sovereignty at some stage in the future. Argued's too strong a word for what actually went on, but it's the only verb that accurately describes the nature of our debates. Drink was usually involved, savage humour and brutal sarcasm always was, and a chuckling audience usually gathered around and invariably joined in. More often than not, there were more girls than guys.

No-one doubted how close we were though, and there was little chance of anyone ever testing our loyalty to each other, but most arguments finished up with a spirited rendition of *"You've Lost That Lovin' Feelin"* and after a few such performances we became known as *The Irony Brothers*. But that was just the start of our celebrity. More scary-looking barmaids followed and our fame spread; at least, much to her amusement, as far as to Úna and one of her Dundalk-based girlfriends. Then the year moved on and in September so did we.

Our move into shared student digs off the Malone Road in Belfast and our nervous start at Queen's were far more subdued affairs, but we settled-in quickly and soon made our mark in both the lecture halls and on the rugby pitch. We had discussed what we wanted to do in life at length over the past year – and we didn't know for sure – but we had a rough idea and neither of us seemed able to just ignore the conflict still simmering-on in Ireland. And so we agreed on the same syllabus. That way we reckoned we could keep each other focussed, keep each other supported, and keep each other out of trouble. 'Trouble' and 'fun' seemed to be George's middle names, and I wondered some days if I was up to the task. His personality tried valiantly to grow along with his size, but the little boy in him was always ready to dart out from under his legs, with sometimes spectacular results. My task was to round him up and take control before he did damage.

We knew when we applied to Queen's that we wanted to put down roots in the Arts, Humanities and Philosophy Faculty, and given the festering political and para-military undercurrents still tugging at the North of Ireland, we knew that we wanted to play an active part in countering *The Troubles – The Sequel*, if things kicked-off again. So we both chose a three-year bachelor's degree in International Politics and Conflict Studies, and then we discussed how we could best put our skills to good use going forward. The work was harder than we'd imagined – uni' wasn't the sixth form we soon realised, and there was no-one to make us do our homework except each other – but then we found a beer before bed was a good way to go about things, and so all I had to do then was keep George's little boy under control. Once we got into our rhythm the relentless grind of study, sport and living up to our solemn social responsibilities carried us to the end of our first Semester.

No matter how frustrating the academic week proved to be, most weekends there was rugby and so someone to take it out on. And come the following summer George would have cricket and I would have the track; but in between there was the slight matter of the Millennium celebrations to square away. There was a party or two for some reason or other pretty much every week on campus, and so there was no way we were going to let that one go unnoticed, except… I had already made tentative arrangements to mark sunrise on the Millennium with someone else. With Úna. She'd resisted the temptation to visit us in Belfast until we got thoroughly settled in, and I'd only seen her twice in four months when I'd gone home, so for me the New Year and spending sunrise with her was a must.

George knew Úna well, and they both liked each other thank God, so notwithstanding the parties he was giving up on campus he simply invited himself along. We partied in Newry until midnight anyway, and then at 6 am on the 1st of January we began our climb to the top of Slieve Donard, the highest peak in the Mountains of Mourne. Sunrise wasn't until 8.46 am and thankfully it was dry. Although we'd pledged we were going to do it anyway, George would have moaned like hell if the weather had turned. Despite its eight hundred and fifty metres' height, not quite three thousand feet, Slieve Donard's a fairly simple climb and we were confident of doing it in a little over two hours. George had only imposed one condition, and we'd met it.

"So long as we take meat, cheese, bread and Champagne," he'd demanded, "then I'm up for it," and so that's what we had in my rucksack; plus two flasks of tea and another two of soup in case it turned ugly. In the event it was a cold, sharp and crystal clear morning, and but for the mist we'd have been able to see Belfast thirty miles to the north; Dublin fifty miles to the south; and the Isle of Man, something in between, and across the Irish Sea directly to the east. What we still saw though, in the sleepy half-light of a brave new millennium, was the faintest smudge and sparkle of fireworks from all three. 'Twas quite the moment.

New Year's Day in 2000 was a Saturday, so once we came down off the mountain the three of us made a day of it. We ambled around Newcastle and had a drink by a pub fire, and then we had a late lunch, Úna's treat 'for two starving students', she said, in the Victorian grandeur of the Slieve Donard Hotel right on the beach. That evening we dropped George off in Dundalk to see his folks, and Úna and I headed back up to Newry to spend the rest of the weekend with ours. No Midnight Mass for me, my God-shaped hole was still empty and waiting, but it had been quite the day and my cup runneth over.

I caught up with everyone's news and Úna invited herself to Belfast for the following weekend. 'Now I know you two are OK,' she said, 'and that I won't be cramping your style.' She offered to drive me all the way back and it killed me to say no, but when she learned that I'd arranged to board a specific Belfast train in Newry, and that George would already be on it having got on in Dundalk, she withdrew her offer anyway. But she made me promise that the next time I was headed home I'd ask her to come and collect me. I agreed before she'd even finished saying it.

The news from Newry and thereabouts was pretty slim, and so I checked Ma's latest scrapbook to see if they were holding out on me. Little did I know it was the last one she'd ever keep. As I turned through the pages, 1999 tapered away from not much at the start of the year to nothing by July. Maybe it was over after all, I dared to wonder. With the Real IRA still effectively in-hiding after Omagh, '99 turned out to be the quietest year by far of the then-dormant Troubles since it had all begun thirty years earlier.

In January there'd been a shooting by the Continuity IRA in Belfast, an attack on the Woodbourne RUC Station; and then on the 27th, the former Provo Volunteer-turned-Supergrass-cum-Whistleblower, Eamon Collins, was found dead in Newry. Despite the Provisionals' ceasefire, everyone believed he'd been killed by

South Armagh PIRA whilst he'd been out walking his dogs near Barcroft Park. He was stabbed and beaten so badly that the RUC thought initially he'd been hit by a car. Brendan Curran, himself a former IRA Volunteer and by then Sinn Féin Chairman of the Newry & Mourne District Council, said, 'As far as I am concerned, Eamon Collins was a dead man walking. I am not sad at his death. He will not be missed. I have no feelings for Eamon Collins.'

Sinn Féin's President and alleged former Provisional IRA Army Council member, Gerry Adams, put it more simply and said that the killing was 'regrettable'. Then he added that Collins had 'many enemies in many, many, many places.'

I read on. In March solicitor Rosemary Nelson, who had defended a number of Republican clients, was assassinated by the Loyalist Red Hand Defenders - killed by a car-bomb in Lurgan, County Armagh; in May the Continuity IRA attacked Lisnaskea RUC Station; and then a few days later an alleged drug dealer, Brendan 'Speedy' Fegan, was shot dead by Real IRA gunmen during a busy lunchtime in the Hermitage Bar, on Canal Street in Newry. Aye, peace in the border counties of Northern Ireland, I could see, was coming along nicely. And then in June, a telephone bomb-warning using a recognised CIRA codeword, warned of a five hundred-pound bomb in Russell Street, Armagh; but no bomb was ever found.

And that... as far as Mum's last ever scrapbook went... was about it. Done. Although it's probably worth mentioning that just after Christmas over twenty thousand people were evacuated from Kempton Park Racecourse, just beyond Twickenham to the south-west of London, following yet another CIRA hoax bomb-warning. The Dissidents were proving to be a pain in the arse right enough, but the Provos they most certainly were not. Thank God for small mercies.

And so against that backdrop we hiked, drank and sang our way optimistically into the year 2000. Nay, into a bold new millennium. But then we soon realised that its first year wasn't going to be nearly as quiet as the 20th Century's last, when on the 20th of January, the Real IRA announced an end to its ceasefire. Yet every cloud has a silver lining, so Grandpa Peter used to say… and so once again George and I were confident we'd have a job of work to do beyond uni'. "Sláinte".

Golden Dragon Year

At the end of our first year of studies George and I realised we had our work cut out. We were enjoying ourselves, if that's the right phrase, but we were having to work way harder than we had ever imagined. So for a while we stepped back and looked around to make sure that we'd made the right choices. We didn't look around for long thank God.

Our rugby had taken a step back since our studies had leapt to the fore, but we were still playing, still enjoying ourselves, and we were still two of the best four in the Queen's First XV; despite many of them being in their senior year. Two of the best four was a seductive place to be, and for a week or two we looked longingly at the burgeoning world of the professional game and wondered if maybe that should have been our future. A hundred and twenty-four years after the founding of the Rugby Football Union, and after just two Rugby World Cups, in 1995 the game had finally gone fully professional; a fact not lost on George and I back in '99 as we decided our futures. George was already pretty set on a career in the Garda, but I wasn't really set on anything yet; and in the year when the Royal Ulster Constabulary transitioned so awkwardly into the Police Service of Northern Ireland, I didn't feel it was likely to be in the police.

Had the change in rugby codes happened five years earlier and had the professional game been more established, I think we might have gone the other way; but the first few seasons seemed less than straightforward even for full international players who'd taken the plunge. And so we got back to our books and back to our plans for a better tomorrow. But then in 2000, when we were caught like deer in our faculty headlights and looking around once more to make sure we'd done the right thing, the Five Nations annual rugby championship became the Six Nations... and over a beer we checked every which way to see if we had any Italian ancestry so that we might play at the full international level.

Guess what? We didn't. Although we did discover we both had a liking for caffè corretto (corrected coffee, an espresso with a shot of Sambuca in it), and for girls with sultry Italian looks and long, thick, jet black hair. That was a bit of a joke I was glad George shared with Úna the next time we saw her, because the upshot of that I will share with you in the next story.

So, with our dreams of rugby stardom parked indefinitely, and with another round of exams looming large on the horizon, we got back to what we should have been doing all along. That brought its own frustrations, as we quickly learned that there was far more to the background of the Troubles than the limited first-hand knowledge we had been so confident of before. And ours was a pretty straight forward conflict; trying to understand some of the other international terrorist scenarios playing-out around the world was essentially a contradiction in terms. They were beyond understanding, and most, it seemed, were beyond any meaningful intellectual description as well.

We buckled-down, worked harder, played less and sought more, from anywhere and everywhere we could learn it. I thought I had a pretty good handle on the Troubles having grown up in South Armagh, but I soon realised that was virtually a war within a war and that other students from Belfast, Derry or elsewhere, could put a whole different spin on things with equal conviction and clarity. I learnt as much from George as from anyone else, and through being so close we discussed things in far greater detail than we did with others.

Just where we lived and were raised, for example, meant that we had a vastly different understanding of the Provisional IRA and many of their sordid activities. Whilst I had observed far more PIRA attacks than had he, George routinely saw a greater number of prominent IRA players than did I, and often in plain view. The overwhelming majority of attacks took place across the border and in the North, but at the height of the Troubles Dundalk had been home to more than a hundred and eighty *On The Run* terrorists, or OTRs in Brit speak, which riled him even more.

Our discussions had two lasting effects on not just us, but on a small group of fellow students from our social circle and who were chasing the same degree. The first was that when George went home to Dundalk, he'd no longer get up and walk out of bars if a former Provo came in; he'd stay and listen and watch and learn. And the second was that when he told us that, half a dozen of us formed a select study group and went in search of 'former' Provos in and around Belfast. Just having George with us meant that we got a fairer hearing than might otherwise have been the case, and a couple of the rest of us looked like we could take care of ourselves too; but the two girls in the group were the real ice-breakers, and unsurprisingly they would often come away with the most revealing exposés. 'Girl-power at work,' they said, and George and I quickly learnt never to fight it... but to revel in it.

Neither of us had steady girlfriends in the first eighteen months – our status as the *Irony Brothers* ensured we were never short of female company – and the nearest thing I had was a six-month something with a female athlete I'd competed with in the summer and which lasted until the Christmas of 2000. But then I got seriously immersed in the preparation for my Barrett Paper, for my dissertation in my final year, and girls became an add-on once again. Besides, after my special birthday present from Úna in the January of 2001, I focussed on middle-aged women again for the longest while. George reckoned I was crazy, yet he happily took on my share of the girls our own age as well as his own; and he never said 'no', I also noticed, to the better looking mates of the various cougars I hooked up with. He was a man of no principal whatsoever, what more can I tell you?

Our Irish-based studies inevitably took us deeper into the mercurial world of the Dissidents, and once RIRA's abandoned ceasefire receded further behind us so did the level of activity slowly climb again. They never came close to the sustained and deadly complexity of the Provos – what they called war was more like the early fumbling attacks or hoax warnings of the Provies at the start of the 1970s - but they did serious damage nonetheless, and occasionally they killed. But crucially, they blundered around and festered-on just enough to prevent Northern Ireland from returning to normality in its entirety.

In May 2000, CIRA called upon the Provisional IRA to 'hand its weapons over to those who were prepared to defend the Republic'; and even had they done so, the form book showed that they would have been unlikely to use them. Two weeks later, however, RIRA mortared one of the colossal Brit look-out towers in South Armagh, at Glassdrumman, then just days later they set-off a small bomb on Hammersmith Bridge in London. They followed that in June with another device in the capitol, on a railway line at Ealing Broadway; and then back in Ireland, the following day, by a device on the property of Peter Mandelson, the Secretary of State for Northern Ireland.

During the second half of the year the Dissidents were responsible for another dozen similar incidents, only two of which impacted on me and George directly. On the 30th of June, a Friday, RIRA bombed the main Belfast to Dublin railway line near Meigh in South Armagh, and so interrupted our journey home for a long weekend; and then on the 22nd of September, the cheeky fuckers fired an RPG-22 anti-tank rocket across the Thames at the HQ of MI6, the Secret Intelligence Service – a building affectionately known to Londoners as 'The Blancmange'. That impacted on us in as much as it was also on a Friday, and so on a whim our study group begged, stole or borrowed the money for six cheap return flights to London, and we went to canvas the views and opinions of any eye witnesses we could lay our hands on.

Much to our surprise we found a few – although we found even more pubs, but the London prices kept us pretty well in line – and the consensus was that it was just London being London, and the Dissidents being the ineffective and almost farcical follow-on to the Troubles that the Brits had come to expect. We noted in our presentation when we got back, however, that these were the same Londoners that had been putting up with much worse for the past thirty years, and that their parents and grandparents before them had also had to put up with the Blitz; the threat of Nazi invasion; the Battle of Britain; and ultimately, Wernher von Braun's V-2 rockets in the final days of World War II.

The Dissidents, we concluded, were essentially a small and senior cadre of radical former Provos who just couldn't let it go, and then a following of lesser would-be terrorists, militant Nationalist idealists and younger wannabes who'd missed the war and so wanted their chance to fight beyond the PIRA ceasefire. But 'fight' was a relative term, and we also concluded that they'd never have anything like the infrastructure, complexity, sophistication, organisation, communication, weapons, explosives or widespread support that the Provos had enjoyed from 1970 onwards. But that didn't make them any less dangerous on the wrong day.

It had been a busy year of political developments too, and so George and I had to buckle-down to make some sense of the macro-level events that we hadn't tracked as closely as the terrorist incidents. We'd actually got our priorities arse about face, we sheepishly admitted to the rest of our study group, but then in our defence we put that down to our border mind-sets and our Dundalk-Newry perspectives. All four of them jeered playfully at our feeble argument, and thereafter *Irony* was out and we were renamed the *Bandit Brothers*.

For the first half of 2000 there'd been a seemingly endless flurry of political and quasi-diplomatic activity. Back in May, Northern Ireland Secretary Peter Mandelson, had offered to cut troop numbers if the IRA kept its promise to disarm; then the next day Sir Ronnie Flanagan, the RUC Chief Constable, said that five military installations were to close. About then two independent arms inspectors, Cyril Ramaphosa, who in 2014 would become South Africa's Deputy President, and Martti Ahtisaari, a former Finnish President, arrived in Northern Ireland to report to the Canadian Head of the International Decommissioning Body, General John de Chastelain.

Still in May, David Trimble, who was the First Minister of Northern Ireland and the leader of the Ulster Unionist Party (the UUP), said that he believed PIRA's offer to open its arms dumps for inspection meant that its thirty-year war was over. Then at a crucial meeting of the UUP Council, he only narrowly won a vote to re-enter a power-sharing government with Sinn Féin. He won by just three percent, with four hundred and fifty-nine votes; but that meant four hundred and three of the ruling council still voted against the motion... it was going to be a long hot summer.

In June the Brit government announced that five hundred soldiers were to be withdrawn, which would bring troop numbers in Northern Ireland to below fourteen thousand and so the lowest since 1970; and the IRA announced that it had opened its arms dumps to the international inspectors. Ramaphosa and Ahtisaari subsequently confirmed the Provos' claim to Prime Minister Tony Blair. But then in the July, the Province's latest bloody sectarian fiasco began to unfold.

On July the 2nd the Northern Ireland Parades Commission banned the Drumcree Orangemen, a Unionist ancient order, from marching along their traditional route through the Nationalist Garvaghy Road in County Armagh. Prior to the ban the security forces had been reinforced by two thousand or so troops and police to cover the Loyalist marching season. For several years before that, troops had all but been removed from the streets in most areas of the Province, and they were only deployed in direct support of the RUC. That night, and then again the next day, police had to clear Loyalist demonstrators from Drumcree Hill under a barrage of bottles, stones and fireworks, and the violence had soon spread across Northern Ireland.

On July the 5th, and following a third night of rioting, British Army engineers had erected a huge steel barricade across the Drumcree Road; and by the 11th, Loyalists were attempting to block other roads right across the Province. To add fuel to an already raging Unionist fire, on the 28th the last so-called political prisoners – the vast majority of which were Republicans – were released from the Maze Prison under the terms of the Good Friday Agreement. A violent feud ensued between opposing factions of the Loyalist community – between those who to some degree supported the agreement, and those who didn't – until on the 21st of August two men were shot dead in Belfast and troops returned to the streets. The situation was only eased the following day when the Loyalist paramilitary leader, Johnny 'Mad Dog' Adair, was re-arrested and sent back to prison.

And so the situation festered on for months, although it was calmed somewhat by a statement from the Northern Ireland Secretary in October: As dissident Loyalists agitated still harder for IRA disarmament, Peter Mandelson warned them that if the power-sharing executive between the Unionists and Sinn Féin was allowed to fail, then they could face joint rule by London and Dublin. That to Unionists and Loyalists was unthinkable, and if nothing else it focussed a lot of minds and shut a lot of mouths.

Two days later the First Minister spoke in defence of power-sharing at the UUP annual conference, and although he was booed by about a third of the delegates, the other two thirds gave him a standing ovation. On the political front at least then, some measure of calm returned; even when in January 2001 Peter Mandelson was replaced as the Secretary of State for Northern Ireland by John Reid, the first Catholic to hold the post. Reid was a Scot, and he'd previously been the Scottish Secretary, but he was Roman Catholic nonetheless, and so no-one doubted that we were living through momentous times.

About then an advertising campaign was begun seeking recruits for the new Police Service of Northern Ireland. Catholics especially. The PSNI was destined to replace the RUC, the Royal Ulster Constabulary, and although Republicans protested angrily that they had not yet signed-off on the new force, few doubted that it would come about. But even fewer believed that it would really be made up of equal numbers of Protestants and Catholics. For maybe a week or two, George and I seriously considered being amongst the first-few of the few; but we judged that the time wasn't right and so we both got back to our mainstream studies, and I got back to the faculty proposals for my Barrett Paper for my final year.

Christmas inevitably saw a break in the proceedings, which both George and I spent with our families; as did the New Year, which we spent back in Belfast and with our many admirers. Only my birthday present from Úna surpassed our New Year celebrations, and that got my year off to about the best start imaginable. But there was more to come. In Chinese astrology the Year of the Dragon comes around every twelve years, and then a Golden Dragon Year, like 2000, every sixty.

Some believe that such years can change the course of history; although by its end I reckoned they were a whole year out. Because 2001 changed everything.

La Dolce Vita

The biggest deal at the start of 2001 was my 20th birthday; although not to me, just to everyone else. I was so stuck into my studies and the research proposal for my dissertation that I was having trouble seeing it as anything other than yet another birthday. By the New Year though it had all been sorted for me, so all I had to do was pretty much turn up and follow my instructions. George and Úna had combined forces to ensure I did as I was told, and the McCormac-Kennedy family plan comprised a three-part celebration.

My actual birthday was on a Tuesday, and so in the middle of courses. So, the first party was to be the Saturday before and on campus – and that one my mum didn't want to know anything about – followed by a second at home in Newry the next weekend. George was coming home for that too, and he was going to stay at our house. But then on the actual day, on the Tuesday evening after uni', I was to have a night of five-star luxury in the Europa Hotel – the main part of Úna's present to me – followed by a late start because of no classes in the morning. She'd also intended to buy me an engraved wristwatch, but she let my mum and dad do that and she got me a 3G mobile phone instead. Don't laugh, 3G was state of the art back then, and everyone knew it. She'd been going to buy me a BlackBerry, but BlackBerrys didn't have *voice* back then and she wanted to be able to talk to me more often; so she'd elected for a phone rather than a keyboard. Thank God she did, for several reasons you'll soon read about.

A night in the Europa... and the family were all in on it... so my heart didn't race quite as quickly as it might have. Besides, George was in on it too, and he and Úna were sufficiently close by then that if she had a secret agenda then George wouldn't have been able to avoid some sleazy innuendo. Nonetheless I was fascinated, and so Tuesday couldn't come around quickly enough.

Úna had said she'd see me at the bar at 7 pm, and so I put on the smartest trousers I owned, wore my best shirt with an open collar, and packed the coolest-looking overnight bag I could find. And of course a warm jacket to get me there. This was Belfast in January after all. She'd already explained in front of the family that she wouldn't be able to stay for more than one drink, but she said she'd get me checked-in and settle the bill and then I was to make the most of all the hotel had to offer and to spoil myself. I knew her well enough to know she was telling the truth... mostly... but then a tiny part of me hoped that this was just a cover story, and that now I'd left home for good then maybe she was planning to stay there with me. Hey, it's good to dream.

I was there a few minutes early and she was already at the bar. She looked fabulous as always, but I was pretty much able to discount sex straight away; she was wearing a tasteful silk blouse, but with smart jeans... and that wasn't her style. If this had been all about seduction, I would have known it instantly – and instead I knew it wasn't. We embraced warmly anyway - I hadn't seen her for three weeks, since Christmas - and she smelled amazing. But there again, Úna always smelt amazing.

She ordered a second cocktail, got me a whiskey and dry ginger, and then caught up with my news. After a while we moved to a table on our own, and there she gave me my room key and explained where the spa was and so on. Then after chatting easily for nearly half an hour, she said she'd see me at the weekend and got ready to leave. We both stood, we kissed lightly and then hugged warmly, and before we stepped away from each other she casually introduced the rest of my 'birthday present'.

"Oh, by the way," she purred as we separated, "seeing as I couldn't stay over too, I thought I'd feel happier if I left you in good hands for the night."

I suddenly became aware of someone on the edge of our space, and so I half turned to see who it was. It was the vision of a dark-haired angel, was my first impression, and my face in that instant must have been quite a picture. But unlike Úna in the rowing boat eleven years beforehand, this angel wasn't wearing all white... she was all in black.

A beautiful late-thirty-something face, framed in a mane of long black hair, was smiling at me eagerly, laughing almost, and I saw in an instant that she was wearing the exact same black sequinned cocktail dress that Úna had worn for Éamon's wedding reception. The next instant was dominated by an immediate hard-on. As with Úna before her, it came to just above the knee and it was V-wired, strapless and bra-less; except if anything she'd had to squeeze an extra inch or two of breasts into the top of it. When I looked back at Úna she was grinning even more broadly.

"Neill, this is Maria..." Úna waited a moment for the penny to fully drop, "and if you go and see the barman you'll find he can make you a caffè corretto as well."

"Oh my God, are you Italian?" I asked Maria.

"Not quite," she smiled with a South Down accent, "but I can speak Italian if you want to close your eyes and pretend."

Úna giggled and studied my face, so I uttered a nervous chuckle so as not to be left out.

"My father's Italian," said Maria, "and my mum was made to learn, so we grew up speaking both."

"Umm," Úna added, "and Italian's quite sexy, right Neill?"

I blushed, then from somewhere I found the manners to pull out a chair for our stunning intruder and the two girls sat. The barman appeared within seconds and put a large gin and tonic in front of her. He couldn't help but snatch a glimpse down into her gaping cleavage, and I couldn't help but follow suit.

"But so you're Irish then?" I stuttered as I sat back down. It was a stupid question and I wished I hadn't asked it.

"Yes, I am," Maria giggled, "but I have some very Italian habits. Will that make up for it?"

Úna chuckled too, but then she bought me a moment to regain my composure whilst she explained a little more.

"Maria's dad was an Italian Prisoner of War, you see. He was captured in North Africa in 1942 and then brought to a POW camp here at Rockport."

"Rockport?" I queried lamely.

"Yes, not far from here," Úna said, "and then when Italy surrendered to the Allies in 1943, he became one of thousands of Italian 'co-operators' and he worked on a farm out by Killarn."

"Jees, what, and so then he stayed here?"

"Yes, that's where he met Maria's mum. She was in the Women's Land Army... in amongst all that hay..."

Both the women looked at each other and giggled, and I sensed a not-so-private joke.

"Yeah, she was *one* of them right enough," Maria laughed.

"He's a charming man," Úna continued, "I've met him loads of times. He's seventy-six now," she smiled at Maria, then looked back at me, "but he's an even bigger flirt than you are."

I blushed hard again, but I didn't feel much of a flirt for the moment. I tried a come-back but I shouldn't have bothered.

"Seventy-six?" I babbled, "but then he's your grandfather, surely, not your dad?"

"Oh, he's cute," Maria said to Úna, "I'm going to have to be especially kind to him," and then to me she said, "but no, I'm nearly forty, and Úna tells me that makes me the girl of your dreams."

She had no idea how right she was. That was almost the age Úna had been when she'd worn that dress in front of me five years beforehand – *and* very nearly *not* worn it – and I could only pray that this was headed where I thought it was and that it wasn't some cruel but phony wind-up. But not for my birthday, surely? No, that wasn't Úna's style either. Or so I desperately hoped. As if she'd read my mind, Úna stepped-in and put me out of my misery.

"Listen you two," she said casually, "I've got to get going; but Maria's seen you several times before Neill, from a distance, and she's always teased me that if I can't look after you properly, then she'd be happy to step-in and do it for me." She fixed me with her electric gaze and flared her eyes. "And so I thought your 20th would be the perfect time to take her up on it."

If there was any noise anywhere in the bar, then I couldn't hear it. For a moment all time stopped, but I knew I was expected to respond in some way.

"Er... well, if you two aren't winding me up," I uttered as confidently as I could, "then happy birthday me, and I'd love to."

"Love to what?" Úna teased.

"Don't embarrass him," Maria smiled. She was too late.

"Seen me where?" I mumbled as confidently as I could.

"Um, well playing rugby of course," Maria said, "several times in fact, and er, I saw you once here, about six months ago, when Úna brought you along for a meeting in Belfast."

"Oh, yeah, I remember that, but I don't..."

"No, we didn't meet, but that was my building that Úna brought you to, and I saw you outside my office... *most* of the girls had a peek in fact."

I blushed again and they both smiled at my awkwardness.

"Yes, lucky Maria," Úna grinned sheepishly, "there could have been quite a queue if I'd been selling tickets."

"There you go again," Maria smiled, "trying to embarrass him... I thought you had to be getting back to Newry, and then Neill and I can explore the hotel together."

"Right then, I will," Úna chuckled, "and I trust you two will have the time of your lives. Happy birthday my darling, I'll see you on Saturday. Sleep well."

Then she stood, kissed me on the cheek, turned, and with one last smile behind her, left us to it.

There was a short silence, which I was determined this time Maria wouldn't have to break. I swallowed hard and hoped that when I went to speak that something would come out.

"So, umm, have you eaten?" I said nervously.

"No, and you know Una's kindly covered dinner already?'

"Yes, I know, she's kind of covered everything."

"So time for you to just push back and enjoy. Or for *us* to push back and enjoy, if you'd like?"

"Yes, of course..."

"But unless you're starving," she added tentatively, "then I thought maybe we could order room service later?"

"Oh, sure..."

There was another short silence, so she helped me out.

"Because if we go into dinner, I'm only going to pick at something tiny anyway," she smiled, "I hate feeling too full when I'm having fun." Then she smiled again, an amazingly disarming smile, and I was disarmed immediately.

"No, got it..." I stammered, "me too. So maybe another drink then?" I tried gamely.

"If you like. What's that?"

"Er, Power's and ginger..."

"Right. Well I've just got a fresh one, so nothing for me, but if you want another whiskey and ginger then help yourself. But..."

she purred shamelessly, "there's Champagne already in the room, if you fancy that instead?"

"Oh, cool. Umm. Champagne then…"

Maria stood and gathered up her purse and her drink,

"Bring the whiskey with you," she smiled, "Úna's already signed for all of these. All you'll have to do is take care of anything else we order."

"Got it."

I stood anxiously, downed the rest of my drink in one, then picked up my key card and my bag and motioned for Maria to lead the way to the lift. As we stepped off I wondered if Úna had got us in the same room as well. She hadn't (but I learned later on from Maria that she had tried to).

The short journey to my room – our room – was carried out in silence, although we both smiled all the way. Me nervously, and Maria with confidence and an air of faint amusement. Then as the lift stopped and before the door opened, she leant in and kissed me lightly on the lips. Just like Úna she smelled wonderful, and her lipstick tasted of pure decadence. Then she led the way to the room; she'd obviously been up there with Úna before I had arrived. When I saw her overcoat across a chair and heard Jazz FM playing quietly over the room sound system, I knew she had.

We made our way across the room and gravitated towards the desk. I put my overnight bag on it and the key card, Maria her purse. She kept a hold of her drink for the moment and then pointed to the two bottles of Champagne in two separate ice-buckets across the room.

"Úna didn't want us getting thirsty," she chuckled, "but it's there when you want it."

"No, I'm good," I explained, "but can I pour you one?"

"Not just yet, thanks. I'll finish this first…" she sipped her gin and tonic, "but why don't you sit on the end of the bed for a moment. We've got one more surprise for you."

I looked around and then did as I was told. Whatever it was I doubted that it was going to hurt, and so my mind was racing as much as my erection was aching. I wondered fleetingly if she could see it, and then just as quickly dismissed it as irrelevant. I felt pretty damn sure she was going to see it in a minute or two. At that precise moment I loved Úna more than I ever had.

Maria finished her drink and walked slowly across the room towards me. Once she was directly in front of me she put one of her high-heeled feet gently in my lap. I glanced down at her delicate foot and recognised the shoe immediately.

"What the...?" I grinned.

"Úna said you might recognise these," she purred.

Recognise them! They'd been seared into my brain for the past five years. Without being told what to do next, I put one hand behind her silk-covered calf and unbuckled the shoe with the other. It actually took two hands for a moment, but I replaced my hand on her calf – although slightly higher this time – as soon as I could. It felt wonderful.

I finished unbuckling the fine leather strap and removed her shoe. And just as before with Úna, I could see the top of one stocking and a suspender strap but no more. And also just as before, I became even harder in an instant.

Then Maria put her naked foot down and replaced it with the other, but this time as she did so she hitched-up her dress ever so slightly to make it easier. That meant I could see both stocking tops and more than a mere glimpse of her panties too. She saw me looking – she couldn't help but see me looking - and it was clearly what she'd intended... and for just a moment I wondered if they were Úna's as well. Probably not, I reasoned, and thank God I had the sense not to ask her. Then I unbuckled the second shoe.

Once I'd removed it and held the back of her calf as before, she lifted her dress a little higher and replaced her stockinged foot back on my groin. In case I was in any doubt about what she was doing, she gently teased me through my trousers with her toes.

227

Huh, I wondered who'd told her to do that? Before I could decide what to do next, she spoke.

"Now we might be wrong," she smiled down at me, "but right about now, Úna and I reckoned you might be thinking that you've got some unfinished business under this dress..."

I looked up at her and I had to swallow for fear of dribbling like an idiot, but again she spoke before I'd had to.

"So... *finish*... and a very happy birthday from both of us."

I swallowed again, and then slid my trembling hand slowly up the inside of her thigh and gently stroked her through her panties. She didn't say a word, but she smiled down at me and gently squeezed me again with her toes.

"Don't stop, that feels nice," she said, but she lowered her foot to the ground so as to be sure of her balance. I carried on as she'd told me to and she lifted her dress high above her waist to make it easy for me; then she purred something, several sentences' worth, in Italian. I nearly came on the spot. Whatever she'd said, she made sure I knew to carry on, and so I stroked her through the thin material as calmly and confidently as I could.

"Slide your fingers inside my panties," she urged, and from that moment on she repeated everything in Italian as well... until the time when no explanation was necessary. Then she spoke Italian only, in between all the little moans and the sighs and the gasps. For long blissful seconds I stroked the wonderful, slippery folds of her ecstasy, and then the warm, wet firmness of her bud. After maybe a minute she lifted her dress even higher, and then eventually she pulled down the front of her panties and urged me on in Italian yet again.

There was of course a whole wonderful world I hadn't explored at all yet, so explore I did. I have no idea if I was doing what she was telling me, but she moved against my fingers rhythmically and she seemed more than happy with the outcome. Then eventually she slowly pushed me back on the bed.

She whispered for me to move even further up the covers and as she did so she calmly unbuckled my belt, undid my trousers and fly, and pulled everything down over my hips. She looked more than happy with what she found. Then she took a'hold of me and worked me skilfully for something less than a minute. Next she took me in her mouth and worked me even more expertly for about the same length of time. And then, at last, she stood up, stood back, slipped out of her panties and climbed back on top of the bed with me. She lifted her dress so I could see her cunny, her suspender belt and exactly what she was doing, and then she lowered herself gently down on top of me. Slowly at first, but then further, harder, deeper... and eventually faster.

Still more Italian streamed from her, and there was even less need for translation. She moved rhythmically the whole time, and the closer we came to our orgasm the harder she ground down on me. But not once did she stop smiling at me or gently biting her lip.

I came quickly, after maybe only three or four minutes; but she still rode me hard, without a word, and she wasn't far behind me. When she came it was really powerful - I'd seen enough juvenile female orgasms by then to know that – and even after we were spent it was unlike anything I'd known with any young woman my own age. Then she kept moving against me for long minutes, slower and slower, until eventually she spoke-up to make sure that I didn't. This time it was in English.

"Shuusshh," she put her fingers to my lips, "don't say anything for a minute, just lay there and feel good."

I felt fucking marvellous, and any embarrassment I'd been expecting to feel was overwhelmed by a warm and intoxicating smugness. Eventually she stopped rocking against me and she bent all the way forward and kissed me on my mouth. It was a long, warm and very deep kiss, several in fact, which brought me almost as much pleasure as what we'd just done. Almost.

I put my arms around behind her, and although her dress was minimal and there was much bare flesh, it was still there and I longed for her to be naked. Me too, and I suddenly felt stupid because I hadn't even got to take my shoes off. We'd barely pulled my trousers and pants below my hips, and everything else was still as it had been when we'd entered the room.

"Hmmm," she grinned into my shoulder, "that was pretty intense. And..." she smiled...

"And what?" I filled the pause anxiously.

"And... the best thing about you being only twenty," she whispered, "is that older guys never really get that hard anymore. Not even close. And in just minutes..." she lifted her head and giggled, "you'll be that hard all over again. Lucky me."

Before I could fret about it any further, that or my trousers being unceremoniously around my ankles and my shoes still on, she began to move against me once more. I was frightened for a moment that she was about to start again immediately, and I wasn't sure I could manage – in fact I was pretty certain that I couldn't – but she eventually sat up, proudly astride of me, and smiled down at me like a goddess. When she spoke this time it was in a whisper, as if Úna was outside and listening through the door.

"And *that* was as good as we've always reckoned it would be." She looked me deep in the eye as if to say, 'It's all good Neill, don't worry, girlfriends talk and Úna gets it,' then she continued to purr, "But now we need to get out of these clothes, and then I can *really* spoil you for your birthday."

"Right..." was all I could manage.

"And Úna said to tell you many happy returns, by the way, which I took to mean many happy repeats - and so I'm enjoying this for both of us remember."

God bless Aunt Úna, I thought, and God bless Grandpa Peter and his positive outlook on the world: Life is *most definitely* where you're at... get on with it!

Ave Maria

The only problem with having the highlight of your year in January is that the cold, wet, dark and dreary weeks that follow seem even more gloomy and miserable. And what's more, they seem to drag on forever. The months at the start of 2001 were no exception. At the end of a week's mind-numbing studies we'd usually have a game of rugby to lift our spirits, but George and I could never remember a year when we'd looked forward to the spring so much. We were used to playing in cold, wet and windy conditions - welcome to Ireland - but several of the games that winter were played in driving snow; and that's when I knew for sure that I wasn't descended from Vikings.

Still, one of the immediate benefits of that post-birthday period was that I had my new mobile phone, and better still, Maria had my number. After our first night in the Europa on my birthday she became one of the more pleasant ways to wrap up against the

Irish winter, and she would call me often enough to tide me over when my studies prevented me from pursuing girlfriends in a more conventional sense. That, I'd discovered, was usually more trouble and effort than it was worth. Don't get me wrong, there were some cute girls at Queen's and I always enjoyed the outcome, but the whole cat and mouse palaver of pursuit, stand-off and negotiation before the deed could be done, cut way too deeply into the little spare time I had. With Maria there was no pretence or pre-amble, and we both wanted the same thing; so we happily took what we wanted, and quite often. Maria was mesmerised by my youthful stamina (which is a polite way of saying how hard I could get and for how long), and I by her luxurious Mediterranean charms. I even picked up a smattering of Italian.

Thirty-nine-year-old Maria McLaughlin had been a good friend of Úna's for nearly twenty years. Professionally she was Úna's mirror-image in the Belfast insurance industry, and they'd met at a convention there in 1982. Úna was five years older than Maria; but crucially that meant five years ahead of her in their chosen sphere, and so she became her role model, her mentor, and following Maria's divorce a close girlfriend. Over the next two years she was to become something of an irregular girlfriend to me too. Or the 'third spoke of our wheel' as Úna put it. 'Hardly', I would tease, 'I'm not doing the other spoke'; to which she would always just smile, put a hand on my cheek and say, 'Ah, but in your mind you are my love, dream on.'

Maria's domestic situation was vastly different to Úna's though. Whereas Úna had her own home and a small but select stable of boyfriends - a couple of which had been for several years at a time by then - Maria lived with a man ten years older than her and they both had other partners as and when it suited them. It struck me as bizarre, and it struck Úna as kind of sordid and far too restrictive for her lifestyle, but then once I became one of Maria's monthly distractions it struck me as absolutely fine.

She would pick me up from campus maybe once or twice a month and we'd simply get a room somewhere for as long as we could get away. It was usually rugby that interfered, not studies, and for the longest time George Kennedy would plead with me to be my substitute for if Maria called and I couldn't make it. But it meant we didn't get out much, Maria and I, that's not what our steamy relationship was all about, and so my hiking with Úna and the easy intimacy we continued to enjoy remained the main spoke of my wheel. I think Úna had known that would be the case all along and our relationship changed yet again – in a good way - and it soon became clear to me that she was enjoying me vicariously through her frank and salacious girl talk with Maria.

That was fine with me, it was even more of a turn-on than just having Maria; knowing that everything I touched, licked, stroked or whispered was probably going to make it back to Úna. But then after just our third rendezvous Maria told me something that caused the penny to drop even further into place. Maria said that she was the girlfriend with whom Úna had arranged for me to stay at the Mount Errigal Hotel on the night of the Omagh bomb, but which, of course, had never happened. When I heard that we both joked that we had three years' catching–up to do, and some weeks we damn near made it; but the one thing we never did was go back to the Mount Errigal itself in recognition of that dreadful day. She was a woman of some integrity, I was pleased to learn, as well as a lady of great skill and considerable charms.

And so, back to my coursework and the preparation for my dissertation. My target was to have my research proposal ready by the start of my second year, so in September 2001. That meant I had to get cracking, and my teachers had spotted a few potential problems with it already; not least of all, who I was hoping to interview and how? The dissertation would be simply entitled 'The Barrett Paper', and subtitled, 'The Procurement, Capabilities and Psychological Impact of the Provisional IRA's .50 Barrett Rifles'. It turned quite a few heads at QUB when I first submitted my proposal, and I faced enormous pressure initially to develop a 'research question', but the more people I met with to discuss it the more support I began to receive from the faculty.

George's dissertation was going to be about the Troubles too, entitled 'Ireland's Impervious Border – Fact or Fiction?', and so we hoped a lot of our research would overlap. With that sort of synergy in mind, but with the university regulations clearly in sight as well, we were both starting on our final projects much earlier than most. Right from the start I had bold and innovative plans for my exploratory research in my second year, especially over my literature review and what I was hoping would be my background reading and the pool of human sources I hoped to use. But peace hadn't long broken out, and so most of the information I sought still wasn't in the public domain. Worse still, in Northern Ireland a lot of it was still highly classified. Needlessly it appears years later, but at the time quite understandably.

Although Wikipedia was launched a week before my 20th birthday, it would take a year to create the first twenty thousand articles, and I would have finished my studies and graduated before it reached its first hundred thousand. Today, in 2017, it boasts over five million. But that was of little use to me back then. Despite Queen's having been superbly equipped with IT, back in 2001 the 'Web' - and digital encyclopedias in particular - were still in their infancy. So that meant I had to read a lot of books, essays, newspapers, American magazines, manuals and any other hard copy I could find; and then read, and read, and read some more. But the real problem was that much of the data I *hoped* existed did so within the military domain, and I feared they would be less than forthcoming towards a twenty-year-old 'oik' from Derrybeg. I couldn't have been more wrong.

After weeks of floundering around in circles and of being frightened and uncertain of where and when to stick my head above the parapet, I had a crucial breakthrough - Mrs Kennedy. Sarah Kennedy, no relation to George, was a forty-eight-year-old teacher elsewhere in Queen's School of Politics, International Studies and Philosophy, and a little birdie in the library had told me that she'd once been an officer in the Ulster Defence Regiment as well. When I approached her and invited her for a coffee to the canteen, I found that not only was that true but that her husband still was; and he was a major in what had been 7/10 UDR, one of the three Belfast Battalions of Northern Ireland's home-defence regiment. She had heard nothing about my proposed dissertation, but when I'd finished explaining exactly what I hoped to achieve she was keen to see it flourish. She agreed to be my supervisor there and then. What's more, she had a plan... which was a hell of a lot more than I did at that stage.

I had started to believe that key elements of what I was seeking were out of the question: to get access to a military library and maybe some unclassified military data; to spend time with British Army small arms experts; and to be allowed to interview soldiers who had patrolled South Armagh at the height of what I was calling 'the Sniper era'. She on the other hand had got quite excited. She thought if no-one ever asked then it couldn't possibly happen, but she judged that the time, the nature of my request and my apparent credentials – ie. a *good boy*, but from Bandit Country South Armagh – were all perfectly aligned to give it a try.

Sarah reckoned that if I wrote a letter to the Chief of Staff at HQNI, the Headquarters Northern Ireland, then in the current political climate she thought I might get a fair hearing. The letter, she suggested, could best be walked through the system by her husband Charlie, and then at the very least I'd get to meet-up with someone and then they would either say yes or no. Simple as that. I liked her no-nonsense manner straight away, and by the time I graduated two years later I considered her a close friend. The fact that she was extremely pleasant to look at and had a mischievous way about her had relatively little to do with it. Relatively little.

The more we worked together during that first semester the more we became impressed with each other. My research proposal got her nod of approval second time of asking (a record, she told me), but she tinkered with my letter to HQNI and sent me away to re-write it four times before she gave it to her husband to put into the system. And the moment she knew I was *really* serious, she said, was when we spent a whole day together at her home – her, her husband and I - and she realised the full extent of the background reading I'd already done.

In fact, I'd prepared a fifty-page synopsis for them of what I'd already learned from open sources, some of which they could scarcely believe. But there again, they hadn't had the benefit of receiving bundles of magazines and newspapers from the USA like I had, from our distant relative Patrick McCormac IV in Boston; Úna's idea and more of that later. I already knew, for example, a fair bit about the three essential components of my paper: the procurement of the Barretts from the USA; their capabilities and 'battle proven accuracy', so proudly vaunted by their Tennessee-based manufacturer; and that by all accounts they'd had a more devastating effect on troop morale in South Armagh than any other weapon or tactic throughout the Troubles.

The first and last of those three components, we agreed, were going to be the hardest to research, evidence and then pin down as theses; whereas the middle element was going to be the toughest to expand beyond mere technical data. But I had a plan for that too, and Charlie Kennedy fancied that if HQNI gave their blessing to helping me at all, then he might be able to arrange for me to fire a Barrett M82 on the army ranges at Ballykinler with someone from the army's Small Arms School Corps.

Vis-à-vis the Provisional IRA's procurement activities, I'd suggested that there had been four main initiatives; one of which spanned the whole of the Troubles and three of which followed clearly discernible eras. The one that spanned the Troubles saw PIRA acquiring weapons from anywhere and everywhere it could, including from Spain (from ETA circa 1970); from Czechoslovakia via the Netherlands (in 1971, although the five-ton shipment was seized at Schiphol Airport); then RPG-7 rocket launchers from an unknown European source in 1972; AK-47s, SMGs, RPG-7s and grenades from the PLO, the Palestine Liberation Organisation, in 1977 (in a shipment from Lebanon via Cyprus, but which was seized in Antwerp); up to a hundred Heckler & Koch G3 rifles that had been stolen from a Norwegian Reserve base in 1984; and two consignments from the Netherlands, in 1986 and '88 (the first of which was seized by Dutch police in Amsterdam, and the second by the Garda in County Meath).

Then the three clearly discernible eras, I suggested, were the George Harrison era of American-sourced weapons, from pre-1969 until his arrest by the FBI following a sting operation in 1981; the post-Harrison US era, from '81 to the end of the Troubles, but which saw as many shipments seized as delivered; and the Libyan era, from 1985 to '90, when huge quantities of weapons, explosives and ammunition were supplied by Colonel Gaddafi during his undeclared terror campaign against the US, the UK and their allies.

The George Harrison in this case was not the famed Beatle from Liverpool, but a native of County Mayo who'd emigrated to the US to source weapons for the IRA's 1956-62 border campaign. That made him the right man in the right place for the start of the Troubles in 1969. So prolific were his activities from then until the FBI shut him down in 1981, that the Bureau had set up a task force to counter just Irish paramilitaries; and so widespread, lucrative and long-established were the various fund-raising initiatives amongst Irish Americans throughout the country, that millions of dollars were in play routinely. By the time of Harrison's arrest, my open-source research suggested that he'd provided about two and a half thousand weapons to the IRA and maybe a million rounds of ammunition. That's potentially a lot of dead soldiers.

But the Barretts came in the post-Harrison era, very much so, and articles I had read suggested that at least two of them had been bought and shipped six months into the Provos' seventeen-month-long ceasefire. They were part of a consignment sold by a Cuban living in Cleveland, Ohio, to an Irishman who subsequently shipped them home to the Republic of Ireland. And yet the first Barrett to be shipped, I reckoned, based on articles I'd found in the Los Angeles Times and several other newspapers and magazines, had probably been smuggled to Ireland by a man called Martin Quigley, just before his arrest in Pennsylvania in 1989. Quigley had been studying computing at a university there, as part of a wider PIRA scheme to combat British Army counter-measures against radio-controlled bombs, but he'd got caught up in a weapons procurement scam at the same time.

And then yet another Barrett had been shipped in pieces from Chicago to Dublin, where it had been re-assembled and passed to the South Armagh Brigade. And so on. The Kennedys agreed that the supply of funds and weapons to Ireland from America - where both were so freely available – was a story as old as the hills, but the Barretts specifically had written a new and terrifying chapter into the annals of the Troubles that they felt was worthy of closer inspection. Sarah felt sure the faculty's Dissertations Committee would agree, and Charlie thought that at least someone in HQNI would be supportive as well. Our review of the other two main components went much the same way, and at a little after 10 pm Sarah dropped me back off at my dorm with a smile and a 'Well done'.

Well done indeed, and I shared my promising news with George over a beer before we both turned in. 'So that had been the easy part', he noted: all the discussions and the scoping and the design. Then all I had to do was turn my bright ideas and eager intent into tangible results. He laughed and readied me for sleep with a variation of one of my own favourite sayings: 'Hey, your dissertation's where you're at fellah - get on with it.'

...From Little Acorns Grow

It was Úna who'd first pounced on the Patrick McCormac connection in America as another source for my research, but there again it was only Úna who'd retained any contact with him. That was largely because it was also Úna who'd calmed him down, poured him a stiff drink and then put him on the train to Belfast after his brush with the masked Provos in the Derrybeg in 1984.

He'd always said how grateful he was, and so she'd quickly upgraded their Christmas cards-only friendship and arranged for my bundles of newspapers and magazines. But then she'd gone one better, and asked if he'd host me for a research visit the following summer if she paid for my flights to and from the States?

'Absolutely,' was his immediate reply – it would give him enormous street cred and a chance to show off his peeps - and so she handed that off to me to turn into a reality in the coming months. We agreed on August 2002, and if George Kennedy could find the funds he was invited too. Just having an Irish youth called

Kennedy staying with him in Boston got Patrick the Fourth pretty excited, and he felt sure there must be some connection to JFK if he dug around back far enough.

That spurred George on to get a part-time job and he tried to talk me into it as well. But I already had one - it was Maria - and between her, my main coursework, research for my dissertation, rugby and the meagre pickings of a non-Maria-based social life, I didn't reckon I could fit anything else in. I was only getting home every other month as it was, and so that's about how often I saw Úna too; but we spoke on my mobile every few days, and at least once a month she'd come into Belfast to hook-up with me, or with me and Maria, for a meal and a drink.

George started saving his pennies as a barman in one of the pubs in the city centre; but after sorting a couple of nasty incidents in his own inimitable style, they offered him twice as much to be a bouncer and so he was set. At one point he was earning so much he started to think twice about his studies and his plans for the future, but then he got a B+ on a key assignment and he suddenly saw the world more clearly again. And I worked with him when I was short of cash, so we certainly weren't as poor in our second year as we had been in our first.

At last our long awaited spring arrived, and everything in life seemed a little brighter. I got an initial response from HQNI via Charlie Kennedy, and I was told that an officer from the RAEC, the Royal Army Educational Corps, would be in touch with me via Sarah Kennedy in due course. That was great news, and Sarah was even more excited than I was, but in due course turned out to be another two months further down the road. The Peace Process was lurching through its inevitable growing pains, and so staff officers at HQNI were clearly under some pressure.

A meeting was eventually arranged for Monday the 2nd of July, but on the 1st David Trimble quit as Northern Ireland's First Minister and so my meeting was postponed. Trimble called upon Tony Blair, the British Prime Minister, to suspend the Northern

Ireland Assembly and the other institutions set up under the Good Friday Agreement, until or unless the political deadlock could be broken and there was clear progress on the decommissioning of PIRA weapons. Powerful stuff, and so trivia like my request got moved to one side - but it wasn't ignored altogether. And so my meeting was eventually re-arranged, rather ominously, for Friday the 13th of July. But then, when that week saw the worst rioting in Belfast since the IRA Hunger Strike twenty years earlier, it was postponed yet again until the Wednesday the 1st of August.

The appointed day duly arrived and Sarah Kennedy drove me to Thiepval Barracks in Lisburn, where we were met by her husband Charlie and eventually walked into the HQNI compound itself. Charlie sorted all the temporary passes and led the way, then he left us to it and went off to meet with others elsewhere in the big glass-fronted building. After a short wait Sarah and I were collected by a pretty young corporal, led out of the main building, taken across the road and into a conference room in a sprawling two-floor complex of Portacabins opposite. She brought us coffee and biscuits and then went to find the RAEC captain who was going to talk to me.

He arrived soon afterwards. There was no more waiting – which impressed me, we could see they were all pretty busy – and he introduced himself as Eric Lawrence. He had a strong and reassuring handshake, a never-ending forehead, and eyes that could have floodlit a rugby match. He was a thin, wiry man, but no less imposing for that, and his smile suggested that the IRA were as good as beaten already. He was wearing what Sarah later told me was barrack-dress uniform, so with a short-sleeved, open-necked shirt, no tie, no medals, no ribbons, and so no signs of the sort of military paraphernalia which I'd expected. But this was the British Army of course, and I already knew from growing up in Newry that they weren't big on badges or flashes and baubles.

He didn't know Sarah, or her husband Charlie he said, and he greeted us both affably and then sat us back down behind our coffees. The biscuits were already gone. I was a student, what more can I tell you? He put my letter and my synopsis down in front of him, which he said he'd read, and then he apologised for the two postponements before continuing.

"I'm really sorry this is only just happening," he said, "but my understanding is that you're engaged in your research now and that your crucial year will be next year, so hopefully we haven't held you up too much. Well, next year as in commencing in September of course."

"Yes," I said. Sarah smiled and nodded her agreement.

"And Mrs Kennedy, I presume," he smiled back at her, "is your supervisor for your dissertation? I know she's not actually one of your teachers."

"Correct," I answered.

"Good, well like I said, I'm sorry for the delays, but it's pretty busy around here these days trying to cover all the options. You know, more conflict, no conflict; Northern Ireland Assembly, no Assembly; IRA weapons, no IRA weapons..." he chuckled gently after he'd said it and we were too polite to answer, "but we're all getting dragged into the staffing of this many-headed monster at the moment, whatever our day jobs are."

"I can imagine," Sarah said.

"Yes, well," he smiled, "it's interesting times for those that are interested, but I'm afraid no-one from the Provisional IRA has yet handed-in their Barrett rifles; so your project might be a lot more topical than you realise."

"Right," I stuttered, "is that a problem?"

"No, not at all," he shook his head, "but it really might attract wider interest than just earning you your degree."

"I'm sure it will," Sarah piped up, "I've been amazed at some of the thing's Neill's turned up already, just from all the material he's amassed from the US."

"Yes, I saw that in Neill's synopsis he produced for you back in March." He moved his copy to the top of the documents in front of him. "Your husband sent me a copy for that first meeting in July, which of course was postponed; but some of that, surely," he tapped the paper in front of him, "is from official US sources, isn't it? And Neill's got some sort of a relation working in the government there, is that right?"

"No, it's all just from papers and magazines and things," she answered, "Charlie and I were amazed. But in a country where you can buy guns over the counter like cigarettes, well I suppose they're far more open about who they've been sold to as well."

"I guess," said Lawrence.

"And no," Sarah continued, "Neill's relative is hardly that, he's six or seven generations down the line..."

"Seven," I added, "his ancestors left Newry in 1846."

"Right..." Sarah continued, "and he was just a junior staffer back in the Reagan Administration, but I don't think he's anything to do with the government anymore, is he Neill?"

"No, not anymore," I shook my head, "he's a realtor now, which I think is like an estate agent."

"I see," said Captain Lawrence, nodding, "and so not really a direct relative either then?"

"No..." Sarah continued, "not at all, so what Neill's pulled together already is quite remarkable."

"Oh, agreed," said Lawrence, "and I've got to say, the way you've structured and written your synopsis for Mrs Kennedy, Neill, has impressed me too. It's a good bit better..." he chuckled, "than some of the things I'm having to staff now from some very senior officers. Huh, well done you, I don't suppose you want a job in HQNI do you?"

We all laughed, but I'm not entirely sure he was joking.

"So," he carried on, "here's what I suggest. I've allowed an hour for this meeting, if you two have the time for that?"

We both nodded.

"And so in that time there's a good few questions I need to ask you, vis-à-vis security and so on..."

"Yeah, especially seeing as I'm from the Derrybeg," I added helpfully; although I'm not sure it was that helpful.

"Right," Lawrence laughed, "well first let me assure you that's *not* a problem, Neill, but it does make you more than a little unusual around here, I have to say."

We all laughed out loud again, but Sarah and I a little less confidently this time.

"And then, after that," Captain Lawrence continued, "that may not leave much time for talking through your dissertation in any detail."

"Oh..." I murmured.

"So, if I might make another suggestion," he went on, "why don't we arrange for you to come here again next week, but for a whole morning or an afternoon this time; and then maybe, with Mrs Kennedy's blessing," he looked keenly at Sarah, "I might be able to help you in some way with the academic aspects of it too. You know, a second opinion sort of thing, but from a military point of view; although I wouldn't dream of contradicting Mrs Kennedy over anything..."

"Sarah," she interjected, "please call me Sarah."

"Oh right, but I can promise you that Sarah. I won't meddle at all. I'm not embedded in the academic machinery at Queen's like you are, and my last degree was a few years ago..."

"No, not at all, I'm sure that would be a great help, thank you," she said, "and I'm pretty sure Neill would appreciate it?"

"Absolutely," I grinned. "More help the better."

"Well not necessarily," he laughed, "that's not been my experience. Your questions should always start and finish with Sarah here, but I'll muck in and help out in any way I can."

"Please do, Neill's right," Sarah nodded. He nodded back.

"So let me get on with all my questions for now then," said Lawrence, "and then we can really drill down into your research material and your wish list from us next time we meet."

"Sounds good to me," I said, and I looked across at Sarah for moral support. She was nodding enthusiastically.

"But I do have one question, Neill," he added, "while I've got you sitting here, and which occurred to me when I re-read your synopsis; because it's sort of connected to some issues were having to work through at the moment."

"Go on," I said, fascinated.

"I mean, seeing as you've done all this work and given this so much thought, and you're obviously highly intelligent..."

"Oh, I don't know about that," I blushed.

"Oh you are, Neill, that wasn't just an opinion," he tapped my synopsis again, "so I wanted to pick your brains on something as a completely independent yet enlightened observer."

"OK, if I can help I will."

Sarah shrugged with a raised-eyebrow, but she looked as fascinated to see what was coming as I was.

"Well," Lawrence continued, "based on the huge amount of stuff you seem to have read from the States in recent months, I wonder if you can suggest why, or indeed if, you think the IRA might have most of their weapons dumps in the South? Or maybe I just mean their biggest. It was one of your conclusions, if you recall, and you also alluded to it several times."

"Yeah, right, and er, no, no I can't, based on anything I've read, but I do have my own theory about that though. On, y'know, like their *deep*, long term dumps maybe..."

"Go on," Captain Lawrence nodded thoughtfully.

"Well I guess it's just basic maths really, it's not like complex analysis or anything..."

"OK, but tell me your theory," he urged me on. Sarah was waiting expectantly too. She hadn't heard my thoughts on this; only George had, and he had agreed.

"Um, well I reckon because the Republic of Ireland is about three times the land mass of Northern Ireland, and it's a lot less populated in places as well; and because there's three or four times more security forces dealing with the Troubles in the North than in the South..."

"More than that, in fact," said Lawrence.

"Right, well," I continued, "then surely that means there's six or seven times more likelihood of finding things in Northern Ireland than in the South. Right? And probably even more chance than that in real terms, just because of the sheer amount and sophistication of your equipment and procedures in the North. I mean, it's been over thirty years now, and billions of pounds' worth of effort and tactics I would imagine..."

"Hmm, interesting," Lawrence nodded slowly, "some of that's absolutely right, and *all* of it's very thought-provoking," he added thoughtfully. "But, and I have to ask you this obviously – because this is where living in the Derrybeg might be relevant – are you sure this is just your theory, and not based in any way on something you've heard over the years."

"God no," I chuckled, but it was a nervous laugh and I saw immediately what he was asking, "no, I've never heard anything like that, ever, and y'know, I don't have any mates like that. Not a one, I can assure you."

"No, no," he smiled and reassured me, "I can believe that; we *know* that most people are nothing whatsoever to do with it all, even in the Derrybeg, and I've got to tell you it's a rare treat to be able to sit and share such thoughts with someone from that environment, but I just had to be sure this wasn't based on more than just your own deductions."

"No, it's all just in my head, I promise you."

"And I believe you," he said, "which is why I really am looking forward to going through your research material with you now next time. That's quite a picture you're painting there."

"Aye, I promise you... just struck me as obvious I suppose. Y'know, if you could hide everything in a kid's playground or in a cemetery, which one would you choose? So I thought that was a no brainer."

"Well," he laughed, "I've never heard Northern Ireland described as a kid's playground before, but I can't fault your logic."

There was a short pause while we all smiled smugly at each other, then Lawrence took up the reins again.

"So right then, before I crack on with these other questions though, can I rustle you two up some more coffee and biscuits?"

"Yes please," said Sarah. I nodded my agreement, and much to my delight Captain Lawrence went off to find the pretty-looking corporal again. Without meaning to be cruel, her uniform fitted her much better than his did.

Now I don't know how closely you've been following this particular story, but it may not surprise you to learn that Captain Eric Lawrence wasn't exactly who or what he claimed to be. His rank and name were real, I found out from JC in 2010, but not his real job or his cap badge. He was in fact from JC's organisation, although over the next eighteen months he did everything he said he would and more; and had JC not been deployed in the Balkans at the time he said he would have met me instead of Lawrence. And it probably won't surprise you either to learn that Lawrence already knew the answer to his 'Weapons dumps in the South' inquiry, but that had been a test question for me. It would appear I passed, because then several other people took an interest in me whenever I visited HQNI in the coming months.

One was a woman called Emily Rankin, or 'Em' as she liked to be called. Eric Lawrence introduced me to her in the first week of September when she just happened to track him down to the conference room where we were meeting. She was after a lesson plan he'd used the day before for an Educational Promotion class – on the cooperation between international terror groups – and when Eric told her who I was and what we were discussing, she stayed and chatted for half an hour. She was a colleague, Eric said, although that day she'd been teaching in civilian clothes, and she said she'd love to see my dissertation once it was finished.

I agreed of course, and then the three of us chatted over coffee about what Eric described to her as my 'thoughts on IRA gun-running'. He explained also the scarcely believable collection of open-source research material I'd been able to amass from the States. Em asked out of interest did my latest American articles include anything about the three Provisional IRA men arrested in Bogotá two weeks earlier, and who had since been charged by the Colombians with training guerrillas from the FARC. I answered that yes, several of them did, and that one magazine had reported that they'd worked with the rebels in the south of the country for over five weeks, training them in the use of explosives and other tactics. And, I added, according to the Colombian army, a fourth IRA man had been arrested some days later.

Em claimed not to know about the fourth man and so I told her what I'd learned, but then we went on to have an entirely separate conversation about three suspected Real IRA men who'd been extradited from Slovakia for planning to buy weapons. She seemed really interested in everything I had to say, and eventually she told me I was 'a font of useful information'. On the half hour though she said she had to go, but she became a regular visitor to my sessions with Eric in the coming months and we often spent as much time talking about Queen's, my courses, and education in the round, as we did about international terrorism and my project specifically. Following my graduation the next year, however, Em said she had a huge favour to ask: could she have her own copy of my finished dissertation?

Of course, I replied, and I gave one to Eric Lawrence for the Garrison Library as well; but months later Em insisted on taking me out for a farewell lunch and to say thank you. Of course I accepted that too, and I should imagine by now you'll be even less surprised to learn that Emily Rankin wasn't quite what she said she was either; and it was she, who towards the end of lunch, dropped her cover and recruited me into the Security Service.

Great oaks from little acorns do indeed grow.

The only other highlight of the first nine months of 2001 was George and I playing rugby against Blackrock College the weekend after I met Em Rankin. It was the first time we'd played them since 1997, but this time we'd been starting-picks for the Queen's Firsts, rather than short notice emergency replacements for an injury-blighted Dundalk. It was a good feeling and a great game, and afterwards we were hoping to find Tommy Bray among the supporters. We didn't.

Tommy Bray had been the teenage prodigy in the last game who'd given us such a lesson on running searingly straight lines and tackling like a demon; but he was long gone according to a couple of the guys in their team. They said he'd just completed a four-year law degree at Trinity College Dublin (at his father's urging no doubt), and he was about to join the Irish Army and work his way into the Army Ranger Wing, their Special Forces. That was hardly a surprise, and neither of us doubted for an instant that he would make it. God help his would-be enemies.

And thus, notwithstanding all the hard work I knew I was going to have to put into the rest of 2001, the following year and my trip to the States were looking pretty good before they had even started. I said precisely that on separate occasions to no less than George, Úna, Maria, Sarah Kennedy, Eric Lawrence and my parents. But that, of course, was a smug thought I'd allowed myself to have before we'd got too far into September.

My bad...

Where's The Arizona?

Just before 3 pm on a Tuesday afternoon I was deep in study, even deeper in thought, and deeper still inside the Seamus Heaney Library at Queen's. It was one of my numerous daytime visits to our on-campus home from home, and for once I wasn't grazing in the canteen at the same time. My night-time vigils there were even more frequent, and some evenings only the endless coffee and the snack machines kept me going. As it was I'd not long eaten, and I was actually reading something important. I'd just turned a bewildering page and I was concentrating hard on a conclusion I didn't entirely agree with, when my mobile phone vibrated abruptly in my pocket.

I hardly ever got calls on it during the day, and so it made me jump. Not least of all because I was in a quiet zone, and although I had the ringer turned off I still felt guilty. It was a library after all... and I was going to have to speak or let it ring out. Or more accurately, let it *throb* out. I did the latter.

In fact, I pondered, I only ever got calls on it from one of a dozen or so people period. Pretty much only from Úna, Maria, George, or one of a handful of people from our year. My parents never called it. Jees, I think my mum still believed the radiation it emitted was going to make me sterile, and at the end of a lot of the more salacious weeks on campus I hoped she was right. So as I fumbled around in my jeans pocket to extract my phone, I wondered which of them it had been.

Before I could find out it vibrated again, and this time I could sense its urgency just from its wild convulsions in my hand. I took it outside as quickly and quietly as I could and waited for it to ring a third time. It did so almost immediately.

"Hello?" I said.

"Where are you?" George's unmistakable voice boomed.

"In the library…"

"Come to the TV room now. Quick as you can." Then he hung up without further explanation.

None was necessary, just from the tone of his voice, and in the two minutes it took me to get there I imagined all manner of ways in which the Provisional IRA might have broken their latest fifty-months-old ceasefire. Despite the raw urgency of George's demand, however, I knew it wasn't some dire message of personal bereavement or concern; because had it been, he would have swum the Irish Sea to tell me to my face.

No, it was something equally shocking, I felt sure, but something detached and remote from us that demanded he not move away from the television. What historic building in London I wondered, or what royal or other notable personage who'd pressed the flesh of the people rather too closely, was no more?

Well that at least was answered the moment I stepped into the TV room, and it was clearly neither of those; because about forty stunned people were stood in a half-circle watching live video of what was obviously New York from a circling helicopter. I recognised both the Empire State and Chrysler buildings in the

251

first few seconds. There was smoke billowing from the top of a skyscraper and I thought at first I was seeing a real-life rendering of the movie *Towering Inferno*. George saw me enter and slid around behind all the others to talk to me at the back of the room. Before he could tell me what was going on, one of our study group at the front hollered to me.

"Jesus Neill, come and friggin' watch this. Do you think it's terrorists?"

"Is what terrorists?" I asked George.

"A plane's flown straight into the World Trade Center in New York. I mean smack into it, dead centre..."

"What, a light aircraft you mean...?"

"No, an airliner..."

"An *airliner!?*" I repeated uselessly. George's face provided the only answer I needed.

"Crashed into it? Or flew into it?" I asked instinctively.

"What's the difference?" one of our mates asked.

"Flew into it," George replied with absolute confidence. He knew exactly what I was getting at. "Flat and level, dead centre, fully under control, and at full speed by the looks of it."

"Full speed?" I queried, "what, no flaps or anything?"

"None," George nodded angrily, "and at about three times normal approach speed for a landing I reckon; and y'know, it's Manhattan for God's sake, there *is* no friggin' runway."

"Terrorists then," I said without hesitation.

"How'd you know that?" the mate demanded.

"Coz it can't be anything else," George snapped.

"Why not? Can't it just have crashed?" our naïve but well-intentioned mate tried again, "Jesus, airliners crash all the time..."

"Not into pencil thin buildings in Manhattan," I shook my head, "at three times their normal speed and in a restricted area. That's some feat of flying even if the pilot *meant* to do it, but with all the safety systems they've got on board that thing there's no way in the world that was just an accident."

"I reckon you're jumping to conclusions," said another towards the front, "you two see terrorists everywhere."

"Only when there's signs all around you, Jesus," George protested, "you listen to Neill Mac, and see if he's not right."

"The Taliban then," someone shouted from the front.

"Don't be stupid, not in New York," hollered another.

"Then maybe it *is* just a crash?" said a third.

"What do you think?" George asked me quietly.

"Not the Taliban... I don't think, but some other Middle-Eastern group right enough. I reckon that crowd that tried to sink the *USS Cole* in Yemen last year... al-Qaeda or something."

"The crowd that issued a fatwa against America?"

"Aye, them, two or three years ago, and they tried to blow-up the US embassies in Africa too, remember."

"Jesus... y'reckon?"

"Yeah, and a bunch of jihadists tried to blow that place up once before, remember," someone else weighed-in, "about eight or nine years ago."

An immediate debate broke out amongst all those present. I didn't join in, because no sooner had they started baying at each other than the TV news re-played the video of American Airlines Flight 11 striking the North Tower between floors ninety-four and ninety-nine. I was the only one in the room who hadn't already seen it, remember, and no matter how loud all the others were chattering I couldn't hear a thing. I was for the moment deaf, dumb, paralysed and transfixed.

'Shocked' hardly describes the sensation that swept over me, and for a moment I thought I felt myself faint... and yet I'd clearly remained conscious and standing. I swear I felt the blood surge through me like a massive blush, starting with my ears, mouth, neck and chest, and then cascading down through my stunned body to my leaden feet. I tried to put a hand to my gaping mouth, but my arms wouldn't move. Then before I regained full control of my senses the room fell stunned and silent again, as the fleeting outline of United Airlines Flight 175 sped into the picture and slammed even faster into the second tower. A huge arc of flame and debris inscribed itself along the plane's now imaginary route, and a massive fireball obscured the building.

For an instant we had all thought we were watching yet another replay but from a different angle, but as it dawned on everyone that we'd just seen a second airliner strike the other tower... then the wailing and the gasps started anew.

"Oh my God, there's another one," wailed someone.

"Jesus, they're going to destroy New York," said another.

"Who the fuck's *they*?" cried a third, "Neill's right."

For the most part only people's jaws were moving, some in silence and some with gasps or unanswerable questions, but every other muscle in the room seemed frozen at the moment of the second impact.

"Oh God, oh God, oh God... all those people," a female voice suddenly sobbed from the far side of the room.

"Jesus Neill," George exclaimed, "she's right, do you reckon there were people in there?"

"In that plane?"

"Aye."

"Yeah, in both of them," I stammered, "and thousands in those buildings too."

"Oh hell no..." was all he could say in response.

The whole room continued to watch in what passed for stunned silence, with just the odd groan or an expletive for a commentary. For a bunch of the nation's brightest young things, no-one could find a single intelligible word to describe what they were seeing or feeling. Some sat down in shock, some wrung their hands in despair, and a few turned in circles to stare at others but for no obvious reason. You could tell most of the Catholics in the room – but not me – because they were crossing themselves and muttering quietly to their clearly helpless God.

Then after maybe twenty minutes a new viewer burst into the room, and although she moved quietly towards the television and the front of the crowd her eyes and cheeks were streaming tears. She would be the main focus of the next half an hour. Her and the gruesome spectacle on the screen, as scores of people trapped above the flames were clearly starting to jump hundreds of metres to their death.

"Lizzy..." someone called to her to distract her from the grotesque images, and then he forced his way to her side.

"Oh my God," Lizzy murmured, "my uncle's in there."

With the realisation that the room suddenly had a casualty in its midst, as opposed to a rabble of helpless and guilty-looking voyeurs, a small posse of friends and Samaritans gathered around her to console her and establish details.

"Where is he?" asked one.

"Are you sure he's in there?" tried another.

"I don't know," Lizzy sniffed optimistically, "he said there's loads of buildings to the World Trade Center, but I don't know which one he works in."

"He might be OK then," someone shouted.

"He'll be OK anyway," shouted another, "unless he was right up there at the top. Hey, chances are he's somewhere else."

"Or already out of there," the first tried again.

And so Lizzy was lifted up and then dashed back down for the next twenty minutes, until it eventually dawned on someone to be proactive and get her moving.

"We'll call him," shouted the helpful voice from a flank. "Do you have any numbers?"

"Back in my room..." Lizzy mumbled.

"Jesus, you're kidding," said a young fellah with a South Belfast accent, "do y'know how many thousands of calls will be clogging up New York right now? Millions probably."

The girl who'd suggested calling in the first place shot him a vicious look, and then she pulled Lizzy away and towards the door with more words of encouragement.

"Come on," she said, "let's go and see what we can do with those phone numbers anyway. Someone'll know something."

As she left the room my final guilty thought on her plight was that there must have been thousands of similar scenes being played out in front of televisions right across America, and that their anguish must have been many times worse. In New York especially, I shuddered, where countless frightened loved-ones must have been glancing at an indentation in an empty chair, or at a hopeful telephone hanging feebly on the wall, and then – reluctantly - back at the horrific pictures on their screens. And were there still more attacks happening somewhere else, I wondered? Were these the only two, or were they two of many? My thoughts skipped ahead to Boston next year, and I wondered if we'd still go? And should I get a black tie from somewhere?

Once Lizzy and her escorts had left the room, a new debate had started. Someone guesstimated that there might be as many as five thousand people killed in the various buildings nearby; and another speculated that it might be even more, and that several hundred were probably trapped in the lower floors. At that point, maybe fifty minutes after the second plane had struck, a young engineering postgraduate student called Shannon added her two penn'orth, and so the discussion began anew.

"Well they're dead if they are," she said gravely, "and any emergency services who are in there with them, because I reckon those buildings are going to collapse sometime soon."

"Surely they won't," said another.

"Surely they will," Shannon persisted, "they must."

"Why?"

"Don't forget it's not only shit that flows downhill," she answered matter-of-factly. "There's tons of burning aviation fuel, and God knows what else by now, cascading its way down through those buildings. I mean, I know we can't see it but it's happening. Jesus, two whole airliners just exploded inside of there... and the temperatures must be astronomical."

"I guess," said one of her doubters, "but they still won't collapse, surely? You know, if they survived the impact in the first place an' all?"

"Well I hope to God you're right, but I doubt it," Shannon said. "I don't know what the internal layout of those two towers is, but they've got an enormous external steel skeleton. That much I do know. And if that gets superheated, at some point it'll just wilt and collapse. It'll have to."

"Really?" someone gasped.

"Really," said Shannon. "You're talking about thousands of tons of burning rubble now, being held up by just superheated metal stilts... just imagine it."

George and I looked at each other, and I think we'd both just been thinking something similar. And although I could follow what she was saying, I just couldn't get my mind around what we were looking at and so I chose not to believe her.

Six minutes later, she was proved absolutely right.

As if watching the two planes engulf the towers in flame wasn't traumatic enough, watching the buildings then plunge and fold-in on themselves was even more shocking. When the North Tower succumbed and was peeled to the ground like an overripe banana, still more cries and wails filled our TV Room; and the thousands of tons of dust seen boiling through the streets and alleyways below caused one young guy to be physically sick. That was the beginning of the break-up of our impromptu assembly, and once we'd cleaned-up his puke people went off to find other TVs elsewhere in smaller groups.

As George and I backed towards the door and took one final look at the mayhem in New York, he muttered:

"Jesus Neill, where's the Arizona in all of this?"

"The what?"

"The Arizona, the battleship… where the hell is it?"

"What? I don't get you," I snapped, suddenly angry, "what the hell are you on about?"

"Where in all that rubble and dust is the *USS Arizona*?" he shook his head slowly. George often spoke in riddles, but he'd stumped me this time. I knew he wasn't making light of things, he was trying to make a point, but I didn't get it.

"I mean this is Pearl Harbor all over again," he said.

"Oh, I get what you mean now…"

"Like total destruction out of nowhere. From out of the sky and without any warning. Fuck Neill, so do you reckon they'll have awakened a sleeping giant again too?"

"God, I don't know," I mumbled.

"I mean…" George stumbled across his words like the victims in the rubble, "what do you think they'll do about this?"

"America? I don't know," I repeated.

"But shit, there's gonna be a war with someone."

"I guess."

And after having grown up in the middle of a war that was never called a war – except by the Provos – and after watching a nation tiptoe around the law, be mindful of people's civil rights, respect the integrity of Ireland's borders and the sanctity of its non-combatants… that's the security forces I mean, because those are things the terrorists never did… then I wasn't sure what the Bush Administration would do next. Revenge I hoped… and although I trusted it would be done within the Rules of War, I hoped it would be waged on a biblical scale.

It hadn't occurred to me until what George had just said that we might be on the cusp of a real war. An honest to God shooting war, where events on the scale of Pearl Harbor would be avenged by whole armies and with total commitment. And so I wondered what might be our part in such a general mobilisation; and if not total war, then I wondered what did I want *my* part to be in preventing such carnage in the future?

Beyond Ground Zero

The post-9/11 world was different. There's no other way to describe it, and within a few weeks it was clear that things were never going to change back. Nothing was ever going to be quite the same again. It must have felt the same for tens of millions right after World War II, but on an even bigger scale. It was probably even worse after World War I, but back then you didn't share it with the victims in your own living room. People were hardier back then, and that had been a different sort of shock, which one dealt with alone and carried with you for evermore.

And so the post-9/11 world was somehow greyer, starker and less intimate. Even those who hadn't been effected by it and who claimed they didn't care, couldn't just pretend it hadn't happened. Thanks to our 21st Century media, it reached into lives and our nightmares and our living rooms, and touched everything and everyone with its bony white fingers of death - and it left them colder and somehow contaminated.

Even Úna was depressed for a while – something I'd never seen before – and it left the whole of the Free World in what she described as 'A state of more and less'... a world that was more stern, uncertain and overbearing, yet less trusting, inclusive and tolerant. The only good thing to come out of it in the short term was that my brother Éamon sought me out for a pint in 'The Bot', in the Botanic Inn on Malone Road. He brought my sister Maud and her husband along with him, but if anything we agreed even less on the rights and wrongs of the world than before we'd all left home; and so it wasn't something we ever repeated. Sure, we all lived in Belfast for the time being, but in terms of who should be entrusted with sculpting our future, then we might well have been spawned on different planets.

For a start the Peace Process in Ireland was spurred on immeasurably, and George and I reckoned correctly that funds for the IRA from the States would dry-up virtually overnight. At the very least they'd slow to a trickle, and I wondered what sort of a reception we would get in Boston the next summer. There was a strange buzz around Queen's, and for a while anyone who was in any way studying international conflict or terrorism took centre stage. But then soon after the US-led invasion of Afghanistan a month later, and once the horror of 9/11 itself started to recede in people's minds, the pacifists came to the fore again. But that, in my experience, is pretty much like student bodies everywhere.

All hungry young minds dream of a liberal Utopia, and most journalists and wealthy actors too I reckon (it's amazing how fame and fortune brings inalienable wisdom and humility. They should try hunger, rape and subjugation). Me too, and of a world without war or violence of any kind. But unlike most of them, I also weigh my dreams of a perfect world against the bestiality and wanton violence of the real world I've been forced to grow up in; and so I know there must also be resolute forces of law and order. George unsurprisingly agreed, as did a reassuring number of the others in our sphere, and it was about now that he started to become known as *King George,* because of his forthright views on justice and his irrefutable reign on the rugby pitch.

The reception I got from Captain Lawrence and others at HQNI changed too. It was a subtle change, and not one that anyone brought up and actually discussed on any of my visits, but I felt more included and more trusted when I next went back. Maybe it was something Lawrence or Emily Rankin had said after our last meeting – now with hindsight I know who she actually was – but I think it's just that the world had changed, and I, irrespective of where I was born and raised, was suddenly perceived as being unquestionably in their corner. They realised immediately I was outspokenly on their side.

Emily was the first to really want to talk about 9/11 in fact, and she correctly guessed that because of the amount of American publications I'd read I was actually more knowledgeable about al-Qaeda than were most of the military community back then. For a start I seemed to know a fair bit about its exiled Saudi Arabian leader, Osama bin Laden, when few others had even heard of him. And when I then brought in over three hundred articles of interest and allowed her and Eric Lawrence to photocopy them, I was treated as virtually a part of their team. Hey, it had immediate benefits for the research, planning and prep of my dissertation, and so I didn't really think about it beyond the next meeting.

It's amusing when I look back though, and more than a little embarrassing, that 'the team' I suddenly felt more a part of seemed to have relatively little to do with educating soldiers, and more to do with informing intelligence officers. I feel absurdly naïve with hindsight, but back then I simply felt privileged and lucky to be making so much progress with my studies and my new associates. In my defence though, no-one ever asked me anything about Newry, the Derrybeg or the Provos, nor even anything about the Dissidents still active in South Armagh, and so it never occurred to me that I was being cultivated. Duh. Life, remember, is where you're at – no matter how unlikely it might sometimes seem – get on with it.

The first breakthrough at HQNI was when Eric Lawrence and a couple of Skill At Arms instructors took me to the ranges at Ballykinler. There, after ninety minutes of what they called 'dry training', they laid me down behind a Barrett .50 and had me fire at targets at two hundred metres. The first thing that struck me was the sheer size of the beast. It was over twice the length of the rifles I'd seen the soldiers carrying in South Armagh, and resting as it did on a bipod it looked more like the M-60 machine gun I'd seen in a Provo roadblock with Úna just below Ballsmill – except longer. The M82 I fired had a twenty-nine-inch fluted barrel. The next thing that struck me was the noise; the first shot I fired sounded more like a canon than any rifle I'd ever heard. But the recoil... not so much. Despite never having fired any sort of a rifle before, I hit all five targets with embarrassing ease.

Then they raised some different targets at four hundred metres, and although I missed the first one – high and very slightly right – I hit the next four dead centre. Then they re-loaded the ten-round magazine with just five rounds and had me shoot at a single target, which would fall when hit, at six hundred metres. They told me to aim at the centre base of the target, and five times out of five there was a mighty *crump* of the rifle and the target fell back as if mortally wounded and in slow motion. Then they'd bring it back up for me to knock down again.

They had two things left to show me.

The first involved another five rounds fired at yet another fall-when-hit target, but this time at a thousand metres. That was to show me how even a novice could do lethal damage with this weapon, and the South Armagh snipers had been far from novices. Before I fired they told me that the maximum effective range of the weapon was eighteen hundred metres. That's its *effective* range I marvelled, of just over a mile, but they added that the round would carry with lethal kinetic energy for six thousand and eight hundred metres... that's four and-a-quarter miles! I missed the first two, just, and they spotted for me with binos and corrected my point of aim; but I knocked the next three down easily, a full and satisfying second or more after each round had left the muzzle. And that sound... that amazingly reassuring sound of might and invincibility, will stay with me forever.

But then the next thing actually unnerved me. The final thing... and undoubtedly the last word. When I'd done firing one of the two instructors took a giant watermelon out to a hundred metres and set it down in the middle of the range. Then he came back, casually loaded the Barrett and shot it. The effect of that will also stay with me forever – Google it if you're curious – and I was overwhelmingly thankful that the soldier I'd seen killed by a Barrett in Bessbrook hadn't been shot in the head.

Two months later and with graphic images of exploding watermelons still seared into my brain, Eric Lawrence called me to say they'd found three soldiers for me to interview. We agreed a day the following week and Charlie Kennedy picked me up and drove me to HQNI. Eric Lawrence wasn't available and so Emily Rankin sat-in with me as agreed. Captain Lawrence had made it clear at the outset that even with HQNI's permission to interview any soldiers, they would have to be genuine volunteers; they couldn't simply be ordered to share their innermost thoughts about when they'd patrolled South Armagh several years earlier.

What they'd managed to come up with, Em told me, was a representative cross-section in terms of age, length of service and previous combat experience. The youngest was a twenty-six-year-old infanteer, who'd been twenty when he was based at Forkhill; the next was a twenty-eight-year-old dog handler, who'd been just twenty-one when he'd been deployed all over South Armagh by helicopter from Bessbrook Mill; and the last was a thirty-five-year-old warrant officer who'd been a platoon sergeant in Crossmaglen back in 1993; the year seven men were killed by the sniper teams in South Armagh, four of which were with a Barrett.

Despite their varying prior service and vastly different levels of combat experience, all three men told pretty much the same story: the Barrett undoubtedly had a more demoralising effect on troop morale than anything else they'd ever known. Even more, said two of them, than when they believed that their body-worn electronic counter-measures had not kept up with the latest IRA radio-controlled bomb technology. Other statements from two of the three were particularly significant I thought.

The first was from the search-dog handler, who for six months was terrified every time he jumped out of a helicopter into the lush green fields of South Armagh. *If* one of the Barretts was out there that day, he'd fret, then he was certain he would be in the crosshairs because he and his dog were a specialist agency and the Provos would know to kill him. And *if* he was in the crosshairs, he knew that the sniper couldn't miss and he couldn't possibly survive the massive forces involved in being hit.

And the second was the warrant officer, who'd seen it all before but had been a wise-old platoon sergeant patrolling daily in the capitol of Bandit Country: Crossmaglen. He said something very similar to the dog handler, when he declared:

"Jesus Neill, you saw what that thing could do when you watched it kill that young lad in Bessbrook. There were no half measures with that thing, and if you were hit... what was left of you stayed hit. And if *he* was out there that day, and if it was you he was aiming at, then you knew you were going to die. No maybe, no receiving just a flesh wound, special body armour or not."

I asked him the same questions that I'd asked the other two, but with several tours of South Armagh under his belt I found his answer to a question about the threat from IEDs particularly revealing. I asked him was he not just as fearful of being killed by one of the IRA's unbelievably powerful and effective Improvised Explosive Devices? His answer was hauntingly forthright.

"No, in a nutshell. Despite the fact we knew that was far more likely. The way we all felt about the bombs down there, was that if we got caught by one we just hoped it would be a biggun and that we'd be stood right next to it. And see if it was a firefight, well bring it on, and there's drills for that and we fancied our chances. But if it was that fucking Barrett, Neill, then Jees, that was something else. And if he was out there that day, well... then all bets were off and you just hoped he aimed for someone else but missed. Sounds cruel, and I know it doesn't sound very loyal to your mates, but that's the truth."

And it pretty much was the truth. Indeed, after all the terrorist prisoners were released in accordance with the Good Friday Agreement, one of the South Armagh snipers himself said, 'What's special about the Barrett is the huge kinetic energy... The bullet can just walk through a flak jacket.' Trust me, the soldiers had known that all along! But he was also right when he went on to say, 'South Armagh was the prime place to use such a weapon because of the availability of Brits. They came to dread it and that was part of its effectiveness.'

It would appear from my interviews that the soldiers had known that all along too, and the South Armagh man's succinct reflection would be the closing words of the final conclusion of my dissertation. Lest we forget.

Waifs and Wolfhounds

My 21st birthday in January 2002 was something of an anti-climax after the Europa extravaganza of the year before - and 9/11 was a bit to blame for that too - but it still involved Maria and a night of sin and debauchery nonetheless. Good job I was still more Samaritan than Catholic, and that my God-shaped hole was in those days being used to store data.

Because of the endless grind of my studies though, only two things really stand out to me from the early part of that year. The first was in April when Patrick McCormac IV sent me some newspaper cuttings from the US he thought I would be interested in, and coincidentally Emily Rankin called me the same day about the self-same news item. It concerned the head of the Colombian Army telling a congressional hearing in Washington DC, that at least seven IRA men had been in his country training FARC rebels;

and so Em and I met-up for lunch at The Empire Music Hall on Botanic Avenue the next day to compare notes.

And the second thing indirectly concerned Emily too, but I didn't know that at the time. In May, three members of the Real IRA from County Louth were jailed in London for thirty years following an MI5 sting operation. The Security Service personnel involved had posed as Iraqi intelligence officers and arms dealers, and for the first time ever I began to wonder if that was a vocation I might be suited for. I discussed it with George Kennedy, and he made two astute observations that pointed me heavily in that direction: He said that if the Troubles or anything like it ever kicked off again, then my South Armagh accent would be worth its weight in gold; and he added that for operations against almost any other target imaginable, he couldn't think of anyone less likely to be suspected of being 'a Brit' than a wild-eyed boy from Newry. Wise words from an impeccable source, and they lit a flame which flickered away for the rest of the year.

It's a subtle difference between fate and destiny, and, call it what you will, when Emily Rankin popped the question after I graduated I was pretty much trying to work out how I might best apply to join MI5 anyway. I call it providence. Clive Ellis had once called it serendipity. 'Twas karma I know now.

And then the warmer weather threatened and so did the marching season. I was glad I was going to be away for a large chunk of the summer, because as with the last couple of years in Belfast it was characterised by still more riots. Despite that I recall that I was struck by two strangely contradictory remarks from two united senior police officers. Although on closer inspection they weren't actually contradictory... and they showed both how far the Peace Process had come - and yet how far it still had to go.

The first suggested that the war with the Provisional IRA might truly be over: when in July, Belfast's top policeman praised its leading members, for quelling any threat of severe Republican violence during one of the most provocative Loyalist parades of the year. But the second showed that the bitter sectarianism that had spawned the Troubles in the first place still blighted Northern Ireland, when in August, and after rioting in East Belfast, the acting Chief Constable warned that his officers 'were at breaking point'. And yet, despite its grave implications, I had an unusually detached outlook on the second statement - from about three thousand miles away to be precise - because for the last three weeks of August, George and I would read such things over breakfast in our very own copies of the Boston Globe in America.

Úna dropped George and I off at Dublin Airport and we flew direct to Logan International on Saturday the 10th of August. We would be there with 'Patrick the Fourth', as we secretly called him, until the 31st. Patrick McCormac was by then forty-eight, just divorced, happy to be so and quite comfortably off. He lived in a well-furnished four-storey terraced home in the fashionable Back Bay area of the city's south-east side, tucked in behind the trees on Commonwealth Avenue and less than a minute from Boston Common and the Public Garden. He had four spare bedrooms and more bathrooms than he could possibly get around, so George and I had a room each and we wondered if we'd ever see each other. Hey, we joked, we were in Boston – enjoy it – but the Derrybeg it most certainly was not.

We actually got on with Pat the Fourth much better than we'd thought we would, and in his own environment he was a good laugh and a gracious host. He took our first week off from work to show us around, and our last so we could do a few things together, but he left us to our own devices for the middle week so we could crack-on with our research. More of that in a while.

We spent most of the first day learning our way around the public transport system and checking-out a couple of Patrick's favourite restaurants and diners. What with an extensive subway system (the first in America), and with rail, commuter rail, light rail, trolleys, buses, ferries and streetcars (the oldest continuously working streetcar system in the world), the Massachusetts Bay

Transport Authority – often referred to as 'The T' – made it pretty simple for even us to get around. Add to that that there were four subway stations on three different lines within just minutes of Patrick's home, then we were pretty self-sufficient from the off. Jet lag caught up with us that first afternoon though, and so we called a halt for the first day and re-charged our batteries for the second.

It was all pretty overwhelming in fact, and no matter how much of America we'd seen on the television or in the movies, nothing and no-one had fully prepared us for the sheer scale of things. The actual area of Boston was almost exactly twice that of Belfast, as was the population of the city at six hundred-thousand, but then its metropolitan area was home to more than four million people (Jees, the whole of Northern Ireland is less than two) and Greater Boston boasted over eight million. But probably the starkest contrast to a young man from the back and beyond was the skyline. While it's hardly New York, its Manhattan-like profile - with the Charles River and busy waterfronts on three sides - still bristles with more true skyscrapers than any city in the British Isles bar London. Yup, we were in the United States of America for the first time ever, and all around us was proof positive.

The next day saw us up and out pretty early for a breakfast of crispy bacon, scrambled eggs, pancakes and maple syrup. Hey, when in Rome... but the one thing we couldn't get our heads around for the first few days was how to order hot black tea with milk, not cream; and then to get it hot enough to properly brew the tea. Quite apart from which, very few people understood a fucking word we were saying. Tomato, tomayto; milk, cream; twit, twot... it was very easy to say things that no good Catholic boy should ever say and not even know we'd said it.

Pat the Fourth quickly became our interpreter, although if the truth be known he was bluffing most of the time as well. Still, our accents – understood or not – were quite the chick-magnet, and when Patrick realised there were going to be considerable fringe benefits for him as well, he started taking us to more and more places to meet more and more people.

On the fourth night, and once we'd got our jet lag tamed if not licked, we unintentionally resurrected the *Irony Brothers* for an impromptu 'The band's back together' one-off performance. But that was such a success in the various Irish bars Pat dragged us around afterwards, that it became the quickest and most comic way to make inroads to the Irish-American community we wanted to hang out with. By the first weekend Pat was taking calls from a few different girls every night, and so much so that he had to start telling some of them we'd moved-on to do research in New York. That was partly true in fact, but more of that in a while.

That first weekend he also took us along to watch pre-season training at the Boston Irish Wolfhounds Rugby Club, and needless to say they took one look at King George and tried to get him to emigrate straight away. But all joking aside, we had a brilliant evening socially and we were asked to play the first forty minutes of a pre-season friendly the following weekend. They were just being cheerful hosts of course, and we knew it, but come the day they were so impressed by our play that they kept us both on for the whole game. A match that they won in style by the way.

Then, with two weeks still ahead of us and much to do, we tapped into the people we'd already met and made plans for the following week. We were fair set and ready to go, and until then we'd hardly had to do a thing for ourselves. Well done Pat the Fourth, and fair play to the genuine warmth of the Bostonians. And I should point out that a couple of them in particular kept us far warmer than we'd ever dared to dream. "Sláinte" to Madison and Kayla... 'twas a pleasure.

I read in my Boston Globe in the first week we were there that the city attracts about a third of a million college students from all around the world, and that they contribute nearly five billion dollars a year to its economy. Somehow I didn't think the thousand dollars we'd managed to save and bring with us was going to have much of an impact, and so I wondered if we might outstay our welcome. Not a bit of it, and even when we made a point of telling people what we were researching and why, they couldn't do enough to help us.

With or without Pat the Fourth, wherever we went we were either expected – word clearly spread fast – or we were instantly welcomed the minute we opened our mouths. And a huge part of being so welcome meant that someone else usually picked up the tab. We were allowed to pay for a few things - I only know that because our money slowly went down - but I can't remember what, and drinks hardly ever. We made all sorts of promises to reciprocate if any of them ever made it to Ireland, which we meant at the time, but God help us if any of them ever turn up. Jees I love Boston!

Although we intended to do any 'interviews' we thought appropriate in the Irish pubs in Boston in our last week, we knew we wanted to spend a couple of days from our middle week in New York as well. We wanted to see the place apart from anything else, but we also wanted to get into some of the Irish pubs, clubs and bars there in the hope of talking to two types of person in particular: anyone who had, or maybe still did, donate money 'to the cause'; and anyone who'd witnessed the horror and awe of 9/11 first hand. If we managed to find a few people who were both then all the better, and just eleven months after it had happened we thought we stood a fair chance. What a massive and fortunate miscalculation – people who'd witnessed 9/11 were everywhere, and only too willing to help.

When Pat the Fourth had first put out his feelers on our behalf, two old boys in Boston had said they'd see us through the whole 'interview process' once we got there. They were called Kevin O'Callaghan and Kieran Lennon, and they were true to their word. O'Callaghan had owned his own bar until he was sixty, and by the time of our visit he was on some committee or other in the Boston Irish Cultural Centre; and Lennon had been a teacher, after which he would write the odd article as a freelance for the Boston Irish Reporter. Both were now in their 70s, both drank nothing but Guinness and Jameson's Whiskey, and both were great craic.

Lennon was the natural leader of the two and O'Callaghan was the showman, and they pretty much owned one end of the bar in Doyle's Café. Doyle's was at the junction of Washington and Williams, about five minutes from the Green Street T Stop and so less than half an hour on 'the T' from Patrick's home. They chatted to us at length in that first week, despite being interrupted half the time by young women coming over to introduce themselves, but they seemed to enjoy that too and so we all just got on with it. But apart from their own candid and insightful opinions on 'collecting for the boys' in the 1970s and '80s, they organised two invaluable opportunities for us in our remaining two weeks.

The first was to send us to a particular bar in New York where they had a couple of friends of the same generation and outlook as them, but where the owner still proudly collected for the Dissident Republicans back in Ireland; and the second was to arrange an interview with Pete Best, a fifty-six-year-old former Provo turned American citizen who now lived in Boston but who wouldn't be in town again until our final week. Quick as ever, George jumped in with one of his sarcastic wisecracks:

"Jees Kevin, its's a shame you're not a McCartney 'stead of an O'Callaghan, then we could have brought three of the original four Beatle's back together…"

And to be expected, the pair of them were quicker still:

"Aye, Lennon, McCartney and Best," said Kieran Lennon, "like we've never heard that one before."

"Smart arse," O'Callaghan grinned and took his turn, "and see big George, if you've really got any of John F Kennedy's DNA, then it must have come from the laundry maid that stole a pair of Marilyn Monroe's knickers."

Touché, and the conversation about the absent former Provo moved on. Pete Best was also no relation to "that Loyalist friggin' wild-child, George Best", said O'Callaghan, but he at least conceded that he was the greatest soccer player he'd ever seen. No, Pete Best, Lennon explained, was originally from the Ardoyne in North Belfast, but in Best's own words he'd, 'seen through the Provos for what they were and seen the whole murderous cycle of violence for what it would become'. After the introduction of Internment and what Best called the Ballymurphy Massacre in August '71, and then Bloody Sunday in Derry just five months later, he upped-sticks and left Northern Ireland for America in 1972. And he'd never looked back.

Best had worked for the tobacco giant, Gallaher's, in the R&D Division of its titanic York Street factory in Belfast; but when he'd been offered a job by a visiting executive from RJ Reynolds Tobacco Co, in Salem, North Carolina, he'd jumped at the chance and they'd sponsored him. In doing so he'd also jumped-ship, from what he thought was the Provos creaky vessel heading inevitably for the rocks. Although it took another thirty years, he hadn't been wrong. Kieran Lennon described him as being 'in over his head' in something he no longer believed in, and which frightened and sickened him in equal measure. He said that Best would be back in Boston for our last week, and that he'd already said he'd be happy to meet-up and help us.

But first there was the humungous prospect of taking-on the Big Apple. George and I, Kieran, Kevin and Pat the Fourth, all sat down over a Jameson's or two and came up with a plan of action. Then all we had to do was stay sober enough to carry it out.

American as 'Big Apple' Pie

The four days George and I spent in New York were even more of an eye opener. I'm not much of a city guy, even now in my thirties, but New York was something else. I loved being able to stand on a street corner and know I could eat just about any food in the world within two blocks; and despite all the history and the magnificent ancient buildings right across the UK, I thought Grand Central Terminal was the most awe-inspiring building I'd ever entered. The New Yorkers too, if you spoke to them twice and so punched through their brusque initial response, were some of the warmest, funniest and most optimistic people I'd ever met.

We'd talked-over our options with Patrick the Fourth and he'd explained that New York was about a four-hour train ride and the fare was in the region of fifty bucks; so it wasn't something we were going to be able to do daily. He'd suggested three nights in the YMCA there, and then to cram-in all the research we could by day and by night. Oh, and to leave a little time for the new young things he knew we'd meet while we were there.

So that's exactly what we did; and by presenting ourselves wherever we went, stating our business and simply asking people if they had been in town for 9/11, we got all the interviews we could handle. It worked everywhere we tried: cafés and diners, coffee shops, pubs and delis, and even a few people waiting in the massive concourse of Grand Central Station. It was as if they *wanted* to talk about it - eleven months down the road and to strangers from a different world – as though it was in some way cathartic. And so we were more than happy to listen and learn.

Kieran Lennon and Kevin O'Callaghan called ahead to a number of Irish bars where they knew people, and so we spoke to all the closet-Provos and wannabe Irish Republicans that we could have wished for. The consensus everywhere though, and across all generations, was pretty much the same as Pete Best told us the following week: they all admitted to contributing freely to 'the hat' whenever it was passed around at some quasi-Irish function or other, but little thought was given in the 1970s or '80s to exactly what people were donating to.

Indeed, after sinister developments like Internment and Bloody Sunday early-on in the Troubles, most Irish-Americans believed they were genuinely helping to bring an end to the British occupation of an oppressed Catholic nation. And much of it, he pointed out, was historic anyway, when whole families or other groups decried the despicable acts of the English against the Irish – just as they did against American Patriots every 4th of July – as if both were just yesterday and still going on.

Then, after a lot of years, he continued, a growing number of Americans realised that the Catholics in the North were actually the minority community; and so they also reluctantly began to accept that the British troops there had been supporting the democratic rights of the two-thirds Protestant majority. What's more, the fighting was not only on streets that were as much a part of Britain as were, say, Hawai'i to America, but the actual murder and carnage of the IRA was being taken to innocent civilians on the equivalent of the US mainland or its overseas dependencies.

"Yeah, but even more so than Hawai'i," George protested, ever the Royalist, "seeing as Ireland was invaded way back in the 12th Century an' all, and Hawai'i was only annexed by America the start of the twentieth."

Precisely, and suddenly things didn't seem nearly so cut and dry. And 9/11 merely drove the point home even deeper.

"But then many in America still don't know that to this day," Best would say… and then he'd add cynically, "or maybe they just don't want to know, because it's not nearly as romantic a notion that way."

It was only in the 1990s, he said, that the penny really began to drop, once British soldiers *and* their family members were being killed in Europe, and when huge bombs in London and the north of England started ripping the heart out of cities well away from Northern Ireland. Cities that many Americans claimed as their ancestral homes. *Then* some started to question where their money was going.

Until then it had just been something Irish-Americans did without question, with a grin and a little jig, like buying cookies from the Girl Scouts of America. There were a few more sinister financiers of course, who knew exactly what they were donating to and how their money would be spent; but Kieran and Kevin never pointed us towards any of them, and sure enough such people existed the world over and in support of any number of causes. Doubtless the Soviets would have argued that about us, all of us, in Afghanistan in the 1980s.

But then there was Declan Callahan. Not only didn't he care where his money had gone, he was still collecting.

Callahan's Bar was in the aptly named Hell's Kitchen area of Manhattan, just off 9th Avenue in Midtown West. Upon entering, our eyes had to adjust to the sudden darkness, and until they had the pub's few lamps and the odd neon signs lit pretty much only themselves. Daylight, it seemed, only crept in when someone let it, and several faces turned to watch us shut it firmly back outside once we'd come in. Irish paraphernalia cocooned the bar and the word *Rebel* was much in evidence.

We headed straight for the counter and got ready to show our passports for ID, and for the moment we still couldn't see much of anything else. That soon changed though, and a pretty young barmaid with a never-ending cleavage stepped out from a backlit mirage of bottles and mirrors to greet us.

"Hi, what can I get you guys?' she smiled beautifully.

"Er… two pints of Guinness, please," I stuttered.

I was still waiting to have my ID checked. Although we could drink legally from eighteen in the UK and Ireland, we'd only been twenty-one for a few months and so we'd got used to being carded in the past week. She'd taken one look at George towering above her though, and so clearly hadn't bothered. She nodded her approval and made a start on our pints.

"Anything else?" she smiled.

"No, not for now…" I smiled back.

"Nothing to eat?"

"No, maybe in a while, but I see you've got Power's behind the bar there." I was just starting to be able to see anything other than her lily-white cleavage.

"Yeah, of course," she said, a little surprised.

"Oh, it's just not everywhere here has it. Some places only have Jameson's."

"Well we've got it…" she teased with just a grin, "and if here's here, where's there?"

"Northern Ireland," I smiled at her quick wit.

"South Armagh," George added. He'd stopped saying he was from Dundalk or South of the border, unless we got into deep conversation, and saying South Armagh for both of us was kind of the truth and it gave us enormous credibility when we asked our research questions. To those that knew anything, that is, and our barmaid seemed to be somewhere in the middle.

"Um, that's bad isn't it?" she asked as she waited for the first pint to settle and started on the second. "That's like the Iwo Jima of the Troubles isn't it?"

We both laughed. Despite her Irish-red hair and her pale freckled skin, she sounded one hundred per cent American; and she can't have been that much older than us, so what the hell did she know about the Troubles? But we'd never heard it put that way before; it was funny, and she seemed quite sharp.

"Huh, used to be," I replied, "but peace has broken out now, don't y'know."

"You think?" she said. "Declan reckons they're just taking a breather before they get going again."

"Well I hope Declan's wrong," said George. "So is he your boyfriend then?"

"No, my boss," she chuckled, "God, he's nearly forty."

"Your boss here you mean?" George persisted.

"Yes, this is his place." She passed George's pint to him.

We glanced at each other and nodded that he must be the Declan of Declan Callahan fame. The one that Kieran and Kevin said still collected for the Dissidents.

"But I'm guessing your Dad was a Marine?" I asked, to keep George off the subject. Tact wasn't George's strong suit.

"Yes," she giggled, "how did you know that?"

"Iwo Jima," I answered. "Y'know, the famous photo of the six Marines raising the flag..."

"Oh, was that Iwo Jima?" she flared her eyes thoughtfully.

"And so is he Irish? Your dad?" George asked. "You've got the colouring right enough, but we can hear *you're* not."

"No, nor is he, but he's closer than me. Four generations ago I think. His people came after the First World War but before the Great Depression, does that sound about right?"

"Aye, does," I nodded, "so in the 1920s. Probably gangsters then, your dad's people?"

Our new friend laughed heartily and she topped off my pint and slid it towards me.

"And yours were comedians, I suppose?" she grinned.

"So what's your name?" George asked.

"Jan."

"No, I meant your surname?"

"Oh, Calhoun."

"Well Hi, Jan Calhoun, that's sure Irish enough. I'm George Kennedy, and this here's Neill McCormac. Pleased to meet you."

Although it seemed kind of silly we all shook hands. It was a very Irish thing to do and she seemed to know that.

"Look Jan," I began, "we were hoping to meet up here with two older guys on the hour, so we're a little bit early, but..."

"So you're the *Irony Brothers*..." she grinned. "Am I going to get a song later?"

"Maybe," George beamed.

"Right," I smiled, a little embarrassed, "so I suppose you knew we were coming?"

"Yeah, your fame precedes you, and your two old boys are sat at the back there..." she nodded into the darkness at the back of the bar. "Tom and Brian. They're cool."

"Can we get them a drink, d'you reckon?" I asked.

"Not yet I wouldn't have thought. They've only just got one, but I'll come over in a little while to check."

"Yes please, that'd be grand," I said.

I picked up my pint to move to their table, but George clearly wasn't done teasing Jan yet.

"So what else did they tell you?"

"Sorry?" Jan said.

"You said our fame precedes us. What did they tell you?"

"Just to make sure I stayed my own side of the bar," she grinned. "They said I needed to watch you around the women."

"It's just our accents," I offered lamely.

"That's not what I heard," Jan grinned. "That's how it starts maybe, but then you're far from all talk is what I heard."

I grinned and backed away cheekily; she returned it with interest. George became uncharacteristically shy and followed me to the two elders' table. The younger-looking of the two, Brian, stood to greet us. He shook my hand first because I was leading.

"You must be Neill?"

"Yes." I wasn't sure how he knew, but then when he spoke again I realised.

"And this giant of a fellah must be King George then."

Then we shook hands with his friend.

"Take a seat you two," said Tom with a quick nod.

We all four just chatted for the first thirty minutes. They heard all our thoughts on New York and Boston – where we'd been, what we'd seen, what we'd done and who we'd met – and then they picked our brains clean on *The Old Place* and what was *really* going on with the Peace Process. They had about as much faith in the media as we did, we joked, but they seemed genuinely buoyed by our assessment that the Provos were serious about disarmament; and although they weren't totally convinced, they listened with interest to our thoughts on the chaotic nature and so ineffectiveness of the Dissidents.

"Don't be telling Declan Callahan that though," chuckled old Tom, "he'll pin your ears back for the next hour if you tell him anything negative like that."

"Really? It's kind of positive if you live in Ireland and in amongst it all," I said cautiously.

"Yeah, and therein lies your problem," Brian chuckled, "Declan flies his sorry ass to Ireland about once every five years, then comes home to dream he's really Michael Collins."

Good, humour was going to be OK and they clearly weren't of the same mind as Callahan. And so we began to chat in earnest.

Their thoughts on habitual American fundraising for so-called Irish rebels mirrored Kieran and Kevin's exactly, which was why they'd pointed us to them in the first place we reckoned. But it really did seem that it was the general consensus on the streets as well, and most we spoke to said there was no appetite for supporting such things since 9/11. New Yorkers, all of a sudden, had tasted the bile of terrorism and mass murder for a so-called cause, and they now saw the world very differently. And so did we... one of the many places we'd visited was Ground Zero.

Brian and Tom, both with the surname Lynch but not in any way related, were interesting characters in their own right. And so we spent several hours in their company and then had dinner with them in a different Irish Pub two blocks away. They both tolerated Declan Callahan rather than respected him or his views, and they found his continued efforts to collect for the Dissidents disturbing; but they had mates in his bar and they'd drunk there forever, so they still went in there from time to time. Callahan was out of town, but that was good news for me and George, they said, and so they answered everything we would have put to him on his behalf. And with objectivity and candour, they promised.

Unlike most we'd met around the 'Irish' community, for them Ireland really was *The Old Place*, and they'd both emigrated to America together in 1945. They'd both served in the British Merchant Navy right through the Second World War, and both had sailed to and from the States repeatedly. Brian had been torpedoed but survived three times, and Tom just the once; but then they'd finished-up the war on the same munitions freighter, became firm friends and then both stayed in America to jointly set-up and run their own plumbing business. I immediately thought of my dad and what might have been. And then the next day we headed back to Boston for the busy weekend ahead.

On Friday the 23rd, Pat had managed to get three tickets to watch the New England Patriots in a pre-season game of American

Football against the Carolina Panthers; the first actual game in their brand new Gillette Stadium. So he took us and proclaimed us lucky mascots when New England won 23-3. The next day we had our own game of rugby for the Wolfhounds, which we won by exactly twice that score, 46-6, and after which we added a few more enthusiasts to our burgeoning fan club. Then on the Monday, he took us to Fenway Park to watch the legendary Boston Red Sox. Despite the magnificence of the Gillette Stadium (George and I both dreamed of playing a game of rugby somewhere similar one day), Fenway Park was remarkable in another way: it had been home to the Red Sox for ninety years, and it was the oldest ballpark in Major League Baseball. Thank God they beat the Anaheim Angels 10-9, and good job he took us on the Monday... because they'd lost on the Saturday and the Sunday. And so our record as lucky mascots remained intact.

The third week with Patrick was amazing, and it was far more about leisure by then than research. Apart from sampling all the sights, sounds and history in Boston we hadn't found yet, we crossed the river to visit Harvard and then got right out of town to places like Cape Cod and Hyannis Port, Lexington and Pioneer Valley. But the highlight of our final week was doubtless sitting down with Pete Best and hearing his tales of the first three years of the Troubles - yet told not by some history book, but by someone who'd been inside the Belfast Brigade at its inception.

Just like Brian and Tom in New York, Best was quite the character. He was bright, very forthright and insightful, but he also had a wicked sense of humour and several times he was hilariously self-deprecating. One of the funniest stories he told us got even funnier eight years later when I heard it again from John Conway in 2010, but from the exact opposite end of things – from JC who'd been there at the time with the Paras. Pete Best's version was told as follows.

"Jees, then about three years after I'd left Belfast I got a letter here in Boston, well in Salem actually, before I moved up here, but from an old mate back in the Ardoyne in 3 Bat PIRA..."

"3 Bat?" I queried, I'd heard it before.

"Yeah, so for your research I suppose you'd call it the 3rd Battalion of the Belfast Brigade of the Provisional IRA. Aye, 1975 it would have been. He said it had been a rough couple of years, y'know, since I'd left an' all, and that he wasn't sure there was a quick finish to things even remotely on the cards..."

"Jesus," George growled, "and thirty years later he wasn't friggin' wrong was he."

"No, he sure wasn't," Pete chuckled, "but then he says that 3 Bat were taking shit from the rest of Belfast for allowing the Paras to do some sort of a PT test through the Ardoyne."

"A what?" I asked, somewhat confused.

"A bloody PT test, you know, a squadded-run." Pete was already chortling to himself at what he knew was coming. "At least that's what a couple of the ex-para guys in the Brigade reckoned. They reckoned it was a thing they did called the BFT, the Battle Fitness Test, and to prove a point they did it right through the streets of the Ardoyne."

"You're kidding?" George piped-up.

"No, and nor were those cheeky fuckers. There was about thirty or forty of them apparently, from 2 Para in Flax Street Mill, and they were all formed-up three-abreast, in just boots, green denims, red PT vests and rifles at the trail... you know, carried by their handles and down by their side."

"You've gotta be kidding," George protested again.

"Nope, not a bit of it. But see, they had magazines on their rifles, and I'll bet they were full of fucking bullets right enough."

"Jesus," said George.

"Aye, and there they were, says Mike in his letter, up one street and down the next, all perfectly in step and all dressed-off in their dead straight lines, and then off away into the distance. Mike said they reckoned they'd never live it down."

So, eight years later, and when I was in London with JC for those two days, he mentioned Flax Street Mill and said he was based there for his first tour of Northern Ireland; and so I repeated Best's story as apocryphal for him to maybe shoot it down. But no, he did exactly the opposite.

"Christ no, he's telling the truth," he laughed. "Or whoever sent him that letter was, that really happened."

"How so?" I asked. "Pete Best said they weren't wearing flak jackets or anything. No helmets, no nothing."

"No we weren't, I was on that thing. God, I'd forgotten all about that." He laughed inwardly and then carried on explaining. "Bloody hell Neill, I'd only been in the unit a few weeks, and so I thought, 'Brilliant, so this is how it is in Battalion... and I guess this is taking it to the enemy'."

"So was it a real test then? A BFT Best called it."

"Well, yes and no really. We ran it exactly like the first part of a BFT, in threes, in step, twenty files deep or something, and he's right, we had our rifles at the trail. Fuck," he laughed, "in fact it was the first time in my career I'd ever been allowed to use the carrying handle on my bloody SLR."

"Jesus, I didn't really believe him..."

"Well he's right, except we didn't then run the individual part, the timed best effort, we just ran right through the Ardoyne to piss 'em all off and then buggered off back to camp."

"So what were you wearing?" I asked, still seeking some sort of verification.

"Umm," he thought for a moment, "the usual stuff for a BFT. Boots, puttees, denims, a red or white PT vest – but my recollection is everyone was in red – and a loaded rifle of course."

"So no helmets?"

"No."

"No berets?"

"Oh, maybe, but I don't think so. No."

"And no body armour or anything?"

"Nope, definitely none of that thank God, those old flak jackets were clumpy as hell, but no. Just routine PT kit but with a loaded rifle. It felt bloody marvellous now I think about it, we reckoned we were the kings of Belfast after that."

"Aye, that's what the guy said in his letter to Pete Best, Mike someone... and they, apparently, were the butt of Belfast's jokes for months after that."

"Yeah, I'm sure they were. Job done then, well done that company commander. I can't even remember who it was now."

What was it, I wondered, with JC and serendipity?

Anyway, back to August 2002 and our final meeting with Pete Best in Boston. So, apart from his amazing insights – although amazingly out of date – the most telling thing he said came right towards the end of our final meeting. Probably fittingly so. About collecting for the Provos, he'd pretty much confirmed yet again that for years people gave blindly but without knowing what to, and doubtless in some cases without really caring. But then after 9/11 nearly *everyone* cared.

And yet as for the way forward under the Dissidents who were trying to keep it all going, he said he couldn't see it; and nor, for the record, could those he was still in touch with in Belfast. He summed it up succinctly for me when he said:

"See Neill, right back at the start in 1969, if you were a red-blooded Catholic in Belfast or Derry and you had any balls, you had no choice but to fight. We kind of had to. Y'know, and seriously, there was a helluva lot that needed sorting. But now... well now there's nothing to fight for. They've got it all. And in some ways, they've got it better than the Protestants these days."

"Except a united Ireland?" I said. "They haven't got that."

"No, but they will in time, even Mountbatten believed that; but my reading of everything that's ever come out of Dublin is that they wouldn't want the North... Jees, too much friggin' baggage, and it's still as divided as ever."

And in 2002 it was. The truly scary thing though, is that in 2017 I'm not so sure it's that much better.

Gettin' Away Clean

After three years at uni' and so away from home, I was a pretty forgotten figure in the Derrybeg. Good. That was for the best. Especially for my parents if it became known I'd gone into some sort of government service with the Brits. There wasn't a sign of Fin Magee or his cronies anywhere over Christmas 2002, and Shaela Keane, who'd so kindly popped my cherry back in '96, proved equally scarce on the horizon. Shame, I'd kind of hoped to bump into her just once more for old times' sake.

The week I'd graduated there were a few back-slaps and well-dones from close friends and neighbours, but then on the morning I actually slipped away to live in London in a flurry of light snow, I did so while the Derrybeg was still yawning itself awake. It was a scene in Irish towns and villages as old as time itself, as one of an imponderable number of kids from a large Catholic family grew up, packed a suitcase and walked solemnly out of their street to find a new life somewhere else. Anywhere else usually, but I was one of the lucky ones – I had some money, an address, a job and a plan.

Úna drove me to the airport, of course, and there were no tears from her because she'd already made it clear she was going to come and see me monthly in London until one or other of us got bored with it. My mother cried enough for both of them. I teased Úna that I'd rather she sent Maria, but then she surprised me at the end of January by bringing her anyway. No threesome sadly, but I had more than enough stress built up by then to have made Maria's trip worthwhile.

George Kennedy had travelled up to Newry and spent his Christmas with us too, and he was starting his Garda training in County Tipperary on the same day as mine with MI5 in London. But of course, going home for the New Year to him was just a hop and a skip back across the border, and so he'd come to me and not the other way around. Besides, he loved spending time with his second-family and in the North. The other Kennedys came to the airport to say goodbye too, Sarah and Charlie, and I received a touching note from Eric Lawrence and Emily Rankin – but no face time of course. Just a wee footnote on Em, and as a mark of her professionalism: I only appreciated a couple of years later that it was only *after* she'd successfully recruited me into the Service that she told me she'd like to debrief me in detail on all those people I'd met in the United States. That's integrity. Quite a girl, and quite the role model for a while.

I left the week after Christmas because my training was due to start at Thames House on the 6th of January, but it felt like the start of so much more than just a new and uncertain year. The light snow followed us all the way to Aldergrove Airport, and rising above it – as the aircraft eventually did – seemed to promise a bright new start in England. How many millions of Irish émigrés had nurtured such ideas in the past four hundred years I wondered, and would my own path be any less challenging than theirs? As a timely reminder not to get too carried away with it all, the weather as we touched down at London Heathrow was even worse. Welcome to England, and a Happy friggin' New Year.

Úna and my dad knew I'd joined the Security Service, and of course George, but they didn't think my mum would ever be able to handle it. Not until peace at home was assured at least, and assured meant something far more permanent and reliable than the corrosive misery seeping out of the Dissidents like a festering wound. So not yet at least. And my siblings were all kept in the dark too, largely for their own protection. They were all told I'd joined the Home Office, and that through my work there – or on occasion as a part of the NIO, the Northern Ireland Office – I felt I could have a hand in shaping Ireland's future. Kieran and Eílis were fiercely proud and wished me well; Margaret thought I could have done better for myself; and Maud, Éamon and their Belfast clan of Kellys thought I'd sold them out and that I should be trying to change things from within Sinn Féin.

Me leaving brought about a lot of other changes at home over the next two years as well. Eílis moved on a year later, and Kieran didn't. He still lives with mum and dad today, and he works as an electrician in Daisy Hill Hospital. That's a five-minute walk to work for him, and maybe six going home because it's more uphill; but otherwise that's pretty much his life... and for him it works. Úna's still Úna in every way that counts, but with Eílis and I gone even she unfurled her wings and started travelling more often and more widely. Within a couple of years of me leaving she was away from Ireland as much as she was there, and once she'd hooked-up with Dermott McCracken again they decided to move in together so both could have some company in their later years. Good, because I'd always liked Dermott.

From Heathrow the weather didn't get any better, but my mood lifted as I started to realise that the planning for my future was at last over. What I'd considered my future until that moment had miraculously become the present, and so at long last I could actually begin to live it. But then just as quickly I realised that living it was going to be about as far from the glamourous world of James Bond as I could get. The proof began immediately. I gathered up my bags, heaved them into the luggage bins in the bowels of my No. 726 bus to Bromley South, and then headed across grey, wet and wintry fields for three hours to a small two-bedroomed flat on the rural edge of Bromley. Dry Martinis, Aston Martins and even faster women were going to have to wait.

Bromley is historically in the County of Kent, commonly referred to as the Garden of England; but it has since 1903 been a municipal borough of the capitol, and since 1965 an actual part of Greater London. In short that simply means it's one of London's larger suburban towns, but it's still perched on the very edge of Kent's green and rolling woodlands. That at least made me feel at home almost immediately, but the two main reasons I'd found a place there was affordability and a relatively quick commute to Central London. The other link to home that I hadn't appreciated until I got there was that I lived not ten minutes from RAF Biggin Hill, the former Royal Air Force fighter base where my Grandpa Peter had served throughout World War II.

It hadn't been an active air base since the late-1950s, although it was now a thriving commercial airport, but the RAF still retained a toe-hold around St George's Chapel and what was once the main gate, where two full-sized replicas of a Hurricane and a Spitfire still acted as gate guards. During the war, fighters based at Biggin Hill had claimed no less than fourteen hundred enemy aircraft, at a cost of over four hundred and fifty aircrew, and it was a little bit of McCormac history I had no idea I would be so close to while I put down new roots. I would walk or run there often in my first year and once the good weather came, but then as I expanded into my new and challenging life… not so much.

Still, life in Kent was good, and although I didn't know it at the time I would spend the next four years living there; until I moved in 2007 from T2 to G9, and so also from Bromley to West

Dulwich to be closer to Thames House. There were some great real ales to be had in Kent, and some wonderful country pubs still left in which to enjoy them; and so I quickly discovered those I could walk or bus to, and a bunch of others further out that Úna and I would drive to when she came to stay and she had a hire car.

I didn't bother with a car myself for the longest time. There was no need initially. Throughout my training and my first few months in a section, I had no social life, and so a car in Central London was just a liability. And a bloody expensive one at that. Plus, I could use my London Transport season ticket on buses, the tube and for rail into and out of London; so why would I drive anywhere until there started to be anything in my life but work?

Yet the real casualty of my personal life for the first couple of years was rugby. The nearest team I could reach out to was Beckenham RFC, which played in the London Division 2 South League - and so at level 6 in the hierarchy of English rugby. Not quite what I was used to; but they were gracious enough to let me play when I missed most games, and even more training, due to the nature of my work 'at the NIO'. It wasn't until I moved to Dulwich that I started playing more regularly again, for the equally gracious and understanding Old Alleynians; but by then rugby had become a part-time leisure activity, rather than my main reason for getting up in the morning. Those days, alas, were some years in my rear view mirror and receding fast.

I didn't really bother with girlfriends a lot either, for much the same reasons as rugby or a car, and that would prove to be the story of my ad hoc and largely non-existent lovelife until I met Katy Owen at the beginning of the NEON case in July 2015. At one point the year before that, I even started to wonder if it would still work if I gave it a run out! By then all my holes – my God-shaped hole, my rugby-shaped hole, and my girl-shaped hole - were all filled with duties and work, and I wondered if I'd ever clear them out again for action another day.

But as discreet transitions go, from one vastly different environment and lifestyle to another – especially where there was a degree of secrecy required as well – I think it all went pretty well. So did my first Civil Service pay check, rapidly, and so for a while I just hunkered down and got used to the life of a student again.

Regnum Defende

At a little after 9 am on a cold, grey and overcast Monday morning in January 2003, I emerged from Victoria Station into the bedlam and the fumes of Central London. I then began a twenty-minute walk which I would come to cherish in the coming months, and certainly once the weather had broken, but only after I'd tried and rejected all other options. That twenty minutes was the last stretch from Victoria to Thames House, and no matter how I attempted to complete it, it took about the same time.

The tube was a nightmare, and even if I was squashed-up against an attractive young woman, by the time I'd been elbowed through overburdened turnstiles, abused by some transport Nazi for unintelligible misdemeanours, and then manhandled down escalators and spewed onto my platform, we'd both be more in the mood to make war than find love. And besides, where the hell would I ride to?

Thames House was annoyingly encircled by Underground stations, but it wasn't actually near to any of them – a deliberate ploy no doubt, to confuse already bewildered enemies of The Crown – and so why would I put myself through all that? London's legendary double-decker buses weren't much better, although through my government-subsidised season ticket that would be my preferred method of hop-on-hop-off transport around the city for the next six years. And from the upper deck, I quickly learned, I could see so much of interest at the same time.

London's equally famous black cabs were the way to go right enough, but only if I was off to a meeting somewhere and the Office was paying... but to and from work, and out of my meagre beginner's budget, forget it. And so I would walk; and in all but the foulest weather, when I would jump onto a passing bus, it would be either the last peaceful moment at the start of my working day, or the first blissful moment of my journey home. Usually the only blissful moment, and in the four years of commuting into Victoria from Bromley South I only ever got a seat for the eighteen-minute train journey three times. And that was the fast train. I *never* got a seat for the twenty-four-minute slow train at all - and suddenly, Boston to New York looked quite civilised.

So, my route that morning in the cold and the drizzle, that told me that I may have left Ireland but I was still gallingly in the British Isles, took me half the length of Victoria Street, until I turned right into Artillery Row, on into Greycoat Place, and then onto Horseferry Road and the start of my run for home. Thames House was nearly eight hundred metres along Horseferry Road, or rather Lambeth Bridge was, and for the last ninety metres I'd stroll proudly past the front of the building and then turn smugly into the Neo-Classical grandeur of its triumphal main entrance. I had no idea what life held for me in the future, but even then, on my first day, I knew I'd arrived! Exactly where I'd arrived at, and just how insignificant I was, would become clearer in the coming weeks and months.

After about a year of walking those same streets every day I'd discover a more direct route - albeit only slightly - but if nothing else it would offer a bit of variety; and on days when it really mattered, it might save me a whole minute. Or so I liked to think, but that sometimes felt like a lifetime. On those occasions I'd cut down Wilton Road, through Neathouse Place, onto Vauxhall Bridge Road and then left onto the western and northern sides of Vincent Square. That way I could at least walk along two sides of a huge green playing field, just the colour of which never failed to remind me of Ireland.

Come the summer months I'd cut past there during the day as well if I could, just to watch the kids from Westminster School play cricket. Or maybe I'd watch their forebears: the Old Westminsters, or the Eton Ramblers, the Oundle Rovers, or maybe even a Lords and Commons XI from Westminster Palace and the Houses of Parliament. Stirring stuff, which never failed to remind me why I was working in defence of the realm. Everything for a while was so English... so *not* Newry, but there again neither was it Boston or New York. Now I had first-hand experience of other lands, I looked at everywhere with a fresh eye. For me, life had truly begun.

Then from Vincent Square I'd turn onto Maunsel Street and emerge into Horseferry Road, maybe fifty metres short of the Coroner's Court (and the morgue, where the nameless corpse later identified as IRA elder Cahal Brady would lay for several months in the spring of 2016. I would be looking for him by then, except at that stage we still wouldn't know he existed. More serendipity?) And then so back onto my original route to Thames House and my final approach from the rear. I'd use the same route some days going home too, and boredom, repetition and the ludicrous desire to get to one's platform maybe a minute earlier, can do strange things to a man's grasp of reality.

I often wondered if daily commuters into London *had* any meaningful grasp of reality. To me it became just a necessary trek to get to my place of work, but I knew it would only be for a few years at the most. Then I'd be moving-on to pastures new and challenges a-plenty in some new appointment, and so I was able to keep it all in perspective. Or so I hoped. It was already a journey of three parts, each of which I could make interesting in some way if I chose. Firstly, I had a twenty-minute bus ride from home to Bromley South Railway Station. I would catch that bus at 6.30 am, and barring delays it would get me onto the fast train before the hour. Then after an eighteen-minute train ride, standing of course, I would finish up with another twenty-minute walk to Thames House; or maybe another bus if it was raining heavily.

Aye, I could do that for a couple of years, I thought, and I would try and find something new and interesting to observe about London every day. Most days I managed. But... during that eighteen or twenty-four minute train ride, when I would stand and teeter back and forth in between all the other itinerant passengers, I would study the faces of those around me and look for signs of life. Those who were seated especially... those who clearly got on before the rest of us hapless pedestrians - and so also much earlier - and who seemed to be as wedded to their particular seats as would be a Red Sox season ticket holder. What stare-downs or train-rage took place earlier in the journey, I wondered? Poor bastards. And in *those* faces I would often see the sallow complexion and the hollow stare of someone who'd been doing that self-same journey every day for thirty years or more. Faced with that, I vowed, I would walk into the gates of Provo hell armed with just a baseball bat, before I would ever succumb to a death like that. Some of them looked as if they'd passed already.

So if I hit all my connections perfectly, I could be entering Thames House just seventy minutes after leaving my front door near Biggin Hill. And most often I did. But if a single link in the chain failed, then a two-hour journey wouldn't be unusual. Either way that would get me in well before nine, and usually long before eight, and for many in the building 10 am was considered the start of the working day. Lucky them.

My training and selection when it started varied between mind-numbingly tedious and absolutely terrifying. Not that there was any danger involved – although predictably there were a lot of *Boys' Own* type stories of derring-do from some unlikely public school old boys – but because of the self-inflicted pressure of tests and the constant selection process. Some of the classroom work was interesting… some!… but that's what I'd just done for the past three years. Or was it nine? But right from the off, for me the most stimulating training by far was that which introduced us to the world of covert operations and contact intelligence. I say which *introduced* us, because it took me less than my first year to realise that the training just prepared us to toddle along… and that learning to walk, trot and then run was something we largely learnt the hard way and over a number of years.

Thank God I was a fast learner, not prone to incompetence or gullibility, and that I seemed to have a triple-helping of street sense from my upbringing in Newry. That and my accent put me in good-stead straight away, even in London, where I found myself launched into any number of unlikely places to get alongside someone from the *Old Place*.

Despite that, all I really got to bear-down on for my first three years after training was a desk and a computer work station, because first I had to learn my craft and then I had to pay my dues. I worked initially as an analyst against the Irish target in T2, in T2A to start with and then later in T5C, but then I followed the changing dynamics in the building and moved to work against Islamic extremism in G-Branch. At the time many of our resources were all headed in the same direction, as were rising media interest and wider public concern. And, of course, ever-closer political oversight and scrutiny.

Two years earlier, on what became known as '7/7' in 2005 to be precise, coordinated suicide attacks on the London transport system during rush-hour had killed fifty-two people and injured over seven hundred. The year before that, al-Qaeda inspired train bombings in Madrid had killed over a hundred and ninety people and injured nearly two thousand. The overt face of terror had changed and so we were having to change with it. In 2007 I moved to G9C, where quite apart from anything else I gained invaluable experience against non-Irish-thinking minds and methodology.

I also gained a new home for the next two years: one half of a Georgian semi-detached house not two minutes from the railway station at West Dulwich. That for many in Thames House was a terrifying prospect, as my regular commute into London would be through the so-called urban battlefield of Brixton, but for someone raised during the Troubles in South Armagh... well. It was a much better, much cheaper and much closer home than the one near Bromley, simple as that, and so I made the most of everything it had to offer. That included some spectacular food, a couple of new casual girlfriends, and a lot more rugby than I'd managed to play since I'd left Queen's University.

In 2009 I was due to move back to Northern Ireland to be an agent handler in T8NI, based in Hollywood just outside Belfast. But my swan song in G-Branch got me into the right frame of mind more surely than any of the specialist training I'd had to complete. Pretty much my last act there was to have a walk-on part in a long-term sting operation against several wannabe Islamic Extremists in the North of England.

It was, I immediately realised, to be the mirror image of the operation which had attracted me to the Service back in 2002; when covert operators had posed as Iraqi intelligence officers and arms dealers to catch Real IRA would-be gun-runners. But this time I was the bait, and my role was to portray a former Provo from South Armagh to identify would-be Islamic martyrs at large in our community. Score!

Then, and only then, did I *really* know I'd arrived.

March ou Crève

Bill Wallace was one of the first characters I'd looked up to upon my arrival in Thames House. Looked up to as a would-be mentor that is, because I was actually a few inches taller than him. He was the Head of T8NI back in 2003 when I'd arrived, and right at the end of our training he'd been one of the role players who'd flown back from Ireland to take part in our final exercise. But over and above that he'd sought me out several times for a chat during breaks over coffee, and he didn't try for an instant to conceal his interest in my background and where I'd grown up. I knew then he was sizing me up as well as just getting to know me, and I think I also knew back then that he probably had plans for me and my Newry accent further on down the road.

But it was a long and busy road for both of us, and so we didn't see much of each other for the next couple of years. In 2005 he'd moved back to London and become the Head of T8 for the second time – it was he who'd set it up in the 1990s – and then he'd spent the best part of the next five years there. But three meetings between us that stand out to me though, were in 2006, '08 and '09. The first was when I was just finishing-up in T5 and about an assessment I had made; the second was in my final year in G9, and concerning a Counter-Islamist operation I'd played a major part in; and the third was my pre-T8NI interview, which he carried out as Head of T8 before I'd been confirmed as landing the job. One short part of that interview best summed-up just who he was, what he wanted of me, and why I respected him so much.

"So Neill, I know you're very close to your family, and that's a good thing, but do I take it from what you've just said that you don't intend to go home to Newry too often."

"Not at all Boss, to be honest. There's plenty of places we can spend time together without having to go within thirty miles of Newry or the border, and so I didn't want to put my parents in that position."

"Fair enough. But what about you though? Would you be entirely comfortable driving around there for yourself?"

"Oh absolutely. That's not what I meant."

"But what about *by* yourself? That's a different question."

"Even better."

"Really?"

"Aye, for sure, but that's why I've got no intention of going home there. I kind of thought the only time I'd go anywhere near South Armagh, the border or anywhere in the South itself, would be if I was working. So I'd not reckoned on going to those places at all for any other reason."

"I see. And how likely do you think that is?"

"Well... umm, very likely, I'd kind of hoped."

"OK, and what about if you're right, but I wanted you to stay-over some nights? Say in a hotel or something."

"No problem."

"And so what about for a *lot* of nights, and maybe not in a hotel? Maybe even if I wanted you to move into somewhere, you know, supposedly as a resident for a while?"

"Still no problem. Look Boss, I see what you're getting at, and I'm absolutely up for it. Honestly. To be blunt, if we don't exploit the hell out of my accent while I'm there this time around, then I reckon we'd be missing a golden opportunity."

"Go on."

"Well there's places I can't and shouldn't go, obviously, but not so many, and *that's* why I don't intend to put my face around that region at all except for if it's on business."

"OK, I hear you, and we'll come back to that in a moment," he'd nodded thoughtfully, "but if that were to be the case, then let me also just check the Circle of Knowledge statement you've made on your application form here. Tell me *precisely* who in Ireland knows you're in the Service."

"Right, well, apart from anyone actually *in* the Service, or anyone at HQNI who might know from when I was recruited, it's a pretty short list."

"Let me reassure you there's very few at HQNI who know Neill, that I can promise you; although they'll get to meet you soon enough of course. That is, if you're successful here today and you start working with them, but go on..."

"Simple then. It's my father, my auntie, a guy called George Kennedy in the Garda who was at Queen's with me, and that's it."

"Not your mother?"

"Nope."

"Would she have objections?"

"No, quite the opposite, but we didn't reckon she'd cope with knowing very well."

"We?"

"Me, my dad and my aunt."

"That'll be... Aunt Úna?" he looked at his notes. "She seems to be quite a level-headed person?"

"She is."

"And so you trust her with that knowledge?"

"One hundred per cent. She wouldn't even confirm it to you if you asked her. She'd flip-it-off as natural as day, and then refer you back to me. But..."

"Sorry..." he'd begun to interrupt me, "go on."

"I was just going to say that she'd call me first to say you were asking. Just in case you shouldn't be."

"Right," he chuckled. "Well I guess I needn't worry about your Aunt Úna then."

"No, and nor need I Boss, for the record. Even the Provos around Cross' back in the day wouldn't have been able to get that out of her, and we ran into a few of those in our time."

"Really?"

"Oh aye. She used to drive me everywhere when I was growing up: to Gaelic footy, and then to rugby, and then we'd walk the Donegal hills together, things like that. I mean everywhere."

"And you're still close now? Correct? I see in here..." he glanced towards his notes again, "that she sponsored your time in America when you were going through Queen's."

"Yep, pretty much paid for the whole thing, but she's done well for herself over the years. She could afford to."

"Yeah, I can see that here too." He took another look at his notes and read in silence for a full minute at least.

"Listen," he suddenly paused and he held my gaze before speaking again, "I'm going to ask you a very personal question, and so you don't have to answer, but I'm just curious is all."

"Go on."

"Are you two lovers?"

"No," I smiled.

"Were you ever?"

"No, but not for the want of trying."

"Go on," he chuckled, "that feels like a very honest answer, so carry on being so honest."

"Simple, I'd have been her lover in a heartbeat – wanted to be – from, oh, about the age of fourteen I reckon, and right up until I came here, but she never would. She's way smarter than that and she didn't want to hurt either of us or her sister."

"Your mum?"

"Yes."

"Well that is honest. Of you I mean... well, maybe both." He stared at me for the longest three seconds of my life before speaking again. "So what about now?"

"No, she's safe now," I smiled. "Now it's me that wouldn't."

"Why?"

"Because of all this," I glanced around his office. "Because of the Service and my integrity an' all. I've made it 'til now without, and she was right – she's always right – and now it could only end badly. She deserves better than that, Boss. We both do. And so now of course, do you and the Service."

He studied me again for a while, and then without making a note anywhere he revealed the merest hint of a smile and asked his next question as though we'd never broken step.

"And where's George Kennedy now?"

"A detective in Dundalk. Just taken his sergeant's exam, which I'm confident he'll ace."

"Will you tell him you're back?"

"I was hoping to, but only when Tony says it's time." Tony Moss was the current Head of T8NI in Northern Ireland.

"Good. Yes, I agree. But you should. And I see you trust him implicitly too," he tapped his file again, "and earned over a lot of years by the looks of it?"

"Exactly."

"So just those three?' he confirmed.

"Just them."

"And not your siblings I see."

"Correct."

"So what do they and your mother think then?"

303

"What I've told them: I'm in the Home Office, which means on occasion in the Northern Ireland Office, both there in Ireland and here in London; and so not something they should be making too well known around the Derrybeg."

"Quite, and you think they believe you?"

"Aye Boss, I do, and so does my dad; but they all take their steer from Úna. If she says I'm in the NIO and she never seems to question it, then they'd take that as gospel."

"And what about the two with Republican leanings? Your, er..." he looked down at his notes, "your older brother Éamon, and your sister Maud, and of course their Belfast families?"

"Same, although they're quite outspoken in saying that I shouldn't work for the Brit establishment at all; but it's nothing militant, and Úna kind of sorted them out too."

"Your auntie? How?"

"The last time they were all together apparently, without me that is, and they were slagging me off because I wasn't there."

"Go on."

"Well according to my dad she said something like, 'At least Neill's got the balls and the smarts to try and change things, unlike you all talking behind his back, and if he's so wrong then why don't *you* all become active in Sinn Féin and put him straight.' Aye, fair told 'em by all accounts."

"And why don't they? Become active in Sinn Féin?"

"Too lazy. Simple as that."

He laughed.

"Your Aunt Úna is clearly quite the backstop," he chuckled, "I wish we could clone her and make her standard issue."

"No way," I protested playfully.

"Why?" he smiled.

"And then have some other guy in the Office doing her? I've been waiting years, over my dead body."

Bill Wallace suppressed a barely restrained belly laugh. He'd liked that one. His smile lit the whole room for a second or two, and then he got back to business; but any remaining ice was well and truly broken.

"And what about these other two Kennedys? Sarah and her husband Charlie? From university. She was your supervisor and is ex-UDR, and he was, er… still is a serving major. Correct?"

"Correct."

"So what about them?"

"Well, I can't be sure Boss, but not from me they don't know; and I don't reckon they did back then just from the things they said and did. So no, I don't think so."

And so we continued. When we'd finished my interview about thirty minutes later I'd been expecting to be told I'd hear in a day or two. Instead he'd said we were done, he stood up, shook my hand firmly, and then added:

"Welcome to T8 Neill. We're clearly lucky to have you. And unless you have to rush home to Dulwich, I'll stand you a pint somewhere in Whitehall while you tell me about you and Úna and your various run-ins with the Provos."

And so that's exactly what we did.

I went off to Northern Ireland several months later, fat, dumb, happy and keen as mustard, and the next time we had such an in depth personal chat was when we next worked together in B7 (Training) in 2014. Oh, I saw plenty of him once I was in T8NI, and whenever he was visiting Ireland or if I was in London; but he was only running T8 for my first year, and then they pulled him into G-Branch for his operational experience.

So, off to Northern Ireland, and that left only one other loose-end to tie off: Maria McLaughlin. I'd discussed my concerns with Úna first, and in truth I hadn't seen Maria for the past two years anyway; since I'd moved to G-Branch and to Dulwich and my hours had gone through the roof. But now I needed to meet her and to tell her I was back in Ireland, but working at the NIO and so vulnerable vis-a-vis her common-law 'married' status. Maria understood. We discussed it over a great dinner, we agreed to meet platonically from time to time and as a foursome with Úna and Dermott, and – I hope you're really impressed by this – we didn't even do it once more for old times' sake. Although it took every ounce of will power I had.

But then here's the thing about life: as one door closes, remember, another often opens, and as I said goodbye to Maria I said hello again to Tommy Bray, the charismatic half-French rugby centre who'd run rings around me and George Kennedy at Blackrock College back in 1997. George and he had met up after a rugby match the year before, in Dundalk and whilst Bray had been home on leave from the army. But Tommy's real news was *which* army, and George updated me on my last trip to Ireland before I moved back there in '09 to begin my new job.

Tommy had finished-up his law degree at Trinity College in late-2000, but then, more to his father's disappointment than disgust – his dad was a High Court Judge in Dublin – the following year Tommy had joined the army and not the bar. After his first year learning his new trade in the infantry, the next three were spent in the IDF's Ranger Wing, the Irish Army's Special Forces. That merely inflamed Tommy's itch for soldiering, he told George, but it never really managed to scratch it. And so, through the action he saw there, next he migrated naturally to the 2emeREP, the 2nd Foreign Parachute Regiment of the French Foreign Legion. France had a much bigger military footprint than Ireland, he'd explained, 'and it gets involved a lot', he'd told George with a glint in his eye. Hence, he spent the next three years in the 2emeREP and in the French Special Forces Brigade. That's where he'd been serving when George had met-up with him, and we discussed the pros and cons for an Irishman serving in the French Army.

"Well, no cons really," George pointed out, "because he's fully bi-lingual remember, and, y'know, he's half-French anyway. He lives in the old family home in Lyon; he's got dual-nationality; and 'soldiering's soldiering,' as he puts it; so he just wanted to take it to the next level. Huh, sounds a lot like you in that respect."

"Aye, I guess," I replied, and I ignored his cheap shot at my OCD-approach to work, "but I was thinking more about all the cultural differences... y'know, like having to think, act and take orders in French an' all."

"Yeah, but not really; it's instinctive, he says, and it's him giving most of the orders now anyway, coz he's a Captain. Besides, that's just how it is in the Legion he reckons; and even if you say he's really Irish, or even mostly Irish, that just puts him in the seventy per cent of non-Frenchmen in his unit."

"Jesus, that many?"

"Aye, even more he reckons. Nearer seventy-five per cent. They've only got to be able to speak French apparently, otherwise nationality's not an issue; although he's only able to be an officer because of his French citizenship."

"But seventy-five per cent..."

"Yeah, for the rest. Providing you can shoot straight and die, he reckons, you're in... although he did say the training was something else as well though," George chuckled into his beer. "Marche ou crève, he reckons..."

"Is that 'March or die'?"

"Yeah, it's their unofficial motto..."

"So what's their real one?"

"Jesus, can't remember," George shrugged, "he told me but you'll have to ask him."

And so in time I did. They've got two: *Honneur et Fidélité*, 'Honour and Fidelity'; and *Legio Patria Nostra*, 'The Legion is our Fatherland'. As opposed to motherland... clever.

Anyway... the upshot of it all was that once I got back to Ireland full time, George hooked us all up for a few beers. And then after that, whenever Tommy was 'home' on leave again, we'd all get together as and when we could. Tommy's parents still lived in Drogheda, and his dad – although retired – was still a big wheel in Dublin legal circles and with Interpol, for whom he'd worked in

Lyon in the 1980s and '90s. Plus Tommy was single, and so he had more money than God.

What with his regular army salary, Special Forces pay, near-constant add-ons for back-to-back deployments, and then the fact that by being away for nine or ten months of the year he had few opportunities to spend any of it, Tommy had bought himself a small place in Dublin too. The three of us had some rare old nights there, and I got to know his couch quite well. Kennedy was too long for everything, including Tommy's only spare bed; but I deferred to George's ugliness always and so the couch was as good as mine.

And so in 2009, as I arrived back in the Province to settle into my new job, what actually awaited me in T8NI? A great bunch of people, a vastly changed Northern Ireland, and a lot of hard work, that's what.

Even since the last time I was there on leave less than a year before, there had been significant changes. Peace wasn't yet something that was guaranteed for the Province's future, far from it, but it had pretty much become the daily way of life for the time being. The checkpoints had totally gone from Belfast city centre, except for at peak periods like Christmas or for increased threat levels, as had any routine evidence of soldiers on the streets; but... the police were still armed, the Dissidents were still around, and so were the peace walls between most sectarian enclaves in Belfast and other urban interfaces. And so becoming 'normal' by the rest of the Free World's standards was still some way off. As someone pointed out to me in my first week back, stretches of the eight-metre-high peace walls had been in place for over forty years by then... so twelve years longer than the Berlin Wall!

The Dissidents were actually something more than just 'still around'. Although they were nowhere near as sophisticated as the Provisional IRA, even thirty years earlier, they were still pretty busy and getting busier. And tragically, they were still taking lives. In January the Real IRA shot dead two British Army soldiers in County Antrim, and then in March the 'Conts', the Continuity IRA, shot dead the first policeman killed in Northern Ireland since 1998 – the first of my mum's brave new millennium.

So... there was still plenty for us to get our teeth into and I knew I was in for a busy time. Good, that's exactly what I wanted, and I had done since I opted to join the Security Service back in 2002; but for me personally there was even more to be done than I had realised. Tony Moss, my new Boss, had a special plan for me. But just for me. It was a good plan, and Bill Wallace had given it his unqualified support, but it was also a total surprise; to me at least, because I didn't know a thing about it until I got there.

As my plane dropped below the sunny, white and fleecy clouds into the rain and the near-permanent twilight of an Irish winter, it all had an ominously familiar feeling to it.

'Welcome home, fellah,' it seemed to chuckle haughtily, 'Welcome back to Northern Ireland, and a Happy friggin' New Year yet again'.

Utrinque Paratus

Tony Moss, the Head of T8NI when I first got there, was an extremely bright and capable graduate of the Bill Wallace school of agent running. Or rather a graduate, with honours, from Bill's first stint in T8 back in London in the '90s. It was no accident then, that as Bill was half way through his five years running T8 for the second time, from the start of 2005 until almost the end of 2009, Tony found himself working there again also. And it was even less of an accident that upon Tony's promotion later that year, Wallace and the then Head of T-Branch sent him to Northern Ireland to head up the budding section there.

I'd had plenty of dealings with Moss, all good and none disciplinary thank God, because he'd also inherited Bill Wallace's sense of fair play and no-nonsense command and control. And by all accounts his sense of humour. That suited me fine, some others not so, but it also meant he expected me to dive straight in and not pause for too long to check the temperature of the water. And so that brings me nicely to the Moss-Wallace plan for my first year...

Tony explained that he didn't want me to be known to most of the section's current stable of agents. Quite simply, he wanted as few of them as possible to even know that we had a South Armagh 'speaker' in the office. It wasn't that he didn't trust them - although that was a stringently objective filter always - it was just that it was a rare and precious secret he felt we should keep to ourselves for as long as we could manage. And, he shrewdly calculated, it would also ensure that I got cracking in the search for new agents of my own. Clever men, because that's exactly what I did.

One of the first came from the most unlikely source... Úna. And it came, unbeknown to her, at an extremely helpful time to the section overall. As did another about a year later, which also fell out of the blue so to speak, and from none other than Tommy Bray. Both worked out well and so the die was cast, and I was given more and more leeway to try evermore innovative ideas. Most successful recruitment operations were the culmination of many months of sheer hard graft and more than a few setbacks – some took years – but Úna and Tommy Bray got us off to a flying start with little or no effort and no real risk of exposure. And as in all such enterprises, nothing breeds success like success - and so other opportunities were exploited along the way.

First let me tell you about Úna's contribution.

With the loss of thousands of British soldiers regularly patrolling the streets, and their instinctive propensity for writing detailed reports about everyone they spoke to or anything that happened, the search for good agent potential had become a ball-breaking and often thankless task. Enter Úna... stage left, and over a much needed cocktail in Hillsborough one evening.

"Listen Nephew, don't answer if you don't feel you can, but if I told you about a fifty-something-year-old haulage contractor from just outside Newry, who had been pulled-in by the police for a smashed rear light and had blamed some Real IRA man he'd pissed off, would you find that interesting at all?"

"Aye, but only in passing." I said. "However..."

"However what?"

"However, I know you well enough, Auntie, to know that twinkle in your eye means that's only half the story."

"Maybe," she teased, "so what if I also told you I reckon the same guy was being pressured by the Real IRA around his home somewhere to help them out in some way?"

"In what way?"

"Oh, that you'll have to ask him yourself, but given that he owns his own trucking business, or two trucks anyway, I'd guess it's something to do with that. Or at least I'm pretty sure that's what the Real IRA think he's up for."

"Well, maybe, but that's a bit of a stretch just because..."

"No, I'm pretty sure that's what they think."

"Why?"

"Because he's got prior form, as the police would say."

"In what way?"

"Well I'll tell you."

And once we were quite alone, she did. She told me that the man, when just a youth, had been arrested in the 1980s for moving a weapon for a Provo neighbour; but that the charges had been dropped because the evidential chain had been broken. His name was Séamus Fox, and that reputation had stuck with him however. Now, thirty years later, he was desperately trying to make a go of a small hauliers' business comprising just him, two trucks and two other drivers, and he was being strong-armed by someone in the Real IRA to move gear for them too.

"How do you know all this?" I asked her.

I should have known better, and I had no doubt that once she put her mind to it her in-depth research was probably better than my own. And what's more, after thirty-five years in the insurance business in South Armagh and along the border, her sources almost certainly were.

"Wives talk," she grinned, and then she laughed a dirty laugh, "and so do husbands, by the way; but on this occasion I'm talking about the most intimate secrets of a young wife I know."

"Jesus."

"And that's a lesson for life too remember..."

"What is?"

"Wives talk... and don't you ever forget it. I don't want to hear you've had it cut off one day."

"Very funny. Chance would be a fine thing, and I'm way too busy these days. So go on then, what sort of a wife would be telling you this?" I asked.

"A police wife, here in the North, but... and here's where I think you might be able to do something with this without it ever coming back to me, *she* heard it from a Garda wife in Dundalk. That's where the guy got pulled-in... by the Guards."

"OK. And so this Fox character actually told them he was being intimidated by the Real IRA then, did he?"

"No, of course not, not in so many words. I've worked that part out for myself from a couple of things I've heard on the insurance network. Y'know, like a sort of protection racket they're running against small business types. And especially guys like him with past form, to try to get them to help in some way. And he's cropped up a couple of times now."

"So how can the Garda help? Why do you say that?"

"Ah, because supposedly he said to the Guard that pulled him over, 'Jees, sorry, I know I need to get that fixed, but that's down to some Real IRA fucker I've pissed off. He smashed it, because I told him what I thought of him and he knows where I park this truck.' You see now?"

"Got it. And the Guard let him off?"

"Yeah, just with a caution apparently."

"OK, and that's useful to know, but so how could I have come to hear about something as trivial as that though?"

"Trivial?"

"No, not what he said, the potential's great – and thank you, honestly – but how would I happen to hear about the traffic stop of some spotty-faced Guard in Dundalk?"

"Jesus Neill, you must be tired. How on earth have you got by without me these past ten years?"

"Y'know, I often ask myself that. Especially whenever I climb into my cold and empty bed." She laughed. "Go on," I grinned stupidly, "I'm clearly missing something obvious here."

"Well isn't that something that Detective Sergeant George Kennedy might stumble across? And if this Fox character in the report lives in the North, and if George just happens to know somebody in the North who could look into it, well then…"

"Jesus Úna, you're a star. You know that? How *have* I got by without you?"

The rest after that was pretty simple. Recently promoted Detective Sergeant George Kennedy had indeed found the report, and he'd arranged for me to talk to the young Garda face-to-face to make sure I was clear on the exact wording, context and inflection of his encounter with Fox. He'd even offered practical support if I'd somehow wanted to follow it up in the South, so the unsuspecting Newry man wouldn't make the obvious connection with the Brits until I'd had a chance to break the ice. I didn't take him up on it on that occasion, but he had sewn an important seed for another case that was just around the corner.

To cut a long story short we actually got Fox to deliver two pallet loads of local granite to a supposed landscaping project inside Hollywood Barracks, where I met him as the man who would sign for the delivery. With our matching accents we'd got chatting right away, and given my surroundings it had been a quick and simple process to drop cover and say that 'I understood from the Garda…' and so on. He was indeed under duress from

RIRA, and he was grateful for an opportunity to have someone to ease him out of his predicament *and* get back at them at the same time; and so we'd shown him some safe and secure ways for him to show his gratitude. It had become a very happy marriage.

Séamus Fox was one of the easiest recruitments I ever made – thanks to Karma, Úna and George – and he soon turned out to be one of our most productive sources working against the Real IRA in South Armagh. Better still, there was the added bonus that if his trips to Hollywood Barracks ever became known to RIRA, and if they then took an interest, then we'd have a heads-up on whatever they were planning at the outset.

Then it was Tommy Bray's turn.

Soon after I'd arrived back in Ireland and got settled-in, I'd looked George up and we'd set-about picking up where we'd left off. We both worked silly-hours and so we couldn't get together that often, but we had a secure phone-link and we spoke on that maybe three or four times a week. It was usually work, sometimes social, but after one of those calls we'd got together to catch up and for a pint in Banbridge. Banbridge was pretty much half way between Dundalk and Hollywood, and fairly discreet for both of us. Plus, George had announced that Tommy Bray was in Dublin on leave and he was seeking our advice on a sensitive matter.

Tommy knew what we both did by then. He'd moonlighted for George on a couple of reconnaissance tasks in Dundalk and although he'd not worked directly with the Service, Tommy had worked on deployment with the SAS and so on several occasions with some of my counterparts in MI6. I'd declared him as a Social Contact as soon as I got back, and so he was a known and cleared quantity to the office as well.

Tommy was en route to Fort Bragg in the USA, to start a three-year tour as a French Special Forces Exchange Officer with US Special Ops Command. Before he'd shipped-out, and on his last trip to Drogheda to see his parents, he'd been sought-out and spoken to by a former colleague from the Rangers. Tommy rated his colleague, Des Tierney, as a high calibre soldier and a man of considerable integrity, so he was keen to help him if he could.

Amongst other things Tierney had been a sniper. He'd left the Rangers two years after Tommy had joined the Foreign Legion, and he'd worked until a few months beforehand as an Adventure Training Instructor in Connemara. Originally from Ardee in County Louth, less than twenty minutes from Tommy's family home in Drogheda, Tierney had recently inherited his maternal grandfather's timeworn cottage in Castlewellan, in the North in County Down. Although pretty run-down and in need of repair, it was just a stone's throw from the landward side of the Mourne Mountains and from Tollymore Forest Park; so Tierney was living between the two homes and was determined to set-up and run his own adventure training company from Castlewellan. As a result, he'd moved-in some weeks beforehand and started working to that end. Enter three goons from the Real IRA.

A couple of months after Tierney had arrived, he'd been chatted-up in a Castlewellan pub by a local man from Kilcoo and by a mate of his from Downpatrick. That had happened several times, but as more of his background was confirmed in casual conversation so their interest in him had changed. And then after a month or two more, they'd approached him one night at his grandfather's cottage. That time though, they were accompanied by a Dundalk man called Tim Docherty. Docherty was known to George as a Real IRA suspect from the Muirhevnamore Estate in Dundalk; although Docherty hadn't hidden that fact from Tierney and he'd stated his business pretty clearly. The three men had wanted Tierney to give sniper-training to selected members of their Newry-Castlewellan unit. He'd refused.

They hadn't left it at that though, and further approaches and minor acts of vandalism around his Castlewellan home had driven him to seek Tommy Bray's advice or assistance. Tierney had been hoping for the latter, and between them he'd hoped they'd simply disappear them, but Tommy stressed they should use legal means only and so his advice would have to do. Bray had thought immediately of George Kennedy, and because Docherty's RIRA unit was in the North and because of the Newry connection, George had immediately thought of me. I'm glad he did.

Tierney was up for it, and so in less than a week we had all the clearances and blessings we needed to ease Tierney into the Real IRA unit concerned; and in Tierney himself we had a tough, resourceful, bright and willing agent that would benefit any network hugely. What we also had was at least one RIRA unit whose sniper and other attacks would fail consistently... for one mysterious reason after another. Game on. And a substantial added bonus was that Tommy Bray was now fully indoctrinated and on our books as a facilities agent as well. George and I saw him off to the States in style, and then we looked forward to the next time he was back.

There were other new cases of course, some grander some simpler, yet all vital to our efforts to save lives, protect property and enable the peaceful way of life trying so hard to take root in Northern Ireland. But if the first eighteen months of my three years in T8NI were busy, then the next eighteen could only be described as manic. But they were also great craic and highly productive, and so apart from some sort of a steady girlfriend for the first time ever... what more could a young and dynamic professional guy who was approaching thirty ask for?

Life, remember, is where you're at... blah, blah, blah. And so I just got on with it.

That year, 2010, saw not only *my* real breakthrough in the section, but also that of our team and of an era of jointery with our counterparts in the South. We had been aware for some months of a growing yearning in the-as-yet-still-dormant former Provo constituency, for a resurgent IRA that was nothing at all to do with the Dissidents. Some sort of 'rebranding and rebirth of the real thing', as one of our agents had put it, and so we'd been focussing whatever resources we could on just that.

Names were still few and far between, and indications of their intent and current progress were even rarer; but we'd made a start and it was clear that there was a new and scary threat looming on the horizon. One name that had cropped up several times, however, was that of a man called Joe Gorman; and if he wasn't already the leader of what at the time we were calling the new IRA, or NIRA amongst ourselves, then he certainly appeared to be its rising star.

Without further direction we started to build a case against him and those in his orbit, in an attempt to stay one step ahead of them if they became a current and lethal threat. The case built quickly – he was vulnerable in several ways. But then before we had to decide whether to arrest him, or simply monitor him to drastically increase our knowledge of the group overall, what Tony Moss called an 'intelligence pearl' presented itself and effectively made the decision for us.

As our knowledge about Gorman grew, so did a mass of data surrounding his wife, Finella, and a number of loyal cohorts. Finella back then was a still very presentable fifty-two years-old. Gorman was a few years older and one of the things we'd learned was that he'd never let her fall pregnant because he didn't want her to lose her figure. She'd been seventeen when they married and she loved kids; he didn't, and that was the end of the argument for the next thirty-five years. That had become a major source of anger and resentment, we learned, as had a number of other things we were still picking up. Not least of all, we were unclear as to why Gorman should be so worried about his wife's figure when he was seeing-to half a dozen young mistresses at the same time. We were onto something big, and it became my charging buffalo to bring down before we missed our chance.

In terms of establishing a number of different potential motivators for Finella Gorman to turn against her husband, things moved quickly. We learned a lot in quick time and from a number of different sources –human, technical and from surveillance – but the problem we were going to have was how to get alongside her. They lived in a former Provo enclave in the gut of West Belfast, where everyone knew everyone else, everyone knew everyone else's business, and where strangers were spotted in a heartbeat. Back at the height of the Troubles and in that area, it might easily have become a covert operator's *last* heartbeat.

After months of compiling dozens of leads and snippets, and of tracking not only the extent of Gorman's infidelity but also the depth of what I felt was surely his wife's resentment, I was ready to go. But how, where and when would I be able to put my case to her? I'd brainstormed her possible motivating factors to a standstill, and I was confident that if I could get in front of her under the right circumstances they boiled down to three essential things: she was sick and tired of his philandering; she was fearful of the new IRA campaign he was planning; and strongest of all... she was hell bent on revenge!

I hadn't even considered the South, we'd had no reason to, and then just when I was fearful that she might just up and leave him altogether, she walked, figuratively speaking, right up to our pearly gates and stepped inside.

We learned from one of our other agents that Joe Gorman had just gone an affair too far, and that his wife had found out through a relative of the young girl concerned. But we also found out that as part of a revenge getaway, Finella Gorman had stolen Joe's cheque book and was off for a pamper weekend in a five-star Dublin hotel. He didn't even know yet, but we did, and the information, bizarrely, was fairly common knowledge amongst a bunch of Belfast wives. We had just three days and much to do, but the prize potentially waiting for us at the end of our race meant that almost any effort was worth it.

I instantly thought of George Kennedy and how he might be able to help, but then on a whim of inspiration I walked into Tony Moss and suggested we go one better. I reasoned that seeing as we only had seventy-two hours left in which to plan, prepare, deploy and execute – *and* in which to attempt the torturous inter-governmental and cross-border clearances that we were going to need – why not approach the Garda and suggest a joint case from the outset? Tony had been looking for such an opportunity for ages, or was it Bill Wallace or 'T' back in London? Whoever it was, Tony fairly leapt out of his chair to make it happen, and so it did.

London, the NIO and the Home Office gave their respective blessings immediately – all at the secret level of course – and so our liaison with Dublin began the same day. As JC had suggested when I'd met him in London just days before, the HUMINT world might usefully have adopted the same motto as the British Parachute Regiment... *Utrinque Paratus*... 'Ready For Anything'; and if we were going to be ready at all, we had an enormous amount to do and very little time in which to do it.

Tony and I drove immediately to Dublin and met, briefed, cajoled or brainstormed for the whole of the next day; and then the day after that we deployed. Or rather I did, into a room in the same luxury hotel that Finella Gorman was already booked-into the following afternoon. I was supported by the two CSB case officers, one male one female, who were going to be my co-handlers from the outset. The CSB was the Crime & Security Branch of the Garda – some of its sections would equate to the Garda Special Branch in old parlance – and we reckoned they would prove essential for the smooth running of the recruitment pitch (especially if Gorman reacted badly), and then helpful, to say the least, to the case going forward. The various political entities in the approval chain were beside themselves at our 'dynamic and proactive spirit of cooperation', and dozens of senior people on both sides of the border – and on both sides of the Irish Sea – anxiously awaited news of our joint operation. Tea and medals for Tony, I reckoned... all I wanted was a successful outcome.

I wasn't disappointed. None of us were.

That's Doable

It was a relatively simple thing to do, so we set it up and did it. I was on my way out of the hotel and stopping off briefly at the front desk, just as Finella Gorman was about to check-in. Job done. Then as she approached the desk I stepped back and let her deal with the receptionist before I did. That went well, and so we exchanged our first glances, our first courteous gestures and our first smiles, but no conversation - which is exactly what I'd intended. Later on she glimpsed me again going to the pool that evening, when she was turning-up for the first of several spa sessions. That trip must have cost Joe Gorman a fortune, but I pretended not to have seen her. The same thing happened at breakfast on the Saturday, although that time I gave her a friendly nod as I left the dining room.

Late morning, we saw each other once again in the spa area – me going for a swim yet again and her for a massage – and this time I gave her an embarrassed smile and a friendly little wave, as if to say, 'Oh, Hi again, but I'm not a stalker, honest.' She both waved and smiled back, and hers clearly said, 'What a shame, you can stalk me as much as you want.' But that was it until two hours later in the bar.

Our team had noticed that Finella Gorman liked her cocktails, or maybe she was just punishing Joe even further, but on the off chance that she'd see me sat at the bar – or simply stop for an afternoon cocktail of her own – I went there after a snack lunch and had a whiskey and dry ginger. Sure enough, as she left the dining room she approached, smiling, and so I turned on my stool and stood to greet her.

"You look lonely, drinking there all on your own," she said.

"No, thoughtful actually, but I'd love you to join me if that's what you were about to say."

"Thank you."

"And if not…" I continued with a smile, "then forgive me for being so forward."

"Oh, no," she grinned, "course not. No apology necessary."

"Please…" I pulled a stool out for her.

"Thank you," she purred, "besides, it was me that spoke to you. I hate to see someone drinking alone, and we've met now, what…" she grinned, "four times already?"

"Yes," I laughed, "I suppose we have, four or five I guess. And so now I can put a voice and a conversation to that beautiful smile of yours." It was beautiful, Joe Gorman was clearly stupid as well as ruthless.

"Thank you," she beamed, and she climbed carefully onto the stool so as not to reveal more thigh than was appropriate.

"So you're obviously staying here too," she began, "and you like to swim I see. Business or pleasure?"

"Business," I answered warmly, "although it just became a pleasure too, what can I get you?"

"Thank you twice more," she smiled even more broadly, "once for the drink and once for the compliment. I'll have a Sangria if that's OK?"

"Course it is," the barman had heard her order so he gave a little nod and made a start on it. "And what about you? You like to relax in the leisure centre too I see, and so I'm guessing your stay is entirely pleasure."

"Very much so. I'm going to treat myself into the ground," she grinned mischievously, "but maybe mine just got a little bit more enjoyable too."

"Well thank you too, ma'am," I lifted my glass.

"So, business you say... and you're here in Dublin...?"

That was obviously a question, so I gave her the answer I'd rehearsed more than a dozen times. My CSB colleagues thought I was mad, but I knew exactly how I wanted things to progress. That didn't mean I was right, but I knew what I was hoping to achieve; and when they'd suggested that I might be able to get her to accept dinner, I'd simply replied, 'Aye, I reckon that's doable.'

They'd inevitably roared with laughter and asked, 'What is? Finella Gorman or dinner?' to which I had replied, 'Both, but only dinner's going to happen on my watch.' They laughed again, and I smiled, but they knew from the way I'd said it I wasn't joking.

"I work for the British government," I told her matter of factly, "so I travel a lot."

"Oh wow, what here in Dublin?" she asked.

The barman slid her cocktail towards her and so there was a natural pause of a second or two.

"No, umm, I don't know how to answer that exactly."

She didn't look concerned, just curious. So I dangled my line a little further. She sipped her drink.

"I guess I work wherever I'm sent. Y'know, for like a few weeks or months at a time. As I said, I travel a lot... it's a large Commonwealth, and it was once an even larger Empire."

"Right," she smiled and sipped her drink, "but Dublin's in the *former* Empire isn't it? So how does that work?"

"Good point," I chuckled, "but I'm here to do with the Peace Process."

"Oh, I see," and she looked suddenly thoughtful, but still not anxious or concerned. Fascinated, was the word I'd use to describe her expression. "Well that sounds even more interesting. And will it work?"

"The Peace Process?"

"Yes."

"God I hope so. Don't we all?"

"Yes, of course," she sounded sincere, "but I'm just a little surprised that's all. You sound like you come from around the border somewhere?"

"I do, and if you go back far enough one of my forebears was probably responsible for drawing the damn thing up."

I laughed, and so did she.

"So you don't agree with the border?" she chuckled.

"Not really, and hopefully one day it won't be there, and I certainly don't agree with where it is."

"I'm not with you, where should it be?"

"Well, I'm from South Armagh, for example, and so *we're* on the wrong side of it for a start..."

"Oh, you should be in the South you mean."

"Exactly."

"I've never heard that from a Brit before," she chuckled, "that doesn't sound very loyal to the Crown."

"Oh, I'm fiercely loyal, to everyone I'm ever involved with, that's what I do... loyalty... but I just don't happen to agree with everything they say or do is all."

"The government you mean?"

"Exactly."

"No, well you wouldn't be alone in that back home, I'm sure," she laughed again. "So what do you do exactly?"

"Umm, that's even harder to explain. And to be honest I'm not allowed to, but the best way to describe me is as a sort of a peace-maker. A sort of diplomat I'd guess you'd call me. I try to keep the peace and sort-out bad stuff... y'know, so we can all keep shuffling forward towards a better world."

She cocked her head and clearly didn't know what to ask next. Good, it was like *she* didn't want to spook *me*. I continued.

"I'm a sort of Father Theresa you might say."

"Oh," she looked confused, "so are you a priest?"

"God no, not nearly saintly enough," I laughed. "I suppose what I mean is I *aspire* to be a Father Theresa, in terms of the big picture and making a difference; but there's a few too many sins seeping out of my confessional for that. And I actually have to bang heads together from time to time. So that's not very priestly."

"Oh I don't know about that, you should meet some of the priests I grew up around."

"Yeah, I'm sure," I chuckled, "In Belfast?"

"Yes, my accent?"

"Aye."

"Ballymurphy. Have you heard of it?"

"Of course," I laughed, "have you heard of Crossmaglen?"

"Touché," she smiled warmly and lifted her glass for me to clink mine, and so I did. "Crazy places, both of them..." she said, "so here's to being away from home."

"I'll drink to that. Away from home can be good."

"And I'll definitely drink to *that*," she smirked, "away from home for me right now is about perfect."

I'd sewn all the seeds I wanted to for the time being and I was delighted with how well it was going, so in my judgement it was time to bail for the afternoon; but I couldn't let that remark go without passing comment. I decided to do both. It was fifteen minutes to the top of the hour, so I reckoned I'd take the plunge and then give her a little time and space to reflect.

"Look, er, Mrs…" I glanced down at her wedding ring to show I understood she was married.

"Finella, call me Finella," she said. I extended my hand and shook hers gently.

"Aidan O'Connor," I replied.

"I should remove these by the way," she fiddled with her rings, "I'm not exactly married at the moment."

"Oh…" I feigned shock, "not exactly, what does that mean?"

"Long story."

"I see…"

She didn't answer. She smiled awkwardly instead.

"And I'd love to hear it," I carried on cautiously, "but I'm not sure I should say what I was about to now?"

"Go on," she looked a mixture of flattered, disappointed and curious, but still not in the least bit nervous or hesitant.

"Well, I was going to say I have to go, I'm being picked-up for a meeting at three…"

"Oh…" her disappointment was palpable.

"But if you're still here tonight, I was also going to suggest that we have dinner this evening."

"Oh, yes, I'd love to."

"Honestly?"

"Yes, definitely, I'll have pampered myself to a standstill by then. Reckon I'll have quite the appetite."

"But are you sure? With your marriage thing an' all?"

"Positive. That's not a problem, trust me. That's just some nonsense in my life at the moment…" I looked sympathetic, "and I shouldn't really wear these." She fussed with her rings again. "It confuses people."

"Well if you're sure, then great, just say a time."

"You say a time, I'm the one relaxing. You have a meeting."

"Seven."

"Here at the bar?"

"Perfect. Sorry, um… Finella?"

"Yes, Finella."

"Sorry Finella, but I've got to rush off now…"

"No, it's fine, I hope your meeting goes well."

"God, so do I," I looked suddenly grave and ominous, "it'll be war again for all of us if it doesn't." Then I smiled and she laughed, hard. Very hard. I signed-off my bar bill, nodded her a cheeky smile and then backed away.

"Seven," I confirmed.

"Looking forward to it." Then she turned back to her drink with the smug and satisfied expression of a fifty-year-old woman who'd just proved that her charms were as potent as ever.

At 6.50 pm I walked into the bar and Finella Gorman was already there and one drink ahead of me. Although I'd called down and booked a table, she hadn't used my name and so she was sat on a barstool again. This time she wasn't so shy about her thighs, and she'd put on what was clearly a favourite cocktail-style dress. The effect was alluring and she had good legs. I was wearing a suit, and so it would appear that we'd both correctly read each other's perception of what dinner should be about. She looked pleased that I'd made the effort. Good, because I knew that I was soon to disappoint her.

"Good evening," I said. "Good, glad I'm not overdressed… you look absolutely stunning."

"Thank you Aidan, and you look pretty handsome too," she grinned. "Very smart. You really do know how to make a girl feel special I've noticed. Is that one of your duties as Father Theresa?"

"No," I smiled, "sadly it's not one of my *duties*… but I like to think it's one of my skills as a man. Life's too short to want to make a girl feel anything other than special."

"Huh, that makes you a pretty rare breed." Her attractive and smiling expression had never changed, but for an instant her voice had become harsh and cynical. She realised and recovered quickly though. "I wish all men felt like that."

"Of course," I winced, "I can only imagine. And I wish all beautiful women thought that was as special as you seem to."

She smiled.

"Then it sounds like we'd both have more fun," I added.

"Hear hear," she cocked her head playfully. "And is that what we're going to do?" she raised her glass, "have fun?"

"Ah, see I thought we were going to have dinner," I grinned mischievously, "but I hope we're going to have fun as well."

The contrast with her husband must have struck her from our first meeting, but still I didn't mention him. Not yet. And I hoped that nor would she. It wouldn't be hard to come across as more charming than Joe Gorman, and I knew we would talk of little else once he cropped up in the conversation soon. But there was no hurry... and every reason not to.

We chatted easily for a little while and flattered each other with more innuendo and non-verbal cues, then I suggested we stay at the bar and order from the menu there before sitting down. I had a whiskey to go with her cocktail; we chose our meals; selected a bottle of wine; and only then did I help her down from her stool and did we move to our table. She showed a little more thigh as she climbed down and she made sure I'd noticed... I made equally sure I didn't comment.

Easy conversation continued throughout the first course, and by the time our main arrived it had progressed cheerfully to a little flirtatious banter. Despite me coming from South Armagh she had teased me playfully about being a Brit, and in the end it had become even more good-humoured and more about our regional differences than anything. The 'Townie and the Bogger' she teased. We had already gone over what we'd both been up to since we last saw each other at lunchtime, although she'd not been too nosey about the nature or the venue of my meeting. It was inevitable though, and I was ready.

I had warned her earlier, after all, that I wasn't really 'allowed to explain' exactly what I did, but inevitably she came back to some of my earlier comments and tried to tease more out of me. Despite that, of two things I was as certain as I could be: she seemed to have no interest in my status or how it might be of use to the new IRA or her husband; and she seemed fully relaxed and totally un-phased by the fact that I was some sort of 'a Brit'. And so I judged that my window of opportunity was opening slowly, and that I should step through it as soon as I saw the right moment. It wasn't long in coming, and after the main course it felt just about perfect.

"So, Father Theresa," she had teased, "just how much of a diplomat were you this afternoon? And so are we still at peace?"

"We are indeed... for today at least," I smiled. "Peace in our time, as Neville Chamberlain so famously said."

"Yeah, but he was wrong, wasn't he? Didn't war follow straight afterwards?"

"Aye, he was," I sniggered, "but hopefully I'm not. You'll know as well as me that there's more than a few people out there trying to change that."

"Huh, tell me about it."

"Oh Finella, I could. Do you really want me to?"

"What?"

"Tell you about it?"

"Oh, well... no, not if you're not allowed to..."

"Some I can. Some I want to."

"Well yes then, I'm interested obviously, but I was just teasing though really," she giggled.

"No, I know you were, although there's things I'd like to tell you. But... y'know, we're having so much fun here..."

"Exactly."

"And we seem to be getting on so well..."

"I agree entirely."

"...that I thought I'd like to tell you *exactly* what I'm doing here in Dublin. You know, tell you the whole truth as it were... so that you don't feel later on that I've been deliberately trying to mislead you."

"Oh, right. No, I'm sure I wouldn't think that."

She looked puzzled, and by way of solving it she decided to clarify the situation.

"Look Aidan, if you work for the government and it's all secret, then of course you can't tell me. But that shouldn't stop us having fun, should it."

"That's precisely how I feel."

"Good, well there you go then," she beamed, "and I won't tease you about it anymore. Let's just get on with the fun bit."

"Oh I'm up for that, and I really do mean fun by the way – you are an amazingly frank and open person, and I am so enjoying your company, truly – but so I think it's time to share the secret part of it with you too."

"Oh... but can you do that?" she was suddenly hesitant.

"Yes, but I feel I need to, out of fairness..."

"Oh..." she said again, "well whatever you think."

"You see I can do pretty much whatever I want," I smiled, "and I think it's time to share something with you."

"Oh wow. I'm all excited now. What?"

"Well, I hope you still are in a minute, but it's all the wrong sort of excitement I fear."

This time she didn't reply, and she was clearly a little anxious about whatever was coming next. My clear impression was that she thought I was going to turn all 'Father Theresa' on her, and pronounce some moral judgement on what we were doing. If only it was going to be that simple.

"In fact, Finella, I must. Now's the time. Because I'm a frank and open person too, and scrupulously honest, and so I don't want to go any longer without telling you exactly what I do and why I'm here in case it damages the trust I think we've established."

"Oh wow, oh my God. Well now I'm more confused than excited," she smiled, but this time she wasn't totally convincing, "but I'm trying hard not to be scared."

"Oh please don't be that. There's no need to be that at all, and I doubt if you'll ever be as safe as when you're with me," she pulled a quizzical face, "but please let me explain just what sort of a diplomat I am; a sort of peace-maker I told you earlier."

"Go on, so is it really about the Peace Process then?"

"Oh yes, my meeting you mean? One hundred per cent about the Peace Process. And more vitally important than you could probably imagine... but it was also about you."

"About *me?*"

"Yes, Finella, you're the real reason I'm here."

"*Me.* Why?"

"Because I knew you were here and I wanted to meet you."

"Why?"

"Because I think you could play a major part."

"What, in the Peace Process? Me?" she laughed nervously. "How on earth can I do that?"

"Because I reckon you're here to punish Joe..."

"Joe! You know Joe?"

She was clearly alarmed, but she glanced around quickly and didn't let the rest of the room see. For a moment or two my South Armagh accent must have overridden everything else I'd told her, because it was immediately obvious she thought I was an IRA plant conspiring with her husband.

"Did he send you here?" she demanded quietly. Not even a hint of denying she knew him, or who she was. "Are you one of his border cronies? So what's this then, are you trying to lure me into bed so the shoe's on the other feckin' foot or something?"

"No, God no," I smiled, "and no again. No to all three of those things unfortunately. I'm sure payback like that would be great fun for both of us, but that's not what I'm here for. I am really who I told you."

"A diplomat?"

"Well, I should probably clear that bit up a little..."

"But a Brit?"

"Yes, an official from the British government, and here in Dublin specifically to see you."

Her face turned suddenly stern and her beautiful smile was a thing of the past. What replaced it looked angry and vicious.

"To trap me you mean?"

"No Finella, quite the opposite. You can get up and leave whenever you want. You can leave now... but I hope you don't, I'm enjoying your company..."

"Fuck you."

"And I haven't finished explaining," I added quickly.

She went to speak but I gently beat her to it.

"And you can go and tell anyone you want as well... feel free, seriously, but I hope you don't do that either. That would be awkward for both of us, but far more awkward – and possibly dangerous – for you, don't you think?"

"Was that a threat?"

"God no, that was a warning. A friendly warning. I meant I was worried about what Joe would do to you, not us. We wouldn't do a thing, except be sad at a missed opportunity. A missed golden opportunity I might add."

"A golden opportunity for what?"

"Well, let me explain, and then as I said if you don't think my idea is a good one, then why don't we just finish a pleasant meal, try to enjoy each other's company as much as we had been until now, and then I'll walk out of your life forever. I promise."

"Right now? Forever?"

"After our meal, yes. If that's still what you want."

"So look. If I hear you out and say 'no', you promise there's no strings attached."

"I promise."

"Just for listening?"

"Just that."

"You soft twat, you must think I'm stupid."

"No, I think the exact opposite, that much is very clear. Which is why I think you'll listen."

"Because you want me to tout for you, right?"

"God Finella, I know what you're getting at... and so 'yes' is my totally honest answer..."

"Well fuck you twice then."

"...but listen, I detest that word, and what you're asking about couldn't possibly be further from what I'm proposing."

"So what are you proposing that's so different?"

"That I honestly believe we can help each other."

"Fuck you three times. The answer's no."

"But you're still here I see."

There was a deathly hush between us and neither seemed to breathe; but all around us the hum of life circled our table as though nothing had happened. She swept a glance across all of them, but no-one was taking the slightest interest in us. In that way she'd handled it well and it seemed to give her strength.

"Go on."

"Well I believe you're done with Joe and his philandering, but you know he isn't going to change..."

"So how can you help with that?"

"Well, maybe we can't directly," I was brutally honest yet again, "but if you're looking to sound off about it, you can't run to a Dublin Hotel every time - come and talk to me. And if there's anything to be done, maybe we can do it together. And if there isn't, then at least there's ways you can get revenge by helping us to keep some other people alive."

"So set him up you mean?"

"No, not necessarily..."

"So how else can you help me get revenge?"

"Many ways, think about it, but that's just the negative side of this. There's a lot of good you could be doing at the same time."

"Like what?"

"Joe's planning some evil things, Finella, I'm pretty sure you know that..." her jaw was set and she said nothing, but neither did she deny it, "and it's my job to prevent them from happening."

Not a word, and so I kept going.

"Simple as that, and I could use some help... as I'm sure you understand. Now if life got awkward for Joe at the same time, well, that's the bit that might make you feel you had a voice."

Still not a word. A short silence was fine – time to think and reflect – but an endless hush was bad. I pushed on.

"And look, I'm pretty certain in my own mind that you're as much against all that carry-on as I am. You're not Joe, Finella, I'm certain of that..."

"You don't have a clue who I am."

"Well, we'll just have to agree to disagree on that, and like I said, I reckon you're as much against it all as I am... and so I hoped we could work together. I hoped Finella, we could save lives together."

Silence again.

"I know that all sounds pretty melodramatic, but guess what... that's the shit that's going to happen if Joe gets his way. That's the real world, his world, and I'm just telling you the truth."

"Yeah, right. That'll be for the first time."

"But I am. About everything. I have all along."

A sudden look of fear seared her pretty face, and I was fairly certain it wasn't anything I'd said; it was a thought she'd conjured up for herself.

"And so how do I know you're *not* from Joe after all? How do I know he's not testing me?" Fearful scenarios tumbled behind her eyes and cast ghoulish shadows on her cheeks. "Well you're wasting your time, I'm no tout. For all you know I could be even more militant and Republican minded than he is, got it? And so you can go back and tell him he's fucking testing me for nothing."

She had suddenly become more frightened than angry, and so I had to reassure her that I was who and what I'd said I was and not one of her husband's South Armagh envoys. Apart from anything else, I needed to get her voice back down again. She was still whispering, but it was a damn sight louder than it had been.

"Well, for what it's worth I'm pretty sure you're neither of those things," I said, "I've been studying you for a long time; and I'm equally sure by the way, that apart from feeling neglected, and cheated, and taken for granted, that you personally are also horrified at the prospect of what Joe's planning for the future. Just when it was all over almost, and Belfast was almost at peace..."

She fixed me with a piercing stare.

"Yeah, great speech," she growled, "but how do I know you're not one of his boys? And if you are by the way, you really are barking up the wrong tree... because I'm not going to tout for you any more than you're going to get to fuck me."

"I'm not Finella..."

"It's Joe who screws around on me remember," she carried on without a breath, "not the other way around, and I'm just here chilling 'til I calm down. And chilling with you was fun, whoever you are, but nothing's happened here except dinner; so you can toddle off back to Joe and tell him to get fucked."

I didn't answer, I merely smiled and waited for her to calm down a little.

"What's so funny?" she demanded, but still quietly.

"That you think I'm here from Joe."

"Oh yeah, well I don't think so. So why are you smirking?"

"Nothing's funny, but I've got to tell you... you looked quite magnificent then. I'm kind of sorry that message is never going to get delivered to Joe, I would have liked to have been there."

She wanted to laugh, I could tell, and she was no longer hyperventilating. In fact, I think she really believed I was telling her the truth about my credentials; but she retained a stern expression and she knew that her life depended on getting to the bottom of her latest question. If she was wrong, it might be the last mistake she ever made.

She went to speak, but we were saved for the moment by the waiter who came to clear our plates. I ordered two large cognacs without even asking her, and she didn't object. She watched the waiter leave and then turned to me again.

"So, Mr Diplomat. Prove who you say you are, and *then* I can tell you to go fuck off."

"Fair enough."

"Fair's got nothing to do with it. You've tried to trap me whoever you are, so that's exactly what I aim to tell you."

Only *aim* to tell me... bingo, I was getting there.

"OK, but if I *can* prove who I am, and explain why I'm here, then I like to think that you'll hear me out."

She didn't answer and neither did she move. Not a muscle.

"Well just look at this for a start," I took out and discreetly passed her an official Security Service badge: big, metal and heavy, and in a wallet-sized leather case. It was just like a scene from an American detective movie and the crest was emblazoned with the characters 'MI5'.

"But you'll probably need something more concrete than that," I added, "something that I can't have had forged or knocked-up just to fool you."

She didn't answer again, but she studied the badge and the case carefully and held on to it until I'd finished. She even smelled it to see if it was real leather.

"So what if I told you that I knew you were coming here from the phone call, which only you and one other person know about by the way, that you made to Jeanette Breen four days ago?"

Silence and a long hard stare. I sensed her legs move under the table, but nothing else did. I continued:

"And I'm pretty sure you're one hundred per cent certain Jeanette won't have told Joe, am I right? Or anyone else for that matter. I mean, tell me Finella, honestly, is there anyone in the world that she hates more than Joe?"

She went to speak, but didn't. I continued carefully.

"And that clearly isn't something Joe knows, true? Because if he knew some of the conversations you and Jeanette have had, he'd have dealt with her a long time ago. And... well... maybe you too, Finella? You know that's not out of the question. Even you."

Finella Gorman continued to study me long and hard as she processed what I'd said. The call I described was real, and I had no intention of explaining how I really knew about it, but I'd pressed the buttons I wanted to and then I threw her off the truth with a deliberate fabrication.

"And before you ask how I know that, I'll tell you; as an example of how this whole trust thing is going to work between us if you think you want to help me."

Not a flinch.

"Well, I understand, but I'll tell you anyway. Well done you, by the way," I began, "for using a call box and not one of your own phones, but... and I know this means it's blown now, and I'm prepared to take that chance... *that* pay phone, in *that* particular store is monitored because you're not the only one that knows that trick. Please don't ask any more, I won't tell you. Any more than I'd ever tell anyone about you."

She studied the badge again and then closed its case and slid it in silence to the middle of the table. Precisely in the middle. Silent or not, I took that as a promising sign of mediation; and so I left her her space to construct the next part of her negotiation. I smiled ever so slightly and sipped my wine. I had to sip twice before she next spoke.

"So, if you've been studying me as you say," she eventually murmured, "why do you even think I'd help you?"

Bingo again, and I was half way through my window.

"Well, I reckon it boils down the three things, essentially, but now I've got to know you a little I can imagine that there might be a whole lot more as well."

"What three things?"

Before I could answer, the waiter came with our cognacs. I waited for him to leave and then continued.

"OK, first I think you're sick and tired of all Joe's affairs..."

"Maybe. But I'm still no tout."

"Then I think on top of that you're sick and *frightened* of what he's up to."

"I'm not frightened of Joe."

"No, I believe that, but of what he's planning for Northern Ireland I think you are. Jees Finella, for the *whole* of Ireland, and God knows how many people in the UK too."

She just shrugged, so I continued:

"And I know you don't have kids – and why – but an awful lot of people you care about do; I know that too."

That hit a raw nerve. Two maybe?

"Maybe. And last?"

"And last but not least, you don't strike me as the sort of woman who's just going to leave it at that."

"You mean payback?"

"I guess I do. But payback and peace."

"About payback you're right, but there's a whole lot of other ways I could do that without getting involved with you."

"But better ways? I don't think so."

"Maybe, but there's sure as hell safer ways."

"Against Joe? You think? I don't agree."

That struck a chord, and for the next thirty seconds she scrolled through all the ways in which he could hurt her... and, I like to think, through all the ways in which she perceived that I could prevent him.

"So..." there was a long pause before she spoke, "payback and peace, huh? So all this flirting then's been a complete fake? You've just been dangling me a carrot?"

"No, I've been getting to know you. And you me I hope."

"But how could I? You didn't tell me who you really were."

She fixed me with a stare again, but this time it was more pleading than severe. I edged a little further through my window.

"Oh but I just did, Finella, surely you can see that? And at the earliest *possible* safe moment. And look, nothing I told you before that was untrue; it was just only half the story, until I felt you could cope with all of it."

That really flummoxed her, and she thought long, hard and deep for maybe two minutes before she spoke again. When she did her whole demeanour had changed. It was as if for the past ten minutes she hadn't been able to catch her breath, and now at last she was breathing normally again.

"True, but the flirting still wasn't real, was it?"

"Yes it was," I smiled, "the flirting's been genuine, and I've enjoyed every minute of it; but sadly Finella, it's back to the real world now, and unfortunately it's not actually leading anywhere."

"Not even to get what you want?"

"No, not even. Now you've heard me out, you either *want* to help me or you don't. I can't make you... and I wouldn't try."

"Really. So it's not heading anywhere? So like we're not going to have an affair or something? I mean, isn't that how you're going to meet me? In hotel bedrooms an' all?"

She'd said it. 'Going to meet me...' Nearly there! I climbed the rest of the way through my window.

"Nice thought, bad idea," I smiled, "and that unfortunately is how James Bond gets to do it; I'm not so lucky."

"But we could, couldn't we, so you get what you want? That would be a good way to hide it, wouldn't it?"

"Why? Would you *want* to have an affair?" Meaning, 'have you decided you're going to work with me?'

"Absolutely. It's my turn don't you think?"

"Fair point, and although two wrongs don't make a right, as they say... *I'd* certainly say it's time to do *something* about the way you're treated."

"And so are you going to help me with that?"

I smiled, a deep, warm and understanding smile, but not one which would raise her expectations I hoped.

"Yes, if you like, with the 'do something about it' part, but not with the 'having an affair' part, no."

There was a pause. A long one, while she rolled her empty wine glass around in her hand. Her expression showed she was once again a willing and compliant partner in what was going on, but it was a crucial moment and I knew it. I too looked relaxed and un-perplexed, but that was far from the truth.

"So if you don't like the word tout, wouldn't you rather make this an affair?" she grinned. "Seriously, that might be the best solution for both of us. I'm a good bit older than you I know, but that could still be a lot of fun, I promise you."

"Yes I would," I smiled, and I ignored the tout reference completely, "but sadly that's not what I'm proposing here. And, for the record Finella... you look amazing. I'm damn certain it would be a lot of fun."

Whatever she was actually thinking, she couldn't contain the smile that suddenly appeared on her face from just the words I'd used. She shook her head gently and continued.

"Oh I *know* what you're proposing Aidan, and now I'm over the shock of it all I'm not saying 'no' to that necessarily, but couldn't sex just be a part of it all too?" She tilted her head, smiled coquettishly and gently bit her lip. She was good, and she was enjoying herself. "Not even just this once?"

I couldn't help but reflect on being sat on Úna's bed in the Europa Hotel when I was just sixteen, and when I was tumbling through the exact same emotions but in reverse. God knows what this woman had been through in the past thirty years, and her eyes were pleading with me to simply let her have her way. But sadly, just like in the Europa thirteen years earlier, it wasn't going to happen.

"To seal the deal, you mean?" I gently joked.

"If you like."

"Oh and I *would* like, Finella. I'm sure that under different circumstances I would like that very much..."

"But...?" she waited, "I can hear there's a 'but'."

"But that's still not going to happen. Like I said, it's a great thought but a bad idea," a line another handler would borrow in a similar situation the following year, "and it's your safety we'd be messing with, Finella, not your virtue, and I'll *never* mess with that under any circumstances."

There was another long pause, during which I poured her more wine and her sad and pleading eyes became as bright and feisty as at the bar at lunchtime. She gently nodded and mouthed the words 'Thank you' rather than actually said them, and I pulled my best hopeful face.

"Can we get coffee to go with these brandies?" she asked. Her tone now was as soft and seductive as it had been at the start of the meal.

"Of course, I'll call him over when he reappears."

But then she picked up her wine in silence, not her cognac. She took a sip, kept a'hold of her glass and leant slightly forward into the glow of our candle. Then she paused mid-word, thought for a moment longer, and looked softly but enthusiastically directly into my waiting eyes.

"So tell me..." she gently closed my window of opportunity behind me, "how do we do it? Let's get the bastard."

Keeping the Spare Room Spare

Finella Gorman was given the MI5 codename FINCH, and in relatively quick time she proved to be a songbird of quite exceptional talent. She had indeed been planning to leave her husband Joe, despite whatever revenge he might have sought as a result, but after agreeing to work as a part of our team she also agreed to stay as long as we wanted her to. She knew that he'd be taken down eventually – one way or another – and far from being uneasy about that, she relished the day.

The recruitment of 6026 a year later went pretty much the same way, although this time there had been several months' worth of leg-work and research done by the CSB handlers in County Kerry before I even showed my face. *Twenty-Six* was Kaye O'Brien, one of Joe Gorman's longer-running affairs, and we'd actually learned of her through FINCH. FINCH didn't know her, they lived three hundred miles and several worlds apart, but she knew all about her and the sort of woman she was. She knew because Twenty-Six originally came from Belfast, and so she knew people that O'Brien knew as well. Friendly people. Helpful people. Discreet but divisive people from the biggest *village* in Ireland, and who liked to keep the wife of the Belfast IRA's rising star thoroughly informed. And she knew that her husband Joe would be using and abusing O'Brien in exactly the same way as herself. The only difference that marriage made to her husband was that FINCH was the one he'd always come back to... eventually. The one who washed, and cooked, and covered for him. The one he owned and so didn't have to impress. The one who had no choice. Well now she did.

Because Twenty-Six lived deep in the Republic of Ireland, in a tiny harbour village called Loughsmalley, she was also run as a joint case and she'd also been recruited in the South. There were five such cases taken on in my three years in Northern Ireland, two women and three men, and they gave me just as much satisfaction as several of the more highly placed agents in the North. And one of the most amusing debriefs I had was with one of them, a former senior Provo who envisioned a circumstance, not unlike Brexit, whereby the British Army was back on the streets fighting to *achieve* a united Ireland instead of prevent it. Because this time, he predicted, the Brits would be deployed in support of the democratic wishes of an eventual Catholic majority.

"Hey, that would be a turn up," he chortled, "seeing as the last war you had against a one-third minority only lasted thirty-eight years. Good luck with the next one then."

"Yeah, well," I teased, "the political backdrop could well come about – if and when that majority becomes a fact – but the military scenario you're suggesting isn't likely. I'm not sure the bulk of Republicans in the North would be too happy with giving up all Her Majesty's benefits and their welfare packages, any more than Dublin would be to take them on."

"Aye, reckon you're right about that bit," he laughed, "but it's interesting to ponder nonetheless. Just think about it. See if all the Loyalists – so-called Loyalists by then of course – turned their not insignificant number of guns on the British Army, then that would be a cracker. Jesus, Dublin and the Irish Army might even be a part of it all by then, because how much would you be able to count on the bulk of the police in the North if that happened?"

"Careful what you wish for," I humoured him.

"Hey, 'We'll be out by Christmas', the Taoiseach might say. Shit, does that sound familiar?" he laughed again. "But here's the real difference though fellah: without the border to hide behind, all those Loyalists want to watch it doesn't finish up being more of a Dunkirk than a thirty-year guerrilla war. Or maybe their very own Arnhem... for trying to go a parade too far."

Food for thought, and think about it I did; quite often once I returned to London. (And not least of all some six years later, when on the 23rd of June 2016, the successful 'Leave' vote in the Brexit Referendum made it just a tad more feasible overnight.)

2011 was just as busy, just as productive, and just as rewarding by its end. It's highlight, funnily enough though, was undoubtedly a fortnight's leave taken at the start of the year in March. It was the first leave I'd had for over a year, and Tony Moss insisted that I take a minimum of two weeks and get right away somewhere. So I took fifteen days, and George and I flew to the States to kill two birds with one stone - and hopefully nail another two in Boston: the fondly-recalled duo of Madison and Kayla. We flew into Boston and spent St Patrick's Day and the next with Pat the Fourth, and then we took two days to drive all the way to Fort Bragg in North Carolina and spend a week with Tommy Bray.

Tommy was in his second year there of three, and he was about to deploy again for God knows how many months. 'Come now,' he'd said, 'or maybe miss your chance forever.' We drove the eight hundred or so miles at a fairly leisurely pace: straight down 'the 95' and so through Rhode Island, Connecticut, Philadelphia,

Baltimore and Washington DC, where we spent the night. Then we carried-on down through Richmond and Petersburg in Virginia, past Rocky Mount and on to Fayetteville and our rendezvous with a bronzed-looking Tommy.

Tommy was enjoying his time in the States, and more to the point he was *really* enjoying his time anywhere but Stateside and deployed on almost constant covert fire-fighting missions in war-torn corners of the Special Ops world. There, at the cutting-edge of Special Forces tactics, techniques and procedures – not to mention world-leading combat technology – he honed his already innate skills as a 21st Century Celtic *Ninja* and became a key player in a number of multi-national operations. And so he thrived. Partly because he spoke both French and 'American' like a native, but mostly because he seemed born for what he was doing.

It didn't hurt either that he also spoke passable Spanish, German, Italian and, like all good Catholic Irish boys, Latin. And if you speak Latin, he pointed out over a beer in Fayetteville, you could get your mind around most of the languages of the Old World. That had made him the *de facto* liaison officer for a number of high-risk but high-yield NATO operations, and so he'd become much sought after for a whole host of multi-national tasks. His Spanish had been more helpful to him in the States than his English, he'd joked, although he'd than added that in the situations he was on about he wasn't really joking; and yet it wasn't whilst serving in the US that he'd first had dealings with the CIA, but five years before that in the Central African Republic and whilst still in the French Special Forces. Another story for another day.

Like us Tommy had taken a whole week's leave, and so the three of us – and on one memorable night the six of us – spent our middle week around Virginia and the Carolinas and as far out as the Chattahoochee National Forest. 'Twas 'awesome,' to use the local vernacular, and we wished with hindsight that we'd gone to see him in his first eighteen months. The only shame of the whole trip was that when we headed back up to Boston, we didn't go also to New York and re-visit Callahan's Bar in the Hell's Kitchen area of Manhattan. And what a shame, because five years later I realised that if we had, we'd have almost certainly run into one Michael McCann, aka NEON, while we were there. Lucky him.

The rest of that last year for me in T8NI was a little fraught though. Just fraught, not unpleasant, but hard work nonetheless. Tony Moss had moved on and the new section chief, although no less professional, wasn't nearly as robust as Tony for his first year. Especially with London. A lot of his job – and to be honest I'd been disappointed that Emily Rankin hadn't been selected in his stead – was about keeping the section in the public eye. By which, of course, we meant the exact opposite: it was about keeping the section, the Service, and most definitely our operations and day to day activities *out* of the public eye, but very much on the desks and in the minds of our esteemed masters in London.

I was assured by others that a great deal had changed in the Service since the end of the Cold War, and then even more and more quickly since 9/11. Not all for the better. But the biggest changes by far in the whole mindset, priorities and day to day management of the Service came with the dubiously labelled 'End of the Troubles'. Oh, the thirty-eight-year war was over for sure - that was by then official, and no-one that I knew was suggesting that its imminent return was even remotely likely - but we in Northern Ireland were struggling to understand just how far some people had taken their eye off the ball.

'What ball?' I could even imagine some people saying, and the ball, however big it was or wasn't at that stage, was just starting to be kicked around again by growing numbers of a resurgent IRA back in Ireland. The comprehension gap between Belfast and London had always been wide, but on a bad day the Irish Sea could seem as formidable as the Pacific Ocean.

One of the consequences of that mindset was that half way through 2011, I received my marching orders to join our Training Wing in Thames House at the end of the year. That was a huge compliment, and a job I would normally have looked forward to, except that the order to move came very early in the life of several new cases. That meant there were going to be difficult days, even more difficult meets, and several delicate handovers. Such was war in the shadows instead of on the battlefield, I had told myself... get on with it. And more to the point, when I'd discussed it with Bill Wallace for his advice and guidance (who I knew would become the Deputy Head of Training the following year), he'd pretty much told me the same thing, "Don't fight it Neill, do it."

"Hey, nothing's ever perfect," he'd said over a pint in Whitehall, "but you've got to find the positives and work them. This time it's that in eighteen months from now you'll know your way around the Training and all the main courses, and then I'll arrive as the day-to-day Boss... so *then* we'll make things as damn near perfect as we can."

"Aye, I guess so I suppose," I'd said gloomily; at which he'd realised my disappointment and frustration, and so sutured both once and for all.

"Look, you're not wrong Neill, but here's how to do it: state your case, say your piece and stand your corner; but *then* follow the final order and don't fight the damned inevitable. And because it's inevitable, get on with it... and save your energy for something that can be changed."

"Yeah, I'd kind of worked that out for myself, it's just those brand new cases I'm worried about."

"They'll be fine, and so will the handovers. It's just not perfect, that's all... and no-one ever said this place was perfect."

We just looked at each other and laughed spontaneously. I felt better already.

"Look, in a nutshell, Neill, I'll see you in Training Wing in about eighteen months... that's good, not bad, get on with it."

Get on with it I did, boosted by the news that shortly after I left T8NI, Joe Gorman was made the Chief of Staff of the new and fledgling IRA; and so the work of FINCH, Twenty-Six, and several others in his sphere became even more important than before. Vitally important, we learned with hindsight, because whatever other shortcomings the new IRA was working through it was proving to be alarmingly secure. But that became just an excuse for another pint – Bill's head and heart were always in T8 – and yet another debate about how we'd set the world to rights once he joined me in Training in twelve months' time.

With a settled two or three years in London ahead of me, followed by maybe a couple more in another section in Thames House after that, I also set about the business of trying to recruit a long term girlfriend for the first time ever too. Except, unlike most of my operations, that didn't seem to go so well. Jees, I tried maybe a dozen over the next three years, but none lasted for more than a few months. I was thirty going-on thirty-one by then, and so pretty set in my ways, but that wasn't really the problem. The problem was much simpler than that.

Firstly, I worked horrendous hours for weeks on end and I was forever cancelling things at the last minute. Next, no matter how charming, disarming and subtle I tried to be, the inevitable secrecy about work sometimes became so obvious that it crushed any possible rapport. It certainly crushed any passion, and usually – thanks to pagers and the mobile phone - at the crucial moment. But lastly, and decisively, no woman I had ever tried dating in the past dozen years had come even close to my unrealistically high expectations. Úna's fault... and maybe more recently, Maria's.

At least I got my housing selection right, and so avoided any messy complications on that front. I'd thought of returning to the Dulwich area, but I knew this time around and with a little more cash to throw at my rented accommodation, I could live a bit better and get a bit closer to Thames House than that. After a lot of advice and some painstaking homework, my choice was pretty simple: a one-bedroomed cupboard in Pimlico, just beyond my price-range and a five-minute walk from work; or an affordable three-bedroomed Victorian terraced house in Balham, just two minutes from the station and fifteen from the office. Hello Balham. But then my next big decision was truly inspired.

Even on the budget for rent I'd set myself, I knew taking-in a lodger for at least one of the other two bedrooms would help massively. The third and spare room, I was determined, would remain spare; for the likes of Úna, George, Tommy Bray when he was in town, and so on... or maybe even Maria McLaughlin from time to time. And so I set about advertising for a house-mate for the other room. I was prepared to take any age, either sex, any colour, and just about any political, religious or environmental persuasion, so long as it was someone I reckoned I'd be able to get on with and with a bit of humour. I kind of hoped it would turn out to be an attractive young female... but at least forty-nine per cent of my already frail common sense was telling me not to go there. And bingo.

The very first applicant turned out to be a girl who'd just moved to London from Cardiff, and more crucially she was from the more sensible compartments of my dreams. She was twenty-six, fit, attractive, hilariously funny and she was determined to stay single... but best of all, Bev was gay as a maypole. No, not best of all – the best was yet to come. My new long-legged lesbian-lodger was none other than a working Graphic Artist, most were unemployed, in... get this... Lingerie and Sleepwear Design. Score! We were both utterly safe from each other, and so safe also from any messy complications and bestial temptation, but some of the impromptu fashion-shows I had to endure in the next four years were beyond my wildest dreams. So, although my God-shaped hole remained depressingly full of work stuff and not tantalising new possibilities, at least I'd found a very settled home situation in which to empty it each night.

The first person to ever come and use 'our' spare room predictably was Úna, who came to stay the first weekend I wasn't working and once I was fully sorted. It was only Bev's second day since moving-in, and so she was still going through her 'shy' stage

– a relative term – but her attraction to Úna was obvious and Úna's encouragement unforgivable. I forgave her anyway, and so too did a chuckling Bev, and in pretty quick time they became great mates. But despite my many fantasies, only mates.

The next to stay, unexpectedly, wasn't George Kennedy but Tommy Bray. Tommy stayed four whole days at the start of 2012; and although we called George to see if he could get across to join us, that time he couldn't. Most other times he did, and no, before you ask, he never did manage to convert Bev. Tommy had completed his time in the States and upon his return to his headquarters in the Pyrénées-Atlantiques city of Pau, he had unexpectedly terminated his service with the French Army and joined Interpol two months later. It seemed to surprise everyone but him, and so it must have had something to do with his father's influence, I suggested.

"Yeah, sort of. Kind of yes and no really," he said. "Mostly I just got tired though... y'know, literally tired. Frig Neill, that's a young man's game, unless you don't mind taking a back seat, and I do. So I let him talk me into it," he laughed. "Him and some of his old cronies in France."

"Aye, fair one. But I thought he was living in Drogheda?"

"Yeah, he is, but he and my mum live between Louth and Lyon the same as I do. But theirs is more based on the weather."

"Nice work if you can get it."

"Aye, well that'll be me in a few years then I hope."

"Yeah. So how did your dad get to serve in Interpol then? If he's always been a judge an' all?"

"Something to do with working with the Allied Powers in Berlin I think, y'know, in the 1970s and as a judge I mean, but then in 1989 he joined them full time for a few years because their HQ moved from Paris to Lyon."

"Got it, and that's where your mum's from. So is that where they met?"

"God no, I was already ten then..."

"Oh, of course. I wasn't thinking."

"No, it had something to do with his decision right enough, but nah, they met in Berlin in 1977, and get this..." he laughed, "I was born at the start of 1979, so that must have been a bit of high-speed international cooperation, don't y'think?"

Huh, a bit like George and me with Madison and Kayla in Boston then. 'Twas just a shame I didn't seem to enjoy the same good fortune in London. I guess Irish accents don't have the same effect over here.

Work in B7 though, in the Training Wing, proved to be the exact opposite of my love life: it was enormously satisfying. Once I became established, I learned things almost daily that hadn't been nearly so obvious in the field, and then when Bill arrived and added his vast operational experience I discovered what was on the flip-side of almost every coin I handled. Training gave me the big picture – upwards, downwards, sideways and into countless other organisations - so that when I next went back to operations I had so much more to offer. And as for the satisfaction of passing-on everything I could to others, young and old; well that remains one of the highlights of my career so far.

But training provided constant challenges too, and so it was a good job that was the frame of mind I was in during the first few days of July 2015, when Bill Wallace took me into his office to discuss the latest report from 6026 in Loughsmalley.

As the pace and gravity of the situation in Ireland had picked up again over the past year, I had often been called to a secure phone or to a video conference with T8NI. It had usually been to add my thoughts on something one of the agents had said, or maybe just to answer the odd question harking back to their recruitment. But this was different. This time Bill was asking, and through him Maggie Allinson and so the whole of the branch.

Margaret Allinson was the Head of T-Branch, the Service's Irish desk, and so known throughout the building as 'T'. She was also a lifelong friend of Bill's – they had joined the service together the year I was born – and she was most people's best bet to be the next DDG, the Deputy Director of MI5. Bill recounted a top level meeting she'd called earlier, with just him and several of her section chiefs, and then went over the Twenty-Six report that had prompted it. In essence it said that Joe Gorman had met in Loughsmalley with an as yet unidentified IRA Elder, and that they had discussed a forthcoming spectacular attack that, in Gorman's words, would 'make history'.

Much of it didn't make sense, we agreed; welcome to the world of contact intelligence. Our information to date suggested the IRA weren't yet ready for large scale attacks; and if it was to be on the UK mainland, which was Bill's gut instinct, then they weren't ready at all. What the report meant by 'forthcoming' wasn't at all clear either, and irrespective of our assessment of IRA readiness, it didn't give any clear indication of whether it would be in the coming days, weeks or months. It hinted, however, that it would probably be later rather than sooner - an unenviable call for an intelligence officer to have to make, and a potentially huge stick for politicians and the media to beat us with later. But such veiled threats were just grist to Maggie Allinson's mill.

Bill's main concern had been for 2016 and the hundredth anniversary of the Easter Rising in Dublin. I knew that already, and he knew that I agreed with him; but it was only then that I learned that Maggie Allinson also shared our fears. Hence the meeting she had called, and her directive for Bill to include me in all his actions going forward. As unlikely as it seemed on the face of it, and from such a fringe-access source, the report demanded much closer scrutiny than was normal. Twenty-Six's sub-source, after all, had been Joe Gorman himself, and so 'T' wasn't taking any chances. Since 9/11, no-one did.

Despite our full-time day jobs in B7, Allinson had wanted Bill to lead on branch-wide analysis of what the Twenty-Six report really meant for the mainland; and so also of the who, what, why, where, when and how we should be paying closer attention to until we knew more. By the end of the month T2 had produced a list of hundreds of people we should be looking at more closely, and in pretty much every corner of England, Wales and Scotland. T5 produced a similar list, although much shorter, of those from the Republic of Ireland who might suddenly have come into play as well but who weren't already under our purview. But Wallace and I, with Allinson's blessing and concurrence, produced a much shorter list; a list of only potential Cleanskins.

By mid-August Bill and I had reduced T2's list of hundreds to thirty-six Possibles of our own; and by late-September we'd got it down to just four Probables. Then we set to work in earnest to learn more about those four than even their own parents knew. But therein lay our first setback, and one of the four, Michael McCann, didn't even have parents; both were as dead as the trails we were attempting to follow into his past. That still didn't make him unique, so we scrutinised all four until or unless their profiles became clearer. But then in the October, after a hastily arranged police surveillance follow from Yorkshire back to Central London, we'd narrowed it down still more to just one Favourite: McCann, MI5 codename, NEON.

NEON, Smoke and Mirrors

With the help of that sharpest of tools in the intelligence toolbox, hindsight, we now know that forty-five year-old Michael Joseph Mary McCann had moved to London in the June of 2013. Once there he'd set himself up in a modest flat in Fitzrovia in the shadow of the BT Tower, and in an unremarkable studio in West Kilburn. He was a Dublin-born citizen of the Republic of Ireland and an established professional photographer, whose niche area of his art in recent years had become the imaging and illumination of skyscrapers and other high-rise structures.

Immediately prior to that NEON had spent six years as a mature student in New York, where he'd added three-back-to-back master's degrees in Photography, Imaging Arts and Digital Media to his 1992 honour's degree from Manchester University in England. But piecing together any details of his life before that took time and a disproportionate amount of cunning, effort and resources - although there was a clear and carefully documented trail to nowhere once we dug deeply enough. And yet, by the end... by Easter 2016 and the sudden discovery of *exactly* what he'd been up to... we had learned the following.

He'd been born into almost Dickensian urban poverty on the 12th of January 1970 in Coombe Women's Hospital, Dublin. His parents were Patrick and Anne-Marie McCann. Anne-Marie had been a pretty and vivacious seamstress, his dad a drunken sot six years her elder. Within a year Michael also had three siblings and the family was as complete as it would ever be: one brother four years older, Patrick; one sister two years older, Mary; and a sister one year younger, Sinead. But by 1987 all of them except Michael and his dad were dead - and his father would follow a mere five years later. Furthermore, they had all passed in violent or tragic circumstances, and brother Patrick's death was especially telling.

The first to die, when Michael was just four, had been his mother; who was in every sense the centre of his new young universe. And he was hers, although she pretended not to have a favourite. She was killed in the Dublin and Monaghan Bombings of May 1974, when the Ulster Volunteer Force slaughtered thirty-four people (if you include the full-term unborn child of one of the victims) with four separate car bombs within minutes. She had been just twenty-nine and at her most beautiful, people said. The bomb that took his mother also killed his sister, Mary, it also claimed his maternal grandmother, and it severely maimed his younger sister, Sinead... all witnessed by four-year-old Michael, who had been holding his gran's hand at the time.

But significantly it never killed his brother, Patrick, who'd been playing football at school that day. Although never proven, Michael allegedly did that himself: eight years later with Patrick's own hurley stick after eleven-year-old Sinead had given birth to his baby. And then, to complete Michael's teenage despair, Sinead took her own life five years later still; to end the pain and misery of her existence and the shame heaped upon her by a judgemental

Catholic church. NEON's father, Patrick Snr, was the only natural death in the family – that's if you count dying in hospital from chronic alcoholism in 1992, aged fifty-three.

Not that NEON really knew his father. That wasn't quite the horrific shock or the final blow to his emotional security that you might imagine. Michael wasn't with him when he died, and in fact he hadn't seen him at all for nigh-on ten years by then. The last time he'd *ever* seen him, was when he'd finally turned the tables on him and beaten him unconscious back in 1983. So, notwithstanding the vile terrorist that NEON eventually became, it wasn't entirely for no reason.

From the ages of four to twelve Michael was moved from pillar to post to live with a succession of relatives, half-friends and half-humans - girlfriends most of them, of his drunken and abusive shell-of-a-father. But when thirteen-year-old Michael eventually left his Dublin home for good, to live initially with the Christian Brothers in the West of Ireland, unbeknown to him at the time he had embarked upon a ten-year rite of passage. It would take him through a complex maze of yet more 'relatives', attractive and very sociable aunties mostly, to a privileged nest under the wing of a secret benefactor, Frank O'Neill. O'Neill was at the time at the zenith of his power, as the IRA elder who for forty years had enjoyed a majestic reign from deep in the shadows of militant Irish Republicanism. And over the next ten years NEON was effectively 'raised' in his image.

McCann was slowly but surely schooled and blooded in the arts of war, of deception and of life, until at last he was a beacon of charm and a consummate warrior. And, with no adverse or subversive traces to his name, that also made him the ultimate Cleanskin. Thus he became one of O'Neill's secret weapons; kept out of the Provisional IRA and the Troubles, and kept-back for greater things another day. That day, O'Neill had always intended, was to be Easter Friday 2016 - the one-hundredth anniversary of the Easter Rising in Dublin.

Their goal was pretty simple – to detonate a former Soviet backpack nuke at the top of the BT Tower on Easter Friday - but the various multi-national sinews of their plan couldn't have been more complex. The acquisition of the device, three of them in fact, had been through McCann's close association with a Muslim Chechen warlord, Ruslan Barayev. He had first met Barayev at a terrorist training camp in Libya, but then over the next twenty years they'd become devoted comrades whilst fighting together in Soviet-occupied Afghanistan, in Kosovo, and in Barayev's native Chechnya – against the Russians yet again. O'Neill had facilitated the weightier parts of the plan through time-honoured links to senior Middle-Eastern terrorists, and NEON - Michael McCann - was the tip of their spear pointed at the very heart of Great Britain.

Through McCann's long-established and fully functioning business cover, he had secured the contract to stage a laser light show for the fiftieth anniversary celebrations of the BT Tower. To achieve it he would fire laser beams across Central London from the tower – five of them, one for each decade – at pre-positioned light-prisms on five other high-rise buildings or structures across the city; some of which required Home Office authority just to visit. That was one of the things that first brought him to our attention; and were it not for other unrelated events that forced us to look at him more closely, it may well have been the double-bluff that caused us to discount him altogether. And then, of course, other major distractions, like the attacks in Paris and San Bernardino in November and December of 2015, further took our eyes off what was still only half a ball.

Having gained authority for full and regular access to the BT Tower for a nine-month period, NEON's next challenge was to so embed himself within the routine there, and so ingratiate himself to its security staff, that he worked painstakingly to gain an 'insurance policy'. That policy was to be in the shapely-form of one Karen Wallace, a forty-year-old nymphomaniac Shift Team Leader who ran one of its four security teams. McCann had identified Karen through months of research and surveillance, supported by his only two conscious-contacts in London: Cahal Brady, another IRA elder, and Briege McConnell, an eighty-one-year-old IRA widow and facilitator enacting the role of McCann's grandmother. And the most secure and easily achieved route into Karen Wallace's bed, they had concluded, was via the bed first of her vulnerable younger sister, Sarah Price.

So sex was clearly one of NEON's weapons of choice, we later confirmed, but what we also quickly established was that it seemed to be an irrepressible obsession as well. Even an addiction maybe. And so it proved, over time... when he was tripped-up at the eleventh-hour by his own Achilles heel.

Notwithstanding that, from our initial interest at the back-end of 2015 until the discovery of NEON's plans on Easter Friday the following year, he managed to defeat the myriad tentacles of our security infrastructure until it was almost too late. And he did that essentially by turning our modern and high-tech procedures back on ourselves; by exploiting our increasing dependency on digital supremacy and automation, and by boring us witless with day upon day, week upon week and month upon month of exactly that which he *wished* us to see. Thus, through that dependency, he created gaps in time, in our certainty of his location and in our coverage of the tasks that he *couldn't* let us see.

And then, as is so often the case, we were distracted yet again at a crucial moment – not just us, the whole world was – by the Daesh suicide-bombers at Brussels Airport and at Maalbeek Metro Station just three days before McCann's planned attack; and by a bungled IRA car-bomb near Heathrow with just twenty-four hours to go. Two attacks at two major airports within forty-eight hours... and by two radically different organisations... the world held its breath. But despite the intelligence frenzy that followed, there were still those amongst us, thank God, who prized gut-instinct and the perpetual analysis of human behaviour as their primary intelligence tools.

And so last Easter we dodged a bullet – or to be more precise, a six kiloton nuclear blast a hundred and eighty metres above the centre of London. A blast from a former Soviet ADM, an Atomic Demolition Munition, that – although only a third of the power of Hiroshima - would have killed at least a million people and devastated several square miles of Central London. Indeed, it would have vapourised a few hundred square metres of it, but literally... everyone and everything within its insatiable core. And as if that wasn't sickening and scary enough, as McCann evaded capture and escaped to God knows where, in the following weeks we unearthed evidence that he had control of at least one other device. With the great game won in just the nick of time, there also came the realisation that the great search had only just begun.

So what more can I tell you? The whole story of those nine months is well worth reading about. It's a story of painstaking analysis, review and conjecture, and of fruitless surveillance, gut-instinct and bold calls; but also of a successful outcome – just – thanks as much to luck and to fate as to the thousands of man-hours thrown at the problem.

NEON refers to just Michael McCann himself, but other MI5 codenames cover other aspects of the whole complex and sorry saga. Operation STELLAR embraces everything about his would-be attack; from the first ever report from 6026 about Joe Gorman and Frank O'Neill, to the discovery of McCann's device on Easter Friday and the titanic follow-up. Op BOLAS concerns the continuing search for NEON; Op CLARION is a crucial bugging operation... and there are others.

And I say 'fruitless surveillance', but there I must correct myself. There were in fact hundreds of hours of some of the most detailed and comprehensive data imaginable, both human and technical, but after it was all over they merely confirmed the danger of an adversary who knew how to turn such methods back on us to prove his lie. And, of course, to ensure his ultimate escape and his enduring freedom.

Despite the failure of NEON's attack, the impact globally was huge and seemingly never-ending. Now, in 2017, far from abating, it merely seems to be increasing all the time - and a new President Trump certainly isn't going to let it go anytime soon. It wasn't only in Ireland that swift and drastic action was taken. There the whole world had got to watch on their televisions, when it manifested itself in armed conflict and nearly two hundred arrests against Joe Gorman's still-born IRA. And the immediate result was that their new and final campaign – Frank O'Neill's campaign - stumbled and fell before it had got fully into its stride. But elsewhere hammers fell in secret.

Executions took place in Iran and deep inside Daesh and al-Qaeda; arms dealers in the former Soviet Union vanished before they could be questioned; and even Ruslan Barayev went to ground. The United States launched an unprecedented covert assault on just a concept for want of an actual target; intelligence agencies were turned inside-out; and some governments upside-down. The failed *coup d'état* in Turkey in July 2016 was but one example, because Daesh, at the height of its power and wealth in 2015, had moved NEON's device right across Iran, Turkey and the Mediterranean without detection.

And whilst it was inconceivable that anyone in the Middle-East would spawn such a deformed alliance ever again, the whole of the developed world remained on tenterhooks at how close it had come to a nuclear catastrophe. And more to the point, at who might be next? The fear was not that McCann's device was to be an opposing book-end to 9/11, but that it was just a new and bloody chapter of a tale with no ending.

And so with NEON vanished and with no discernible trail to follow, life – eventually - carried on. It didn't go back to normal, it would never do that, but it carried on nonetheless. But so did the search; and so although I was promoted and sent back to Northern Ireland as the Head of T8NI, as far as coordinating MI5's intelligence collection on NEON was concerned, I remained the pivotal node. I was going to be in Ireland after all; I had all the contacts; I'd recruited most of the key agents surrounding Joe Gorman, and later Gorman himself... and so I was deemed to have the best 'feel' for what was what and for what was needed. Or to put it another way, I was judged to be the steadiest hand on the poisoned chalice that was full to its quivering brim.

Probably the clincher though, was that I had also become the main proponent of the unsubstantiated theory that NEON was still somewhere in Ireland or the British Isles. I had made my bed, as one superior put it, and so I'd been sent to lay on it.

Interregnum

As if the run-up to Easter 2016 hadn't been hectic enough, the bewildering twelve months that followed proved to be many times worse. To say that the world was in shock at what NEON had *nearly* managed to do was an understatement of Clintonesque proportions. But then I, as the hub of the wheel for Op BOLAS going forward, was under significantly more pressure than Hillary had ever been from the FBI. Unless, of course, you include her post-election assertions that she was scuppered by their untimely release of information. A part of me felt for her – I was getting to know that feeling well.

But first let me gallop through a few other related events that had gone on during that period. Somewhere back in the fog of 2015, for example, Tommy Bray had stayed with me in Balham and we'd gone into the city for a feed and a few beers to celebrate his early promotion within Interpol. After only three years he'd been made an Enquêteur Principal, a Senior Investigator; his qualifications for which had boiled down to his impeccable law degree, his even better brain, and the ten years he'd spent in the Special Forces of not just one but three developed nations. Plus, I suppose his father may have had some influence too - but neither of us mentioned that, and nor would it have changed his worth to their organisation one jot if true.

NEON wasn't even NEON at that stage, but I'd had a hunch that what Bill Wallace and I were looking at was potentially huge; and so Tommy had offered to help me, on or off the record, should the need arise. It did, and he did, several times. Tommy was one of those who'd also thought the clock was ticking, and he too had been convinced that a resurgent IRA was bound to make its move over Easter 2016. And so he'd subsequently proved invaluable (off the record) prior to the discovery of McCann's device on the Easter Friday, and then no less crucial to our follow-up efforts (on the record) after his attack had failed and once we began our worldwide enquiries into Ruslan Barayev and others.

I guess in some ways it was payback. I'd helped Tommy out with a few enquiries since he'd joined Interpol, all very much above the counter, but then one day he'd asked me to give him a little 'hands-on' support for an ad hoc task in West London. I'd expressed my discomfort with doing anything in the capital off the record, and so he'd told me that if I wanted to declare it I should; but then when he'd explained what it was I'd agreed, and so we'd just got on with it. It wasn't even a formal Interpol task, it was a favour for a fellow officer whilst he was in London on a different investigation; but the subject matter was a pet peeve of mine, and the task was simplicity itself... and so it had been done.

Tommy's Lyon-based colleague had been working on a major paedophile investigation, and he'd wanted to put a name, a location or even just a face or a phone number to an anonymous darkweb address they'd found. Enough was known to deduce that the man was based somewhere in West London, and so seeing as

Tommy was going to be in town anyway they reckoned that had given them options. Tommy had set up a false-flag approach on the web and then he'd arranged to meet said paedo' in a café at the seedier end of Edgware Road; the close proximity of which to Kilburn made our border-area Irish accents the perfect cover. Tommy had wanted me along for a bit of back-up for the meeting itself, and then for the ability to carry-out a two-man follow afterwards if possible.

The meeting had been pretty straight forward, at which Tommy had paid a hundred pounds for a black-market DVD; although both our first instincts had been to drag the guy across the table and castrate him with a broken coffee mug. He was fat, sweaty, middle-aged and as disgusting as his smile, which when he curled-back his bloated lips revealed a mouthful of unkempt teeth and a fog of bad breath. He'd brought a minder too, a burly-looking youth in a track suit that had clearly never been anywhere near a sports facility, but thank God the minder didn't smile at all.

I had spoken only when spoken to, but when I had my South Armagh brogue had complemented Tommy's Dublin-Louth burr perfectly. Then, when they'd left, and after we'd both made simple changes to our appearance, we'd tailed them discreetly and housed them at an address not far from St Mary's Hospital in Paddington. Job done, and about three months later I'd noted with satisfaction that the address was amongst a dozen raided right across London by the Vice Squad.

In fact Tommy saw a lot of such jobs 'done,' and I saw that day as a bit of harmless moonlighting to contribute to the greater good. With hindsight though, the only thing that never really gelled with me back then was how Tommy could have traded *such* an exciting life in Special Forces for the relative tedium of being what amounted to a supranational liaison officer. It just wasn't Tommy. I was right, but it would be a while yet before I knew it. Interpol officers from the one hundred and ninety member states don't make arrests themselves. They are not armed, they don't 'take people down' and they don't pursue criminals per se. Nor do they put people in an Interpol jail – there's no such thing.

Instead their officers facilitate the smooth passage of vital intelligence, they bring about the sharing of multi-national police procedures and best practice, and they ensure the furtherance of international cooperation between widely disparate police forces and cultures. Laudable aims and a vital job... but it was far from the Tommy Bray I'd come to know. Maybe he was simply as tired as he'd told me back in 2012, and so maybe he'd reckoned that a change was as good as a rest? Or maybe not. It would be another two years – and so right about now - before I finally learned the rest of the story.

Then, on a completely separate occasion about a month later, I'd celebrated George Kennedy's promotion too: to Detective Inspector and still working out of Garda CSB in Dundalk. Just like with Tommy, we'd gone into Central London, had a meal and then a few scoops afterwards; but unlike Tommy, George had insisted that we finish-up at a strip club in Bloomsbury. He'd been the life and soul of the party, and he must have put three or four times his new pension in an unbelievable number of waistbands... but it didn't stop him from staggering back to my Balham home and trying to convert Bev to blokes yet again.

No joy, bad luck George, but *Bellissimo-Bev* as he calls her had got the last laugh when she'd teased him almost to the point of self-injury with her latest batch of homework. Within a couple of months of that weekend I was scooping drinks with George again, but this time in Dundalk – less the strippers – during my working trip both sides of the border to learn whatever we could about NEON. And so the spirit of cooperation with both George and Tommy was alive and well. Good, because it was about to prove a game-changer.

The other humungous breakthrough towards the back-end of 2015 had been a positive development in my lovelife. Well, not so much a development really – seeing as I didn't really have one to improve – but more the discovery of someone who was stunning, quick-witted and bright, and yet daft enough in a few crucial ways to find me half-attractive. Her name was Kirsten Owen, universally known as Katy, and she was the twenty-four-year-old analyst from T2 who had become so invaluable to Bill Wallace and I in our quest to expose NEON.

In no time at all we'd progressed from a few much-needed drinks after work most days, to something in the same ballpark as a meaningful relationship. I guess when I'd first known I was really onto something, was when I'd taken her home to meet Bev, my attractive lesbian-lodger; and far from showing any signs of jealousy, they'd become firm and lasting friends overnight. Even after the time, weeks later, when Bev had insisted on giving us both a full-frontal fashion show of her latest batch of would-be lingerie. What a find... both times.

Katy was highly intelligent, bubbly, even prettier than I'd allowed myself to admit, and frighteningly good at her job; and she'd wanted to learn whatever she could from the likes of Bill Wallace and me. That suited me just fine, because there were plenty of things I wanted to teach her too! At last, and just when I was beginning to think it would never happen, I had a real long-term girlfriend... no, a partner no less... and younger than me for once. And just in case I hadn't been totally convinced for myself, it would appear that pretty much everyone else had decided for me. Bill Wallace and his wife Pam treated her like a daughter-in-law from the off, as did my parents when they eventually met her, and so too did Úna - what more can I say?

2016, once it had eventually come and gone, had been a year of two very unequal halves: the anxious and intense three months until Easter, and then the frenetic and bewildering nine that followed. The nine months *after* NEON's failed attack and his subsequent disappearance. We'd had an abundance of data and material to look at retrospectively, both physical and forensic, but from the instant he'd vanished late on Maundy Thursday – aptly named by many Catholics the *Thursday of Mysteries* – he'd been as lost as Malaysia Airlines Flight 370 – but with significantly less clues. And he has been ever since.

With the discovery of his device and the two intelligence reports that eventually exposed him all having come within hours of each other, the penny had dropped far too late for us to do anything except look for the dust from his hasty departure. There had been none, and we now know that's because there hadn't been anything rushed about it. It had been as methodically planned, as meticulously covered and as carefully executed as everything we'd observed in the previous nine months. So that had left us painstakingly piecing together all that had happened, but without a clue of where he was or what might come next.

We'd been further constrained for the first month by the Herculean attempts of the government and its closest allies to keep a lid on the fact that NEON's bomb had been a small nuclear device. But when that leaked, at the end of April, the whole shape and nature of international condemnation and cooperation had changed; and on the cooperation front we began to receive help from the most unlikely quarters.

The CIA had stepped-in with unconfirmed historic reports about an Irish Foreign Fighter in Afghanistan in the late-1980s and '90s; the crucial input of an Iranian defector had given us a half-lead on the sometime-location of a second bomb; and once the Soviet origins of the device had at last been proven, a scarcely believable level of support had been forthcoming from the Kremlin as well. But it had still been over a month before we'd enjoyed anything like a breakthrough in our worldwide search for NEON. And then after waiting so long for nothing - much like a London bus - several half-leads, false-leads and promising clues had all appeared out of the gloom together.

The greatest benefit of the public announcement about the device though, had come not from the inclusion of countless other nations and agencies, but from the cause and effect it had

had among NEON's own terrorist cohorts after his disappearance. First-off, the discovery of the device had brought forward hundreds of arrests in Northern Ireland in the early hours of Easter Friday; and so the launch of the IRA's overt campaign had collapsed immediately. As a result, Joe Gorman had gone On The Run deep into Southern Ireland and he had been replaced as the IRA Chief of Staff by Kieran Hagan, his former driver. Better still of course, for us, was that Hagan's car remained the target of Op CLARION and Hagan himself had begun to spend even more time dribbling pillow talk into FINCH's ear.

We hadn't benefitted initially from the enormous ructions in the Middle-East though, because most of those had taken place with extreme savagery in the desert or deep in secret bunkers. But then our ambush and search of a hide in Wales, that had previously housed NEON's second device, had uncovered two of Ruslan Barayev's former fighters from Lithuania. They were a married couple from the hills of Gudžiai, near the Belarus border, living and working under the auspices of the EU on the Llŷn Peninsula as shepherds – and of course as guardians for NEON's device. But then, when cornered by armed police, they had killed themselves with potassium-cyanide suicide-pills rather than be caught and questioned. At that point we'd confirmed not only the full multi-national complexion of NEON's planned attack, but the fanatical commitment of those involved.

Not to be outdone, such total commitment in Ireland had been best demonstrated by the massacre of Frank O'Neill – the former IRA godfather – and seven of his closest aides at his farm deep in the gut of Ireland. At the same time as those killings an accomplice of O'Neill's and five of his men had been similarly slain in Sheffield, in the North of England. Kieran Hagan had ordered all fourteen executions, just as he had prepared the IRA statement released the same day from Dublin:

"Volunteers of Óglaigh na hÉireann, the Irish Republican Army, today executed all those responsible for planning and attempting the heinous bomb attack in London on Easter Friday 2016. Their cowardly and inhumane intentions besmirched the very principles and revered memories of our courageous forebears from one hundred years before, and the Army Council states categorically that they did not act in its name or on behalf of the Executive. The traitors executed today, both in the shadow of the Slieve Bloom Mountains of Ireland and those in England, have paid the ultimate price for their betrayal; others, who continue to tarnish our brave and honourable conventions, will pay the same price in their turn. Resolution of the current conflict demands an inclusive and negotiated settlement of our sovereign claims, and the IRA will not be deflected from its just and principled cause by such bestial and mindless actions. All similar traitors be warned."

And warned, by all accounts, they were. But for us, the investigation of just those killings had opened-up a new forensic jamboree, as had the discovery of a mobile phone in a waste-bin near the BT Tower. It was subsequently linked to the unidentified body of another IRA elder in the morgue nearby, and that elder had turned out to be Cahal Brady. Brady had been Frank O'Neill's lifelong partner-in-crime and, we'd learned from DNA profiling, had been his half-brother as well. Even more surprising, and we still don't know if NEON himself is aware of it, was that the same DNA analysis had revealed that NEON, Michael McCann, was Frank O'Neill's biological son. And yet, if and when I will ever get to use *that* pearl of knowledge against him, will remain for the time being a question without answer.

What we did get to exploit though was Joe Gorman's increasing vulnerability to Kieran Hagan; as he lived his life in safety and On The Run deep in Southern Ireland. That resulted in me approaching him under the cover of darkness and under the influence of extreme fear, and so his recruitment in the June as T8NI agent HEEL. But although he could tell us nothing about NEON's likely whereabouts – he'd never even met him, although he knew of his existence as a Cleanskin in London – he would prove invaluable in the future in disrupting the activities of Hagan's new IRA.

And yet despite all of that, and despite the combined anxiety of most of the Free World's intelligence agencies, the first real lead with regard to McCann's likely whereabouts came from a fairly junior analyst in Thames House and from his speculative conjuring with NEON's Computer KSA – from Keystroke Signature Analysis - should NEON have ventured online at any stage. And it transpired that he had, some weeks before, but it was enough to have placed him in the hours following Easter Friday in the tiny village of West Runton in Norfolk. At last a firm lead.

From there we now know he bought a second hand car, for which sightings ran out soon after - almost certainly when he changed the number plates - and which he subsequently used to clear his hide in Wales. After that we now think he disposed of the car in a Lanark breaker's yard a week later; and if so then he probably continued east across Scotland, because we believe he spent the next six months masquerading as a Russian merchant seaman in Aberdeen, on Scotland's north-east coast.

But if correct so far, at least all of that tended to support our much-contested view that he probably wasn't in hiding abroad - as his deliberate trail at Easter had suggested - but somewhere in plain view and still in Ireland or in the British Isles. Our reasons for thinking that were many and complicated, and they were more cerebral and circumstantial than digital or substantial. As a result few other nations or agencies agreed with us, neither at home nor abroad, and so few others joined that particular part of the search with any vigour or confidence; but carry on searching we must, and it would be under my direct purview until further notice. Lucky me.

And so in short, the past couple of years have been an appalling interregnum in the normal run of things: between the relative order and predictability of my existence in Training Wing before it all kicked-off, and the sheer bedlam of life in the Service and in Britain post-NEON. But y'know... in spite of that, I suppose the double-icing on 2016's smashed and crumbling cake, was Katy's move to T8 in London as a handler, and my return to T8NI in Ireland as the section chief the following Easter.

And once I got there I reckoned I was there through fate, through relevance and through good fortune; and if it couldn't be Emily Rankin, then it would damn well have to be me. So I set out to make her and Bill Wallace proud.

Ménage à Trois

I arrived back in Northern Ireland just before Easter 2017, and so a whole year after NEON's failed attack in Central London. One of the earliest things I did was to begin taking stock of my life for the first time since I'd joined the Service fourteen years earlier. I didn't mean to, it just began and never stopped. It was a sub-conscious thing to start with, very, but it quickly became a deliberate and rejuvenating process and so eventually a source of good ideas. And it wasn't because I felt the need, but simply because all of a sudden I lived alone and so I had the time.

It's not that the hours aren't still long in T8NI, they are, but now I'm the section chief I'm kept even more under wraps from the agents than last time I was here. Apart from the odd Boss-Meet as and when needed, by and large the only sources I get to see now are those I recruited; and even then only on rare and special occasions. And I travel a lot. A hell of a lot. I go to and from London at least twice a month, usually more – that's good thinking time -

and, as I promised him at the height of the NEON enquiries, I go to Dundalk quite often to spend some time with Detective Inspector George Kennedy. *King George* doesn't have a crown yet, but he got his three pips in near record time; and he's onwards and upwards in the Garda for sure. Good for them.

I spend a day or two a month with George, and if I travel further afield in the South he will usually come with me. He says it's to hold my hand, and we do have some great craic, but it also means the Guards are in on everything we set-up at the outset and so it's about as efficient as an intelligence sharing initiative can be. If I know him then he'll have given me an Official Contact number and told Dublin that he's running me; but that works just fine for me and cross-border cooperation, between our two organisations at least, is as good as it's ever been. And then I go every few months to Mullaghmore as well, to stay with retired Garda Inspector Ned Boyle and his wife Briana. When Katy can next make it over for a long weekend she's going to come with me, as did George and Bill Wallace recently.

Ned and Briana Boyle are a wonderful old couple in their seventies, and you only have to pass their front door for Briana to start cooking for the whole of Ireland. But my original interest was in Ned only, her devoted husband of fifty years and the man who'd held the only key – well, half a key - to NEON's early teens. Back in 1984 Ned had been the Garda Sergeant in the same village as NEON's Christian Brothers' school, and so he'd *attended the scene* after the death of a priest there, Father Joseph Devine. I say he *attended* rather than *investigated* - his words not mine - because in Ned's opinion that was the one thing on the day that he was never really allowed to do. Investigate.

His mere presence seemed to be an embarrassment to the other Brothers, to the vicar forane and to Ned's immediate superior – whom he hadn't called by the way, but someone had - and so all he was allowed to do was observe, tie-off loose ends and then submit his final report. A report which was challenged at the time because of some of its conclusions, and which subsequently disappeared from the system anyway. All three copies of it. Ned was the new boy at the scene, having only just moved to the village on promotion from Mullaghmore; where he'd been one of the gardaí at the time of Lord Louis Mountbatten's murder by the South Armagh Brigade of the Provos in 1979.

Admiral of the Fleet, The Earl Mountbatten of Burma, a cousin to the Queen and the last Viceroy of India, had been killed by a remote-controlled bomb on his boat. That same day and on the opposite coast of Ireland, my dad had looked-on in horror as still more South Armagh men had killed eighteen British soldiers at Warrenpoint. And so the 27th of August 1979 had an ominous but special resonance for both of us. Ned had known Mountbatten personally; the seventy-nine-year-old naval officer, statesman and royal family member would look-him-up during his frequent visits to Mullaghmore, because Ned's grandfather had been serving on his ship, *HMS Kelly,* when he'd perished at the Battle of Crete in May 1941.

Much to the horror of the church and the local community, Ned Boyle's conclusions in his long-since-vanished report had stated the following facts: Father Devine was an alcoholic; he had been drinking heavily at the time of his death; he had summoned several of the boys to his quarters; and he had fallen down a flight of ancient stone steps and was killed by a blow to the head at the bottom. Horrified or not, everyone accepted that part of the report because they had no choice. But he'd also added that in his opinion Devine had been a long-established paedophile (which several of the boys had confirmed); that he believed he'd not fallen, but been thrown down the stairs by one boy in particular who'd rejected his advances; and then that boy had slammed his head against the bottom step because the fall hadn't killed him. And *that boy* had been a muscular, larger-than-usual and self-assured fourteen-year-old called Michael McCann. The same Michael McCann who also kept a hurley stick beside his bed. That part of the report was contested vigorously.

The saga of Ned's missing report was never fully resolved, any more than the death of Father Joseph Devine was, but Ned's recollections and the circumstantial 'evidence' they represented were a Godsend. They were the real turning point in the way some of those involved in Op STELLAR began to view NEON, and so in real terms in the way they more fully supported me and Bill Wallace. And it was a discreet but crucial breakthrough for which I will always owe Ned an enormous debt of gratitude.

So... what else do I do with my spare time now I'm back? Well, the meagre remains of it, less a little bit for sleeping, is spent on my own at home just outside of Belfast or walking the hills or playing sport. Not much sport unfortunately, but enough, including a game some weekends for a rugby club on the Ards Peninsula (for whom JC and an army mate used to play in the 1980s. Still more serendipity, I'm certain.) I see Katy about once or twice a month, if my frequent trips to London fall-in neatly with her meet schedule in T8; and if not then we make time, there or here, at least every other month. 'It won't be forever,' we keep telling ourselves, but for now there's no other way. Since her move to T8 Katy has been well and truly bitten by the handling bug, and unsurprisingly she's proved to be very good at it. Better than me, people in London keep teasing me.

But then the other thing I find plenty of time to do alone these days is reflect. Deeply and often, and on any number of things. Y'know... the usual stuff: life; death (and the million or so Londoners we saved); on yesterday, today and tomorrow (and how the next time we might not be able to); and on the organised chaos, the inconclusive outcome and the many lessons-learned from NEON. And, seeing as I'm still looking for him, on the innermost anything and everything about him I can find to think about. So maybe not such usual stuff.

That's more than enough for any one man to be thinking about, but I'm only glad that I'm doing it in Northern Ireland and not back in London. When I think about what Maggie Allinson, Bill Wallace and a hundred or so others are having to go through daily, I actually feel guilty that I'm back at the 'sharp end' and camping-out on Her Majesty's final Western Front. Far from being safe and sound in the battle's rear area, they are still in the gaze of the world's media and pinned-down in the withering crossfire of a global intelligence feeding frenzy. Good job they're up to it - and I'm glad I'm no longer there to take my share.

It was a difficult period in the Service anyway, irrespective of anything cluttering the tangled desktop of my thoughts. The shock of Brexit in June; the overnight change of Prime Ministers; and Britain's precarious status in a new and uncertain world; had set a pretty chaotic scene before I'd even returned to Ireland. And then countless, mindless, terrorist acts had shattered that world still further. To add to the general malaise, the anxious first steps of the United States' brash new Administration had caused the whole planet to hold its breath. And it's still holding it. Never before had America's chief executive been elected amid such vitriol, loathing and scepticism; and never before had a President thrown out the playbook and promised so much. Over-promised, many believed. As unlikely as his success seemed, we *others* in the Free World wished him well – because after years with no steady hand on the tiller and heading in the wrong direction, America's fate was ours and we had no choice.

According to myriad polls before the US general election – nearly all of which were proven to be entirely wrong - the voters' choice had been a simple one: between bad or worse. And so once that vote was cast, what momentous challenges had faced the eventual incumbent? The tentative pause that followed – a global vacuum of doubt, apprehension, incredulity and fear – seemed punctuated only by still more terrorist atrocities and a seismic shift in the international hierarchy. Thus the pressure mounted on men and women like me across the world, to answer questions which no-one had yet even found the words to ask.

And on a personal level, now I'm torn as well... between three women no less. A difficult and unenviable situation for any man, and at any time. Katy and I have been dating for over two years now, and I feel a mounting imperative to 'pop the question'. We've been living together for most of that time, but the pressure comes from me alone. It certainly doesn't come from her; she's far too busy in T8, and some days I think she forgets I even exist.

Good girl, because some days in that job that's the way it needs to be. Nor does it come from Bill Wallace or his wife Pam, both of whom have clothes for the wedding already picked-out. And nor from any number of our friends, relatives and colleagues who would also be delighted. No, it stems from my own certainty about my choice of partner – our choice of partners – and so from a vague yearning to express the depth of my commitment more clearly. Maybe soon then... but not just yet.

But then there are the other two women... who between them demand far more of my time, thoughts and devotion than Katy ever gets to experience anymore. They are our new Prime Minister, who knows me rather too well having been the Home Secretary for the past six years, and Maggie Allinson, who serves her, the Crown and The Service so faithfully. Katy understands of course, and indeed she's proud to be third-in-line in such exalted company; but for how long?... and under what circumstances might that change?

It's the question neither of us ever takes the time to ask, and so the answer we've not yet had to deal with.

Introspection

As Easter 2017 came and went a few months ago, I was prompted to pause and reflect on NEON in particular. In fact, as we passed the first anniversary of his failed attack - and so the beginning of what I feared might be a lifelong search for him and his second device - I almost *had* to sift and sort my thoughts and my theories to be able to carry on. To prioritise things, I guess, both professional and personal, so as to chart a way forward without that constant dread that I'd forgotten something in my rush to leave the room.

Since then I've been determined to turn all this alone-time and reflection into a positive thing, not a gloomy or introspective waste of time. And so it's given me pause to map *his* childhood and his development against my own. At least all the parts we've been able to find out about. But please don't think it's some deep and pointless flagellation I'm obsessed with - it's merely another attempt to make sure I'm not missing something vital.

It's unnervingly sobering, for example, to think that at fourteen years of age I was terrified of what I might find if I slipped my hand inside a girl's knickers, whilst Michael McCann had just murdered a degenerate priest by smashing his head open on a stone floor. And two years before that even, when I was proud of myself for climbing the hills above Poison Glen with Úna at twelve years of age, he'd just beaten his older brother to death with a hurley stick for raping his younger sister. Or when at four years of age I was surrounded by doting relatives, he had just watched his be blown to pieces right in front of his terrified young eyes. And as I thought more and more about it, I couldn't even begin to imagine his state of mind... much less comprehend his actions.

I thought I'd had a tough upbringing in the Derrybeg - and indeed I had - but when I then tried to superimpose all of my ordeals over NEON's likely trials and tribulations in Dublin's Northside, I was humbled into submission. And then God knows what other encounters he'd had in terrorist training camps, and in bloody war zones that we only partially knew about? In places like Libya when he was just seventeen; or in lethal combat in Afghanistan just a year later, and in the Balkans and in both Chechen wars when still only in his twenties. It was humbling indeed, even for someone from Bandit Country South Armagh.

And so only then, with all that alone-time, did I *really* start to comprehend the sort of man we were hunting. I'd had a healthy but grudging respect for him all along, of course, but only in the benign context of our cat and mouse tumble through the streets of London. It felt like that had been a game almost, compared to what might be required to find and capture him going forward. A chivalrous game of chess maybe, where the all-seeing knights and bishops of the Service had jousted with a swashbuckling con-man and photographer who seemed more at home in a woman's bed than in a slit-trench and under fire in some Medieval moonscape.

In any number of beds, it would seem. But then after a while the other NEON loomed ever larger in my dreams, and so even greater in my plans. The 21st Century gladiator and sometime-Mujahideen that was Michael McCann.

When I was next in London I ran it all past Bill Wallace for good measure. Bill had at last just taken over T-Branch, when Maggie Allinson had promoted and moved into the DDG's post. Notwithstanding the Irish Sea, that made Wallace my immediate superior yet again. Brilliant... the two key players were now in the two key appointments. 'Now we could get things done,' I'd told myself, 'now we'll find the bastard.' By way of celebration I got us a table right at the back of Gordon's Wine Bar, we got a bottle of good Cab' Sav', and then we got into the right frame of mind to discuss it all at length. We were well into our second bottle before either of us thought we were getting anywhere.

"Yeah, I guess it is kind of humbling," Bill said, "and we're certainly dealing with someone who's a lot more substantial than just the charmer we stalked all over London. But he's still only flesh and blood Neill, don't get demoralised and lose sight of that. He's gettable, and at some stage we *will* get him."

"Oh aye, I know that, and I'm not getting demoralised, just frustrated. Right now it's hard to see where and when he might pop up again, that's all. And, y'know... we can't get him until he does, whatever we throw at it."

"True, but if he is in Ireland, like you think he is - I mean, *anywhere* in Ireland – then you're likely to be the first to hear about it, North or South."

"Aye, well I hope so, and that's part of the reason I spend so much time with George and the Guards at the moment."

"Yeah, I know that, and so does Maggie by the way, so don't worry about that fellah. We both know that in real terms we've got you doing two full-time jobs, and so that in some respects both must suffer from time to time. But you know... that works for any number of reasons back here in London, and T5 are especially grateful for what you're doing, trust me."

"Well knowledge is power, and if I keep them all up to date with what we *do* know, and right down to the lowest safe levels, then that maximises our chances of a breakthrough. That way we're all trying to fill-in the same blanks and we're all hopefully looking out for the same hints and clues going forward. But then, it's just... well, y'know..."

"What?"

"It's just, huh, where the hell's he been since September? It's almost a bloody year now, and not a ripple anywhere."

"Yeah, I know what you mean. I'm as frustrated as you."

"I mean, we know he left London maybe as long as twenty-one hours before his device was due to detonate; we know he was in Dover - and actually on a ferry at one point - late on the Easter Friday morning; and then we know he spent the next twelve hours or so in Norfolk, posing as an American called Niall Kelly."

"I know, I know. And is there still nothing of value from the hundreds of security cameras we've checked?"

"No, nothing of *value*. We've got loads of pictures of his arse disappearing out through some door and wearing whatever disguise he was in at the time, so we think we've tied down all his train journeys for that day, but nothing that tells us anything we really want to know."

"Right."

"Like the ferry in Dover, for example: we still can't ID him on *any* CCTV from that phase – over a dozen different cameras - and we pretty much know right where he was stood when he sent those text messages on the Spanish girl's mobile. Canny fucker."

"Because he was stood in dead-ground to the cameras you mean? And so nothing to see?"

"Precisely, and because he must have been in a disguise we haven't been able to confirm yet immediately before and after he stopped her. Y'know, entering or leaving that area."

"What do you mean stopped her?"

"Well, it's just a theory, but I don't think he approached her, I think he was deliberately stood in dead-ground and simply stopped her as she strolled past."

"Got it, but so what did she say?"

"She couldn't remember. Back last year she said he tapped her on the arm from behind, so she feels like she was approached; but of course he could have worked that out to the inch."

"Yeah, I get you."

"But that's just typical of everything that day. I mean, Jesus Bill, this fellah's so crafty with so-called security cameras and so good with disguises, it's actually frightening."

"Except when he forgets."

"Aye, except then – which isn't often – or when he simply doesn't bother."

"Like at the Savoy."

"Exactly. Thank God we've got one or two like that."

"So any more on Aberdeen?"

"No, you've seen the file now I know, and the best I can say is it's thick and getting thicker; but it still only really tells us he was there from April to September last year, posing as a Russian sailor called Yury Borzov. I mean we're pretty certain it was him, although Jack Swain's exhausted the DNA and print search and come up empty because it was all so long ago; but most who knew him think he was the real thing... including a few Russians."

Jack Swain is a retired Metropolitan Police Detective Chief Superintendent, who'd been vital to our team for pretty much the whole of Op STELLAR. He still was to me on Op BOLAS.

"Yeah, well, the speaking fluent Russian part was a bit of a surprise, I'll give you that, but I reckon we'd already decided he was a master of disguise though, hadn't we."

"Aye, and a master of disappearing again as well, damn it."

"Yeah, no shit," Bill rolled his eyes. "And so the past nine months are still a total blank?"

"Yep, as at today they are, but you see we're really only just beginning to ask that question, aren't we; y'know, downwards and outwards to where it counts..."

"Yeah, I know."

"I mean... Jees... we're really only just now starting to get all the Aberdeen stuff out there for police forces to work off. It's frustrating. That should have been done months ago, Bill." Bill was nodding. "But hey... I know about all the political sensitivities... and I've got a section to run, you've got a branch to run, and now Maggie's got the whole friggin' Service to run, and none of us can be everywhere all at once, so..."

"I know," Bill nodded apologetically, "but just get on with your day job, and trust that those running Op BOLAS back here now are doing far more behind the scenes than you are getting to see in Ireland."

"Aye, I do, I do... but maybe I'm a little more trusting about that than I should be. Y'know, there's an inevitable disjoint."

Bill didn't comment out of loyalty to the Service, but his expression told me he felt the same way. Then his half-answer merely confirmed it.

"I know, well maybe now..."

"Aye, maybe," I said a little too gloomily. Bill picked up on it straight away.

"But listen fellah," he smiled in his most fatherly voice, "although we've spent most of the past hour talking about how humbling it is to compare yourself to NEON growing up..."

"Yeah, yeah, I know."

"No but listen, seriously, whatever he's been through, and whatever he's capable of, he's still just flesh and blood like you and me. And whatever he's done, whoever he's fought for and against, we're gonna get him in the end... you know we are."

"Oh aye, I know that. At some stage..."

"Exactly. We'll get him when we do, and not before. Simple as that. And in the meantime, you're doing a pretty important job where you are."

"Aye, I guess."

"Jesus Neill, there's no guess about it, and that's official. Look, Kieran Hagan's new IRA's dead in the water, thanks in no small part to you and your section, and our coverage gets better with every day you're still chipping away at them; so try to keep it all in perspective."

"Yeah, I know."

"Do you? I hope so, because the way Maggie and I see it is this: You're the right man in the right place to spot a lead if and when we get one, and then you're the best man by far to leap all over it when that time comes. You just need your chance, fellah, and then we reckon there's no-one anywhere who would know better what to do with it."

"Aye, well, I sure hope so…"

"Well we *know* so, and so that comes from the DG too don't forget. And so through him from Whitehall as well. Seriously. The whole system's poised and ready to do whatever's necessary when we find him – us, the police, the military, SIS, whatever it takes - but we still reckon that's most likely to come from you and everything you're doing. We all do. So there you have it."

As pep-talks go it was pretty straightforward: 'Get on with it.' And although we're all still waiting for me to get my *chance*, what none of us knew was that our next major breakthrough was just around the corner. Just around the corner, but still temptingly out of reach. It would fall to Tommy Bray to give me a leg-up.

Cabbages and Kings

It had been a windy day in August and we'd just played in our first rugby match of the 2017/18 season for the club's 2nd XV. I knew I couldn't make another game for over a month and I'd brought George and Tommy along as ringers and for the craic; I felt I owed the club at least that much. I hadn't made it to training at all, and they knew with my workload in the Northern Ireland Office I wouldn't all year.

Tommy was in Ireland for just four days, just a long weekend he'd said, and George had driven up from Dundalk specially. We'd all played well, for guys in their mid-thirties that is, and we'd just returned from Ards Hospital where they'd put six stitches in Tommy's gashed eyebrow... he was slowing-up these days, as we took great delight in telling him. Now it was time for a pint in *Grace Neill's*, Ireland's oldest pub.

Grace's sits at the top of New Street, a two-minute walk from the harbour in Donaghadee, and I'm sure a lot of other pubs would dispute its claim to be the oldest. It's the sort of assertion that any self-respecting Irishman would probably be willing to fight over – in defence of his pint, as it were - but its licence speaks for itself. It's had one since 1611, and for the first three hundred years of business it was called the *King's Arms*, but then in 1918 one of its keenest patrons, Grace Neill, died aged ninety-eight, and so they renamed the pub in her honour. If only... I never get to be a regular anywhere for long enough, so I can't see any pub doing that for me; and Gordon's Wine Bar in London already has a name. But *Neill Mac's* sure has a ring to it.

We got our pints, chatted to an old boy on a stool who I knew a little, and then settled down behind a table on the long side bench opposite the bar. It had been a busy month and I was looking forward to a quiet pint with a couple of mates who knew what I *really* did for a living; so no blarney or charades, just a rare chance to chill. We'd worked four back-to-back eighty-hour weeks in T8NI over the past month, longer maybe, and it didn't look like letting-up any time soon. George could have told a similar story, and Tommy... well, who knows, but then he had all his travel on top of everything else. He'd been in three different countries that week, and over seven since we'd seen him two months before.

George, I knew, had more of the same to come. Three days after the 9th of August marches - the Anniversary of Internment – fifty more IRA men and women had been arrested right across Northern Ireland, and now a dozen similar arrests were planned in the South over the coming week. And even before that we'd both been trying to make sense of the mysterious killing in Belfast of Kieran Hagan at the end of July, the IRA's Chief of Staff since the days soon after NEON's failed attack at Easter.

It had been a deliberate hit with a silenced weapon at point-blank range, but who the hell had ordered it? Even more unsettling, it had been in the Ballymurphy and so virtually in his own back yard, so who the hell had actually *done* it? Both of us had been working on any number of unfinished puzzles at the time, but who would replace Hagan – or maybe who already had - was without doubt the most pressing. George and I didn't reckon we'd be playing rugby again any time soon.

Tommy sipped his pint, picked up a magazine that had fallen out of his coat pocket and put it down on the bench. 'Twas time to jack him up some more, and so I did.

"How's your eye?" I grinned.

"Oh, not so bad. Throbbing a bit."

"Can't believe you had it stitched, you big pussy."

I leant forward and prodded it with my forefinger. Tommy winced and pulled his head back and George just laughed.

"Jesus," I continued, chortling, "I had one worse than that playing footy in Carrick' when I was just a spotty-faced teenager; and Úna just closed me up with some Steri-Strip. Good as new."

"Yeah, well I wanted some of those invisible stitches, I've got better looks to think about than you have," Tommy chuckled.

"Aye, he's got a point there, fellah," George added his two penn'orth, "a few more dings and bumps in that face of yours might be a bit of an improvement."

We all laughed aloud, but payback's a bitch – and within moments George had taken a call from his section and he had to return to Dundalk to deal with a fastball. The drive was going to take him over an hour, and so he supped the rest of his pint and set-off straight away. That left just me and Tommy to chill together and wondering what we should do about food. We agreed to finish-up our pints and then take a wander to *Pier 36*, a good pub-restaurant on the harbour's edge. In the middle of the small-talk that followed, Tommy knocked his magazine on the floor again, and this time I passed comment.

"What is that?" I asked. I could see it was a copy of Time Magazine. It had a picture of a US soldier on the front cover and the headline, 'Was He Worth It?', but I wondered what it was about and why Tommy was carrying it?

"Och, I picked it up in the hospital waiting room. It's three years old now, but there's something in here I want to read."

"What, about him?" I nodded towards the cover.

"No, about a piece called ten questions - y'know, like an interview they did - with a former CIA chief about Snowden an' all..." Tommy put it on the table, "but what did you reckon about all that though? About him there, Private Bergdahl?"

"Jesus, that was some nonsense, wasn't it? Talk about keep politics out of war," I laughed.

"Yeah right, if only."

"But I thought he was a sergeant?"

"No, a private."

"You sure? I thought I read something just the other day..."

"Aye, you probably did. When they got him back he was a sergeant, but that's one of the stupid things about it. One of many."

"What was?"

"He was only a bloody private when he walked out of his location and got nabbed by the Taliban..."

"So how does that work? The White House says sergeant."

"Aye, I know they do; but like a lot of other things, that's the way it was made to look and not the way it actually happened."

"Now you've really lost me."

"Aye, well trust me, you're not the only one," he laughed. "I was working with Americans at the time he vanished, and that was bad enough... but then I've met-up with some of them again since his release, and that's just one of the many things that jacked them up so much."

"What, trying to cover it all up?"

"No, kind of the opposite, but what a total fuckup. He was Private First Class Bergdahl when he went walkabouts, and then he was promoted in captivity. Twice."

"You're kidding? How does that work?"

"Nope, wish I were. The guys I'm on about were furious. Just think about it: his promotion in captivity and in absentia; his alleged desertion; charges that were never really dealt with; the bizarre support of the Joint Chiefs; and then his return to active service, by then as a sergeant no less, and alongside others who didn't know where they stood... talk about eroding morale, Jesus."

"Aye, I can see how that would work. It must have been pretty grim for the whole army."

"Yeah, it was, still is maybe, but since when did that bother an administration with a point to prove? And that was only half of what got the guys so jacked-up."

"Go on," I urged. I knew I was about to get an inside-line on something interesting, and so I was genuinely interested.

"Well you've got to remember I was still *Capitaine Tomàs Bray* at the time... you know, so representing the French Army as it were, and so I think the guys I was working with were more embarrassed than anything."

"I guess, I get that."

"Because suddenly *whoosh*, we're all dropping everything else we're doing and looking for this guy, and he'd just wandered off the reservation. Jesus, and the search was fucking huge, and well... y'know, complicated."

"Yeah, I can at least remember how long it dragged on for."

"Huh, it dragged on alright. But so then when I met these guys recently, when I was in Virginia on Interpol business and we all hooked-up for a beer, well he'd not long been released and they were seriously pissed. Fuming in fact."

"Go on."

"Well, quite apart from the whole desertion thing and how that still wasn't resolved six years later, and over a year after his repatriation by then too, they were more angry at the politics of it all than anything else."

"What, the prisoner exchange you mean?"

"Aye, that's a huge part of it, although these guys insisted it was a political trade, not a prisoner exchange as such..."

"Yeah, because the Taliban weren't actually terrorists or somesuch, wasn't it?"

"Well that was CNN said that, but it was the same thinking I reckon, and I think you'll find that the guys who've had to stand there taking rounds see it differently."

"Aye, I'm sure they do," I chuckled.

"See, notwithstanding the 'No soldier left behind' ethos - which is highly commendable by the way – the guys I'm on about don't get how one alleged deserter, who simply wandered-off into the night and got himself nabbed, is a good trade for the Taliban Army Chief of Staff, their Deputy Minister of Intelligence, a former Interior Minister and two other senior-somethings in the Taliban that I can't remember just now..."

"No, that was my thoughts at the time, and a lot of others, but then I always thought there was more to it."

"Well yeah, there was, a helluva a lot more, and that's what jacked them up even worse; because of the agenda coming out of the White House an' all. Y'know, they were pissed about the whole Rose Garden ceremony, and all the fanfares and media hype when they got him back... like it was some huge moral victory for the Administration or something."

"Right."

"But even worse was going-back on the key policy of never negotiating with terrorists. I mean that had huge implications for future kidnappings, and for all other nations as well don't forget; not to mention handing the Taliban the biggest psychological victory against US Forces since 9/11. But what they were *really* pissed about was the mealy-mouthed double-speak coming out of the Administration..."

"What, some of the crazy statements about what a hero he was or something?"

"Well not a hero exactly, but just that. Jees, they were beside themselves when the National Security Advisor said on ABC that Bergdahl had been 'captured on the field of battle' and that he'd 'served the United States with honor and distinction'..."

"I'll bet."

"Yeah, I think you'll find that most of his colleagues thinks he simply walked out of his post, wandered off into the night and was grabbed by the Taliban. That's hardly the same definitions of 'on the field of battle' and 'with honour and distinction' as she was using. Now *that*, they reckoned, kind of summed up what they'd been up against their whole time."

We fell silent for a moment and both finished our beers.

"Well... I hope you feel better now you've got that little lot off your chest," I laughed.

"Aye, I do," Tommy laughed back, "but seriously though, I don't see how any soldier could see it any differently to be honest. Y'know fellah, from any nation I mean. Because now there's five more Taliban *generals* back on the battlefield; some of our previously sacrosanct rules about dealing with terrorists have been torn-up; and yet still more soldiers are going to have to go back out there and face them all over again. So who's fucking idea of smart was that?"

"Aye, I get it. Another pint?" I asked.

"Aye, if you like, or shall we go and eat now, like we said?" He put his hand up to his throbbing eyebrow and checked his stitches. "Do you fancy taking a wee walk along the harbour first, and then finishing up at the restaurant? You've got me going now."

By which I sensed that he meant just the 'walk along the harbour' part, so we could speak more freely.

"Aye, of course," I nodded. I was at the very least curious, and I was ready to eat anyway. And so that's what we did.

We walked slowly and chatted as we strolled: all the way to the boat park to the west of the bay and then right along the promenade around the harbour to the lighthouse at the far end of South Pier. Tommy talked in general terms about some of the military operations he'd been involved in over the years - which was why he'd wanted to leave the pub – because he knew I'd be interested and many of them had relevance to my work. But then he wanted to sound me out on something in particular as devil's advocate; but 'just as a fair-minded Brit' and not as an MI5 officer: 'Summary execution,' as he put it, but specifically as it applied to a total war situation.

"OK," he began, "so imagine we're both in a hot war zone somewhere, and we've identified a proven, top-level, Islamic State terrorist – or y'know, it could be al-Qaeda, IRA, ETA, it doesn't really matter - but for whatever reason he's about to get off on a technicality or something."

"He or she, could that be?"

"Yes, good question, and that's really important."

"And so have we arrested him?"

"No, we can't... or yes, say we have, but he's about to be released on some farcical multi-national absurdity. Y'know, to go straight out and kill all over again..."

"But a known and proven killer, either way? Y'know, not some planner or some Sinn Féin type?"

"Always. And we're not talking about some rabid wannabe jihadist who's hacked off heads in a London street here, or some whack-job pseudo-Islamist who drives a truck into hundreds of people in Nice. We've got to trust that the system will deal with them, as and when they occur - or not - and there is no way to stop incidents like that..."

"Agreed."

"No, I'm talking about committed lifelong terrorists who will plan, direct or actually do things like that time after time after time, unless they're removed from the equation once and for all."

"Understood, and so if that's the case then I reckon the gender's irrelevant... but go on."

"Good answer, I agree, and so if a capture and arrest op isn't going to cut it, unless he's killed in any firefight that might occur, would you support a drone strike?"

"What, to take him out?"

"Yeah."

"Yes, depending on where. Y'know, provided there was due diligence to avoiding collateral casualties and so on."

"Right. So what about an air strike, fast jets an' all?"

"Same answer."

"Cruise Missile?"

"Same."

"What about a raid by Special Forces then? Because all of those others, remember, are kind of blind from the moment of release. Oh I know they're laser-guided an' all, but they still can't read the situation and react to changing circumstances."

"Same answer, I'd still be OK with that, but you said there's no capture and arrest option?"

"No, there isn't, because of the risk to our own troops say; overwhelming numbers of enemy for example, or inner-city or impossible terrain; so it's going to be a kill-only mission, with no intent to capture him alive."

"Well then, I'd still support that, but surely there'd be a risk to our troops anyway... just by putting them in harm's way?"

"Yes, there would," Tommy raised a profound-looking finger, "so that's why all those other remote techniques become so important. Important but blind."

"OK, I get that, clearly..."

"Right. So here's the question I'm leading up to," Tommy said thoughtfully, "and not here remember, but in a total war situation somewhere... what about assassination then?"

"What, by poison... or by an agent or something?"

"Or something, yeah..."

We walked in silence for a moment while I pondered the difference, and it was some seconds before I decided that there wasn't one. Except the moral conundrum for the assassin... and quite obviously, there had been for me for a moment as well.

"No, that's good too," I said with conviction.

"Good. Good to know."

"Why?" I asked. "Is that something you've had to do?"

"Well," he slowed and looked at me resolutely, "I'd be lying if I said no, but it's a gross oversimplification to say yes."

"Of course. I can imagine." I thought about his ten years in Special Forces and I honestly believed that I could.

"Yeah," he glanced at me again, "I think that's why I asked you. You probably can, the vast majority can't."

"So does it trouble you?" I returned his steadfast gaze. "Is that why you asked me?"

"God no, not for a second... no, I just wanted to see how you felt about it all, that's all. Y'know, it's not often I get to discuss it with someone in the same business as it were, but who wasn't stood next to me in the military. And especially because of all the shenanigans you grew up with in South Armagh... that's about as close to a total war zone that the Brits could experience at home; that and the mainland bombings for all those years I suppose. No, I just wondered if or why you'd see it all differently I guess."

"No, can't say that I do... and I kind of wish that we could arrange things like that sometimes."

"Aye, I'll bet you do," he laughed, "but do you really?"

He stopped walking for a moment and studied me closely.

"Yeah..." I thought hard for a moment, "I think I do... but of course we can't, and we never will, so it's just one of those frustrating dreams I'll have to live with. I've got a few, trust me."

"Huh, do you mean NEON?"

"No, not really... although he'd be top of the list," I laughed. "Jesus Tommy, I'd climb over you to get to him I reckon."

"Yeah, if only you knew where he was," he chuckled.

"Aye, well that's tonight's nightmare: where he is right this minute, and where's that friggin' second device? Last night's was where the hell he went to after Aberdeen nearly a year ago."

Tommy studied me again... then grinned.

"Come on, let's go and get that feed," he said, and then he turned and headed slowly off the pier towards the pub some three hundred metres away along the harbour wall.

For almost an hour we'd been talking about some pretty heavy things – in fact, at times, some pretty highly classified things as well - and yet as we walked towards the door, Tommy suddenly started to recite, of all things, Lewis Carroll:

"The time has come, the Walrus said, to talk of many things," he glanced at me and grinned again. "Of shoes, and ships, and sealing wax, of cabbages and kings..."

I stopped at the door and looked back at him inquisitively. Nothing Tommy ever said or did shocked me anymore, but it nearly always made me smile... and so I waited to see what the hell it was he was on about. There'd be a point to it, I knew that much at least.

"It used to be painted on the wall above a coal-burning cooker in the restaurant here," he smiled as he explained. "It was an orange-coloured Rayburn, a beautiful old thing, just like the one we had at home growing up in Drogheda."

I didn't know Tommy knew Donaghadee that well. He'd never said. But he was full of such surprises.

"Huh, God knows if it's still here," he continued, "hope so," and then he mimicked the poem and its metre: "But the time has come, young Tommy said, for our duty ne'er to shirk; so let's go in, and get a beer, and talk of no more work. Agreed?"

"Agreed," I grinned.

And so in we went, with me still smiling broadly. It was the most succinct security brief I'd ever received.

Sermon on the Mount

On Friday evening, six days after we'd eaten together by the harbour in Donaghadee, Tommy Bray called me on my mobile but from a number I didn't recognise.

"Hello?" I answered.

"Neill?"

"Who's this?" Although I thought I knew the voice.

"Tommy."

"New phone?"

"No, borrowed." A burner phone I later learned.

"Got'ya. Where are you?"

"Not far actually. About an hour from you."

"Oh right, so you're not in Dublin then?" Dublin was over two hours by road. "You with George?"

"No, he doesn't know I'm here."

"Nor did I. I thought you went back to Lyon?"

"I did, but I'm back. Just for the weekend again, but no-one really knows I'm here."

"Well I do, so you're wrong about that much."

"What, you knew I'd travelled?"

"No," I laughed, "Jees, that's a bit Orwellian, even for you and your cloak and dagger lifestyle."

"Right, got it, you mean just coz I've called you?"

"Yeah, that's all," I chuckled.

"Touché… I think you know that much French, don't you?"

"Ouais, je t'encule."

"Aye, fuck you too," he laughed. "That was almost correct."

"So what's up?"

"Nothing, but look… I need to see you."

"Need to, or want to?" He had my immediate attention… Tommy didn't usually start conversations that way.

"Need to. Your need, my treat. I've got something for you."

"OK… er, right now or will it keep?"

"Oh, it sure will, it's kept for a year."

My heart skipped a beat as I replayed parts of our dialogue from the week before. That was almost how long we hadn't known where NEON was, and Tommy knew that full well.

"Jees Tommy, don't do that," I tried to sound light-hearted, "anything to do with my year-long nightmare?"

"Look, can you get away to do the Mournes tomorrow?"

The fact that he hadn't answered directly told me that it was. He had something to do with NEON, or at least Op BOLAS, and I hoped that it was important enough to have brought him back to Ireland just to tell me. Wishful thinking, I know, but…

"No, sorry fellah, not tomorrow I can't… but look, come up here tonight if you want? Stay over Tommy. Or I can drive straight down to you… no problem. Are you staying at your flat?"

"No, not tonight, and I really am off the radar, so not your place or mine. What about Sunday? For the Mournes I mean?"

"Aye, I can do that, but are you sure it'll keep?"

"Yeah, I am, but I can hear you're not," he laughed. "You'll not sleep now until you've seen me, right?"

"Arsehole," I chuckled, "Sunday it is then..."

"Seven at the obvious, is that OK?"

"Aye, 'tis."

"And Neill, don't tell anyone. Seriously."

"Yeah, if you say so, of course. Everything alright though?"

"Yeah, grand, but not a soul. Please."

"OK."

"Not Katy, not Bill, not George... no-one."

"Not even Bill?"

"Especially not Bill. You'll see why on Sunday."

That spoke volumes.

"OK fellah, I hope so, but I promise until then at least."

"Aye, I understand, but so will you."

"Cool."

"You still in the same car?"

"Yes," I answered.

"Got it. Then just park-up and I'll come to you."

"Good enough, seven it is. Will you have all day?"

"Yes, 'til my flight on Monday."

"OK. Forecast's good. Do you want to get food or beer?"

"I'll get the beers."

"See you Sunday."

"Aye, you will."

And we were done.

So that Sunday morning I met Tommy as we'd arranged, at 7 am in the Donard Car Park at the north-eastern corner of the Mourne Mountains. I had told no-one I was meeting him - until I found out more about why all the secrecy - although I had said where I was going in case of a chance sighting. But it wasn't an unusual rest-day activity for me anyway, and I had walked various hills with Tommy several times before.

Actually taking a Sunday off without attracting attention had been trickier. I'd worked the past five in a row to make the most of quiet-time in the office, and people had come to expect it.

I later learned that most of my team presumed I'd gone to see Ned Boyle in Mullaghmore... because it was the 27th of August and so the thirty-eighth anniversary of Mountbatten's murder and of Warrenpoint. But I'm ashamed to say that in the excitement of meeting Tommy to see what he had, I hadn't even remembered.

As I climbed out of my car and went to the boot for my rucksack, Tommy was striding across the car park towards me. His smile arrived first, followed by the warmth of his voice, and then all tied-off like an unbreakable promise with his handshake.

"Morning Neill," he grasped my hand firmly, "Jees, what a beautiful day."

"Morning Tommy. Aye, 'tis... unless you're about to ruin it for me," I grinned. "Why all the secrecy?"

"Just that. Secrecy?"

"Really? Why?"

"But literally I mean, total secrecy."

"OK, I'm sensing that right enough, but why?"

"Pub walls have ears," he grinned, "and even harbours like Donaghadee may have many eyes..."

"True," I laughed, "but that sounds kind of ominous..."

"Nah, it's a grand day fellah, and we'll not let anything spoil it for us, trust me."

That was half the problem – I did.

"Sounds like it's going to be an interesting climb though?" I smiled nonchalantly, but my eagerness must have been obvious.

"Aye, we're good, you'll see." He glanced around casually. "But look, if anyone does see us hiking together... then fine, that's something we've done before... but I'm actually hoping that no-one gets to know I've been back this weekend at all to be honest; and then they can't possibly join the dots."

"What dots? What is it? Are you OK?"

"I'm fine, better than fine, and so will you be in a while, but I've got a fair bit of stuff to tell you." He put a strong hand on my shoulder. "Come on fellah, let's climb, and then I can explain the whole shebang."

We shouldered our packs and stepped off through the busy car park. Climbing was a grand term for strolling for the first mile or so, to the top end of Donard Park and then away up the track to the first of three bridges over the Glen River. Then, after rambling through endless forestry blocks of oaks, birch and Scots Pine, at the third stone bridge the real work would begin. There was another group maybe three hundred metres ahead of us and no-one ready to step-off behind, so we pretty much had the track to ourselves. As the trees leant in and hissed their curiosity, the stream fought noisily to mask our words. Content that the stream would win, Tommy began.

"So, before you jump in and cut me off, I have no idea where NEON is right now, none at all so don't be asking, but I'm about to tell you where he was until about two months ago."

"You're kidding. Where?" I stopped dead in my tracks.

"Scotland, you were right..."

"I knew it! How do you know?"

"Ah, well that's not so simple, and that I'll have to explain in some detail... come on."

"But are you sure it was him?" I stayed rooted to the spot.

"Not for certain, no, but ninety-five per cent, yes."

"Christ! So... as Niall Kelly or Yury Borzov? Or as someone else even? Who was he?"

"Borzov, and it seems that he may have been there for the whole ten months since Aberdeen, but that I *can't* be sure about."

"And so have you no idea where he went next?" I asked, almost pleading, "I mean where he might be right now? Not even a hunch or something?"

"No, none at all."

"And can you find out more? What was the source?"

"No, almost certainly not, and I'll tell you what the source was in a moment; but let's keep walking fellah, and I'll explain everything as we climb. Just give me time."

We stepped off, but my heart was in my mouth and I wasn't sure that I could wait. I was breathing like we'd already reached the summit and I couldn't form my words. Despite the enormity of what we were discussing, Tommy just chuckled at my boyish exuberance.

"And you were right about *where* in Scotland too, by the way," he continued. "Presuming that it was NEON, then he'd set himself up right on the opposite coast to Aberdeen, away up in the Highlands in Mulloch."

"Mulloch! That was on my list."

"Aye, it was, and that's crucial, because now we've got to work out how you're going to learn this for yourself."

"Why?"

"Because it can't have come from me, Neill. It cannot."

"Why?"

"Well that's all part of the same story, and that's why I suggested this place. We'll be lucky if I've finished telling you by the time we come down six hours from now. It's complicated."

"You're kidding?"

"No, I wish I were, but there's more angles to this than the Koh-I-Noor diamond. Just hear me out and then you'll get it."

"OK, OK," I said reluctantly, and both my breathing and my pace slowed a little, "but what do you mean I've got to work this out for myself?"

"Because what I'm about to give you must be viewed as lead intelligence only, and I'm passing it in total secrecy. So then you've got to let it lead you to find the answer for yourself, but without ever putting it into the system. You can't share this, Neill, you can't discuss this or brainstorm it with anyone – except me of course – and so you'll have to work it alone."

"Why?"

"Neill, give me a bloody chance, fellah. I told you this was going to take all day to explain; it'll take two if you don't shut-up."

"Sorry," I panted, and he chuckled again at my excitement.

"It *cannot* have come from me, no way, and no-one must know that we're working this together."

"Yeah, but it might not be that simple for me."

"Well it's got to be – and look, I know that, I know that very well - but I reckon we can work it out quite nicely because of what you just said about your list. You'll see."

I wanted to ask him a thousand questions and all at once; but I could tell from his voice, and from just knowing him as well as I did, that the sensible thing to do was indeed to shut-up and to let him explain. No matter how close to bursting I felt.

"So what's the importance of my list?"

"Right, well you were about to concentrate on half a dozen small ports on the west coast of Scotland anyway; so I'm just going to point you to the right one, that's all. And you were going to have to cast a huge net through the police an' all you said, but maybe now you need to keep it much tighter than that."

"Understood, but surely time's of the essence here, so it's going to be pretty obvious once we blunder into Mulloch and start asking around."

"Then don't blunder in Neill. And don't ask around, just sit and listen… and look, maybe that should actually be you. Y'know, continuity is everything with BOLAS and NEON, and that way you can also decide what goes into the system and what doesn't."

"Well everything goes in of course…"

"Really? We might be past that point, fellah. Hear me out today, I mean the whole story, and then you might not feel that way. And by the way, I judge that time's not the issue here - not letting-on that we know he was there is."

"I get what you're saying, but I'll have to hear exactly what you know to really understand…"

"Yeah, I know you will… so let me bloody tell you."

We climbed-on, careful to stay well behind or in front of any other hikers so we could talk freely. When one couple caught up with us, we stopped in a wee clearing for a beer and let them get well ahead again. For almost the next hour Tommy explained that through a trusted narco-contact in Stavanger he'd learned of a five-million-dollar drug-run from Oban in Scotland towards the end of June.

Oban is a small but busy port and resort town in the Firth of Lorn, and it had also been on my list. The contact was a Scottish fisherman from Peterhead, who had no idea of the significance of the name Yury Borzov, and what he knew was only a tiny part of a bigger story. But it was something.

The drug-run had been from Oban to God knows where in an Icelandic-skippered boat. The Scot had no further knowledge of the voyage, the skipper or the trawler, but he knew two of the highly-paid and secretly-hired crew had been Russians; because he had spoken to one of them. The man, in his thirties, called himself simply *Vlad*, and the Scot had no way of getting back to him. They had met in a bar near the docks in Haugesund just over a week ago. Vlad claimed to come from Moscow, but then later in their drunken conversation he had said he lived in Murmansk and he'd been raised there. Tommy had been unable to identify him on a number of police and intelligence databases.

Vlad had protested his violent mistreatment at the hands of another Russian, Yury Borzov, who had knocked him out with a marlinspike and whom he was one day hoping to run into again. They had both been crew on the Icelandic trawler from Oban. He knew Borzov had spent time in Aberdeen, and so he wanted to know if the Scot knew him. He didn't. The Scot was pretty sure that it was only the drink talking, but although he couldn't get Vlad to say any more about the voyage or the skipper he knew that Tommy would be interested in the size of the drugs-haul and the Oban connection. He'd been right - and although Tommy hadn't let-on, he'd been far more interested than in just that.

From the description Vlad had given of his assailant and from a couple of tell-tale statements, Tommy reckoned it was the same Yury Borzov who had worked in a strip club in Aberdeen. And if it was, then our recent discreet enquiries there meant it was highly likely to be NEON. So maybe our next batch of answers, I hoped, were to be found in Mulloch; a picturesque train stop on the West Highland Line beyond the Harry Potter Bridge.

Mulloch was part town, part village and mostly harbour. Its population was less than a thousand, but its characters, I had been told, were a million or more. It was home to an RNLI lifeboat and terminus to several ferries to the outer islands. In its heyday it had been herring-heaven to a thriving Scottish fishing industry, and its railway line had run right onto the pier to get alongside its busy fishing fleet; but now it shipped more tourists than tonnage, and so I'd calculated it was a perfect place to hide – right under the noses of the masses, but so far from anywhere else as to be almost invisible. It had been number three on my list of possibles, after Oban itself and Thurso.

Thurso had been the exception to my thinking, because it wasn't on Scotland's fjorded west coast but at the northernmost tip of the country. That put it midway between a quick dash across the North Sea to Scandinavia - and so maybe to NEON's Chechen cohort, Ruslan Barayev, I'd thought - or a long run down the west coast of Scotland to just about anywhere on the island of Ireland. The criteria for all the ports on my list had been very similar, but in Mulloch's case they had been the following:

It was a small to medium port in the right general area, but a busy one. It had enough commercial shipping for *Yury Borzov* to blend or to have found work, including several outer-island ferries, a number of fishing operations and at least one boatyard. As a result there was almost certain to be a few Eastern-European mariners hanging-out there; there was only one road in and out, so pretty easy for NEON to monitor if he'd had to; and it's on the Highland Railway Line for convenience and so would have given him options. Finally, it was a big enough town to hide in, but a small enough village to keep it all under his watchful eye. Yeah, I could believe it easily, and if Tommy's man was right then I wasn't in the least bit surprised.

Tommy and I talked at length about how we might elicit details about Borzov if he'd lived there for a while, rather than merely make enquiries and then maybe let him know we were onto him. Tommy couldn't do it, I knew, because Interpol had no idea of his interest already – more of that shortly – and even if I could find the time, I couldn't simply drift into town and start eavesdropping. Nor could I divert resources from Thames House, not least of all because Tommy was insisting his information *had* to remain off the record. More about that shortly too.

What we eventually came up with two-thirds of the way up the mountain was something in between, but we reckoned it just might get the job done. Katy was taking two weeks off in September, her first for nearly a year, and she had been planning to spend it with me. I was going to take local-leave so I could remain on call, and thus we would have just pushed-back and chilled in Ireland. But Scotland would fit the bill too, we reasoned, and I had a perfectly capable deputy, so I knew that if I suddenly got the bit between my teeth about my Highlands' Ports List, Katy would be just as happy to do that. Happier in fact, because then I really couldn't be called-back-in easily, and barring a disaster the most I'd have to do was field a few phone calls.

Tommy and I judged that a young, co-habiting and fully-rutting hiking couple would be the best possible cover; and that if Mulloch was the right place then eliciting something about a muscular, ear-ringed and bearded Russian sailor with wild and scary hair, might be relatively easy to do. If that's how he'd still looked when he'd got there. Tommy's Scottish contact said that in Vlad's quest for revenge he had described Borzov as fully bearded and still with an earring, but with an almost shaven head. Either way, or for anything in between, a beard seemed to be the common denominator and I fancied our chances.

My plan was that Katy and I would work south to north and spend two days each in Oban; Mulloch; Ullapool; Thurso; Stornoway and Uig; and that we'd leave Stornoway and Uig until last because they were on islands, and so NEON would have been unlikely to restrict his options that unwisely. And so that meant if we got to Mulloch in the first four days and thought we were onto something, then we'd still have up to ten days in situ to play with. Katy, of course, had to believe it was by chance too. It was indeed a plan, a bloody good plan I thought, and once formulated I couldn't wait to get started on it. But after the joy of formulating a new plan came the hammer-blow of a crucial new afterthought.

"But Christ!" I'd exclaimed.

"What?" Tommy paused.

"Oh my God Tommy, hold on a minute, if he sailed from Oban at the end of June sometime, that could have put him into Ireland easily in time to kill Kieran Hagan in late-July."

"Yeah, he could have, that's crossed my mind too, but that was in Belfast remember, and that's a hell of a conclusion you're drawing from just knowing he left Oban a month earlier."

"I know, but... so Belfast maybe?"

"Aye, maybe, but why the North and not the South."

"I don't know. A double-bluff maybe. Or exactly *because* he's not known there. Feels he can hide more easily maybe?"

"Well maybe. But look, that's tomorrow's question, so add it to your list and you can't draw that connection until you've established when and how he left Mulloch, so..."

"Aye, I know, but that could be something y'know."

"Aye, it could."

And yet as we turned east and followed the Mourne Wall up the steepest and final part of the climb, whether NEON was in Belfast or not, and no matter how happy I was with my new plan, there was one crucial question I couldn't let go. From everything we'd discussed in the past hour or so, it was obvious that this wasn't Interpol information and that Tommy's Scottish fisherman narco-contact wasn't an Interpol source. And more to the point, whomever Tommy was working on behalf of wasn't in receipt of this piece of information anyway – or so he'd said – so who?

"So where's this coming from Tommy? I mean who's this for? This isn't for Interpol, is it?"

"No," he looked at me and read deep into my eyes to see if I still trusted him. That was clearly the truth, and so for then at least I still did. "No, it isn't. So who do you think?"

"Well not Dublin, I reckon I'm pretty certain of that. And so if not Lyon, then maybe Paris? I wouldn't be surprised if you're DGSI or even DGSE?"

"Or?... there's an 'Or' in your voice."

"Is there?" we stopped climbing for a moment and started to get our breath back.

"Aye, there is. Clearly." He studied me carefully.

"And do I need an 'Or', do I?"

"Aye, you do."

"Or the CIA then," I muttered almost guiltily, but it was something I'd been pondering for the whole of the last week. "Y'know Tommy, I could never get my head around you just up and leaving the Special Forces' world and joining Interpol at the end of your three years in the US. It just never made sense to me. Still doesn't. But then after today...?"

There was a long pause while Tommy took a deep breath and formed his next sentence.

"Well you're not wrong fellah." He moved right away from the track, sat on a large boulder and looked straight at me. "Beer?"

"Aye, let's."

I walked across to where he was and waited for my beer, but I stayed standing. We were now ten metres back from the track and so from anyone passing, and in the moderate wind that blew always across the peak not far above us we could talk freely.

"Except it didn't happen like that," he simply continued, "they recruited me way back in 2007, when I was working with their guys in the Central African Republic."

"2007?" I confirmed, "when you were still in the French Special Forces?"

"Yes," he paused and looked me straight in the eye. "So how do you feel about that?"

"Jesus Tommy, I don't know. How do *you* feel about that?"

"I feel just fine... better than fine, but I'm no traitor if that's what you're thinking. It has nothing at all to do with providing information, except what I need to get my job done, and I provide a service that benefits all nations."

I didn't answer straight away, and so he clearly felt he needed to keep going.

"Besides, what am I? See with my dual citizenship an' all, am I Irish? French? American? Jesus Neill, am I a Brit even? I worked with the SAS as much as the Americans back then, and *we* in the British Isles have had pretty much the same national interests for over fifty years now. Right?"

"Right. Pretty much. So what do you feel you are?"

"Irish... Franco-Irish I guess, but Irish as a fistfight."

This time I nodded and took a gulp of my beer, because I didn't think I could swallow otherwise, and then I asked my *real* follow-up question. And yet, after the brief conversation we'd had the week before, I reckoned I already knew the answer.

"Would this service have anything to do with when drones and cruise missiles aren't subtle enough?"

"Aye, it would..." he studied me closely and pleaded with me to be OK with it with his eyes, "like in foreign capitals maybe... or in other crowded cities, or inside so-called Allied nations..."

"Jesus Tommy, move over... I need to sit down."

He did as I asked and gave me both space and time to get my breath back. It wasn't entirely from the climb and he knew it.

"Y'know Neill," he began to speak softly, "sadly I'm a fact of life. Well, of modern life at least, and that I'm needed at all is an even sadder fact. Someone somewhere's going to die a violent death tomorrow with or without me - thousands in fact, right around the world - but for every one I deal with, that's potentially hundreds of innocent people who'll survive."

"Hey, save your breath," I nodded, "I can see all that. And sadder still is that I wish I had the balls and the background to do it too. I'm envious Tommy, not judgmental... but to just look the other way from something like this is huge. For me it is."

"Aye, well... good job we're up here then, because now you know why you can't tell anyone. No-one. Ever."

"No fellah, I know. And so Interpol's just your working cover? Is that it? To put you wherever you need to be?"

"Yeah, just about, although I do a real job of work for them, obviously. And hey," he chuckled to break the ice, "I think I'm pretty good at it."

"And so they don't know?"

"No, not a clue, except for four other people who are also involved as facilitators... y'know, like conscious backstops."

"But the organisation itself?"

"Nothing. No-one. Like I said, not a clue."

"Are the other four Americans? I mean, are there any Brits involved at all?"

"No, not officially, not at the national level, but one of the four is a Brit funnily enough; but he needn't have been. Just is. The other three are two Americans and a Frenchman, but we're all CIA facilities agents as well as functioning Interpol officers."

"So not SIS then?"

"Jesus no, I hope not. No, I don't think so."

OK... so... I appreciate your honesty, and now I've got a thousand more questions, but the first two are why are you telling me this? This is dynamite I'm holding now. And the second is what's your interest in NEON? What's *their* interest in NEON?"

"And I'll tell you – the truth." He lifted his beer for me to clink bottles, and so the deal was done. "But now you see why both you and I can only discuss this with each other, and then I'll explain why you or I must get to NEON first."

"Go on."

"Well, for any one of a hundred reasons if anyone's going to find him before anyone else I reckon it's likely to be you. I mean you personally, while you're here in T8 and in Northern Ireland, not necessarily you the Service. And it won't surprise you to learn that you're not the only nation looking for him. I mean *seriously* looking for him. But yours is probably the most understated and perceptive search going on, you the Brits I mean, and right about now the closest to finding him I reckon."

"And...?"

"And so I can help, as I think I've just illustrated, but that's because I need to get to him first. One hundred per cent. Or you and me together if you like, but no-one else."

"Why?"

"Because then we'll have options."

"What options?"

"Well... let's crack another beer and I'll tell you. In fact, crack-open those sandwiches too, fellah, and then I'll tell you the whole damn thing. Sláinte."

Comfy Genes

So what I'm about to tell you didn't come directly from Tommy Bray - he's far too modest for one thing - but rather from what he did tell me, what I've been able to establish since, and from what I've known since I carried out checks on him and registered him as a Social Contact back in 2009; when I came to T8NI for the first time. And, of course, from getting to know him pretty damn well over those eight outlandish and eventful years. All Tommy told me on the day was the bare minimum he could get away with and until I ceased my relentless questions, and that was just enough to answer the biggest of them and assuage my fears. There were plenty of both.

And yet when I say all he told me was the bare minimum, I'm not suggesting that Tommy was lying at any time - I'm pretty certain he wasn't - but I'm equally sure that there's a whole host of things he never bothered to mention, because I hadn't asked. Aye that, and because he knew I wouldn't want to know. Well then good luck to him, because that's kind of how it has to be, but I'm sure also that they're things both of us hope we never have to discuss in the future.

Tomàs Henri Liam Bray first went to Willow Park School in Blackrock near Dublin in 1984, followed by an international school in France from the ages of nine to fifteen. When the Brays returned to Ireland in 1994, he attended Blackrock College to finish-up his International Baccalaureate before reading law at Trinity College, Dublin. Needless to say he excelled at all of them. But then, more to his father's disappointment than his disgust, and not at all to his surprise, he'd joined the army and not the bar. No-one else who knew him was surprised either; George Kennedy and I certainly hadn't been.

Tommy is two years older than me and his colouring is dark; he has thick sable hair and deep, sparkling brown eyes that warm you with a glance. So unlike me, not a Viking methinks. That and the rest of his undeniably good looks came from his mother's side, he says, as did his fluent multi-lingualism and what he describes as his French table manners. I've never worked out if they're good or bad. His mother is Pascal Margaux Bray, née Leduc, and her lineage in the Lyon region is a mite impressive. His father, Judge Liam Bray, is from County Louth, and his reputation on the High Court circuit is a mite fearsome. And yet... if I had to sum Tommy up in a single sentence - as spooky as it sounds - I would say he was me and NEON incarnate.

From anything and everything I've learned about Michael McCann in the past two years, if you could mash me and him into one body – except for his propensity for evil – then Tommy Bray could have been our twin. All three of us were bright, tenacious and quick-witted Irishmen, and both Tommy and McCann at least possessed that same innate charisma that opened doors with just a smile. There were also striking contrasts of course, like NEON's intent to kill a million Londoners for one, but there seemed to be more that connected us than divided us. Tommy was as complex as McCann, that was for sure - and doubtless as was I - but the very origins of that animal complexity were also the source of the main differences between us.

Tommy and I had been raised in a caring environment by forthright and decent parents; McCann had been bounced from pillar to post until 'saved' by Frank O'Neill and raised as an IRA Cleanskin. Tommy and I had been made tough and fearless through our genes, through sport, and in Tommy's case through military service; and McCann through the bestiality of Dublin's slums and his life as a mercenary soldier. And Tommy and I did what we did best through a sense of duty and in support of law and order; McCann through revenge and on behalf of the IRA. But they both believed fervently in what they did – at least NEON had until Easter '16, we reckoned – which is why, I had just learned, that Tommy is comfortable with the one or two grey areas where his interpretation of justice disagreed with that of international law. There were of course other differences, but under different circumstances – and given vastly different choices - I feel any one of us could have been the other.

When Tommy had set about explaining his role for the CIA, it came across more as justifying it rather than explaining it. He gave me one example of a recent task, quoted one of his controllers who had obviously been stumbling through the same moral maze at the time, and reprised a brief discussion between the same controller and a hawkish senator who liked to keep abreast of classified discussions about the Agency's undeclared Black Ops. To Tommy after one mission the controller had cited the F3EAD Special Forces' Targeting Process – Find, Fix, Finish, Exploit, Analyze and Disseminate – and he had likened him to 'a more resolute Third *F* and an alternative *E.*' And then to said senator, the same man – from the Special Activities Division of the National Clandestine Service – delivered the following off-the-record hypothesis:

'Hey, 'What's the difference between sending a team of Navy SEALs and maybe losing a few; or a fast jet with a smart-bomb and killing a few innocents in the vicinity; or a drone and having the fallout micro-analysed and debated by the world's media for a month or two... or we can covertly send a *'Finisher'* and have no visible consequences at all? No fallout, no aftermath, no witch-hunt, just a clean result. And wherever possible it will be made to look like an own-goal or some sort of an accident.'

Whether I totally agreed with it or not as an MI5 officer, given some of the target organisations we face and some of the skewed rules of war we find ourselves fighting under, it made enormous sense to me. Then the example Tommy gave of a recent *'Finish'* was from his last Interpol trip to the Middle East.

It had been a three-part trip to Iraq, Saudi Arabia and Egypt he explained, as part of a fraud investigation into a former Iraqi Army officer and an as yet unidentified Western arms dealer; but during the five days he spent in Baghdad he'd also had an additional task for his NCS controller.

That one had been particularly satisfying, he said, not least of all because of the countless lives it would save along the way. Based on technical intelligence gained just before his arrival, on his second night Tommy had covertly entered the apartment of an ISIS bomb-maker in the Ghazaliya neighbourhood in the western outskirts of the city. It was a densely populated area, and so Tommy was the perfect tool for the job. The man had his television on loudly to cover the noise of some of his tools, and he worked alone for obvious reasons. He had two so-called guards outside, but they were so discreet as to be useless and Tommy had bypassed them easily - both on the way in and on the way out.

Once inside and still undetected, Tommy observed the man for some time as he concentrated intently on his task, and then he edged ever-closer and cradled a rubber-covered lead cosh in his gloved hands until just the right moment. When there was a brief pause in what the man was doing, and while the device was safely to one side, Tommy killed him with a single blow to the head - a very hard blow – and then caught him as he slumped lifeless in his chair. Then he propped him up just inches from his own device and prepared to leave.

When the bomb exploded fifteen minutes after Tommy's covert departure, thanks to the timer he had set before he left, yet another fanatical martyr went to meet his virgins... the result, ISIS mourned for days, of an appalling own-goal. Neither the forensic examination nor the post mortem that followed – if they even bothered – revealed anything that suggested otherwise. It was nothing whatsoever to do with Enquêteur Principal Tommy Bray, of course, who was visiting from Interpol in France, but he was nonetheless delighted to hear of the demise of such an infamous bomb-maker the next day in police HQ. So too were all of his new Iraqi colleagues, men who suddenly had one less lethal security concern for themselves, their families and their citizens.

Such tasks didn't take place on all trips, Tommy pointed out, quite the opposite. On average he visited between thirty and forty countries a year, generally on his Interpol Travel Document but not always, and for a relatively small proportion of those trips he'd also have an *additional* task to perform. Just six or seven a year for the past five years. So it would be on some trips and not others; never on two trips back-to-back; and it would be in certain carefully selected countries and war zones, but never in some others at all. The UK and Ireland, he assured me, were two such countries where he would never be tasked.

"So what about France?" I'd asked him.

"Huh, France is a concern," he'd smiled dolefully, "and so it's the subject of some pretty intense discussions. So long as the authorities are as effective and decisive as they are at present, I would not be tasked to operate there; but French society is far too deeply penetrated by Islamic jihadism to just ignore. And so..."

"And so what?"

"And so who knows tomorrow."

I was amazed at how totally honest and specific Tommy was being, and I wasn't sure if I was grateful or not. But I was also clear that I was now fully included in his secret and so I could never now simply unlearn it. It was a strangely mixed sensation, and a part of me resented his having shared it... halved it I felt.

"So how are you with that, y'know, I mean as a sometime citizen?" I asked.

"Well, I can answer better as a most-of-the-time-resident, and I hope in future I'm allowed to operate in France too. Like I told you earlier, I feel I provide a service that benefits all nations."

"And so what about NEON?"

"What, in Ireland you mean?"

"Yes, or in Northern Ireland. Or wherever we find him."

"Huh, good question."

"Aye, and it deserves an answer."

"Yes, it does…" he looked at me intensely, but still with a hint of that Tommy smile, "and although it's not one I can give for sure, I feel pretty certain that they'd go after NEON anywhere."

"Yeah, based on what you're saying, me too. Not forgetting the priority has got to be locating the second device."

"Right. And not forgetting that I'm not the only person they could call upon."

"Really? How many are there?"

"I don't know. And I don't know for certain that there are others – I mean maybe I'm the first – but I can't believe that I am."

"Have you ever asked?"

"Yes."

"And?"

"And I still don't know."

"Right…"

"Which makes it even more crucial that you and I are the first two people anywhere to find him. Do you see now? Because then Neill, we would have options, remember."

His options – which were by then our options – were a separate subject, and we discussed them no less intently.

Tommy's account of his recruitment by the CIA in 2007 was, if anything, even more interesting than his specimen Iraqi *task*. To me at least, because it underscored the importance of correctly identifying someone's primary motivating factors *and* their true capabilities. Tommy only told me the essential elements of what I'm about to tell you – modesty again – and the rest I've deduced and added for your broader enlightenment.

When he was first recruited, it was as a human source whilst on deployment with the French Special Forces in Africa, but that was just to get him on the books until they could use him as they'd intended from the outset. He was recruited by a man called Larry Allen, who'd been in Birao or in the capital, Bangui, for some months by then; but the hook had been Allen's knowledge, and so the CIA's, of an incident in Afghanistan the year before. It wasn't used to blackmail him, quite the opposite, but the bait once dangled was eagerly snapped-up by a fair-minded but brutally pragmatic Capitaine Tomàs Bray.

Tommy had first come to the Agency's attention after his deployment to Zabul Province the year before, also while in the French Army but whilst deployed with US Special Forces as a French SF Air Liaison Officer. One man he'd worked with closely there was a like-minded Nevadan, Major Andrew Barclay, and Barclay had seen enough to know that his former college buddy, Larry Allen, should have a closer look at Bray in due course.

It might have been Tommy's shrewd and no-nonsense approach to just about everything he did, or his strong soldiering skills and his fluency in five languages, but it was more likely to have been the way he'd tracked-down and stabbed to death a known terrorist who had evaded justice that day on a bizarre multi-national technicality. Tommy's single-handed night-time execution was impressive enough, done with a knife Taliban-style and bearing the hallmarks of a tribal blood-feud, but the way he'd covered his tracks with the help of just Barclay back in base was nothing short of remarkable. It's not as outrageous as it sounds - despairing fighting men sometimes do desperate things.

Armed with that knowledge, Allen had made sure he got to work with Tommy in Birao and that he'd got to know him well. He was immediately impressed with his skills across the board, but in quick time he also confirmed three attributes that made him ripe for the picking: a steely determination to see justice served – frontier-style and at the earliest sensible opportunity; a clinical readiness to kill, with his own bare hands if necessary; and the depth of his disillusionment with the oft-bungling impotence of multi-national law enforcement. Recruitment as a HUMINT asset followed soon after, and his wholly deniable transition to an invisible hired assassin came about within days. The un-named hawkish senator would have been proud.

It occurred to me in passing that his grandparents would have been proud too – although I couldn't imagine that his father had a clue of his secret role. His mother maybe, now that I could believe; I had met her several times and she was a striking woman in a number of ways, but I could imagine that her son being a state-sanctioned assassin would be just fine with her. Yet my checks years before had revealed that Tommy arguably had a genetic aptitude for his life on the edge, and when we'd made him a facilities agent for the Tierney-Castlewellan Real IRA operation I'd dug a little deeper. To my surprise, even for Tommy, I'd found a number of significant and hereditary links to a life in the shadows of Europe's hot and cold wars of the last century.

Tommy's father was fluent in French and German, I knew, but for reasons I hadn't been able to find out that had seen him working for the Allied Powers in West Berlin in 1977, where he'd met and subsequently married Tommy's mother. I had even less idea what she'd been doing there, but it was pretty obvious it had been in some sort of intelligence gathering role. But Tommy's grandparents on both sides, I felt, held the real key to his evolved personality. They comprised an Irishman and his American wife; a Frenchman and his English spouse; and all of whom during World War II had been involved in some sort of espionage against the Nazis in the SOE, the OSS, in British Intelligence or in the French Resistance. One of them had even managed to work with all four! His grandparents were born between 1918 and 1925, and his parents at the start of the Cold War in the mid-50s, and so Tommy seemed to represent but an evolution of the species.

Bizarrely that caused me to wonder if it was a good thing or a bad thing for mankind that Tommy had shown no interest in ever having kids. And now I was a part of his... God, I don't know, sordid world... or did I mean courageous mission?... what would my answer mean for me and Katy in the future? But for now at least it was a question I shoved firmly to the back of my mind. My more pressing concern, which was also for the sake of mankind, was simply to find NEON.

And so eventually Tommy had finished his explanation and I had finished an endless stream of questions. We'd both long since finished our sandwiches, next we'd finished our second two beers, and then finally we'd stood up, stretched our stiffened limbs, and finished-off our climb the top of Slieve Donard as well.

Despite the million and one things we probably should have discussed on the way down, I'd had a pretty good idea we would descend in virtual silence. Laughter maybe, and the odd wise-crack to go with the odd stumble, but I'd reckoned we were done talking for the day. I'd felt like I was done talking forever. But first there'd been that spectacular view from the summit. It had been a crystal clear day, and so our visibility from the very top to the horizon had been maybe seventy miles.

As we'd looked around we could see not only the Isle of Mann and a huge swathe of the Irish Sea, but the Mull of Kintyre in Scotland and the peak of Mount Snowdon in Wales. And then from on top of the wall and when I'd turned slowly through three hundred and sixty degrees, I'd seen pretty much the whole of the top half of Ireland too. I couldn't help but reflect on being stood on the exact same spot seventeen years earlier with Úna and George Kennedy, and on all that had happened since that sunrise and its brave new millennium.

'Jesus,' I'd thought, 'in another seventeen years, and if I'm still in the Service, I'll be nudging up against retirement'... and I wondered if I'd still be looking for NEON? But if I was, at least now I'd have the Third 'F' and the crucial 'E' to my puzzle as well.

The search for NEON is where we're at. Get on with it.

About the Author

John Benacre was born in the suburbs of London and raised in Kent. He served for thirty-five years in the British Army and held every rank from Private soldier in the Parachute Regiment to Lieutenant Colonel in the Intelligence Corps. Most of that time was spent on Counter-Terrorist duties. He is married to Pauline and has three adult children.

You can follow John Benacre on:

www.johnbenacre.com

CPSIA information can be obtained
at www.ICGtesting.com
Printed in the USA
LVOW12s1639190417
531396LV00004B/794/P